The Midwife's Secret

Emily Gunnis is the internationally bestselling author of *The Girl in the Letter* and *The Missing Daughter*. Her novels have sold in twenty languages. Emily previously worked in TV drama and lives in Brighton with her young family. She is one of the four daughters of *Sunday Times* bestselling author Penny Vincenzi.

Also by Emily Gunnis

THE GIRL IN THE LETTER
THE MISSING DAUGHTER

The Midwife's Secret

EMILY GUNNIS

First published in 2021 by Headline Review
An imprint of HEADLINE PUBLISHING GROUP

1

All characters in this publication are fictitious and any resemblance
to real persons, living or dead, is purely coincidental.

Cataloguing in Publication Data is available from the British Library

Hardback ISBN 978 1 4722 7204 1
Trade Paperback ISBN 978 1 4722 7213 3

Typeset in 11.5/14.75 pt Adobe Garamond by Jouve (UK), Milton Keynes

Printed and bound in Great Britain by Clays Ltd, Elcograf S.p.A.

Headline's policy is to use papers that are natural, renewable and recyclable
products and made from wood grown in well-managed forests and other
controlled sources. The logging and manufacturing processes are expected to
conform to the environmental regulations of the country of origin.

HEADLINE PUBLISHING GROUP
An Hachette UK Company
Carmelite House
50 Victoria Embankment
London EC4Y 0DZ

www.headline.co.uk
www.hachette.co.uk

For Grace and Eleanor – my inspiration

Yew Tree Manor

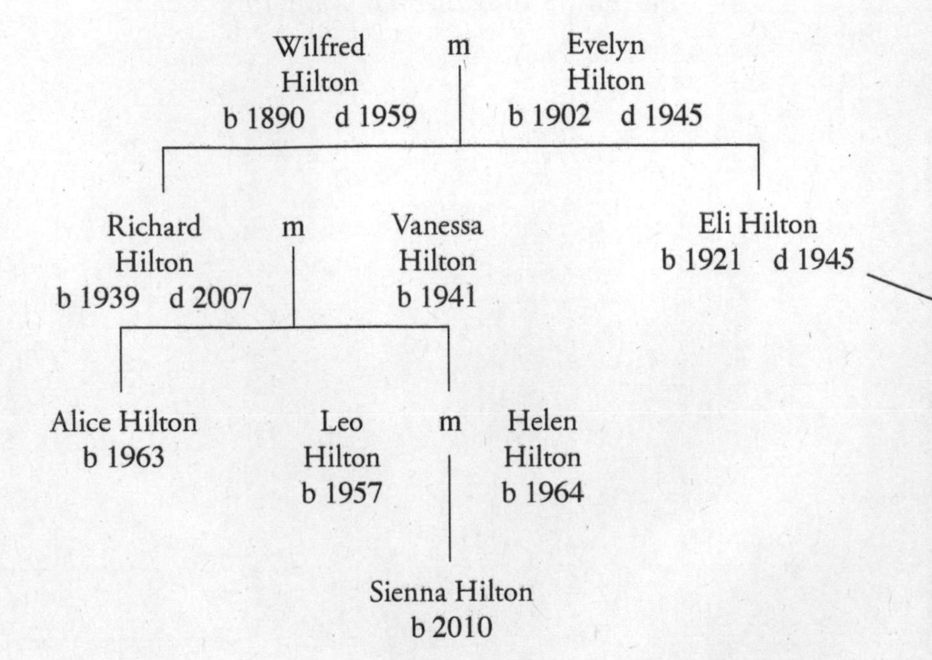

The Vicarage

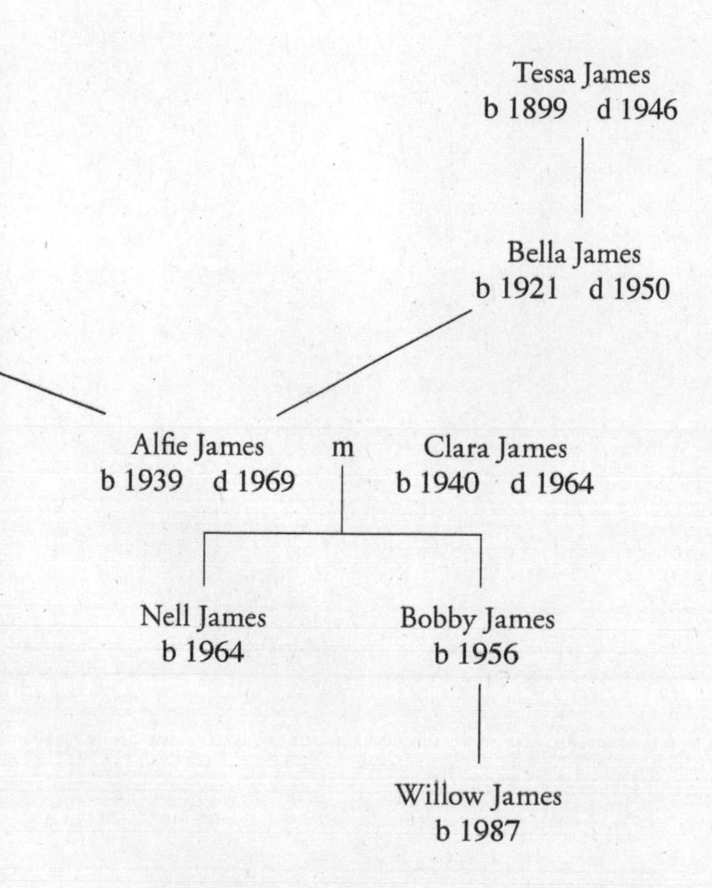

No one does more harm to the
Catholic Faith than midwives

Heinrich Kramer and Jakob
Sprenger, *Malleus Maleficarum*

Unable are the Loved to die
For Love is Immortality

Emily Dickinson

Prologue

Monday, 8 January 1945: Kingston near Lewes, East Sussex

'They're here already.' Tessa James looked out of her bedroom window as two police cars pulled up outside The Vicarage, their beaming lights making her flinch and turn away before rushing back to her six-year-old grandson, who was sitting on the landing shaking with fear.

'Baba, I'm scared. I don't want to be alone in the dark.' Alfie stared hard at her with the James family ice-blue eyes; so hard that she felt the little boy was looking right through her.

He gripped his grandmother's hand as she eased up the top step of the landing to reveal a small room underneath the stairs; a priest-hole, just large enough to fit a mattress and little more, which she had discovered quite by accident when she moved into the near-derelict cottage when she was pregnant with Alfie's mother, over two decades before.

'Climb in now, hurry,' she urged.

Knowing he had no choice, the little boy reluctantly scuttled in, then immediately turned around to look up at her, his black hair framing his cheeks as he started to cry.

'Alfie, listen to me, you must only come out of here if you absolutely have to; you must stay hidden. You have enough supplies to last for five days. I've sent an urgent telegram to Mama; she knows you're in here. She will come for you sooner than that, maybe as soon as tomorrow.'

'What if she doesn't come? What will I do?' he said, starting to sob.

'She will come, Alfie.' Tessa wiped away his tears, needing desperately to close the lid on the secret room before the police burst in and saw the concealed entrance. With Alfie's mother away working as a house servant in Portsmouth, Wilfred Hilton wouldn't hesitate to have the little boy – his illegitimate grandson – sent overseas, probably never to be seen or heard of again.

'Do you promise, Baba? Because I know you always keep your promises.' His tears left trails down his cheeks, muddied from playing outside in the fields earlier in the day. He had run in to escape the rain, around the time the Hiltons' house servant, Sally, had come hammering at The Vicarage door, her clothes soaked through.

'You have to come, Mrs James,' she had said, her eyes wild with panic and panting from running through the woods that connected Yew Tree Manor and The Vicarage where they lived. 'Mrs Hilton's near having her baby and it's stuck. The doctor says she will die if it doesn't come soon. He said to fetch you. He doesn't know what to do.'

Tessa felt her stomach lurch at the thought of Evelyn Hilton enduring so much suffering at the hands of Dr Jenkins. 'Sally, you know I'm forbidden by Mr Hilton to go anywhere near his wife. I have had no consultations with Mrs Hilton; it is the doctor's job to deliver her baby safely.' Fighting back tears, she tried to close the door on the girl.

'Please, the doctor begged me to make you come,' Sally said. 'He said he would tell Mr Hilton he had requested your presence and bear all responsibility for you being there. Please, Mrs James, there's so much blood. He says you're the only one who can save her. They'll both die if you don't. I thought I couldn't take any more of her screams, but she's gone awful quiet now, and that's worse.'

'Where is Mr Hilton?' Tessa enquired.

'He drove off after the two of you quarrelled about your tenancy here at The Vicarage. You see, they had a telegram this morning to say that Master Eli has been killed in action. Mrs Hilton was terrible upset; she went into labour soon after Mr Hilton left. I called Dr Jenkins, just as I was told to, but it's a breech baby and the doctor said he weren't expecting it. He keeps shouting at me to find the master. I've been looking for him everywhere in Kingston village – at the Rose and Crown and the stables. I looked all over, but he's vanished.' The girl was frantic and began to sob. 'Please don't let her die, Mrs James. Please!' She pulled at Tessa's arms, easing her towards the door. 'Richard is only six; he'll be left without a mother.'

Eli Hilton was dead. Tessa still couldn't believe it. Bella's beloved, Alfie's father, killed in a war that was so nearly over. She had been there when Eli came into the world, and soon after had given birth to her own baby, Bella, and the two had been inseparable their whole lives. Eli was like a son to her, and as the servant girl stood staring at her in the rain, she found it hard to breathe. But there was no time to react, no time to scream and cry and weep. She was needed.

'Alfie, stay here in the warm, keep the fire topped up,' she had said, pulling on her heavy black boots and wrapping her shawl around her shoulders before venturing out into the storm.

She had delivered Evelyn's previous two babies safely – Eli and his younger brother Richard – but both births had been tricky. Evelyn was a woman whose labours never seemed to end. She was tiny, her birth canal was small, and attending her required a great deal of patience, which Tessa felt sure Dr Jenkins was lacking. She needed to be able to move around during labour, and had given birth to both babies on all fours on her bedroom floor at Yew Tree Manor. She feared Dr Jenkins would have her in stirrups on the bed, using forceps to try and heave the baby out.

As they ran from the edge of the woods down the stone driveway of the huge Georgian mansion, the memory of her quarrel with Wilfred Hilton that very morning filled Tessa with sadness. 'I want you and that bastard child out of The Vicarage and off my land,' he had told her. 'You bring shame on the Church and shame on my family. I see you trying to hide those women whose miscarriages you induce; do you think that by bringing them here in the dead of night we won't notice? You are a disgrace, Mrs James, with your secrets and herbs and organic medicines. We need real doctors like Dr Jenkins, not God-hating charmers like you, spreading your hatred of proper medical practices like a cancer in our community.'

Ever since she had become a midwife, women had asked how to get rid of the babies growing inside them. She had always listened sympathetically, but she knew it was illegal: people were sent to prison for bringing on a miscarriage. But the law wasn't as much of a deterrent as her instincts – she had devoted her life to saving babies' lives, not ending them – and so instead she offered comfort. She listened and she didn't judge, because she knew that a woman had her reasons for not wanting a baby. She might have too many to care for already, or was so sick from bearing babies that another might kill her – and without her, what would become of her other children? She gave such women herbs that were recommended to bring on their monthlies, but they mostly didn't work. A few women were so desperate they threatened to kill themselves. Those were the ones who troubled her the most. If she didn't help them, they would drink bleach, or do it themselves with a needle or a crochet hook, or by any number of means that often had horrifying consequences. It was a man's world, and few knew what pain a woman suffered for his pleasure.

'And what did they teach Dr Jenkins at medical school?' she had replied to Wilfred Hilton. 'How many babies has he delivered? You don't learn in medical school how to soothe a mother barely old enough to have a child, who's near dying from the pain of childbirth. Or a woman who cannot get her baby out because her birth canal is too narrow.'

'Shame on you, Mrs James. You've bewitched the women of this village with that tongue. I want you out tomorrow.'

As she walked through the house and up the stairs towards Evelyn's bedroom, it was the thought of the bleeding that spurred her on. The baby had turned, and Evelyn would be weak from loss of blood, maybe unable to push the infant out. However Tessa felt about Wilfred Hilton, she had to try and help her friend.

But as she stepped into the bedroom, nothing could have prepared her for the scene. Never in her thirty years as a midwife had she seen so much blood. The white sheets on which she lay, and Evelyn's ivory nightdress, were dyed completely red. Evelyn lay in the centre of the four-poster bed, pale and lifeless, her legs in stirrups, the doctor heaving and pulling at the baby's legs, its head still inside her.

'For God's sake, do something!' the doctor yelled when he caught sight of Tessa. 'The shoulders are stuck, I can't get the baby out. I've cut her, but it still won't come.' He was glaring up at her, panting with exertion, blood caked up to his elbows.

Tessa rushed to Evelyn and gently took her legs down from the stirrups. She knew just from the sight of her, and all the blood, that it was too late to save her. But the baby's legs were moving; there could still be hope for the child. Quickly, she felt Evelyn's abdomen for the baby's shoulder and then pressed down on Evelyn's tummy just above her pelvic bone.

'What are you doing?' the doctor panted, his face still puce and caked in sweat.

'Dislocating the baby's shoulder,' Tessa replied. 'Help me get Evelyn on all fours.'

The doctor looked at her wide-eyed. 'I will not! I want nothing more to do with this!' He picked up his bag and rushed from the room, his white shirt spattered with Evelyn's blood.

Tessa watched him go, knowing what it meant: that he would blame her for what he had done and her work as a midwife would be over. She looked down at Evelyn, then at Sally cowering in the hallway, weeping quietly.

'Help me!' she snapped, frozen to the spot with terror. 'Sally, you begged me to come. Please, Mrs Hilton needs you.' The girl looked up at Tessa, then nodded and walked over to her.

Together they eased Evelyn over, then Tessa reached inside her womb and with a great deal of effort turned the baby.

'Push, Evelyn,' she whispered in her friend's ear as the next pain came. Evelyn used the last of her strength to push, while Tessa pulled as hard as she could, and out the baby came: a beautiful little girl, her long limbs white, her rosebud lips tinged blue.

Long minutes passed as Sally sobbed in the corner and Tessa sat on the floor blowing into the baby's mouth and rubbing her soft belly, trying desperately to breathe life back into the child. Finally she gave up and looked over to see that Evelyn had stopped breathing.

She didn't know when exactly Wilfred Hilton had walked into the room, as Dr Jenkins lurked behind him, but there was no shouting, no raging; he ignored her entirely and walked slowly over to his wife, looking down at her porcelain skin, then at his lifeless child, before pulling the sheet over Evelyn's face. Tessa got shakily to her feet and laid the dead baby in the crib by the door.

'What is Tessa James doing here, Dr Jenkins?'

'She forced her way in, Mr Hilton. When I left, Mrs Hilton and the baby were very much alive,' said the doctor.

'Sally, call the police,' Hilton said.

Fear had gripped Tessa's heart. She thought only of Alfie sitting alone by the fire in The Vicarage, the grandson Wilfred Hilton disowned, and would do anything to be rid of.

'Stay here, Mrs James!' shouted Hilton, but she didn't hesitate; knowing what she had to do, she pushed past the men, running down the stairs and out onto the driveway. Not stopping until she reached the post office in Kingston village, her clothes and hands still stained with Evelyn's blood, she wrote an urgent telegram to her daughter in Portsmouth.

My darling Bella. Come home immediately. Alfie is waiting for you in our secret place. Mama. X

On shaky legs, she'd then hurried home to The Vicarage, and to Alfie, sleeping soundly by the fire.

Bang bang bang. 'Police, open up!'

'Baba, promise me and I'll believe you,' said the little boy as he looked up at her from the secret room, his eyes pleading.

Tessa paused, fearing that to promise would be a lie, but worse, far worse, was to leave a six-year-old boy alone in the dark for days, fearing no one was coming for him.

'I promise,' she said finally, deciding that if Bella had not returned to the village in five days, she would tell the police where Alfie was. Any longer than that was a death sentence for the child. She would do everything in her power to keep him out of the orphanage that Wilfred Hilton no doubt had planned for him, but she would not risk his life.

She leaned in and cupped the child's face in her hands. 'Alfie, if anyone sees you, they will take you away. And Wilfred Hilton will see to it that they hide you somewhere Mama won't be able to find you. This is our only hope.'

Bang bang bang. 'We know you're in there, Mrs James. Open up!'

'You must be brave. Take the key now and lock yourself in.' She removed the ornate key from around her neck, its head engraved with a willow tree, and handed it to the boy. 'Let yourself out whenever you must, but try not to,' she added firmly.

She began to lower down the roof to the room, remembering the day she had discovered it. She had been planning to varnish the dark mahogany stairs, and had been sanding them, pushing hard against the top step, when something had clicked and it had released on a spring. She had taken a candle and climbed in. It was only a small space, barely big enough to lie down in, but somehow it didn't feel claustrophobic. There was a little window at the end, made of blue glass bricks the same piercing colour as Alfie and Bella's eyes, and the room had the feeling of a tree house, a den, a haven. It had immediately occurred to her that, in her line of work, it could prove useful for women who needed somewhere to hide while their bodies recovered from the ravages of childbearing or miscarriage. Women who couldn't bear to go home to their ashamed families or violent husbands.

Bang bang bang. 'Open the door, Mrs James, or we will break it down. You have ten seconds. Ten . . .'

Tessa looked at her grandson, only six years of age, tears streaming down his pale cheeks.

'You are a James, Alfie. I love you. You must be strong.'

The little boy gazed back at her, and suddenly, as if from nowhere, a strength overcame his terror, his tiny frame lifting from despair, trust and courage propping him up as he sat straight and began to let go of his beloved grandmother.

'More than all the stars?' he said quietly, wiping his tears away with his sleeve.

'Five . . .'

'More than all the stars and the moon. Hold on, Mama is on her way. Be silent, my darling.' She kissed his face over and over, his tears salty on her lips.

Bang bang bang.

'I'm coming!' she shouted. She closed the priest-hole door and waited until she heard the little boy turn the lock. *Click.*

'Three . . .'

'I'm coming; please don't break down my door,' she called out.

'Two . . .'

It was less than an hour since she had stood by Evelyn's bedside, since her friend had bled to death in front of her eyes. Since she had laid Evelyn's lifeless baby in the cot beside her bed.

'One!'

She opened the front door and was immediately blinded by the lights of two police cars as four policemen stormed past her into her small, fire-lit kitchen.

'Tessa James, I am arresting you on suspicion of the manslaughter of Evelyn Hilton. You do not have to say anything, but anything you do say may be given in evidence in a court of law.'

'Where is the boy?' one of the officers demanded as his colleagues charged past them towards the stairs.

'With his mother,' Tessa replied quietly.

'We have instructions to take him to his guardian, Wilfred Hilton,' the policeman snapped.

'Well, you can't, he's gone,' Tessa said.

'When? We know your daughter works in Portsmouth. How did you get the boy to her so fast?'

'There's no sign of him.' Another policeman appeared next to them, out of breath from searching the house.

'I put him on the train.'

'He's six years old.' The officer, who had a moustache and pungent breath, leaned in, fixing her with his stare. 'You're lying to us, Mrs James. He's here.' He turned to the other policeman. 'Take her to the station, put her in the cells for the night and I will question her in the morning. I can wait here all night if I have to for the child to come out of his hiding place.'

Tessa felt her legs give way from shock and exhaustion as she stepped for what she knew would be the final time over the threshold of her beloved home. It was Dr Jenkins' word against hers, and Wilfred Hilton would be falling over himself to back him up.

She would never be coming back to The Vicarage.

Alfie watched through the blue glass window, silent and terrified as the police car left, carrying his grandmother away from him. He sat in the dark for hours, barely daring to breathe, as the police thundered around, shouting his name, stamping on the floors and banging the walls, until they finally went quiet.

But still Alfie stayed silent, knowing from the small glass-brick window in his secret room that there was still a police car parked outside.

He lay in the dark, thinking of his mother. As the sun came up, he prayed with all his might that the telegram Baba had sent would be handed to his mother that morning, that she would rush to pack her bag then catch the first train to Kingston and get to him before another long, terrifying night arrived.

Chapter One
Vanessa

Thursday, 21 December 2017

Vanessa Hilton stood at the mouth of the woods linking Yew Tree Manor to The Vicarage and looked down across the fields at the derelict house, the winter-morning sun sparkling behind it.

The developers had already cordoned it off with red and white tape and a huge yellow crane stood alongside a wrecking ball, waiting to strike the walls of the listed building that her son Leo still didn't yet have permission to knock down.

She could see a couple of men in hard hats with clipboards pointing up at the roof and walking round the outside of the house, clearly plotting and planning its downfall. The Vicarage was at the centre of the area that Leo had told her was to be cleared to build ten detached houses. No doubt it would make everyone a great deal of money, but she couldn't remember anyone asking her consent for it to happen. Or perhaps they had and she had forgotten. To her, the developers looked like sharks circling their prey, their desperation to be rid of the old house all too apparent.

Vanessa looked down at her black leather shoes, which were soaked through, and realised her feet had gone numb.

She wasn't wearing the right footwear for walking; she couldn't remember why she had left the house. Maybe she had just come outside to see her granddaughter, Sienna. Maybe she had wanted to get away from the men in the house packing up her life's belongings.

She felt tired trying to remember all the time. The doctor had told her to be patient with herself. That it would be harder to recall people's names and words on the tip of her tongue, but that the distant past would stay perfectly intact in her mind; the things she wanted to forget she remembered, and the things she wanted to remember she forgot.

She supposed she must have spoken to her family about selling the estate, but she couldn't remember the conversation, just a sick feeling of it all happening around her, of the tide going out and not being able to stop it. Conversations out of her control, removal men coming and going, architects brimming with ideas holding meetings in the kitchen. A feeling of powerlessness and worry that followed her around like a shadow, starting every day with a niggling feeling of unease and slowly taking over every part of her so that, by bedtime, she could barely breathe for fear of what she couldn't remember. She had to leave, she knew that. But she couldn't recall why.

'Mum! Are you out here?' She could hear Leo calling her, but she chose to ignore him. The house was so full, so bursting with activity, people bustling about, plotting her removal. She felt like a spider being dusted out of the door on a broom, everyone being polite and kind to her face, offering her endless cups of tea, but quite obviously wanting to be rid of her and a lifetime's belongings as quickly and efficiently as possible. She kept asking Leo where they were moving to, but she could never remember the answer.

She turned and started walking back through the woods, the trees overhead forming an arch. The same ash trees Alice must have passed under the night she went missing. On cold, windy days like this they always rustled, as if they were whispering. Trying to tell her something. If only she could ask them what they had seen of her daughter that night. Where she had gone when she vanished into the snow. They would have watched her bumping into their neighbour's son, Bobby, the last person to see Alice before she vanished. Bobby James. Even now with her mind a constant fog, it was a name and a face she knew she would never forget.

What had happened to Alice after that? Nearly fifty years later, she was no closer to solving the mystery. She only knew what the boy had told the police: that her six-year-old daughter had gone running after her puppy towards The Vicarage. Never to be seen again.

Vanessa took one more look back at the old house, possibly for the last time. She remembered that the planning meeting was the following day – Leo had talked about it that morning – and if they got the go-ahead, she knew they wouldn't waste any time tearing it down.

Looking down at the frail building in the morning sun, she had doubted it would take much force. Nobody had lived in The Vicarage since the night of Alfie James's accident – the same night Alice had disappeared. That had been nearly fifty years ago, and over that time, the once pretty house had gradually deteriorated into a state of complete decay. It now attracted only teenagers and travellers, who would light bonfires in the empty downstairs as they huddled together, the smashed windows and the broken front door providing little protection against the wind or rain.

She herself hadn't been inside for decades; it brought back too many memories of a night she had spent a lifetime trying to forget. For the first ten years after Alice went missing, she would go over and over in her mind every second of the run-up to her daughter's disappearance: what she hadn't seen or noticed; what she had failed to do to keep her safe. It had slowly driven her mad. Now she couldn't bear to think of it at all. She had given up torturing herself. Instead she chose to remember Alice in the grounds of Yew Tree Manor. On her long walks she would picture the little girl up ahead in her favourite red coat, asking endless questions, laughing, skipping, jumping. She felt in the depths of her heart that Alice still existed somewhere, in another world, another place. It was just a place Vanessa wasn't allowed to visit. Yet.

She should have been as glad as Leo that they were knocking The Vicarage down. The house was a constant reminder of the James family, who came into their lives as the First World War ended, and had been inextricably bound to them – by tragedy – ever since.

But somehow the thought of the place being torn down made her sadder than she could comprehend. It was a brutal stamp on the passing of time, a plaster being torn off, the world moving on while she remained frozen in time.

As she reached the other side of the woods, Yew Tree Manor came into sight, and Sienna, her seven-year-old granddaughter, hurtled towards her on her red bicycle. She was so like Alice, it was almost too much to bear. Not just her long blonde hair, but her fearlessness and inquisitiveness; the sparkle of mischief in her blue eyes.

'Hi, Grandma,' she called. 'Daddy's been looking for you.'

'Has he?' said Vanessa. 'Be careful, darling, it's icy. And haven't you got school today?'

'Yes, Mummy's just getting dressed,' the little girl replied as she peddled off down the drive.

Vanessa let out a heavy sigh and exhaustion suddenly took hold. Realising from her heavy legs that she must have been out for too long, she made her way back to the house. As she walked in through the door and laid her gloves down, she could hear Leo on the phone in his study, talking quietly.

Passing the full-length antique gold mirror that had been unscrewed from the wall and was propped up at her feet, she realised that the elderly lady with the stooped shoulders, frail frame and wispy light grey hair was her. She stopped and turned to face her reflection, despite desperately wanting to turn away.

She had never been a classic beauty, but she was good at making the best of what she had: fine features, and a wide smile that never failed to get her what she wanted. Megawatt, Richard had called it; it never failed to stop his heart, like a lightning bolt, he had told her the night they met.

She had always been tall; 'Stick', her father had nicknamed her, because of her long, sun-kissed legs and arms, which she vividly remembered wrapping around his back as he gave her piggybacks on long walks. His interest in her, as an only child, had given her an unshakeable self-belief and an endless supply of positivity that had never stalled – until the night Alice disappeared.

Her thick long blonde hair was now thin, almost white, and cut to her jaw in an effort to hide its insubstantial state. Her skin was pale, almost translucent, and her collarbones were visible under her shirt. She stared into the mirror, her green eyes frowning back at her; in her youth they had been likened to sparkling emeralds, but now they seemed more like cloudy beer bottles. Old age is cruel, Vanessa, her mother had warned, but as a young woman it had seemed other-worldly in its distance from her, yet now suddenly it had arrived.

'The planning meeting is tomorrow. Thanks, yup, I'll let you know as soon as we hear. No, I don't foresee any problems; the head of planning is minded to approve it, which means it's as good as done.' Vanessa could hear the stress in her son's voice through the half-open door.

He looked up and saw her, and within moments he had finished the call and appeared in the hallway, flustered and frowning. 'Are you okay, Mum?' he said slightly breathlessly.

'I'm fine, darling, thank you.' She took off her jacket and hung it on the coat stand. It was overflowing with garments, and as she hooked hers on, another one fell down.

'This thing is about to topple over,' she sighed. 'It would be nice if Helen tidied up occasionally.'

'Sorry, Mum, I'll do that.' Leo scrabbled to pick up the coat at his feet.

'You've got enough to do,' Vanessa told him. 'I don't know how you manage it all, I really don't.'

'I'm all right, Mum.' He frowned gently. 'I didn't know

where you'd gone. You've been out for ages. I walked to the edge of the wood, but I couldn't see you.'

Vanessa smiled up at him. Leo was tall, like his father, and despite hurtling towards his sixtieth birthday, he still had a thick head of fair hair, which was now falling in front of his smiling green eyes. He had Richard's rugged handsome looks, and weather-beaten skin from a life lived outside, but there the similarity between father and son ended. Richard had been a hugely confident man, a bad-tempered bull, attacking life and everyone in it with very little regard for the chaos he left in his wake. Leo, on the other hand, was a born worrier, fretting about what people – mostly his father – thought of him and taking everything to heart. He had spent most of his adult life trying to unpick the mess that Richard had made of the guides, but recently she knew he'd come to the end of the road. Selling up was now their only choice, and one that left him feeling as if he had failed.

'I just wanted to be alone,' Vanessa said. 'You mustn't worry so much about me. You've got enough on your plate; you're going to make yourself ill.'

'I'm fine. I've got the final meeting at the village hall this morning, and I wanted to make sure you're okay before I go.'

Vanessa's gaze ran around the hallway: the overloaded coat stand, the piles of walking boots covered in mud, the mound of dog leads, hats and gloves on the grubby black and white tiled floor. Leo was always working, either on the farm or in endless meetings with architects and planning officials. Whereas Helen, his wife, just seemed to flutter around all day, like a bird with a broken wing, making her presence known, fussing over things that didn't need her attention, and seemingly ignoring the things that did. The house was always a tip, and its upkeep neglected. She cooked for Sienna, but rarely for Leo, and while Sienna was immaculate, Leo always looked a mess. Helen ran Sienna's life like a naval ship, yet Yew Tree, the house that Vanessa had cherished all her life, was clearly of no interest to her. It broke Vanessa's heart every day that Helen so obviously couldn't wait to be rid of it, presumably to get her hands on the money.

As if conjured up by Vanessa's thoughts, Helen appeared in the hallway, making her jump.

'Hi, Vanessa,' she said warmly. 'Sorry, I didn't mean to startle you.' Her eyes fell on Vanessa's shoes. 'Oh dear, you're soaked through. You must be freezing. Leo lit the fire in the sitting room if you want to go in there.'

'Okay, thank you, Helen.'

Vanessa looked at her daughter-in-law for a little too long, as if she were searching for something, some clue as to what really went on behind those piercing blue eyes. She didn't wish to make the girl uncomfortable, but Helen reminded her of the mouse that had made a habit of coming into her kitchen every night for the best part of a year. It would sit in the corner and watch television with her, keeping her company, until one night it vanished as abruptly as it had arrived. She used to pretend she was watching the screen, but really she was keeping one eye on the creature, trying to fathom it out. It looked so sweet and innocent, yet it was constantly on edge, always ready to dart, its whiskers twitching, and with Helen's mousy features and fidgety manner, it was hard not to draw comparisons.

Vanessa had never been entirely sure what Leo saw in

Helen. She didn't dislike the girl as such, but there was so little to warm to. She never really showed her true colours, and always seemed to be wary of her own shadow. Leo could have married anyone – every girl he spoke to seemed to melt in his presence, and from the way Vanessa's friends asked after him, it would seem that any of their daughters would have jumped at the chance to bag him – but he had chosen Helen, someone you couldn't take much offence to but who couldn't really hold her own in a conversation. Helen was fifty-three now, yet she still had such a childlike way about her, so that in some ways she seemed more vulnerable than Sienna, who had been a rather unexpected arrival when Helen was in her mid-forties. Helen had a desperate desire to please, a smile always planted firmly on her lips but one that never reached her sad eyes.

'Did you see Sienna when you were outside?' Helen said as she walked into the sitting room and Vanessa followed. Helen walked over to the window, moving magazines around pointlessly on a coffee table in the corner; one messy pile to another, Vanessa thought.

'Yes, she's having a lovely time on her bicycle. You need to leave for school, though, don't you?' said Vanessa, looking at her watch.

'I think Leo is taking her on the way to his meeting,' Helen replied.

'Maybe you should take her, Helen. Leo looks very stressed; his workload never seems to let up.'

Helen smiled weakly and began gathering her daughter's various bits of paraphernalia strewn around the room and packing them into her rucksack. Sienna was the only thing that seemed to interest Helen, thought Vanessa, watching her. She rarely socialised or saw friends; she and Leo never threw dinner parties or went out to the pub. Her world revolved around Sienna's after-school clubs and play dates and school work, and she watched her like a hawk, pouring every ounce of energy into her. Sienna didn't have a single thought that Helen didn't know about. Helen still slept with her daughter most nights, while Leo slept alone. Richard wouldn't have put up with it for one night, let alone seven years. Perhaps it was a generational thing, but it had been that way since Sienna was a baby. Vanessa had often wondered if that was the reason Leo was slightly distant with his daughter: Sienna adored her dad, but he always seemed a little bit detached around her and it occurred to her that maybe it was because she had come between him and Helen. He had always said he didn't want children, then suddenly, at the age of forty-five, Helen had announced that she was pregnant. Leo wasn't unkind to Sienna, far from it, but he rarely played with her or seemed particularly enamoured or engaged with her, as Richard had been with Alice. But then Helen was so smothering, it was hard for Leo to have Sienna to himself.

It had occurred to Vanessa, in her darker moments, that it was jealousy that drove her irritation with Helen's obsession with Sienna. She'd thought she and Alice had a wonderful relationship, but the fact of the matter was, Helen would never lose Sienna. Not in a million years. She would never let her out of her sight for long enough. But maybe the reason she watched Sienna like a hawk was because of Alice's disappearance. Helen saw what the loss of a child did to a mother; the fact was the repercussions of losing Alice lived with all of them at Yew Tree, still to this day, despite nearly fifty years passing.

'Did you have a nice walk?' Helen asked, bringing Vanessa back to the present as she looked out of the window at Sienna.

'Yes, I walked to The Vicarage. They're all ready to knock it down by the looks of things.'

Helen turned slowly and looked at her, flushing red, but saying nothing.

'It's strange to think of that cold, empty shell of a house once so full of life. I have no idea what became of the James family – Nell and Bobby, wasn't it? Do you know, Leo?'

'What, Mum?' Leo had appeared at the door, frowning. 'Have you seen my car keys, Helen?'

Helen was still staring at Vanessa. 'Um, I think they're on the dining-room table.'

'Try under the piles of papers and newspapers,' said Vanessa. 'It wouldn't surprise me if Bobby James is in prison. Awful child, set fire to the cowshed. Do you remember, Leo?'

'Um, yes, vaguely.' Leo looked over at Helen, who had turned her back to them.

'Vaguely? I'll never forget it. Determined to burn those animals alive, he was. Richard only just got there in time.' Vanessa frowned. 'Where are you going?'

'I told you, Mum, it's the final planning meeting at the village hall. Tomorrow is D-Day.'

Helen walked past them with Sienna's rucksack.

'Why don't you let Helen take Sienna to school?' Vanessa said to Leo. 'I can do us a quick fry-up.'

'I'll get something after the meeting, Mum. Helen, will

you make Mum some breakfast? I've got to go or I'll be late,' he said, finally finding his keys and dashing out.

Vanessa looked around to see Sienna darting into the room. 'Bye, Granny!' she said, launching herself into her grandmother's arms, her cheeks flushed from the cold.

'Bye, darling, have a wonderful day.'

'I'll see you at the meeting, Helen,' Leo called out. 'I'll save a seat for you.'

Vanessa looked at her daughter-in-law, who seemed to have sunk into one of her moods. She didn't like to be around Helen when she was silent and brooding; it made her wary of what was going on underneath the surface. She was always acutely aware of the fact that she didn't quite trust the girl, but she never really knew why and it just left her feeling guilty and rather empty. 'I think I'm going to have a lie-down,' Vanessa said. 'I walked further than I meant to.'

She paused at the bottom of the huge sweeping staircase that curled round to the top of the house. There was a feeling of neglect about the large Georgian manor. The paint on the window next to where she stood was chipped, the carpet on the stairs appeared faded and threadbare, and a number of the tiles under her feet were slightly cracked. The heating was always on low, if at all, so that the house felt constantly cold.

She started slowly up the stairs, each of which was littered with books, items of clothing and newspapers. Her eyes ran along the peeling wallpaper, adorned with various large pieces of artwork and oversized mirrors, until she reached the top, where a photograph of Richard and Leo was propped up against the wall. It was a black and white print of the two of them on a tractor, and she could remember the day exactly. It was July, a hot summer's afternoon, Leo had been about four, and Richard had put him on his knee so he could steer. Leo had cried the entire time, hating every second of it, and Richard had been impatient with him and ended up smacking him. She had been pregnant with Alice at the time; and with Richard baling in the fields all day, for weeks on end, she decided to take a picnic lunch for them to eat during his break. Leo hadn't wanted to go and she had known the whole thing would end in tears, but she still went, because she was lonely: the lot of a farmer's wife.

Like her, Leo hated life on the farm. But unlike her, he didn't try and hide it. He would cry if he fell, wail if one of the animals chased him or if he got his hands dirty. Alice, in complete contrast, loved it as much as her father. The more terrifying the experience, the better. They adored one another, and Alice would cry if he went off on an adventure without her. As soon as she could walk, she would follow him everywhere, returning from feeding the cows or mending a fence on his shoulders, so caked in mud Vanessa could barely see her face.

''Gen, Daddy!' was her catchphrase whenever he threw her in the air, or onto a high wall, or over a ditch, when she would invariably fall and hurt herself as Vanessa recoiled in horror. But within moments she had brushed herself down and held out her hands. ''Gen, Daddy!'

Vanessa reached the door to her bedroom and stopped as she always did to look at the portrait of Alice. A painting she'd had commissioned of her daughter in a red party dress, the one she had been wearing the night she went missing.

'Mummy, why can't I wear my dungarees?' said a high voice. Vanessa looked down to see her little girl's green eyes looking at her questioningly as she walked towards her along the landing. Alice was dragging the red dress in one hand and a blue satin one in the other, and was wearing dungarees sodden with muddy snow from playing outside. Around her mouth were smudges of what looked like chocolate cake, and her cheeks and fingertips were flushed red from coming into the warm. Vanessa took her daughter's cold hands and squeezed them inside hers, rubbing them together to warm them up. Alice's silver link bracelet, which she had bought her for Christmas, with the initial 'A' hanging from it, caught the sparkling lights.

Inside her bedroom, Vanessa walked slowly over to the window and looked down at the driveway. Sienna was waving at her from the car window. Vanessa waved back as they turned the corner and disappeared, the little girl's face still fresh in her mind's eye.

So like Alice, she thought. She was so like Alice, it was almost too much to bear.

Chapter Two
Willow

Thursday, 21 December 2017

Willow James's boot heels echoed loudly as she walked up the wooden steps and across the stage of Kingston village hall, home to hundreds of nativity productions, summer fairs and bingo evenings.

Putting her notes down on the lectern, she hid her shaky hands behind her back and looked down at the sea of faces staring up at her expectantly. She suddenly felt self-conscious about her outfit, having opted for a smarter look than usual: a newly purchased navy blazer and white shirt from Zara, skinny jeans and brown boots. She had blow-dried her dark choppy bob, slapped on her favourite Chanel nude lipstick and gone for smoky make-up as a contrast to her ice-blue eyes. But she was worried she now looked too formal. She had tried very hard to dress casually for the previous meetings with the villagers, in order not to appear too corporate, but she'd felt today that standing up in front of them for the final presentation warranted some war paint.

Peter, the caretaker, had told her proudly that he had put out over a hundred chairs in anticipation of the turn-out, all of which were now filled, with the later arrivals still spilling in through the door. A kind-looking man with white hair and smiling eyes, he had informed her that he had held the position of caretaker for nearly forty years.

As she stood waiting for the cacophony of chatter to die down, she scanned the audience for familiar faces, and spotted her boss, Mike Scott, on his mobile phone. Their client, Leo Hilton – with whom they had been working on the five-million-pound housing development plans for over a year – was just arriving and making his way along the aisle to sit next to him. As usual, Mike was freshly shaven and wearing his signature black polo neck, jeans and long black coat. In contrast, Leo was dressed in a waxed Barbour, mud-covered ankle boots and a baseball cap. On Leo's other side was an empty seat, which Willow presumed was saved for his wife. Willow had only met Helen a couple of times in passing but she was a quiet woman with fine features, who hadn't had much involvement in the project.

Two rows back sat Willow's boyfriend, Charlie, and his parents, Lydia and John. They were beaming at her proudly whilst chatting animatedly to their friends and neighbours in Kingston, where they had lived for over a decade. John gave her an encouraging wink and Lydia waved at her cheerfully.

At last the hall fell quiet, with the exception of a young child screaming determinedly at the back. Willow took a deep breath and forced a smile. 'Hello, everyone, and thank you all for coming,' she said. Although she was leaning into the microphone, her voice barely made a dent in the crowded space.

'We can't hear you, love,' shouted a male voice from the

back as the gathered villagers began to murmur amongst themselves again. Willow felt her cheeks flush and her butterflies intensify as she looked down at Mike frowning up at her from his seat.

She began fiddling with the microphone, tapping it fruitlessly, until Leo came bounding up onto the stage, wisps of blonde hair escaping from his cap, and turned it on.

'There you go,' he said, winking at her.

'Oh, thank you, Leo,' said Willow, as a screech of feedback escaped from the microphone. She clocked a row of middle-aged women near the front all gazing at him adoringly as he jumped off the stage and returned to his seat. In every encounter she'd had with him, he seemed to have an extraordinary effect on people, men and women alike. He oozed charm, but not in an obvious way; he was warm, friendly and kind, often remembering tiny details about people's lives. He was very open about his own imperfections – how he was chaotic, scatty and forgetful, but he was always going out of his way to help. He needed a haircut, and his clothes were often rather threadbare, but he was extremely good-looking, reminding Willow of the cowboys in the Westerns her father used to watch. Sienna clearly adored her father, although Leo never seemed particularly enamoured with her. He wasn't ever mean, but if she climbed up on his knee during a meeting and asked questions, he rarely engaged with her, or if she skipped along on their site visits, he would tell her to run back to the house. But then what did she know, Willow thought. Her relationship with her own father was certainly not going to win any awards, so she had little to go on.

Willow took a breath and began her speech again. 'Good

morning, and thank you all so much for coming out on this cold December day.' Her voice boomed as the microphone finally burst into life. 'It is a great testament to the wonderful community spirit of Kingston, a place I have become well acquainted with over the past year, that so many of you have ventured out to see our final model of this exciting development, which will be presented to the planning department tomorrow.'

She took another breath and looked around, catching the eye of several locals she had worked with over the past year: listening to them and easing their concerns over the increased traffic the development would bring; meeting with them over coffee to allay their fears about losing the village hall; and talking through their queries about the design of the development to take to the conservation officers in Brighton – with whom she had built up a strong, trusting relationship – in order to reach various compromises that suited everyone involved.

'As we reach the end of this process, I hope you know that we are very grateful to each and every one of you who has approached us, worked with us, and supported the vision we at Sussex Architecture – alongside Mr Leo Hilton – share for this sustainable, mutually beneficial and exciting new venture for Kingston. I know many of you are deeply saddened by the prospect of replacing this beautiful village hall and The Vicarage, which you hold so close to your hearts. But I assure you, we have listened carefully, and today we would like to show you a presentation of the new community centre, including a library, that we hope will become the heart of the village.'

Willow turned to the projector screen and clicked on the

first image. It had taken her only a month to design the entire project, made up of ten detached houses and the community hub, as Mike liked to call it. But that had been followed by twelve months of struggle to get where she was now: gathering statements, compiling reports, winning over the various consultants to approve the plans and – most challenging of all – getting the locals on board so that they didn't object to the planning application, which was on track to be approved in just over twenty-four hours.

'Could someone please get the lights? Thank you, Peter – my hero!' said Willow as Peter gave her the thumbs-up from the other end of the hall and plunged them all into darkness. 'I'm going to have to get you a cape for Christmas,' she added, and the audience smiled appreciatively.

Willow began to talk through the image on the projector screen – the first sketches of their development, on a page entitled 'Yew Tree Estate: A Vision Realised', taking her back to the day Mike had called her into his office and announced that she was being given her first major project to head up. After nearly five years of trying to prove herself, of drawing up other architects' sketches, of being stuck at her desk, rarely invited out to site visits or planning meetings, of desperately wanting to create spaces of her own and never getting the chance, she was being handed a five-million-pound project from scratch.

'Now, this isn't going to be an easy task, Willow,' Mike had said, leaning in. 'Not only are we demolishing a listed Georgian manor house to make way for the new homes, but The Vicarage and the village hall are going to have to go in order to get the road infrastructure in place.' He had tapped on his pad with his pen until the paper began to rip. 'This house is important to the conservation area, but it land-locks the whole site; we cannot build around it. It's a large, beloved mansion in the heart of the village, so you need to design the new development in such a way that it looks better than the current building. We then need to find a conservation consultant who will say the design enhances and preserves the area, as well as several environmental specialists to declare how green it will be.'

As he had continued, realisation began to dawn that this house he was describing to her, the one at the heart of the project, was frighteningly familiar. Very quickly her elation had turned to fear as a burning sensation began creeping up her neck.

'Crucially – and this is where we feel you will come into your own – we have to gain agreement from the local area that the existing building is an eyesore. On top of which, of course, you'll need to find a structural engineer to say it's falling apart, which won't be easy.'

'You're talking about Yew Tree Manor?' she had said, her eyes wide.

'Ah, good, you know it. So you realise what we're up against.' He ran his hands through his floppy fringe and sat back in his chair.

'Why does Leo Hilton want to tear it down? It's been in his family for generations. Is his mother still alive?' Willow said, failing to hide her shock.

Mike frowned. 'I think of all the things we are going to have to concern ourselves with at this point, Leo Hilton's mother is not one of them. He's mentioned that she hasn't been well, and that he has power of attorney, which is all that matters. You sound as if you know the family?' he added.

'Oh, no. No. My boyfriend's parents live in Kingston, so they've mentioned Yew Tree Manor. The Hiltons are well known there,' she added, her cheeks flushing.

'That's great if your in-laws live in Kingston; they can help rally local support for us. But if this project is a problem for you, I can offer it to Jim. I thought you'd be over the moon.'

It had been on the tip of her tongue to ask if The Vicarage, her father's home for the first thirteen years of his life, was being demolished too, but that would have aroused too much suspicion. She would find out soon enough. She wondered for a moment if Leo Hilton had asked for her specifically, but she wasn't sure he even knew she existed, let alone where she worked. Even if he did, why would he seek her out?

As her boss stared at her intently, his eyes narrowing, fingers tapping on his chair, every fibre of her being ached to tell him she couldn't do it. Her mind raced at the situation presenting itself: a chance to prove herself after years of studying and student debt. Even when she'd finally qualified as a RIBA architect, she had struggled to be taken seriously in a male-dominated industry. Now, suddenly, a project she could only have dreamed of when she was starting out was being handed to her on a plate, but with the caveat that she had to work with the Hiltons – the family that had essentially destroyed her father's life.

'I *am* over the moon, thank you, Mike,' she said at last. 'I think I'm just a little overwhelmed. It's quite unexpected.'

'Right,' he said, frowning. 'Well, it shouldn't be that

unexpected. You've worked hard, Willow, and we feel you're ready, but if you're not up to it, I need to know now.'

'I'm definitely up to it,' she had said, pushing away the conversation she would have to have with her father. A conversation that, a year down the line, she still hadn't had – and now that the project was nearly complete, a conversation she was hoping to avoid altogether.

But whilst she had managed to push her father out of her mind, another person had crept in.

The great unsolved mystery of missing Alice Hilton, the newspapers called it. Six-year-old Alice, Leo Hilton's little sister, who had slipped away from her parents' New Year's Eve party at Yew Tree Manor in 1969. A little girl looking for her puppy in the snow, who before vanishing into the night had bumped into a young lad by the name of Bobby James – Willow's father.

He had told the police over and over that he didn't know what had happened to Alice, but his handkerchief had been found covered in her blood, and today, nearly fifty years later, the police – and Vanessa Hilton – still suspected he'd had something to do with her disappearance. Over the years, Willow had discovered that her father had been well known to the police at the time, having got into trouble for setting the Hiltons' cowshed on fire. She was sure that had been an accident, but when pressed for an explanation, he had shut down, as he always did.

The police had pushed him for a confession over Alice's disappearance for three days and nights until finally he had snapped, lashing out at the officer questioning him and throwing a chair at the interview room window. After that, he'd been sent to a youth detention centre, where he was beaten and abused by guards and inmates daily until he was finally discharged three years later.

Willow could picture the scene in the police station as clearly as if she had been there herself. She knew her father hadn't hurt Alice, but she also knew that when he shut down and refused to talk, it was easy to interpret his silence as guilt. She had struggled with this personality trait of his countless times in her young life, with her father flatly refusing to ever discuss anything about the past, however much she begged. In the end, she had given up.

It was this deep frustration with his inability to tell her anything about his past that, in the end, had made her accept the Yew Tree project. Perhaps, by working for the Hiltons, she might finally discover some clues about his childhood at The Vicarage, about Leo and Alice and all the things he would never talk to her about. After a lifetime of secrets, it was too tempting an opportunity to turn down.

But almost as soon as she had said yes to the project, Alice Hilton began to haunt her dreams; always in the red dress that the newspapers said she was wearing on the night she went missing. Alice's absence started feeling like a constant presence in Willow's life. She would have been a woman of fifty-four now, but her disappearance had frozen her in time as the six-year-old girl in the red dress. On site visits, as they walked through the plans at Yew Tree Manor, Leo Hilton's daughter Sienna would appear from upstairs, the image of Alice's portrait in the hall, making goosebumps run up Willow's arms as she forced herself not to stare at the little girl.

The door of the village hall slammed suddenly and

Helen appeared at the back, her pale cheeks flushing a deep crimson as everyone turned to look at her. She glanced around for Leo, who waved, and she made her way towards him, whispering her apologies to the audience members letting her through.

'As some of you may have noticed already,' Willow continued, drawing attention away from Helen as her slides finished, 'we have had a beautiful model created of the Yew Tree development for you to feast your eyes on. Please help yourselves to a cup of tea and a mince pie, which Peter has kindly laid out, and we will, of course, be here to answer any final questions you may have ahead of the planning meeting tomorrow. Thank you once again for your time.'

She smiled as the audience began to clap, and made her way back down the steps to where Leo and Mike were waiting for her. Leo put his arm around her shoulder and squeezed.

'Wonderful stuff, great work, Willow,' he said. 'I don't think we've ever had such a big turn-out, even when Alan Titchmarsh came to do a book signing. You should be very proud of yourself, shouldn't she, Helen?'

Helen stared at Willow with her intense blue eyes, which seemed, to Willow, to jar with the rest of her mouse-like appearance. Willow had never known what to make of Leo's wife. She had met her a few times when she'd had meetings at Yew Tree Manor, but although she was perfectly pleasant, Helen always kept her distance. She didn't know if she was imagining it, but Helen always seemed to leave the room as soon as Willow walked into it.

'Yes, definitely,' Helen said, her gaze lingering on Willow. 'You've achieved the impossible.'

'Thank you,' Willow replied, pondering Helen's choice of words.

Leo already had five or six villagers crowding round, waiting to talk to him. He turned to the group of smiling faces nursing their hot drinks.

'Martha, how wonderful of you to come out when you've just got back from your holiday. You look extremely well, I must say; you've obviously had a wonderful time. Hello, Jim, how's your back?'

'Would you like a cup of tea, Helen?' asked Willow.

'Um, yes, please.' Helen glanced over her shoulder at the entrance as if she were looking for someone, or possibly a way out. Willow suspected Helen wouldn't hang around long enough to drink the tea Willow was about to fetch her, but she smiled warmly before walking away.

As she stood at the tea station, she watched Leo hold court. The fact that he was so popular in Kingston had made Willow's life easier, although, in another sense, it had added to her feelings of treachery.

Her father very rarely spoke of the Hiltons, so she had no idea how he felt about Alice's older brother. Racking her brain she could remember only one occasion when Leo Hilton's name came up, in reference to a fire in the cowshed at Yew Tree not long before Alice vanished.

It had been Leo Hilton who had actually started the fire, her father had said, but Leo's father Richard had asked Bobby to cover for him. Bobby had never lied in his life before that moment, he told Willow, but it was the start of his downfall. It was the first time he had crossed paths with the police; something that would tarnish his character for ever. And a moment that changed everything.

She didn't know how she was supposed to feel about Leo Hilton, or whether he really had started the fire for which her father had been blamed. But while she had enjoyed working with Leo, and noted how he made an effort to show everyone how down-to-earth he was despite owning half of Kingston village, she had occasionally noticed flashes of another side to him. An irritable side, which came to the surface occasionally if something wasn't going his way.

As she stirred their tea, Willow observed Helen standing silently next to her husband. Theirs, it seemed to Willow, was a marriage that lacked warmth. They were civil to one another, but quite functional in the way they interacted, and every conversation revolved around Sienna. Helen rarely smiled at Leo, and when she did it seemed rather forced, never reaching her striking blue eyes.

'Here you go, Helen,' she said, handing her the cup. Helen's eyes seemed to sparkle with tears, making them even bluer, as she took the drink without a word.

Mike suddenly appeared at her side and smiled at Helen. 'Sorry to interrupt. Willow, the developers have called. We need a signature meeting with them today, so I'm going to take Leo and Helen to the office now. Are you happy to hold the fort?'

Willow laughed at her boss's request before realising he was serious about leaving her in the lions' den on her own. 'Um, there are a lot of people here, Mike,' she said, trying to swallow her shock as Helen smiled nervously and walked over to her husband.

'I know, but Leo's leaving the country tomorrow and he needs to discuss another proposal for us. Which is entirely thanks to you. You've got everyone here eating out of your hand, Willow. I couldn't have hoped for a better outcome. And don't worry, Kellie's on her way to help you get the model back to the office.'

Willow watched as Helen and Leo appeared to exchange words, before Helen turned and walked out. Distracted by Helen's obvious upset, Willow tried to focus on what Mike was saying.

'Kellie? But she's got enough on her plate. It's okay; Charlie's here, he can help me.' She imagined Kellie, their very outspoken office manager, shouting profanities after receiving Mike's request to drive to Kingston, instead of dealing with the piles of admin on her desk.

'Willow, sorry to interrupt, can I introduce you to my wife, Dorothy?' She dragged her attention away from Mike to see Peter standing behind her, next to a woman she guessed to be in her seventies. She had kind, smiling eyes and a neat grey bob, and was wearing a beige cashmere jumper and grey woollen coat.

'Hello,' said Willow warmly, frowning as Mike led Leo away. Leo turned back and waved cheerfully at her, clearly oblivious to her plight.

'Well done on your presentation,' Dorothy said. 'You've really done such a wonderful job of putting our minds at ease.' Willow noticed the woman glancing over at the door as Helen walked out.

For some reason, Helen's distress and Mike's comment that she had the village eating out of her hand had thrown her. She started to feel panicky as she looked around the packed room, as if they all knew something she didn't. Something about Mike's manner had also altered; the warmth gone, the façade dropped now he felt the deal was done.

'Willow? Are you all right?' said Peter as she dragged her attention back to them.

'Yes, sorry, it's lovely to meet you, Dorothy.' She took Dorothy's hand and shook it.

'And you, Willow. We've lived in the village for over fifty years and know the Hiltons well, so we didn't want to be a nuisance. But it was hard not to worry about the plans when they're going to have such a big impact. I think it helped that your in-laws are in the village and could vouch for you.'

Her attention on the exit Leo and Mike were walking through, Willow finally looked back at Dorothy. She suddenly felt a surge of protectiveness over Charlie's family and a stab of paranoia that she'd been used by Mike. 'Well, we aren't married, but yes, my boyfriend's family have been very supportive.'

'Well, Charlie is a lovely chap; don't let him get away!' said Dorothy, looking at her husband, who took a large bite of his mince pie and nodded enthusiastically. Dorothy appeared to Willow to be quite a dominating character; it was clearly a case of happy wife, happy life in their house.

'I just wanted to ask you about something,' Dorothy continued. 'We were wondering what happened to the graveyard at The Vicarage?'

Willow felt her stomach lurch. 'The graveyard?' she asked, trying not to show her surprise.

'Yes, we live at Yew Tree Cottage, as you know, which overlooks The Vicarage from upstairs, and we noticed that the graveyard has been grassed over recently. When did Leo have it excavated?' Dorothy looked at her intently, waiting for an answer, a crumb of pastry balancing on her bottom lip.

'Um,' Willow stalled, feeling her heart race. 'I believe that was all dealt with before we came on board.'

'I see. I thought it would be rather a long, drawn-out process, but perhaps not. I'm not sure it was an official graveyard, but there were definitely some headstones there. Maybe it was more of a memorial ground.'

Willow forced a smile, her anxiety increasing by the second.

'We're just glad to have you involved in the development,' Dorothy went on. 'I think there was a general feeling of distrust until you came along, but you've painted such an intricate picture, you've really won over the community single-handedly. I mean, it's all very well having someone focusing on the positives, saying there'll be more money for the community, more spent on the roads, all the jazz hands, but until you can see something tangible for yourself, like your model over there, and the plans that are being submitted to the council, it's hard to believe we won't all be worse off.'

Willow became aware that another couple had walked over to stand next to her, waiting for her to finish speaking to Peter and Dorothy.

'Hello, Willow, sorry to butt in, we were just wondering if you could talk us through the layout of the library?'

'Of course. Please excuse me, Dorothy,' said Willow, turning towards the model of the Yew Tree development that Dorothy had commented on. The entire room's focus seemed to be on the cardboard sculpture, the design she had spent an entire year fighting for and putting her career on the line for. *You've got everyone eating out of your hands.* Mike's words, though complimentary on the surface, had an air of arrogance about them; they were disrespectful to her and about the people who had put their trust in her. She felt the heat creeping up her neck and back intensify.

As she turned her attention to the model, conversations with her boss that had made her feel uneasy started to come back to her; when he had asked her to do things that weren't strictly ethical. He had described it as looking at things from a different angle, using strategies to act for your client, not showing weakness, playing the game. And she had gone along with it in the name of doing whatever it took to bank the planning permission and seal the deal. In order to be taken seriously in a male-dominated world.

As she scanned the model, now surrounded by two dozen people clutching mince pies and steaming drinks, a sea of faces looked at her expectantly. She glanced down at the buildings and imagined it beginning to snow. Slowly the cardboard figures going in and out of the library and community centre began to move and, on the other side of the estate, a little figure in a red dress appeared from Yew Tree Manor. As Willow watched, spellbound, the figure left tiny footprints in the freshly fallen snow and walked towards the large oak tree where Willow's father had bumped into Alice Hilton on New Year's Eve 1969.

The clatter of cups and plates and the buzz of chatter faded into muffled silence as Willow watched the tiny figure reach the woods, then disappear, as her breath quickened and the walls of the village hall began to close in on her.

Despite it being the end of the line for the development at Yew Tree and the demolition of The Vicarage being, potentially, only days away, she would never be able to erase that night from their lives. Taking on the project had not helped her to find out more about what had happened to her father, and his sister, Nell; it had only served to make her feel guilty for betraying her father and made her act in a way that, looking back, she wasn't sure she was proud of.

Her father had been right: she should have just left the past alone.

She was playing with fire.

Yew Tree Manor, and little Alice, had a vice-like grip that would never let them go.

Chapter Three

Nell

December 1969

'Up you get, Nell James,' Bobby whispered, shaking his little sister awake. 'It's time for milking.'

'It's the middle of the night.'

'It's not, it's five o'clock in the morning. Do you want to come with me or stay in bed?'

'I'm coming. Don't go without me, Bobby,' said Nell, pushing back the quilt and letting out a yawn.

Bobby smiled down at his funny little sister, with her blue eyes that saw straight through him, their mother's dark auburn hair and a button nose peppered with freckles. She was flushed with just being woken from her sleep. Bobby fetched her dungarees, jumper and thick socks from the end of her wrought-iron bed and laid them down next to her.

'I was dreaming that Molly had her puppies and they were licking my ear,' Nell said, rubbing her eyes slowly. 'Do you think they'll come soon, Bobby?'

'You're obsessed with those puppies, and they aren't even born yet.' He smiled.

'I wish Dad would let her stay indoors by the fire. Those poor babies can't be born in the barn in the snow, they'll die.'

'Well, Dad has got a lot to worry about at the moment, Nell. Puppies aren't really at the top of his list of priorities.' Bobby let out a heavy sigh. 'Get dressed quickly, it's bitter outside. The ground is frozen hard with the ice.'

Nell glanced at her brother. He looked sad, as he always did when their father was in a temper. 'I heard Dad talking to you last night, Bobby,' she said, her eyes wide. 'About the police. What's wrong?'

Bobby looked down at his feet. Nell knew he was upset; somehow she always knew what he was feeling.

'There was a fire, in the Hiltons' barn.' He looked up to see Nell's face stricken with panic. 'It's all right. It was an accident, Nell. Richard put it out, none of the animals were hurt.'

'What do you mean, an accident? What happened?' Nell's eyes started to well up.

Bobby paused for a long time, hesitating before he told her the truth. 'They were burning some old wood. It was too near the barn entrance and it spat some flames on a bale of hay, which caught fire. Luckily, I spotted it from the field and ran to the house to raise the alarm, so Richard put it out.'

Nell frowned as Bobby tried to walk away. 'But why did the police want to talk to you?'

'Because there was quite a lot of damage, and Richard is going to have to claim it on his insurance, so he needed me to say it was my fault.'

'What's in-surance?' Nell struggled with the word.

'Look, Nell, it's nothing for you to worry about.' Bobby slipped Nell's thick woollen socks onto her feet.

'Why did Richard want you to take the blame? You

shouldn't have done that, Bobby, you shouldn't lie. Especially not to the police.' Nell was wide-eyed. 'Who did start it?'

'Leo, but he didn't mean to, he just doesn't think sometimes. Richard was pretty hard on him,' Bobby said quietly, lost in thought; he looked sad, thought Nell.

'Alice says he hits Leo with a belt. I don't like Richard. You shouldn't trust him. He's going to take away our house,' she said.

'How'd you know about that?' Bobby frowned at her.

'I heard Dad talking to the man in the suit who came to the door last night. You were working, and Dad thought I was asleep. I heard the man saying Richard Hilton wants to knock The Vicarage down and build some new houses. He's sold all the land already.'

'Yes, well, Richard has told me he's going to look after us once the deal goes through.'

'But it's not his house to knock down. It's Dad's house. His father left it to him. That's what Dad said.'

'It's not that simple, Nell. You're too young to understand.'

'I'm not. I don't like Richard. You shouldn't trust him, Bobby, he's horrible to Leo.'

'Well, he's nice to your friend Alice. Come on, you need to get dressed. And don't ask Dad about the house. He's not in a good mood today.'

'But where will we live, Bobby?'

'We'll think of something, Nell. Don't start crying. And for goodness' sake don't mention the puppies.'

'Ooh, Bobby, do you really think he'll make them stay in the barn?' said Nell, seemingly forgetting about their impending homelessness. 'Will he let me watch them being born, like he does with the cows? I just hope they live, at least two of them, so I can have one and Alice can have the other. Her mummy has said she can. Alice hasn't decided what to call it yet, but I'm definitely calling mine Snowy.'

'You know you talk more than anyone I know, Nell James,' Bobby said. 'You talk in your sleep, you talk when you're eating, you even talk when you're crying.'

'I like talking. How else do people know what you're thinking?' Nell frowned at her brother, squinting seriously.

'You could try just stopping sometimes and thinking about what you say before it comes out. You can't unsay things, you know; you have to be careful sometimes. Especially now, with everything that's going on. We don't know who to trust.'

Nell began brushing her tangled hair, which always looked like she'd rolled down a hill and picked up every twig in her path. 'I trust Alice, she's my best friend. I tell her everything.'

'Yeah, well, she's also Richard's daughter, so maybe don't for now.' Nell started to well up with tears. 'Oh Nell, don't get upset. Come on, hurry up, you know how grumpy Dad gets if we hold him up.'

On sleepy legs, Nell stepped into her dungarees and pulled the woollen jumper their mother had knitted for Bobby over her head. She looked out of the window, seeing nothing but the black winter dawn, but the familiar sounds she had known all her life at The Vicarage painted a picture of the scene outside. The scraping as the milking gate dragged across the stone floor of the barn, her father slapping the cows' behinds and shouting directions, them mooing their protests as he hurried them into the milking parlour.

'Come on, Dad's got the porridge on,' said Bobby, thundering down the stairs.

As Nell rubbed her eyes, trying to push the thick fog of sleep away, she could hear the cottage coming to life for the day: the clinking of crockery as Bobby laid the table, the kettle whistling on the stove, the door slam as her father came in and spoke to Bobby in the kitchen.

'Nell said she heard you talking to the solicitor about the house. Where will we go when we get kicked out?' Bobby said quietly.

'We aren't going anywhere,' her father snapped.

'I can try and talk to Richard?' said Bobby. 'There might be somewhere else we can rent. He owns other houses in the village.'

'No! This is my home, I grew up here. Wilfred Hilton left it to me in his will and over my dead body are we leaving. You have no idea what that family are capable of. It wouldn't surprise me if Richard put his animals in the field next to ours to infect them on purpose.' Nell heard the anger in her father's voice.

'What do you mean, infected our herd?' Bobby sounded nervous.

'Bessie's not eating, and her lymph nodes are swollen. I'll have to call the vet and separate her from the rest of the herd.'

'They've given us TB? Does Richard know?'

'Yes, he knows.' Their father's voice was grim, and she felt the overwhelming urge to comfort him.

'What if we have to destroy the whole herd? We'll have nothing.'

Nell ran down the stairs and came rushing over to the table, throwing her arms around her father. 'Morning, Daddy.'

'Good morning, Nell,' said Alfie James, looking fondly at his daughter.

'Daddy, can Molly have her puppies inside by the fire? It's so cold in the barn. Please, Dad, please.' Nell gazed at him, tears already forming, waiting to fall.

'Houses are no places for dogs. She's fine in the barn, it's warm enough out there,' Alfie said firmly.

'But it's snowing, and they don't have any fur when they are born. Their eyes aren't even open. They'll be frightened and cold.' Nell's voice began to wobble with emotion.

'Nell, don't start,' Bobby snapped. 'She hasn't even had the bloody puppies yet. I asked you not to say anything.'

'But Alice's dogs are allowed inside.' Nell's cheeks burned, knowing that in mentioning her friend she would touch a nerve.

'Well, they have more space than us,' her dad muttered.

As Nell wiped her fat tears away with her sleeve and blew on her porridge, her gaze ran around The Vicarage, which despite being the prettiest house in the world to her, lacked the warm feeling she had when she walked into Alice's home. Despite the fire, her home always felt a little cold, and there were none of the flowers or rugs or cushions that made Alice's house feel so cosy. They were lucky that the pantry always contained food, but at Yew Tree Manor there were cakes and buns, and a pot of tea with a tea cosy over the top. And little sprinkles of happiness everywhere: pictures, and ornaments, and a smell of perfume in the air wherever Alice's mother walked. Nell was the only girl in her house, and she didn't feel grown up enough to do all the things a mother did to make a home feel the way that boys, with their muddy boots and messiness, had no clue about.

Nell often looked around her own kitchen and pictured Alice sitting at her large oak dining table, the Aga warm, her mother cuddling her as she read her a story, the smell of a roast chicken or side of beef sizzling, the newly tiled floor shining and polished, two fat Labradors asleep with bellies full of food.

She loved her family, but she ached for that picture of Alice on her mother's knee to be her. She couldn't remember her own mother, and her father didn't speak of her much. All she knew was that she had died just after Nell was born. She spent a great deal of time staring at the picture of her over the fireplace, looking at her smiling eyes, and her long wavy hair and wondering what her mother smelt like, sounded like, felt like holding her, playing with her, comforting her.

'Even if our house is smaller, I like it better,' she told her father now. 'Everywhere I look I can remember a happy thing that's happened there.' She began squinting, pointing her little finger around the room as the fire crackled in the corner. 'I can see Bobby dancing with me over there, and cuddling me by the fire over there, and you reading me a story over there.' She started to cry again. 'I love our house. I don't want to move.'

'Don't upset yourself, Nell. Your old dad is a fighter.' Alfie winked at her. 'Maybe stop talking just for long enough to eat your porridge.' He spooned a dollop of honey into her bowl. 'You need the energy if you're going to help Bobby.'

'Can I have some milk?' asked Nell, spreading butter over her cold toast.

Alfie's smile fell. 'Not today, Nell. We shouldn't drink it until we know the herd hasn't got TB. We'll have to pour today's milk down the drain too.'

The mood in the room suddenly darkened as Bobby stared at him in disbelief. 'Dad, we can't pour all that milk away.'

Alfie stood, taking a large slurp of his tea. 'We don't have a choice. It could be contaminated. Now get a move on. These cows won't milk themselves.'

'Why are we still milking them?' Nell said, frowning up at him.

'Because it hurts them if we don't. Cows need milking twice a day, whatever the weather; birthdays, Christmas, they don't know or care. Get the warm water for their udders, Bobby.'

As Bobby lifted a bucket of water from the stove, Nell pulled on her coat and scarf. Biting cold engulfed her as she stepped outside and walked over the cracking ice-covered ground to the milking shed, the glow from the sunrise leading the way. At the end of the Hilton field she could see a large digger, its yellow teeth facing towards her like a monster ready to pounce.

'Bobby, why do we have to separate the cows from their babies when they are born?' she asked.

'Because if the calf drinks all the milk, there's none for us to sell.' Bobby puffed some warm air into his hands and rubbed them together.

'I hate it when we have to take the calves away from their mummies. They cry. Lola tried to hide her calf in the nettles, didn't she, so Dad couldn't take her.' Nell's voice wobbled again.

'She did.' Bobby walked down the milking parlour and started to clean the cows' udders.

'Did my mummy die in a hospital? Did I cry when they took me away?' said Nell quietly, hugging herself to try and get warm as her eyes welled up once more.

'I doubt it because you never knew her. Don't start crying again, Nell, we've got work to do.' Bobby sighed.

Nell closed the milking shed door behind them. 'Bobby, are we going to lose our home?'

'I don't know. Grab a cloth, Nell, we need to clean their udders before we milk them.'

'We will always be together, though, won't we?' she persisted, ignoring his efforts to get her to help.

'Yes, Nell. Look, if you don't let me get on, you're going to have to go back to the house.' He looked down at his little sister, her eyes sparkling in the paraffin light, cow slurry swirling about her feet, her breath coming out in puffs as she stared at him adoringly.

As Bobby returned to his task, Nell wandered to the back of the milking shed, whistling to herself. Turning back to check that no one was watching, she pushed open the door and stepped out into the misty morning. Her boots crunched through the light snow as she walked down to the gate at the end of their field. In the distance she could see the large willow tree that stood yards from the lake that bordered Yew Tree and The Vicarage, the morning birds beginning to gather on its branches. It was her favourite tree, and the place she went to think about whatever was worrying her. As she walked towards it, she looked down at the hand-made gravestones and wooden crosses that littered the ground behind The Vicarage.

She sometimes thought how different this place was to the graveyard at the church, with its smart black or white marble stones with gold lettering and fresh flowers which visitors laid on Sunday when they went to church. But these graves felt like they belonged to people nobody cared about. Like the one that fascinated her; just a mound of soil, piled high with stones, which Bobby had told her was a witch the locals had drowned in the lake at Yew Tree hundreds of years before.

It had no name engraved on the stone, but instead just a symbol of a willow tree carved into a wooden block. 'The stones are to stop her coming back from the dead,' Bobby had explained to her one summer's evening, as Nell stared up at him wide-eyed.

That night she couldn't sleep. She imagined the witch coming back to life, crawling out of her grave; her long black hair tangled with thorns and warts on her nose. She would have flown on a broomstick and made potions in cauldrons with frogs' legs and bats' blood. The idea terrified her, but Bobby told her that witches weren't like they were made out to be in the story books. They were wise women, often midwives, who the Church killed because they were educated.

Nell ducked under the fence where the digger stood waiting and watching. The sun was rising as she made her way across the jagged ground churned up by the yellow-toothed monster. It was a struggle climbing up and down the mountains of turf that the digger had unearthed, and as she neared the willow tree, a ray of sunlight reflected off something shining in the distance.

Her heart quickened and she picked up her pace, walking towards the base of the tree. She looked down to see the corner of a metal tin, which she pulled out from the debris with her gloved hands. Slowly she turned it over. It was made of bronze, with dents and dinks in it from the passage of time. And on its front, dug out in the metal with what looked like a knife, was the word *Bella*. Pulling off her gloves, Nell brushed away the soil covering it. Real treasure, she thought to herself, before slowly tugging it open to reveal an ornate key, its head engraved with a willow tree.

'Nell?' Her father shouted her name, making her startle. She immediately snapped the tin shut and slipped it into her pocket, running back towards the milking shed, and tripping over the uneven earth as her heart hammered in her ears.

'Nell! These cows are coated in slurry; we're going to need more warm water. Get some from the well and put it on the stove.' Alfie stood at the far end of the shed, his face red, holding up a bucket for her to take. As she reached him, he thrust it in her hand and shook his head at her.

'Bobby, do you know anyone called Bella?' she panted, as she rushed past him.

'No,' he replied, continuing with his task and not looking up.

'Nell! Now!' shouted her father.

Bobby pulled an angry face and pretended to salute his father as Nell wrapped her scarf tightly around her mouth to stop herself from giggling. Nell walked back past The

Vicarage towards the well, her imagination starting to sparkle; picturing who this Bella was that the box belonged to. As she reached the handle, she hooked the bucket on and began to lower it down into the icy water below.

A warm glow engulfed her as she reached into her pocket with her other hand, and wrapped her gloved hand around the battered tin, feeling as if she had discovered a secret key to a world that she had yet to discover.

Chapter Four

Bella

Monday, 15 January 1945

'Tickets, please . . . Tickets, ma'am!'

Bella startled awake as the train rattled along the tracks, shocked that she had fallen asleep despite the stabbing pains in her abdomen which had started when she had snuck onto the train at Portsmouth.

As she went to reply to the conductor, another wave of pain surged through her, taking her breath away. Bella closed her eyes, praying for it to pass as the man leaned in, his strong body odour seeping through his musty uniform as the burning pain intensified.

'Well? Hurry up, lass,' he snapped, a drop of sweat trickling down from his brow.

Bella looked around, her sleep-addled brain trying to find a way out, someone, anyone who might help her. It had been fairly easy to get onto the train unseen; the platform at Portsmouth had been thronging with wounded servicemen on their way home from France. As she stood amongst them, she recalled how she had waved Eli off at the station in the winter of 1939, surrounded by a sea of excited young men, off on their adventures to foreign lands. As their sweethearts flourished Union Jack flags, they had all been oblivious to the living hell that Eli later wrote of from the front line. Now, in contrast, they stood still and silent, their skin pale, with dark shadows under their eyes, which were fixed and staring. Some were on crutches, with limbs amputated; others had their arms in slings, and a couple were blinded, tied to their guides with rope. She had been able to merge into a group of them as they climbed onto the train, hiding herself in a corner next to a young man who reminded her of Eli, tall and fair. If only she had spoken to him, she thought to herself now, if only she had stayed awake, she could have moved along the train, but her exhaustion and the rocking movement of the journey had been her downfall.

'One moment, please,' she said, as the pain finally let up and she turned to her scuffed canvas bag containing all her possessions in the world: a woollen scarf her mother had knitted her; a picture of her little boy, Alfie; a thin blanket she had taken from her bed at the merchant's house where she worked as a servant; and a small box containing an emerald engagement ring that Eli Hilton had given her the night before he left for war, when she had no idea she was already carrying Alfie.

And right at the bottom, her empty purse and the urgent telegram from her mother that the housekeeper had handed to her with a self-satisfied smirk on her face telling her to get home immediately to Alfie. She had then glanced, with horror, at the date, which told her that the housekeeper had taken a week to give her the telegram. Had Alfie been in hiding all that time? She still couldn't bear to think about it as the train rattled at a painfully slow speed along the tracks, every second she took to get to him feeling like an hour.

She had already been worried sick about Alfie before receiving the telegram, ever since she had seen the newspaper headlines staring up at her from the doorstep of the Victorian town house where she worked. A black and white photograph of her beloved mother, beneath the headline on the front page: *Midwife facing life imprisonment for manslaughter*.

She had immediately asked her employer for a day's leave, knowing that without her mother there, and with Eli away fighting on the front line, Alfie's welfare would fall to his father's family, who would relish the opportunity to have him sent away.

But her request for leave and an advance on her wages had been refused by Mrs Blackwood, the housekeeper, and she had gone to bed that night terrified of what would become of her little boy. But without any money, or any means to get home, she had no choice but to wait another week for her wages. It had been a torturous seven days, thinking of Alfie being sent away somewhere she had no hope of finding – but nothing could have prepared her for the shock of realising that he had spent those seven days terrified, cold and alone in the priest-hole at The Vicarage.

She continued searching for a train ticket that she knew wasn't there, her hands shaking. The packed train carriage was stuffy and hot, and she felt dizzy and sick as she turned back to the conductor, who had flushed red with irritation as a small child sitting opposite tugged at his jacket.

'I'm sorry, I can't seem to find it,' she said. 'I definitely had it. I must have dropped it when I fell asleep.' She looked at the floor beneath her feet.

'It's against the law to board a train without a ticket.

Please gather your things and we will escort you from the train at the next stop,' the conductor said matter-of-factly.

Another stabbing pain suddenly hit her, sharper than the last, as tears stung Bella's eyes. She had lain awake all night thinking of nothing but Alfie, her stomach starting to swell with the pregnancy that, judging from her last monthly bleed, was nearly three months along.

She had woken at dawn, taken some bread from the larder while Cook's back was turned then set out on the hour's walk to the station. It was as she had been walking along the busy road that the pains had begun. Pains that she tried to ignore as she managed to sneak into a carriage, pains that slowly grew as the train crept along. She knew she was miscarrying the foetus inside her. All she could do was plough on and hope she made it to The Vicarage before she started bleeding. She tried to block out Alfie's terror, the image of her beautiful boy alone in the dark, and focus on what she needed to do to get back home to him.

'Please don't throw me off the train, sir, please,' she begged. 'My mother's house is in Kingston; please let me stay on until then. I'll do anything.' She felt tears sting her eyes, mortified that she was having to plead like this.

'I don't want a scene, miss. Just pick yourself up before I have a mind to call the police and have them waiting for you on the platform.'

The woman opposite with her child on her knee frowned in concern as Bella gritted her teeth through another wave of pain then forced herself to stand and make her way to the doors, where two soldiers were sitting on the floor playing cards and smoking. 'Where are we?' she asked the men.

'Just coming into Falmer,' said a woman with two small children waiting to get off.

'How long do you think it would take to walk from Falmer to Kingston?' Bella asked nervously.

'To walk?' The woman frowned. It's a good two miles over the Downs, so it'll take you two hours I'd say.'

Bella gasped as another wave of pain took her breath away.

The woman looked at Bella, then at the child clinging to her leg. She was poorly dressed, her clothes slightly tattered, her boots worn. Slowly she reached into her coat and pulled out a shilling.

'Here,' she said. 'For the bus. I know you, you're Tessa James's girl, aren't you, from The Vicarage?'

Bella nodded. 'I can't take your money.'

'She saved my little boy's life,' said the woman quietly. 'It's dreadful what's happened to her; she would never have hurt that woman, Tessa's an angel.' The train was pulling into the station. 'You need the number sixteen bus, right by the entrance. Good luck.'

'Go on, git!' shouted the conductor as though Bella were a stray dog. As the train juddered to a halt, she stepped down on shaking legs onto the freezing, dark platform. 'And don't let me see you again, or I'll call the coppers on you,' he yelled from the window before slamming the door behind her.

As the number sixteen bus made its way along the country lanes towards Kingston, Bella managed to doze again slightly as the pain subsided for a while. Her mind wandered to the events of the past year, since she'd last seen her mother and

Alfie. Money had been impossibly tight at home, the women Tessa helped during childbirth were invariably poor and she rarely got paid. In desperation Bella had answered an advert for a scullery maid in Portsmouth so she could help support them both while her mother cared for Alfie. It was just until Eli came home from the war, she'd told herself, then they could marry and be a family.

She had cried for the entire train journey to Portsmouth, but had managed to pick herself up and work hard, settling into her role and even letting herself believe the rumours circulating in the past week that the war might soon be over. Eli would be home and they could finally be a family. Then the morning came when she'd seen the newspaper article describing her mother's arrest, laying on the doorstep she'd been sent to sweep. She'd picked it up with shaking hands and read in disbelief.

> A Lewes-based midwife has been charged with manslaughter tonight after a birth she was attending ended in the tragic death of mother and baby.
>
> Evelyn Hilton, forty-two, of Kingston-near-Lewes, was giving birth to her third baby, a much-longed-for girl, when tragedy struck. Midwife Tessa James missed the warning signs of a breech birth until it was too late. As time ran out for mother and child, she failed to call Mrs Hilton's physician, Doctor Jenkins, and instead attempted to cut the baby out herself, resulting in fatal blood loss and the death of the infant.
>
> Chief Constable Payne of Lewes Police said tonight, 'We have arrested a forty-six-year-old woman in connection with the death of Evelyn Hilton. The hearing will take place tomorrow afternoon at Lewes Crown Court. Our thoughts and

deepest sympathies go out to Evelyn Hilton's husband and young son, Richard, who is being comforted by relatives this evening.'

The *Sussex Argus* tracked down Doctor Jenkins to his practice in Lewes. 'I cannot comment on Tessa James's case, but I will say that the issues it shines a light on are immensely troubling, and sadly nothing new. It is my view that midwives need to be regulated much more stringently. The 1902 Midwives Act specifies, very clearly, that midwives are limited to attending normal births. They are required to transfer care of a labouring woman to a physician in complicated cases, and are restricted from using instruments such as forceps, which they are not medically trained to use. What has happened to Mrs Evelyn Hilton is beyond tragic, but perhaps the good, if any, that can come of this is that more stringent measures are put in place going forward.'

When the housekeeper had handed her the telegram, Bella had immediately made up her mind; she had no choice but to go over Mrs Blackwood's head and go straight to the master. She walked through the house and knocked on the master's door, checking her appearance in the mirror before she entered. Her face was drawn from crying, with dark circles under her blue eyes. Her long black hair, which was scraped back into a bun, highlighted her pale skin and, as she looked at herself in the mirror, she pictured Alfie's piercing blue eyes staring back at her in the dark of the priest-hole, and tried to draw strength from them.

'Ah, Bella,' Mr Collins said as she entered. He walked over to her, unsteady on his feet, his breath smelling of whisky as he strayed too close, and locked the door behind her. 'What can I do for you? I hope Mrs Blackwood is not expecting me to deal with any staff issues, I'm not really in the mood.'

She had smiled politely, a feeling of intense nausea creeping in as his smile lingered a bit too long. There was a piece of spinach stuck in his teeth and despite his yellow grin repulsing her, she found it impossible to look away.

'I'm sorry to bother you, sir, but my son, you see, he lives at home, in Kingston, with my mother. She has been arrested, so I need to go home for a short time to make alternative arrangements for him.'

She hung her head, knowing what would come next as a tear escaped and splashed onto her shoe. She looked down at her curved stomach. Did he know what he had already done to her? Did he know she was already carrying his child? When it became obvious, would he kick her out onto the street like others before her?

'I see. Well, are you expecting us to hold your position here open for you? Because that is quite a lot to ask. I suppose there may be some kind of arrangement we can come to . . .'

Bella's body flushed with a familiar panic as he tugged at his zip, then grabbed her hand and pressed it down inside his underpants, his fish breath making her heave. She closed her eyes, pleading with him to stop, which only seemed to excite him more, and he moaned loudly in her ear. She cried silently, trying to pull away, but he slapped her, pressing her hard into the corner of the desk as she watched the fire burn until he let out a deep satisfied groan. Before long he collapsed in a heap in his armchair, pouring himself another whisky and gazing silently at her as he slurped at it.

'Can I leave in the morning, sir?' she asked as she fought back the nausea and straightened her uniform.

He paused for a long time before replying. 'You can have two days, but we will need you back by midnight on Wednesday, or don't bother coming back at all.' He had glared at her, as if she were a bad taste in his mouth. 'Aren't you going to thank me? There aren't many employers as lenient as I.'

'Thank you, Mr Collins,' she had said obediently, before walking back along the cold corridor and climbing the stairs to her bedroom, where she collapsed onto her bed, muffling her tears with her pillow. It was there she had felt the first cramp and, running her fingers down her leg, discovered a small trail of blood.

'Kingston, final stop, Kingston,' the bus driver said, turning off the engine and looking down the bus to where Bella was sitting. She stood up and glanced out of the window. Down the lane, not twenty yards away, was the gate to the path that led to her beloved Vicarage. She thanked the driver, then stepped onto the snow-covered lane and walked on shaking legs to the gate. Lifting the latch, she opened it and shuffled along the snow-dappled path to the front door of the dim, cold cottage.

Bella slid her key into the lock and turned it, the memory so vivid of her mother standing in the doorway, her arms filled with wild flowers, that she felt like she was passing her as she crossed the threshold. Slowly she stepped in before closing the door behind her.

'Alfie!' she called out, breathlessly, her heart hammering with fear.

There was no reply, and in that moment, another wave of pain took her breath away and she felt her heart break as no reply came. She had failed her little boy; she had taken too long and he had given up hope that she was coming. He had come out of his hiding place and been taken away by Wilfred Hilton, and now she would never be able to find him.

'Alfie!' she called again, tears streaming down her face now. The deafening silence in their family home, usually buzzing with happiness and warmth, was overwhelming her with sadness as she looked around the room for any signs of life.

As the pains came relentlessly again, she wrapped herself in a blanket that her mother had left by the fire and curled herself into a ball, digging her fingernails into her arm and gritting her teeth. As she lay on the cold stone floor, the pains got so bad that she couldn't stand. She was barely three months gone, yet the contractions felt almost as bad as when Alfie was born; in this very room, with her mother holding her hand, the fire burning, flowers on the windowsills and cushions under her head. Bella lay alone, crying, as the pains intensified, so she could barely stand it, until she had felt a gush of blood pour out of her onto the blanket between her legs.

She lay still for a moment, relieved that the worst was finally over, her panicked breathing beginning to subside.

After what felt like hours of laying on the floor in a pool of blood, until she could no longer feel her body from the cold, she forced herself up. Weak and dizzy from her ordeal, she slowly piled up the bloodied blankets in the bucket by the back door.

'Mama?' The voice was faint, but it was definitely Alfie. Bella spun round, and looked up at the wooden steps in front of her. Feeling as if she might faint at any moment, she forced herself to climb the stairs until she reached the landing, where she bent down and pulled at the lid. It was locked.

Bella held her breath and bit down hard on her lip to stop herself from fainting. Her little boy was still in there, in what state she couldn't imagine. She began tapping on the roof of the priest-hole with her closed fist. 'Alfie, Alfie darling, are you in there?' she said, biting down on her lip, trying not to let panic engulf her.

'Alfie darling, it's Mama, please open the door, you're scaring me. I'm alone, there's no one else here. Please, if you can, open the door.'

Bella turned away, looking for something to prise it open with, her eyes falling on the fire iron, but as she pushed her broken body up to walk back down the stairs and retrieve it, there was a loud click through the silent Vicarage. Slowly, the lid of the priest-hole began to creak open.

Bella turned back, and from the pitch-black room, a little pair of bright, smiling blue eyes began to emerge.

Chapter Five
Vanessa

New Year's Eve 1969

Vanessa Hilton stood at her bedroom window in Yew Tree Manor watching her husband weaving lights into the bay trees lining the driveway, their glow flickering on and off in the dark as his shouts of frustration at his son, who was trying to help him, echoed through the grounds.

She glanced down at her watch. One hour until the guests arrived, yet she already felt exhausted to the core of her being. Her head had been spinning for weeks with every detail of this New Year's Eve party, which felt to her like an event they had been building up to for a decade. Yet even with nothing left to chance, the day thus far had been a disaster, from the moment they had dragged themselves from their broken sleep until now.

A snowstorm pounding at the house all night had kept the dogs awake and barking until the early hours, and when morning finally came, they had woken to find themselves without any power. Added to which, the lane outside the house was completely blocked with snow, making their driveway almost impassable until Richard had asked Peter, the gardener, to organise the delivery of a ton of bark to absorb the sludge. After that, he had turned his attention to the lights, which had been placed in the trees the night before and had now blown down or smashed. Several times that day Vanessa had been tempted to cancel. It seemed that Mother Nature was doing everything she could to tell her to stop this event that had been their entire focus and obsession for months.

Bang.

The gunfire had been consistent throughout the day, and each shot had made her bones shake. Alfie and Bobby had begun slaughtering their herd at lunchtime, some of them diagnosed with TB, the others needing to be destroyed as a precaution. It couldn't have been worse timing, in the week that the sale of the land surrounding The Vicarage was going through for development and Richard had served them their eviction notice from their home.

Bang bang.

Vanessa flinched as a faint knock landed on the bedroom door. 'Mrs Hilton?' She turned to see a waitress in a white pinafore. 'I'm sorry to bother you, but we were wondering when the champagne is due to be delivered.'

'What do you mean? It was delivered hours ago. I saw the driver myself. It's meant to be on ice in the cellar.' Vanessa walked across the bedroom towards the girl, her nervous eyes wide.

'I'm sorry, madam, but when we went down to start bringing it up, it wasn't there. We've been looking for Mr Hilton to ask him.'

Vanessa glanced at the floor-length red gown hanging from her wardrobe and tied her dressing gown tighter around her waist. 'Well, we're all going to be drinking warm champagne if it's still sitting in boxes somewhere. Why didn't anyone notify me about this before now?'

The waitress scuttled after her as she made her way towards the top of the stairs, where her children's nanny was walking towards her carrying Alice's red shoes.

'Dorothy, do you know where Alice is? I need to sort out a problem with the champagne and she should be dressed by now.'

'Yes, Mrs Hilton, she's in the guest bedroom – I've laid their clothes out in there. She won't be long.'

Vanessa observed how tired their nanny looked. Her dark hair was scraped back in a ponytail, and she was still wearing her apron, which had flour down it from baking with the children all afternoon to keep them entertained. Despite her efforts to always remain cheerful, it was clear the poor woman had had enough. This party had exhausted everyone, and Vanessa for one couldn't wait for it to be over.

She glanced at herself in the mirror in the hallway and adjusted one of her rollers. Her face was already fully made up, complete with fake eyelashes, and she stood with her fingers spread over her narrow hips, her shiny blood-red nail varnish catching the lights from the vast Christmas tree in the hall below.

'There you are, Miss Alice. Shall we get you dressed in your beautiful red frock?' said Dorothy, smiling at the little girl, who had appeared behind her mother. It was obvious from her slightly swollen, reddened eyes that she had been crying.

Alice shrugged, her dungaree strap falling off her shoulder. 'I hate dresses,' she said, looking up at her mother in despair.

'Alice, I don't have time for this now. Please, can you just for once do what you're told?' Vanessa started to make her way towards the sweeping staircase.

'I can't find Snowy anywhere, I'm worried he's run off,' Alice whined, referring to her puppy of three weeks, which was used to the cold and always running off, having been born in the barn at The Vicarage in the middle of winter.

'Why don't you put your dress on and we can get ready together in Mummy's room.' Vanessa's attempts to hide her irritation were failing.

'My tummy hurts.' Alice wrapped her arms around her stomach and sat down on the landing.

'Alice, please! You've just eaten too many of those biscuits you've been baking with Dorothy this afternoon. And Snowy's probably in the kitchen hunting for snacks.' Vanessa turned to the nanny. 'Dorothy, sorry, do you have any idea where the champagne is? I can't quite believe we have spent a year planning this party; everything feels in utter chaos because of this blasted storm.' The waitress, still waiting for instructions, flushed red, her hands clutched in front of her.

'I think I overheard Mr Hilton telling Peter to leave it outside the back door because it's so cold,' Dorothy replied.

Vanessa shook her head irritably. 'Well, it would have been helpful if he could have let the caterer know that.' She turned to the waitress. 'Could you please go and check if the champagne is by the back door. And make sure you get it on ice as soon as possible. The guests will be here in half an hour.' The girl shot off out of sight.

'Mrs Hilton,' said Dorothy, 'is it still all right if I go at seven?'

Vanessa looked at her watch: it was five to seven already.

It wasn't ideal for Dorothy to leave now. Leo was still outside on the driveway and needed to get ready, and Alice was in one of her sulks.

'Could you possibly hang on a few more minutes and get Leo dressed? There's so much to sort still and I'm rather behind.'

'Why can't Dorothy come to the party?' said Alice, staring intently at her mother.

Vanessa and Dorothy shared a look that spoke a thousand words.

'Dorothy is exhausted from looking after you all day. She doesn't want to come to our silly party.' Even as the words left her lips, Vanessa felt bad that it hadn't even occurred to her to invite Dorothy. It was too late now: she wouldn't have anything to wear, and she'd know it was an afterthought on Vanessa's part because she'd felt awkward.

'This party is for your mummy's smart friends,' said Dorothy, not exactly getting Vanessa off the hook.

'Well, you're the only one who really cares about us all. All the others just pretend to.'

'Alice, don't be rude. If you can hang on a little bit longer, Dorothy, I'll send Leo in now. I'm sorry to ask,' Vanessa said, walking away without waiting for Dorothy to answer.

Down in the hallway, Vanessa pulled her wellington boots on over her stockinged calves and wrapped a fox-fur coat around her silk dressing gown. Taking a last look up at her defiant daughter still standing at the top of the stairs, her arms crossed, her messy blonde curls falling into her eyes, she called out, 'Alice, I'll be back in five minutes, and I expect you to be dressed and ready for the party.'

'Don't worry, Mrs Hilton, I'll help her. We'll be ready in

no time, won't we?' Dorothy smiled gently at the little girl, whose green eyes had glazed over again with tears of frustration.

'Thank you, Dorothy!' Vanessa replied, feeling guilty as she rushed out into the cold December air. She knew that as soon as Dorothy and her daughter were alone together, Alice would be dragging her poor nanny outside to look for her puppy in the snow. It had been a mistake allowing her to have the animal; puppies always caused mayhem, and the damned thing had been peeing all over their newly laid carpet in the run-up to the party.

She took one more backwards glance at the finished stage on which their production was to take place: the soaring ceiling made for showcasing a Christmas tree transported from London; the sweeping staircase decked with boughs of holly and a hundred hand-stitched red velvet bows; the hallway big enough to hold a grand piano for the pianist to play Christmas carols.

The sale of the farmland surrounding The Vicarage had given Richard a much-needed injection of cash to keep their own farm afloat and to refurbish the house. In the years since Richard's father, Wilfred Hilton, had passed away, it had become painfully apparent that he had been hiding a vast number of disastrous business decisions. Wilfred was a man with expensive tastes – for horses, cars and women – and very little work ethic. He had inherited the estate from his father, but had had no interest in the farm or its future, and had burned through most of the Hilton money by the time he passed away, leaving behind only bad debts and broken hearts, including that of his only remaining son, Richard, whom he had neglected for most of his life. Which made his final letter, written on his deathbed, all the more painful.

November 1959
Dear Richard,

I know we have not always seen eye to eye, and growing apart as we have is one of my greatest sorrows, along with abandoning your brother Eli's child, Alfie James. I want you to know that I am deeply sorry I was not there for you more when your mother passed away when you were only six years of age.

When your mother died, in such dreadful circumstances, I wanted someone to blame, for both her death and Eli's. But as my life has gone on and my grief has abated, I have looked back at Evelyn's death somewhat differently. And I have grown to regret my treatment of Tessa James.

For years I tortured myself about what had become of Alfie, and when he came back to us, I felt it was a message from God, a chance to put right my wrongs. I am aware I have left you with some debts, but I am writing to let you know that I have spoken to the family lawyer to inform him that upon my death, The Vicarage will go to Alfred James, for him to do with as he pleases. For years I chose to ignore Alfie's birthright, and I now know I was wrong. We have enough; we do not need another farm, whereas for him it is everything. It is also a small price to pay for what he would have been entitled to were it not for Eli being killed in the war. Bella and Eli were engaged to be married when he left, and after his death, she returned my grandmother's emerald ring, given to her by Eli, which revealed a strength of character few possess. Indeed, had she sold it, it would have saved her from the poverty which eventually killed her.

I hope you agree with this decision. I find Alfie James a most affable and hard-working young man, and I hope that you can find a way to live alongside one another.

With much love and admiration,

Your father, Wilfred

Vanessa had read the letter just before Richard threw it into the fire, causing them to have such an almighty row they woke Leo up. The James family had been a curse on their lives for too long, Richard shouted, and he wished Alfie had never been born. When Richard finally stormed out, Leo appeared with a torrent of questions about Bobby and Alfie James that she'd somehow managed to deflect.

Of course she knew the real reason for Richard's fury; the affection between Wilfred and Alfie had been hard to ignore. Wilfred had neglected his son all his life, farming him out to an endless stream of nannies and tutors. Alfie, in contrast, had been loved, passionately, by two James women. He was made of stern stuff, and at the workhouse he had been assigned to the farm, where he learned his trade through back-breaking toil, so that by the time he turned up at their door aged sixteen, he was able to practically run Yew Tree Farm single-handedly.

Richard had hated his father for favouring another boy over his own son, and now, Vanessa observed sadly, history was repeating itself; the pain in their son's eyes was clear to see as her husband overtly gushed over Bobby James yet had nothing but criticism for poor Leo.

'For pity's sake! Where has he gone now?' she heard her

husband shouting from the end of the driveway for anyone to hear.

'Richard, what's wrong?' she said, hurrying over to him.

'That boy is useless, absolutely useless. He's in a world of his own, wanders around with his head up his arse.' Richard was red-faced despite the bitter cold.

'I'm sure he's trying his best,' said Vanessa. 'He's been out here with you for hours.'

'Yes, well, I'd have been better off on my own,' Richard snapped.

All afternoon Leo had tried to help his father with the lights on the driveway, and Vanessa, watching from the window, had cringed as he dropped things and rushed about getting it wrong. Twice Richard had asked her when Bobby would be arriving to help, but this had been one day when Bobby was not available. He and Alfie were destroying their herd, the echoing gunshots a constant reminder all day of the family's suffering, and helping Richard sort out his party lights was not going to be a priority for Bobby today.

'There you are at last,' Richard snapped as Leo appeared from the direction of the house.

'Sorry, Dad, I couldn't find them,' Leo said quietly.

'What do you mean? What have you been doing all this time? Right, I'll go and fetch them myself, shall I?'

Leo flushed red. 'I'm sorry, I looked everywhere.'

'I'll go, Richard,' said Peter from the top of a ladder. 'It's the blue fuses you want, isn't it?'

Vanessa looked at Leo, his head hung down, biting on his lip. It was a sad fact that Leo was not practical. He hated farm life, and had no natural affinity for it, becoming tired and cold and irritable in a very short space of time. He was tall and lean, but not physically strong, with a long blonde fringe he hid behind, and an affinity for daydreaming with his books, inside, by the Aga.

Bobby James, Alfie's son, on the other hand, was tireless, and could often be seen on his tractor until long after dark, barely stopping to eat or drink. Richard and Bobby often chatted animatedly, and when the boy had finally finished his work for his father, Richard would ask him to give him a hand in the fields with a broken fence or a newborn calf.

Vanessa burned with the cold as the lights finally sprang to life, flooding the path ahead of her momentarily before flickering off again and plunging the driveway into darkness.

'Blasted thing's shorted again,' Richard growled. He was scowling furiously at the uncooperative lights in his hand as he teetered perilously at the top of a stepladder. At six foot three, with olive skin, brown eyes and blonde hair, he was several stone heavier than when he had proposed to Vanessa as a gangly nineteen-year-old by Yew Tree Lake, but he was still undeniably handsome.

'Richard, darling,' she looked up at him, 'why don't you let Peter finish the lights? You need to start getting ready.' An eerie calm had fallen over the grounds now that the storm had finally blown its way through. As if it were taking a breath but was not yet done. She had heard that the lake had frozen over and that more blizzards were coming. She had no idea if the fireworks were going to light, but it was poor Peter's next job to lay them out on the jetty ready for midnight.

'We're nearly there. Just a couple more minutes,' Richard said, not taking his eyes off his task.

Vanessa turned back to the house to see another member of the catering staff rushing towards her as Dorothy, dressed in her coat, reached her in rather a hurry.

'Oh good, Dorothy, you're here. Can you take Leo inside and make sure he gets dressed?'

'I don't need her to dress me. I'm not a baby,' Leo sulked.

'I didn't say you were, Leo, I'm just trying to make sure you're ready for when the guests arrive in about fifteen minutes!'

'I'm sorry, Mrs Hilton, I really need to get going, my sister is due at the house now. Alice is ready, and Leo's outfit is on his bed. I hope you have a wonderful party.'

'I'd be very grateful if you could stay a little longer, Dorothy,' said Vanessa, trying to hide her unreasonable irritation. The woman had already been there all day, but she cursed herself for not asking her to work this evening. She would need someone to put Alice to bed and make sure Leo didn't drink any champagne. She'd presumed Alice would just be by her side all evening as she got ready, but the snowstorm and the chaos that had ensued had put paid to any notions of everything running smoothly. 'I'm happy to pay you extra.'

'She's hardly dressed for a party, Mum, and she's definitely not going to fit into any of your frocks,' Leo sniggered.

'Leo!' Vanessa gasped, glaring at her son. Dorothy and Leo hadn't ever got along; the fact was that Leo wanted his mother, not a nanny, and he'd made no effort to hide it, but lately his behaviour towards Dorothy had shifted up a gear and was becoming unforgivable.

'I'm so sorry, Dorothy, I will talk to Leo about his behaviour. Please stay,' she begged.

'I'm sorry, Mrs Hilton.' Dorothy pursed her lips. 'I've been on my feet since nine, and I have to get back to the dog, and to cook dinner for Peter and my sister, who's coming over. If Richard could let Peter head off soon too, I'd be most grateful. I really hope you enjoy your evening, good night.'

Vanessa was momentarily distracted by the sight of Alice, in a red dress, running out of the front door and across the lawn in the direction of the tree house nestled in a huge oak tree by the driveway entrance.

'For heaven's sake, Alice is outside looking for that bloody puppy. She'll freeze, Dorothy.' But she was gone, already scuttling towards the gate as the little girl disappeared into the darkness.

'Mr Hilton, I'm so sorry to bother you, but it seems that only half the champagne has been delivered.' The man from the catering staff stuttered slightly as he spoke, jumping from foot to foot on the snow-covered ground.

'For pity's sake, are you sure?' Richard yelled from his position at the top of the ladder.

'Yes, sir. It should have been twenty cases, and there are definitely only ten.'

'Leo, will you please find Alice, take her inside, and then put on your suit? I'll be having words with your father about how you spoke to Dorothy just now – I'm not happy about it at all.'

'As if he cares,' said Leo, glaring at her.

Vanessa looked at her son. At twelve years old, he was tall for his age and already as handsome as his father, but in every other way they were as different as two people could be. 'Leo, can you please find Alice and tell her to go inside. I don't like her running around in the snow in her party clothes.'

'No doubt she's in the tree house looking for Snowy,' Leo mumbled.

'That dog will die if it's out in this.' Richard frowned down at them.

'Don't say that to Alice. She's already upset with me. She didn't want to get dressed up for the party. She wants to wear her dungarees,' said Vanessa.

'Well, let her, for God's sake. We've got enough to worry about. Leo needs to cycle to The Vicarage and tell Bobby to come and help me.'

'He can't cycle there now! The roads are lethal and besides, we can't ask Bobby today, they've been destroying their herd. Why can't Leo help you?'

'Because he'll cock it up. I need Bobby to take over from me so I know it's done properly.'

Vanessa looked at Leo, who had visibly flinched at his father's words.

'Maybe we can ask Peter to stay a bit longer. It just doesn't feel right asking Bobby today.'

'Vanessa, could you not argue with everything I suggest, just this once.'

Leo glared at her, then glanced up at his father. 'It's fine, I'll go and get my bike.'

As he ran off into the darkness, Vanessa let out a sigh. 'I need to go and find Alice. I think Leo's right: she's probably sulking in the tree house.'

'Don't you need to get dressed, Vanessa?' said Richard. 'One of us should be ready for when everyone arrives. Leave Alice for a bit. She'll come in when she's cold. You fuss too much.'

Vanessa looked up at her husband. The dark mood that

had descended over him had made her nervous, and she knew better than to make matters worse with two hundred guests about to arrive. But her instinct was niggling her that she needed to get Alice inside.

'Do you have a torch, Peter?' she asked. 'Sorry, I know you need to get home. I won't be a minute.'

The long-suffering gardener nodded and reached into his toolbox, pulling out the light and handing it over, and Vanessa set off down the driveway, the ground squelching underfoot. The thought of what the mud would have done to Alice's shiny red shoes made her wince.

Bang! Bang!

She stopped in her tracks and turned to look at her husband striding back towards the house with the man from the caterers as the sound of Alfie James's gunfire echoed through the night.

'It's been a long day,' Peter caught her eye and called out to her. 'Don't worry, Mrs Hilton, they'll soon be done at The Vicarage.'

Vanessa nodded as she turned her attention to the tree house, and as she walked towards it a feeling of deep unease began crawling through her stomach as she reached it and realised there was no torchlight coming from inside.

Chapter Six
Vanessa

Thursday, 21 December 2017

Vanessa Hilton stood at her bedroom window, watching removal men carrying boxes filled with her belongings out of her house. She didn't know what was happening. Perhaps Leo and Helen were finally having the place painted; it had been so long since they'd had any work done.

Fighting back tears of confusion, she looked out at the lake as the men downstairs shouted at one another.

The house had been so full of people it no longer felt like she had any control over her home. Police diving teams had turned up and searched for Alice's body in the lake but found no trace of her. It would have been the most obvious scenario: that she had wandered down there looking for her puppy; possibly even seen it struggling to swim and going under the water. She might have called out into the night, yelling for help as the house throbbed with piano playing and guests and life. Too loud to hear a little girl's cries.

A house full of people and she had neglected the one person she should have been looking after. She went round and round and round dissecting every detail of New Year's Eve, the last thing she had said to Alice, the last thing Alice had said to her. Who had been the last person to see her; was it really Bobby James? Why had he never confessed? Nearly fifty years later, she was no nearer to the truth, no nearer to finding her daughter's body or to forgiving herself. Her grief changed shape, moulded around her life, so that it became like a stone cloak she carried every day. Alice was still here; she was in the fields and on the swing and in her bedroom. Yew Tree Manor was Alice, and Vanessa knew the answer to what had happened to her was here.

'Vanessa?' She could hear Helen calling her name as she walked up the stairs. 'There you are. I couldn't find you.' She appeared in the doorway, her coat dappled with flakes of snow.

'What are all these people doing in the house, Helen?' Vanessa said, as Helen stared at her, eyes wide.

'We're packing up to leave, Vanessa,' she replied gently. 'The house sale completes tomorrow.'

'Leave? What are you talking about?' She could see Helen tensing up and closing her eyes to try and mask her frustration. Obviously they'd had this conversation, many times before.

'We talked it over, remember, and we decided it was for the best, that it was too much for you to manage now. We're all going to live together, in the house in France Leo told you about.'

'But I don't want to go to France. I don't want to sell the house. I can't leave Alice.'

'Leo shouldn't be much longer, he's just gone to talk something through with Mike at the office. It's for the best, Vanessa, it really is.'

'Best for who?' Vanessa snapped.

'I'm sorry, Vanessa, but we don't have a choice; there's no money left in the business,' Helen said, her lips pursed.

Vanessa scowled at Helen. It was all starting to become a blur, but it seemed to her that Helen had become even more withdrawn than usual, avoiding being on her own with her entirely. She knew her daughter-in-law didn't like her; it had never been voiced, but then Helen was always careful not to show too much of herself or give anything away.

She had done well marrying Leo. Vanessa was sure she had met Helen's parents, but she couldn't picture their faces or remember their names; all she could remember was that they weren't *their* sort of people. She couldn't help feeling that Helen had never been good enough for Leo. It had all been so easy for her, and now that they were selling the house and she was about to become very well off indeed, she owed Vanessa some respect, some kindness – some empathy.

Sienna suddenly appeared at the door and ran over to her, causing the panic inside her to subside. As long as she was with her granddaughter, she would be okay. She remembered there had been a lot of debts – Leo had told her about that, and maybe she had agreed to the house sale. It was all just such a fog from which there would emerge a lightning bolt of information, shocking her brain into remembering again.

'Hello, darling,' said Vanessa, the little girl's presence calming her. 'How was school?'

'Not good at all,' said Sienna, crossing her arms.

'Oh dear, what happened?' Vanessa pulled the little girl into her.

'Ben sat next to me at lunch.'

'Who's Ben?'

'Ben has ruined my whole life, he's really mean to me,' Sienna said, sighing heavily.

'Well, it sounds like Ben likes you if he sat next to you. Boys are often mean to girls they like.'

'Like Daddy is to Mummy?' said the little girl, looking up at her.

Vanessa frowned at Helen, then hugged her granddaughter into her. She looked so like Leo – and Alice – but her nature was more like Helen's.

Sienna would sit back as her father darted around making mistakes and errors of judgement and drink it all in, as if making notes of what not to do when she grew up. Only seven years old, she would ask a question, then wait for the reply and sit for some time with the answer, pondering it in her head until she decided whether to accept it or not. She often knew where lost things were, calmly passing her father his keys or wallet while he rushed about with a red face, sweating and shouting. When she wasn't playing outside, she was a very still child, who would sit with Vanessa and ask her about the parties they used to have at the house and the pretty dresses she wore.

And then Sienna would want to talk about Alice – she would ask about what happened to her. And what she had been like, and whether she was like her. And she was, thought Vanessa, she looked just like Alice, with her long blonde hair and green eyes, though she was calmer and easier than Alice. She had a way about her that made you feel she knew you for who you were, just by looking at you. Sometimes it was quite unnerving to notice her watching you.

'So what shall we do? A game, some cooking perhaps?'

'I think cooking would be tricky, we need to stay up here

really, out of the way,' Helen said simply, as Vanessa glared at her.

'When are we leaving Yew Tree?' She gripped Sienna's hand so hard her fingers turned white.

'We fly out tomorrow. We don't want to be here for the demolition,' Helen answered.

'I still can't believe it's tomorrow. It's come round so quickly, I feel like I haven't said goodbye to everyone properly,' Sienna said starting to cry.

'Did your friends not say goodbye at school today?'

'Yes, they made a card.'

'That's lovely, you'll have to show me. Who haven't you said goodbye to?' Vanessa stroked her hair as the little girl curled into her grandmother.

'Peter and Dorothy,' Sienna said quietly.

'Dorothy?' Vanessa shot Helen a look. 'I didn't know you saw Dorothy, darling.'

Sienna nodded. 'Sometimes,' she said quietly.

'I see,' said Vanessa, forcing a smile.

Sienna jumped up and ran to the window; outside the light was already starting to fade. 'Look, Granny, it's snowing! Can we go and play outside?'

'Shall we build a snowman?' Vanessa said, her spirits lifting.

'Can we really?' cried Sienna. 'I'll get my gloves.'

'It's getting dark, Sienna, I don't think it's a good idea,' Helen said, but it was pointless: Sienna was already out of the bedroom door and halfway down the stairs as Helen rushed after her. At a slower pace, Vanessa followed them along the landing, taking the stairs slowly as she looked down at Helen and Sienna in the porch hunting for gloves.

As she reached the bottom stair, one of the removal men

walked past her and started up the stairs. Vanessa watched him as he reached the top and looked around, then walked along the landing towards Leo's study, glancing back down at her briefly. Something about him was making her uneasy, he didn't seem like the other men, bustling and purposeful. He seemed lost.

'Come on, Granny!' called Sienna.

The boxes in the hall with their coats in were still open, and Vanessa pulled out Sienna's red puffa jacket.

'Why do you sometimes call me Alice, Granny?' Sienna asked, pushing her arms into the sleeves.

'I'm sorry, I don't mean to. I think it's because you remind me of her.'

'Daddy never talks about her. She looked like me, didn't she?' Sienna glanced up at the picture of Alice in the hallway.

'All right if we wrap this?' said one of the removal men, reaching up to the portrait. Vanessa felt herself frozen to the spot.

'Can you leave that one, please?' Helen said, reappearing suddenly.

Vanessa turned to look at her. Helen and Alice were the same age, it occurred to her suddenly. If things had been different, if it had been Helen who had vanished instead of Alice, it might have been her daughter standing where Helen stood now.

'Where is your mother, Helen?' asked Vanessa. 'Won't she miss you when we move?'

'I'm sorry?' Helen flushed red, clearly thrown by the question.

'Your mother, where does she live? I don't remember meeting her.'

Helen glared at Vanessa then cleared her throat and spoke quietly, 'My mother died when I was a baby.'

Vanessa stared into Helen's blue eyes, feeling a wave of intense hatred for her which took her breath away. Helen's mother was dead, so she wouldn't have even been missed. If Helen had died instead of Alice, Leo and Helen would never have met, Leo would have married someone else. Someone she liked, who showed her some kindness, a friend to Alice, the three of them would have been happy together.

'Sure, no problem, we can come back for it,' said the man as Helen walked away.

'Alice wouldn't wear dresses, would she, Granny, just like me?' Sienna persisted as Vanessa felt her legs go very wobbly underneath her. She didn't want to leave this house; she didn't want to leave Alice.

'Yes,' she said, watching Helen walk up the stairs towards her bedroom and close the door, 'she was very funny and clever, and she hated dresses. She just wanted to wear her dungarees. I loved dressing her up in her pretty frocks but she hated it so, most of the time, I gave in and let her wear her dungarees.'

'Did you feel sad when she died?' Sienna gazed at her with her big blue eyes. Her face seemed to be blurring with Alice's, and the room was beginning to spin.

'Yes, we all did. I still do, but you've made me very happy since you were born.' Vanessa felt very dizzy suddenly and made her way over to a chair left stranded in the hallway.

'Where are your hat and gloves, Granny?' said Sienna, clutching her grandmother's fingers. 'Your hands are still cold from when you went out earlier.'

'In my room, I think. I'll fetch them, and you start rolling a big snowball for the base. I won't be long.'

Vanessa took a breath to try and stop the dizziness, then slowly climbed the stairs, the hustle and bustle of half a dozen men, charging in and out of the house, fading away. As she passed, she could hear Helen's radio in her bedroom, and the sound of bathwater running behind a closed door. Then, as she walked past Leo's study, she saw the door was ajar and someone was moving around.

'Hello?' she said, slowly pushing it open.

A man in his sixties, tall and dressed in black, was standing behind Leo's desk. He looked up at Vanessa and froze, his bright blue eyes narrowing.

'I don't think my son would want anyone in here,' she said.

The man nodded, saying nothing as he slammed a drawer shut and then slowly walked past her and out of the room. Vanessa watched him walk back down the stairs and out of the front door, where two of the removal men nodded at him politely; as you would to a complete stranger.

'Come on, Granny! It's starting to settle,' Sienna shouted up as Vanessa stood at her bedroom door watching the man walking away down the driveway as the ground lights flickered on. There'd been something about him she recognised – his ice-blue eyes were hauntingly familiar.

Vanessa wandered into her bedroom, unsettled by the man, and picked up her gloves from the radiator under the window. She looked out again as the man walked out through the gates of Yew Tree just as Sienna ran across the front lawn, towards the tree house in the fading light.

Suddenly the little girl stopped and waved at someone in

the distance. Vanessa glanced towards the woods to see Dorothy and Peter walking their dog along the lit path down to their cottage. Dorothy smiled at the little girl and waved back enthusiastically, before looking up at Vanessa's window as if she knew she was there, watching.

For a moment, their eyes locked, then Dorothy looked away, whispering something to her husband, before disappearing around the corner.

Vanessa had had no idea that Sienna even knew who Dorothy was; she'd thought Helen hadn't spoken to her for years. She didn't like the thought of the two of them having a clandestine relationship. A secret hidden from Granny. It made her out as some kind of baddie. The fact of the matter was, it was Dorothy who had a problem with *her*, who had avoided her. Ever since Alice went missing.

Nothing hurt more than people who said nothing to her about Alice. In the weeks and months after she'd disappeared, many of her friends had fumbled around, not knowing what to say, often saying the wrong thing. But she didn't mind what they said, as long as they said something.

Dorothy was one of those people who said nothing, who crossed the street if she saw her coming. A coward who didn't want to have to see her pain and Vanessa suspected it was because she felt partly responsible. If Dorothy hadn't left the party that night, if she had stayed as Vanessa had asked her to, Alice would be here now, a grown woman, like Helen, with children of her own.

The snow was coming down hard now, and memories of that New Year's Eve came flooding back. Several times that day she had been tempted to cancel; it seemed that Mother Nature had been doing everything she could to tell her something; to try and stop the party that had changed the entire course of her life. If only she had listened.

'Where's Sienna?' She snapped back to the present and turned to see Helen standing in the doorway like a deer in headlights.

'She's outside. I was just getting my gloves.'

'I can't see her from the window. I thought you were with her?'

Vanessa walked past her onto the landing. 'Well, I've only been a minute. Don't get yourself worked up. We're going to build a snowman; she was getting started while I popped up to my room.'

'It must have been longer than that; it's got dark.' Helen's voice was panicked.

Helen hurried down the stairs as Vanessa followed on weary legs, the removal men still hustling and bustling below, despite it being past five.

'Have you seen the little girl who was here before? In the red jacket?' said Helen, walking towards one of the removal men who was holding a heavy box in his arms.

'Not for a little while, sorry. We're almost done downstairs; shall we start on the bedrooms now, or do you want to wait for your husband?'

As she walked towards the front door, Vanessa looked into the rooms off the hallway, shocked at how much had been packed since she went upstairs. Outside, darkness had set in, but the lights along the driveway and lining the lawn lit the way. 'Sienna!' she shouted, suddenly feeling as if everything was slowing down; her senses heightened.

'She was running towards the tree house last time I saw her,' said Vanessa, her voice shaking as Helen frantically searched for her wellies. 'Where have my boots gone? I left them here,' she snapped at one of the removal men, who, sensing her panic, stopped and put down the box he was carrying. She finally found them and stepped around the piled-up boxes by the front door, rushing outside and calling Sienna's name. Vanessa sat on the stairs, pulling on her own trainers, then picked up a torch and stepped into the impending dusk.

'Sienna! Sienna!' Helen called out, running round the side of the house.

'I'll check the tree house,' said Vanessa, heading down the long gravelled drive as fast as her tired legs would take her, willing Sienna to be there wrapped in a blanket and smiling back at her.

Finally she reached the tree house and climbed the steps, sticking her head through the hatch. Her heart thudding, she waved her torch beam around the small, dark, damp room, which was empty.

Only a pile of blankets, cushions and sweet wrappers littered the floor.

As she walked carefully back down the steps, Vanessa turned to see Helen rushing about frantically in front of the house, calling Sienna's name.

It was as if she were going back in time, like watching herself fifty years ago; every torturous second turning concern into blind panic.

Vanessa began to walk back towards the house, where the removal men had suddenly scattered in the darkness to join in the search for Sienna. The final light of the day seemed to vanish suddenly like a black curtain coming down on the day, as a terrifying feeling of familiarity began to creep in.

Chapter Seven
Willow

Thursday, 21 December 2017

'Mike is such a selfish prick,' Kellie said, pulling her auburn hair into a ponytail as Willow and Charlie struggled across the car park with the Yew Tree model. 'Why did he leave you to deal with two hundred OAPs on your own?'

Kellie, the office manager at Sussex Architecture, had been planning a morning of catching up on paperwork when her mobile rang with a request from her boss to take Willow and the Yew Tree development model back to the office. Fuming, she had jumped into her car and driven to Kingston village hall.

'He said Leo Hilton was going away tomorrow and they needed to talk,' Willow offered, slightly scared of Kellie's rage, despite the fact that it wasn't aimed at her.

'Bullshit. He couldn't be arsed dealing with a ton of questions about traffic-calming measures and library detaining now that he thinks the deal is done,' Kellie snapped as a passing couple looked at her nervously. 'Nice of him to acknowledge everything you've done – he hasn't even taken you out for lunch. Un-bloody-believable. Right, shall we head?' Kellie shuddered, wrapping her thick woollen coat around her narrow frame. Kellie had looked quite fragile when they first met, like a porcelain doll, with her red wavy hair and pale skin, but it turned out she was quite the opposite; fearless, with a sharp tongue and boundless energy.

Charlie looked at Willow and then over at his parents, who were standing patiently by their Volvo on the other side of the car park. 'We can follow you to the office and give you a hand taking the model in,' he offered. 'My parents were wondering if you wanted to get some lunch in town. Obviously you'd be more than welcome too, Kellie,' he added.

'I'm not eating lunch at the moment,' Kellie said, pulling out her phone and walking round to the driver's seat.

Willow looked at Charlie, then at Kellie, now tapping furiously at her phone. 'That's really kind of them, but I need to do some work, I'm afraid.' Her guts twisted at the memory of her conversation with Dorothy about the graveyard. The planning meeting was the following day; if they'd missed something as significant as a graveyard, they were in serious trouble – the developers would run a mile. She needed to speak to Mike, and fast.

'Okay,' said Charlie. 'No problem. Shall I say goodbye from you?'

'No. I'll come over,' she said, leaning into the car to tell Kellie she'd be one minute and trying to ignore the heat of her boyfriend's obvious disappointment.

She and Charlie never rowed; he hated arguments, as did she, but for very different reasons. He had announced proudly on their first date, at a pizza restaurant in Brighton, that his parents had never argued in twenty-nine years of marriage – something that was completely alien to her. Her own parents, who had finally divorced after twenty tumultuous years, had only ever communicated with raised voices, throwing things and putting Willow out on the balcony of their flat in all weathers so they could yell at one another.

Charlie was not the sort of man she'd imagined herself ending up with. Whenever she'd pictured her future, it was alone or with someone unreliable, who disappeared at regular intervals, much like her father had for most of her childhood. In contrast, Charlie was dependable, funny and supportive, with a rather apologetic way of speaking. He had reminded her of Clark Kent when they first met in the union bar at Sussex University: good-looking and tall, with smiling brown eyes behind black-rimmed glasses, and a gentle, slightly nerdy manner. They had been rubbing along fine for nearly three years, until this Valentine's Day, when he'd got down on one knee at the top of the Sagrada Família in Barcelona in front of a lot of giggling German schoolchildren. Everything inside her had screamed no, but instead she had managed to mumble something along the lines of 'thank you but I'm not ready'. After which they had walked back down the five hundred and four steps in complete silence.

He had seemed to accept her refusal with grace, but ever since they had been irritating one another. An atmosphere between them that hadn't been there before hung in the air; a huge conversation she didn't want to have. She loved Charlie in a way that made her scared to lose him, but for ever was a long, long time.

'Blimey, Kellie's a force of nature,' he said, pushing his glasses up his nose as they walked across the car park.

'She's great; she doesn't care what anyone thinks. Most of the partners at the practice are scared of her because she tells it as it is, but she's been there so long they can't afford her redundancy payout.'

'Brilliant,' said Charlie as they reached his parents. 'Willow can't join us, unfortunately, as she needs to get some work done before the planning meeting tomorrow.'

'Oh, that's a shame. You've worked so hard on this, you should let us take you out for lunch,' said John, smiling at her warmly.

'I would love that, as soon as this application goes in. It's really kind of you, though, and thank you for coming. I appreciate all your support.' Willow felt her anxiety return as the words left her mouth. She had a feeling of dread that all was not as it seemed. Charlie's parents had been fundamental in getting the support of the local community in Kingston. Did they know about this graveyard? Did everyone know except her? How could Leo not have mentioned it?

'Dorothy said she enjoyed chatting to you,' said Lydia. 'Everyone thinks you've done a wonderful job of representing the community.'

'Do you know her?' asked Willow, trying to ignore her butterflies.

'Of course, she's lived in Kingston all her life, in the row of cottages at the end of the Hiltons' driveway.' Charlie's father said, cutting in on his wife, as he had a habit of doing. Willow had never really had a chance to get to know Lydia, as John was a larger-than-life character who tended to dominate conversations. But from the way he spoke to her – not unkindly, but with a slightly dismissive tone – and the way she accepted it, Willow suspected that Lydia was someone who had sublimated herself to her husband her whole life.

'She said that she and her husband had both worked for the Hiltons. Do you know what she did?' Willow asked.

'I believe Dorothy was the children's nanny – before Alice went missing obviously.' Lydia suddenly looked crestfallen. 'No one talks about Alice any more. I believe Leo's been a tower of strength for his mother. Poor Vanessa, it must be a living hell not knowing what happened to her.'

'Yes, all right, Lydia, no need to be morbid. Willow didn't ask about that.' John shook his head gently, seemingly embarrassed.

'You're right, Lydia, it must be terrible,' said Willow, smiling at her encouragingly. Lydia flushed red and looked at her hands. She was an attractive woman, and bubbly when her husband was out of the room and she was allowed to chat freely. For some reason Willow had never thought of her as a source of information about the Hilton family, but it stood to reason that she would know about them. Helen's obvious upset was playing on her mind, and she wanted to probe Lydia a little more, but she was conscious that Kellie was waiting.

'I noticed that Helen, Leo's wife, left rather suddenly?' Willow said, trying to sound casual.

Lydia glanced at her husband, then back at Willow. 'I suppose it was quite awkward for her and Dorothy. I don't think they've seen one another in a while. It's all very sad, but poor Leo seems to cope with it well. He must have rather a lot on his plate dealing with the farm and the development and his mother's heartache as well as Helen's.' She sighed. 'Such a charming man.'

Willow frowned. 'So Helen being upset was something to do with Dorothy?'

'Yes, Helen is Dorothy's adopted daughter, but they're estranged, I believe. It's all rather complicated.'

Willow's heart skipped a beat at this piece of information, which she tried not to react to. 'As families tend to be,' she added, nodding as Charlie and his parents exchanged glances. She could imagine Lydia and John talking about her, trying to figure out her background, worried about their son falling in love with someone whose family they had never met, a girl they knew so little about.

Kellie suddenly tooted impatiently on the car horn, and Willow turned to her and waved apologetically.

'I'd better go. Thank you again for coming.' She leaned in to kiss Charlie. 'I'll call you later. Have a lovely lunch.'

Willow turned and ran back to Kellie's hatchback, launching herself into the passenger seat as Kellie revved the engine. 'Sorry to hold you up,' she said, clicking her seat belt into place as they screeched out of the car park, narrowly avoiding an elderly couple leaving the meeting.

'Everything all right?' said Kellie as she took the country lanes of Kingston a little faster than Willow would have liked. She heard something topple over in the boot and winced.

'I think my boyfriend's parents were a bit disappointed that I couldn't go out to lunch with them,' she said.

'How long have you guys been together now?' Kellie asked.

'About three years. He actually proposed when we went to Barcelona,' Willow said matter-of-factly.

'What?! Why didn't you say anything?' Kellie looked at her wide-eyed.

'Because I said no.' Willow shrugged.

'Very wise!' Kellie winked at her. 'Actually, marriage is the easy bit, it's when kids come along you get pushed to the limit. And even if you're married to the nicest guy in the world, all the pressure is on the mother and it's totally taken for granted.'

Willow nodded, using her hand to wipe the steamed-up window so she could see out. As they reached the A27, Kellie put her foot down and pulled out into the fast lane, the hatchback's engine roaring with the strain.

'I mean, we do the school run, the washing, the shopping, the cooking, the cleaning, organise the parties, nurture friendships, pick them up and dust them down after every upset. But if dads do any of those things, it gets commented on. Isn't he good? He helps a lot, doesn't he? Aren't you lucky?' Kellie tooted her horn at the driver cutting in front of her, then turned to Willow. 'No, actually, I'm not lucky, it's what he *should* be doing, they're his bloody kids too!'

Willow smiled and pulled some gum from her bag, offering the packet to Kellie. 'I don't really know what my problem is,' she said. 'Marriage and kids just completely terrifies me. I can't even think about it. The idea of someone relying on me too much makes me want to run away, which is something I definitely get from my dad,' she added, thinking out loud.

'You've never mentioned your dad to me before. Is he an architect too?' Kellie lit a cigarette and wound down the window to let the smoke out.

Willow smiled and shook her head. 'No, he's never really had much of a career. He's got a criminal record, so it's difficult for him to find work. We didn't have much when I was a kid; I remember my mum worrying about money a lot when my dad wasn't around, which is why I'm so independent now, I guess.' Willow looked out of the window, surprised at herself for opening up.

'I'm sorry to hear that. It must have been tough,' said Kellie sympathetically.

Willow sighed. 'Hard on my mum mostly. I think it sent her to an early grave.'

'What did he do to get a criminal record? If you don't mind me asking,' said Kellie, turning off the A27 and heading into central Brighton.

Willow paused and fixed her eyes on a cyclist they were overtaking. He was bent forward, pedalling hard, with puffs of breath escaping as he tried to keep going through the bitter cold. Fighting against the wind, pushing forward, an uphill battle: it was how she felt most of the time. She turned to Kellie, and smiled nervously; she rarely talked about her dad to anyone, not even Charlie, but she felt a kindred spirit in her, someone life had also dealt a complicated hand.

Charlie, on the other hand, was a black and white person: his family didn't fight, everything was ordered, talked through and logical. If he knew what she'd been through as a child – stealing food when she was so hungry she couldn't sleep, taking night buses at the age of ten to try and find her father in the pub, lying to the police about his whereabouts when they came to the door because she knew he was drunk and would hit one of them – he would hate Bobby, and she didn't want that.

'He was the last person to see a little girl who went missing a long time ago, when he was a teenager,' she said. 'They thought he had something to do with it. The police were under a lot of pressure to find her. They couldn't prove anything, but my dad was known to the police so they sent him to a really nasty youth detention centre and it screwed him up. He's been in and out of prison ever since.'

She had never spoken to Charlie about her father's past, or Alice Hilton's disappearance. Although Charlie and her dad had met a couple of times, something always stopped her sharing the reality of a father who she loved but repeatedly broke her heart.

'I'm sorry to hear that, hon, it must have been incredibly hard. A friend of mine at college used to talk to me about her dad who was violent, about how she had to watch him beat her mum up, but on other days he would sing to her or teach her to ride a bike or spend hours doing a puzzle with her. You still love them, despite the monster inside; you can't help it.'

'She's right,' said Willow. 'Most of the time you blame yourself when they're failing you.'

'Well, I hope he knows what a star you are. You're the talk of the office, hon. You've done a great job getting this planning application through. Not one, but two listed buildings; it's pretty impressive.'

'You sound like Mike. It's not done yet.' Willow bit her lip. 'I've sold my soul to the devil to get this done. I really hope I haven't walked into a trap.'

'What do you mean?' They pulled up in front of the office and Kellie turned off the engine.

'I'm not sure, really. This morning Mike just made me feel a bit used. And one of the villagers mentioned something that made me nervous.' Willow bit her lip as Kellie looked at her expectantly. 'Apparently there's a graveyard next to one of the buildings we're pulling down.'

'Okay,' said Kellie, frowning. 'Did you do an archaeological dig?'

'No, Mike told me I didn't need to, and it's pretty unusual to do one, unless there's good reason as they're very expensive. They usually wait to see what comes up when they start digging the foundations.' She had asked Mike about it twice, and both times he had been quite dismissive, saying it wasn't necessary.

'But if there was a graveyard there, it would show up in the desktop survey and you'd have to do one,' said Kellie.

'Well, Mike did a desktop survey and I saw it, there was definitely no sign of a graveyard.'

'Maybe it wasn't an official graveyard. A while back on one of our projects they found a dozen or so human remains, and apparently paupers who couldn't afford a proper burial or headstone were often buried near churches, but not in the actual graveyard.'

Willow felt panic rising inside her. Mike had been so cocky at the planning meeting this morning, like it was a done deal. 'Shit, Mike is not going to be happy about this.'

'Hmm, he might already know.' Kellie turned to face her. 'Did Mike invite anyone from the planning department at Lewes council to your community meetings in the village hall?' she asked casually.

'No, I don't think so, why?' Willow felt her heart rate quicken again.

'Because it may be that Leo and Mike know about this graveyard, but Mike's trying to hide the fact it's there until the deal goes through.'

'Presumably a graveyard would put the developers off completely?' Willow asked nervously.

'Just a bit. It's ten grand and about a month's work to move a human skeleton, so to excavate a graveyard can take years. Developers run a mile from them. Incidentally, does Mike have the password to your planning application file?'

'Of course, why?' Willow asked.

'You should check there's nothing in there you don't know about before the meeting tomorrow.' Kellie climbed out and opened the boot of her car, piling up the various pieces of the Yew Tree model to ferry inside.

'Why would Mike put something in there that I don't know about? Surely he realises I'll check it?' Willow asked as they walked along the path to the office door.

'Not necessarily. He kind of relies on people not going back over stuff they've already submitted. He's been known to add things to the planning application at the last minute on a big project – like a few extra flats that the locals wouldn't be keen on. So that when you talk to people, you aren't having to lie to them.'

'But that file is affiliated to my name,' said Willow, staring at Kellie in shock. 'Are you serious?' She felt tears sting her eyes. 'Why would he do that to me?'

'Because this deal is worth a lot of money and he wants to shift it as quickly as possible, which isn't going to happen if there's a graveyard on the site. He probably thinks you'll move on soon anyway. There are no women in this practice for a reason, they treat them like shit because in their mind we have a short shelf life. We have babies, cost them a fortune in maternity leave, then, when we do finally go back to work, never work the ridiculously long hours we did before.'

'But what about Leo Hilton? He must know – why

hasn't he said anything to me? We've been working together for a year.' Willow flushed red, feeling like a gullible schoolgirl.

'He might not know what a deal breaker the graveyard is. Or Mike may have told him to keep quiet about it.'

Willow felt tears sting her eyes. 'But this could seriously affect my career. Blakers Homes are one of the biggest developers in the country; they could sue me, couldn't they?'

'Look, I'm just guessing. I might be wrong. But I've worked here a long time and it wouldn't be the first time Mike's screwed a member of his own staff to get planning approved.'

As they reached the front door, Kellie pushed her key into the lock and they entered the two-storey Georgian office building. Willow followed her in and, as they walked up the stairs to the first floor, they could see a light on in Mike's room at the back of the open-plan office.

Kellie walked over to her desk which was strewn with pieces of paper, sweet wrappers, and framed photographs of her children, and placed the boxes she was carrying on the floor. 'Right, I'll sort that lot later. I've got a shit-load of invoices to deal with.'

'Thanks, Kellie,' said Willow, still reeling from their conversation. 'I really appreciate your help, and I'm sorry I've messed up your day.'

'No problem, I'm used to it.' Kellie winked at her. 'I'd find out what you're dealing with and get some proof before you talk to Mike about it, otherwise he might hide the paper trail. Don't beat yourself up. It's a steep learning curve, your first big project. It's easy to get swept up in it.

In the beginning, you don't realise how it works, but over the years, you learn where the bullshit is hidden.'

Kellie slipped on her headphones and sat down at her laptop, leaving Willow alone with her thoughts. She looked over towards Mike's office. She could hear he was talking to someone in there; it was a familiar voice, one she recognised. She moved slightly closer, and heard Leo laughing. She felt the overwhelming urge to knock on the door and ask them straight out about the graveyard. But if Mike had hidden something, she'd need proof.

Slowly an idea dawned on her. She pulled out her phone and opened the audio app, then pressed record. Taking a few deep breaths, she knocked on the door and waited.

'Come in,' Mike said.

'Hi, sorry to disturb you.' Willow smiled broadly.

'Not at all, Willow, it's good to see you,' said Leo, jumping to his feet. 'Well done again on this morning, great job. The paperwork is all signed with Blakers; it feels like we're home free!'

'I'm looking forward to going out for a celebratory dinner when this is all done tomorrow,' she said, her eyes darting from Leo to Mike. There were pizza boxes and cans of Coke on the desk, and she stepped forward and carefully slid her phone under the lid of one of the open boxes.

Leo nodded and cleared his throat. 'I think unfortunately we'll need to head off quite soon after the planning meeting to get our flights,' he said, 'but we will be back to see how it's all going, and we definitely need to take you out for some drinks, don't we, Mike?'

Mike nodded, stony-faced as Leo chuckled nervously at

the atmosphere. Willow felt her stomach plunge at the change in them both. She had been cast out, all the camaraderie of the past year vanished into thin air. She tried to swallow her racing panic.

'Well, I think it went really well. Everyone seems on board now the plans are all finalised,' she said, glancing at Mike, who looked away. 'Anyway, I won't keep you. I was just wondering if you'd like a tea, as I'm making myself one.' She smiled at them both innocently.

'I could murder a cuppa, thank you, Willow,' said Leo.

Mike narrowed his eyes. 'No, thank you,' he said curtly. 'We won't be here much longer.'

'Okay, one tea coming up.' She smiled at Leo again before turning and walking out, leaving her phone recording on Mike's desk as she pulled the door closed behind her.

Chapter Eight
Nell

December 1969

'Nell, we're going to miss the bus!' Bobby said, taking her hand and pulling her along. They could hear Molly barking by the chicken shed. 'What is up with that dog? She's been barking for hours.'

'My tummy really hurts, Bobby.'

'Come on, Nell, you've just got a cold,' said Bobby, his breath coming out in icy puffs as the snow-dappled ground crunched beneath them. 'We can't miss the bus again, I'll get detention.'

Nell let out a deep yawn. It had taken her ages to get to sleep because her cough was getting worse, and then Christopher the cockerel had woken her at dawn to a strange noise in the cottage. As she had listened to the muffled sound, trying to work out what it was, she had turned to see Bobby sleeping peacefully in his bed, his covers moving up and down with his breathing, a sight which always comforted her.

Slowly she had pulled back her blankets and crept out of bed, clutching her teddy bear, as she sought to find the source of the sound, which was growing louder now. As she walked carefully along the creaking wooden floorboards of the landing, trying not to cough, she saw that her father wasn't in his bedroom. His bed was made, but it was still dark outside and he hadn't woken Bobby for milking, so it couldn't be morning yet.

Had he not come home last night? She stopped, listening carefully to the sound, finally realising that it was someone crying. But where? Her instinct told her not to call out to her father. If it was him, she didn't want to embarrass him. But she needed to know where he was and that he was all right.

As she stood and listened, she could hear him moving around. Finally he stopped crying and cleared his throat. He sounded as near as if she could touch him, but still he was nowhere to be seen. She held her teddy bear tight and started to feel hot, even though it was a cold night. A creeping feeling scurried over her skin as it occurred to her it may be a ghost in the walls or perhaps she was imagining things. Maybe it wasn't him; perhaps he was out at the pub, and what she could hear was a vixen crying outside the window. She walked to the end of the landing, but when she looked down the stairs, all the lights were out and there was no sign of life. She lay down and put her ear to the floorboards. She could hear him more clearly now; he was humming to himself, a tune he whistled sometimes when he was milking the cows. It was definitely him, but it was as if he had suddenly become invisible. She lay transfixed, the sound of her own breathing thudding in her ears.

Suddenly she heard a creak, and the top step began to move. She jumped up and ran back towards her own room, closing the door so that only a small crack remained for her to spy through. Then she watched, utterly transfixed, as the step lifted up like a hatch and out came her father. She could see that he had been crying.

Slowly he lowered the step back down, then walked into his bedroom and closed the door. Nell crept back to bed, her heart thundering and her head buzzing with excitement. A hidden room, underneath the stairs, that in all her life living in The Vicarage she hadn't had a clue about. She looked over at Bobby, still sleeping. Did he know about it? Or had her father kept it a secret from them both? What was in there? What was it for? And the most exciting question of all: could she keep her puppy in there during the day when she was at school? It might bark, but once Dad was out on the farm, he rarely came back to the cottage. She couldn't wait to tell Alice about it on the bus to school. It would be their secret. They could have a special club in there. Nobody would know. She couldn't wait to get in there and have a proper look around.

Nell started to cough again, she hid under her covers, knowing she wouldn't be able to sleep, waiting for the sound of her father's snoring, which eventually came. Slowly she crept out of bed, tiptoeing back along the floorboards and staring at the step as if it were the door to a magical world. Nell ran her finger along the ledge and discovered, at the far end, what felt like a brass ridge. She scuttled down two steps and craned her neck in the moonlight to see a small key hole, and carved in the wood next to it, a small Willow Tree, just like the one on her key. Was this what Bella's key was for? She ran to the bedroom, lifting her mattress silently so that Bobby wouldn't hear and then retrieved the box, easing the key softly into the lock, before turning it, *click*. Then back again, *click*! The sound echoed through The Vicarage and her heart raced with panic.

Her father had left the door unlocked so she must not lock it now. Did he even know there was a key for it? Maybe he did and he knew who this Bella person was. She would love to ask him but she couldn't, because then he would realise she knew about the little room. This was even better, she had a key, that no one else did, so she could lock Snowy in there in the day without her father finding out.

Scared of being discovered, she crept back to her room, staring at the ceiling as excitement and her cough kept her awake until, finally, it was morning, and her father was calling to Bobby to come and milk the cows.

When she got downstairs, her eyes blurry with tiredness, the porridge was on and the fire was crackling away in the corner, but she didn't feel like eating any breakfast. Her cough, which had got worse in the night, was getting so bad she could hardly catch her breath.

'You all right, Nell?' said Bobby, pouring her a glass of water which she drank gratefully.

Everything felt familiar, but her father's face looked sad, with black shadows under his eyes. He sat in silence, his familiar grumbling worryingly absent. She thought back to the night before. She'd never known him to cry, though she sometimes caught him staring out of the window for a long time at the end of the day, saying quietly to himself, 'Your mother loved these sunsets.'

'We need to throw the milk away again today, lad. Two more of the cows are sick and the pregnant one miscarried last night.'

'Okay, Dad,' said Bobby, knowing better than to ask too many questions. 'Did the vet come out?'

'Yes, charged me two crowns to tell me he thinks they've got TB, which I know already. He's taken some blood samples, and he's going to run some tests. But I don't think we should be drinking the milk ourselves any more either. It's not safe. We've caught it from the Hiltons' farm.'

'I'm sure they didn't mean for this to happen,' said Bobby as Alfie glared at him. Dad and Bobby had been fighting a lot, Nell reflected, forcing her porridge down. Bobby could do no right, however hard he worked, and Nell knew it was because he had been working for Alice's daddy a lot. Bobby always said that he made sure he got his own work done first, and that Richard paid him for his troubles. Alfie used some of the money to buy groceries, but Nell knew Bobby was putting the rest away in his money tin. He would often let her come up to Yew Tree Farm with him so she could see Alice, and her father would scowl at them both when they came back. 'We need to stick together, Bobby, you don't know what that family are capable of,' he would say as he slammed things about in the kitchen.

That morning, Nell had looked down at the post on the table, where an envelope with big red letters saying *EVICTION NOTICE* sat on the top of the pile. Bobby saw her looking and put his finger to his lips.

'Dad, what does eviction mean?' she asked, starting to cough again.

'Nell!' Bobby threw his eyes to heaven and got up and put his bowl in the sink.

'Richard Hilton is trying to make us leave our home. But his father, Wilfred – my grandfather – wanted us to have it. So he can't evict us. I'm speaking to a solicitor about it and he says we have a good case. You don't need to worry, Nell, we aren't going anywhere. The only way I'm leaving here is in a coffin.' Alfie pulled on his boots. 'That family cares nothing for us. Richard Hilton doesn't know the meaning of the word loyalty.'

'That's not true. Alice is a Hilton and she's my best friend. And we will be best friends for ever.'

'Yes, well, I think you two shouldn't see so much of each other at the moment. Things being what they are.'

Nell looked at him in horror and then burst into tears.

'Good one, Dad,' said Bobby, as Nell opened the back door and dashed out to the barn, her cough stopping her as she reached the heavy door. She could hear Molly inside scratching frantically to get out and it took all her strength to heave it open before the dog bolted out through her legs. There was no sign of the puppies, but eventually she discovered Snowy hidden between two bales of hay. The other puppies were missing, though, from their den in between two bales of hay and it occurred to Nell that Molly had moved them somewhere. Bobby said animals sometimes did that with their young, to keep them safe. But poor Snowy had been left behind, and was shaking uncontrollably.

The memory of finding Snowy so cold made Nell's heart hurt now as Bobby dragged her along. She had scooped the crying puppy up from the stone floor and given her some leftover fish from supper and some cream. She couldn't have put her back in the barn on her own, she just couldn't.

'Nell James, what is that in your bag?' Bobby had skidded to a halt and was staring in horror at her satchel.

'Please, Bobby, don't tell, please.' In typically dramatic

fashion, the little girl fell to her knees and clasped her hands together as if she were pleading for her life.

Slowly Bobby opened the flap of the satchel and peered in to see two ice-blue eyes and a fluffy white face staring up at him.

'Jesus, Nell! You can't take a puppy to school,' he exclaimed.

'But if I don't, she'll die of cold.' Fat tears started to swell in Nell's eyes as she began coughing again.

Behind them, Molly was barking and scratching frantically at the door of the chicken shed. 'What is up with that bloody dog?' said Bobby. 'Dad's gonna shoot her if she doesn't shut up soon.'

'Oh, Bobby! He wouldn't, would he?' Nell started sobbing then, triggering another coughing fit.

'Of course he wouldn't. Come on, let's put the puppy back in the barn.'

'No! Bobby, please don't. She'll die if you put her in there.'

'But Snowy is with her mummy in there; Molly will keep her warm.'

'No, she's not. Her mummy's bored of looking after her. When I went into the barn this morning, Molly ran out. She's just abandoned her, and I couldn't see any of the other puppies anywhere. They were gone!'

'What do you mean, gone? They won't be far away; she's probably moved them.'

'We need to find them, Bobby, because Alice is getting her puppy tomorrow. She has talked about nothing else for weeks!'

Molly was howling now, like a wolf, scratching so hard

on the door of the chicken shed that it seemed about to cave in. Alfie appeared at the door of The Vicarage, red-faced, bellowing at the dog to stop howling. 'Shut up, Molly!'

'Bobby, I'm too tired to walk,' said Nell. 'I don't feel well at all. I'm so hot.'

He sighed. 'You should probably miss school if you feel that bad,' he said.

'No, it's fine. I want to go.' She thought of the discovery she had to share with Alice. They would go in the secret room together and explore it with Snowy. Maybe even after school today, while Bobby and Dad were working, if Alice's mother would let her come and play. If Dad wasn't going to let her see Alice any more, they needed a place to hide more than ever.

'You can't take Snowy to school,' said Bobby, racking his brains for inspiration. 'Look, I'll put her in the chicken shed just for today. There's a heat lamp in there, she'll be fine. And tonight we'll work out what to do.' He opened the satchel and pulled the whimpering puppy out. 'Don't worry, I'll wrap her up. Start up the hill, Nell, and stop the bus for me. I'll catch you up.'

Nell watched him walk towards the chicken shed. Then she set off up the path, but it was too cold and her coughing began again in earnest. She had barely walked ten steps before she heard Bobby shout out. She turned, her head throbbing, to see him rushing out of the shed.

'Dad!' he cried. There was a panic in his voice Nell had never heard before. Bobby was usually calm, quiet, the opposite of her. She could tell immediately that something bad had happened.

She watched, as if in slow motion, as her dad ran towards the shed. On shaking legs she started walking back down the lane, knowing that whatever was happening wasn't good. She was wearing a thick scarf, but despite the bitter cold, she felt like her skin was on fire, and she tore it off.

Alice had been waiting for her at the top of the lane, and now she came running down to join her. 'Nell, what's wrong?' Her hair was in perfect bunches, tied with red ribbons to match her coat. It always made Nell's heart sink a little to see how nice her friend looked. She wished she had a mummy to buy her pretty clothes and do her hair.

'I don't know, something's happened with Molly.'

As Nell and Alice watched, Bobby carried something out of the chicken shed. It was a heavy sack, and there was water dripping from it. Alfie was struggling to open it, and he pulled out a penknife, tearing at the string tied around it, until it finally snapped. Bobby looked over at Nell, a panicked look in his eyes.

'Stay back, don't come over here!' he shouted.

'What's happening?' said Nell, starting to cry. Alice took her hand and held it tightly, but Nell broke free and began walking towards Bobby, who was kneeling down next to his dad, still trying to open the sack.

She reached them just as her father managed to tear it open and a lifeless puppy fell out, soaked through with water. Bobby looked up at her in panic, ushering her away as her father tried to deal with the horror in front of him. He was pulling the puppies out one after the other. Four waterlogged balls of white fur.

Nell tried to scream, but no sound came out.

'Nell, are you okay?'

She turned back to look at Alice, who was rooted to the spot, stricken with worry. Her brother Leo had appeared and was standing behind her, a smug, self-satisfied look on his face.

'The puppies have been drowned,' Nell sobbed.

Alice began to cry; she turned away and reached for Leo's hand, but he pulled it away and made no attempt to comfort his little sister, who had been counting down the days and hours until she got her puppy.

As Bobby reached Nell she started to cough again, this time uncontrollably, until a metallic liquid filled her mouth. She bent over, crying in panic, as blood began pouring out of her onto the white snow at her feet.

'Oh my God, Nell,' gasped Bobby, turning to shout for his dad.

'Bobby, what's wrong with me?' she cried, her tears flowing into the blood coming from her mouth.

'Leo, get Alice out of here, now!' Bobby barked.

Leo turned away with a look of disgust and began walking up the hill to the waiting bus.

'Alice, come here now!' Leo barked, walking back up the lane ahead of her, as the little girl turned away and followed him, her shoulders shaking from crying.

'Carry her inside, Bobby, I'll call the doctor' said Alfie, as he reached them, his clothes still dripping with water.

'You'll be okay, Nell,' said Bobby, his eyes filling with tears, as he lifted her up in to his arms and carried her inside.

Chapter Nine

Bella

January 1945

'Mama, is that you?' Alfie's voice was barely a whisper as his blue eyes sparkled back at her in the darkness of the hidden room at The Vicarage.

'Alfie! Yes, it's me. I'm sorry, my darling. I'm so sorry.' She reached in as the little boy stood on wobbly legs. He was clutching something, a notebook, which fell to the floor as he climbed out.

A cramping pain took Bella's breath away as he fell into her and began to sob. Sinking her face into his neck, she tried to breathe through the pain and not cry out.

'I'm so sorry, my darling. I'm so sorry I took so long,' she said breathlessly. He was shaking uncontrollably from the cold as she clung to him.

'I thought you weren't coming. They kept calling my name, trying to get me to come out,' Alfie said, his eyes shining with tears.

'Who did? Who was here?' said Bella, squeezing him tight as he climbed onto her lap.

'The police and Mr Hilton. He came every night, but I could see his flashlight.' Alfie looked up at her, tears streaming down his face. 'I thought you weren't coming. I didn't know what to do.'

'You did so well, my darling. I'm so proud of you. Are you hungry? You must be famished.' As she stood up, another pain came. She stopped and bent over.

'What is it, Mama, are you sick?' He looked up at her, his eyes wide.

'I'm all right, Alfie. We need to light a fire. It's bitterly cold in here.' She breathed more slowly again as the wave of pain passed.

'Won't they see us?' said Alfie anxiously.

'It doesn't matter if they do. I'm here now. They can't take you away from me, they aren't allowed.'

He threw his arms around her again. 'Mama, come and sit down,' he said, helping her down the stairs to the rocking chair by the fireplace. Grateful for somewhere to rest, she lowered herself down, as Alfie knelt next to her and gripped her hand. 'Shall I light the fire?' he asked.

Bella looked at the ashes lying in the grate, it was a fire her mother would have lit, the last time she was here. Her eyes fell on the wicker basket filled with wood and newspaper, imagined her mother gathering the wood from the shed and chopping off splinters for firewood. Building it carefully and lovingly, twisting the paper to set it alight.

'Yes, you light it, Alfie, but you must have something to eat first.' She smiled over at him as he bustled about building a fire and looking for matches.

'It's all right, Mama, I snuck out every night and took food from the pantry. It's how I was able to hide in there so long. I knew if someone was coming because I saw the headlights through the glass bricks in the wall.'

'You're a good boy, Alfie, well done.' Pain began to ripple through her again, and she looked over at the pile of blood-ied blankets, hoping Alfie wouldn't see them.

The little boy leaned over and lit the newspaper, and it sprang into life. The grey room was immediately filled with a warm glow as he blew gently on the flame, like he had seen his grandmother do.

'Where's Baba?' he asked. 'Is she all right? The police took her away.'

'I haven't seen her yet, but I'm planning to tomorrow,' said Bella, beginning to feel faint.

'Mama, let me get you something to eat,' Alfie said, pulling a blanket over her.

'No, Alfie, I'm all right. Come and sit with me; I want to be near you.' She reached out her hand which Alfie took, sit-ting at her feet and putting his arm over her legs. She began to stroke his hair as the fire crackled, warming them both. She was so exhausted she could barely keep her eyes open.

'Mama, can I come with you to see Baba?' said Alfie quietly.

'Yes, of course. I won't be leaving you again.'

'Baba left her notebook in the room with me. I read a bit, but I didn't understand most of it.' He yawned loudly.

'May I see it?' Bella said.

The little boy stood and ran up the steps, reappearing a moment later. 'Here,' he said, handing it to her.

It was a leather-bound notebook with a ribbon tied around its middle, and Bella recognised it immediately. It was her mother's patient notebook, which she took with her everywhere and obviously didn't want the police to find. She felt tearful holding it, as if she were holding her mother's hand.

Alfie threw another piece of wood on the fire, and it hissed and popped. Bella laid the notebook on the table next to her and looked down at her son, whose head was on her lap. She ran her hands through his dark hair as tears streamed down her face. The pains in her abdomen were easing now, and her body started to relax; she was home and Alfie was safe.

As the fire flickered and she began to doze off, memories came back to her of the night Alfie was born. Her mother's face deep in concentration, her blue eyes smiling, her thick hair falling in front of her sun-kissed face, encouraging her, telling her to breathe. The fire had crackled gently in the corner as she thought of Eli, not knowing if he was safe or dead, scared or comforted, fighting or captured. She had felt overwhelmed by the terrifying pain but knew she was in the best of hands with Tessa James, the finest midwife ever created on this earth – as was the opinion of every working-class mother in Lewes.

A sort of elation had come over her during those last few moments of labour, and the pain had ceased to matter. Another contraction and Alfie had slid out. A small baby, the delivery so quick in the end that her mother had no time to do anything more than catch the child. They both looked down in shock, the little boy just lying there on the sheet staring up at them as if to say, 'I'm here! Make a fuss of me!' Tessa had cleared his airway, clamped the cord and cut it, then handed him to Bella, as she had done with hundreds of other women. Her mother had healing hands and a knowledge of pregnancy and childbirth that meant she had lost only a handful of babies in her life, and saved hundreds.

And by way of thanks for thirty years of – mostly unpaid – service, she was being dragged in front of a jury, accused of manslaughter.

On her lap, Alfie began to snore gently. Bella felt overwhelmed that she was reunited with him, but still she craved her mother's love; longed for the tea and bread and honey that Tessa had made them once Alfie was safely in her arms the night he was born. As she had cooed over Alfie, wishing Eli were there to meet his beautiful son, she had watched her mother in the kitchen, a woman twenty-two years older than her, who had been up all night delivering her baby but was still bristling with energy, as she was after every child she delivered safely. Whistling a funny little tune she had made up for the occasion.

Despite her exhaustion, Bella found it hard to sleep. She was haunted by the image of her mother in a cell somewhere, no doubt cold and hungry and uncomfortable, tortured by thoughts of what was to come.

Bella had yet to find out the facts of the case, but she knew her mother was a scapegoat. Evelyn Hilton's death had been a decade in the making and she knew that Dr Jenkins had something to do with it. She had witnessed the pressure on Tessa building for years. A snowball of hatred towards her from Dr Jenkins, Father Blacker, the local priest, and of course Wilfred Hilton. Men who viewed birth as the curse of Eve and childbearing as the painful punishment that all women should undergo. They did not want women such as her mother, who barely charged for her services, alleviating the pain of childbirth with herbs, experience and meditation, and doing a better job than men with medical degrees who charged a month's wages for their botched deliveries.

Doctors saw birth as a pathology that needed treatment. Babies should be delivered with women lying on their backs with their legs in stirrups, in sterile and frightening medicalised environments where the mothers weren't listened to and did what they were told. The number of medical men practising midwifery was increasing rapidly, and midwives, like Tessa, bitterly resented the invasion of their territory. Most men, her mother said, who started in general practice, had only the dimmest idea of the conduct of normal, let alone complicated births, and learned by harsh experience, often killing mothers and babies who would otherwise have survived. Mothers like Evelyn Hilton, Bella reflected.

But try as he might, the local women still shunned Dr Jenkins in favour of Tessa, and he resented it bitterly. They had gone to her for years and they didn't like the doctor, who had no sympathy and grew impatient waiting around for a baby to be born. He pulled out forceps and medical equipment when they weren't needed just to hurry things along so he could go home.

It was obvious to Bella, from conversations she overheard, that women were more comfortable with Tessa than with Dr Jenkins. He didn't know how to comfort a mother in the throes of childbirth, or young women, terrified and often barely into adulthood and not ready to birth babies, to whom he would talk in medical terms they didn't understand.

Bella's eyes drooped, the rhythmic movement of Alfie's deep breathing and the fire too comforting to fight. As she drifted away, she felt her mother standing next to her, holding out her hand. Slowly her mother led her out of the front door of The Vicarage, to the field behind the house. The sky was red, the moon full, as they walked along the hedgerow to a deadly nightshade plant with purple bell-shaped flowers and shiny black berries, which she had warned Bella of as a child. Now, though, she turned to her daughter and began slowly plucking the berries from their stems and placing them into Bella's cupped hand as the sky turned black.

Bella woke with a start and let out a moan of pain as her uterus contracted. The pain slowly subsided again and she gently moved Alfie and threw another log on the fading fire. It started to burn with a roar as a gush of cold air came down the chimney. Her arms shaking with the weight, she took a bucket, filled with water from the well, and hung it over the fire.

While she waited for the water to heat so that she could wash herself, she walked across to the front door and opened it. The sun had risen, revealing a stunning winter's day, crisp and bright; the sort of morning her mother loved. The sun on her face gave Bella the strength she needed to step outside, and as she lowered herself onto the stone bench outside the door, she looked over at the chain that her beloved mare, Ebony, was usually tied to in the summer months. Selling the horse before she had left for Portsmouth had broken her heart, but they had desperately needed the money. Ebony had taken her out of herself, made her forget how much she missed Eli; on bad days she would pull Alfie into the saddle and take off across the open countryside until sundown.

She squinted in the intense sunshine, looking up to the far field and beyond, to the hedgerow containing the deadly nightshade. Her mother had spoken to her in her dream to tell her that she would rather die than live a life behind bars. If she was convicted of manslaughter, she would be trapped in a cell, with no access to fresh air and sunshine, grass or trees. Everything she lived for would be gone; flowers, the beach, the sea, but mostly her and Alfie. She would survive for a year, maybe two, until she died of a broken heart. She would want to take her own life in a way that meant she was in control, so that it was her choice; to die as she had lived, independent and fearless. If the time came, Bella didn't know if she would have the strength to hand the berries to her, knowing they would kill her, but she owed it to her to be strong if her mother asked it of her.

As she stood, she heard a rumbling noise, distant at first, then louder, and the ground beneath her feet began to tremble. She looked around, her head throbbing from the cold, her stomach aching still, to see a man on horseback thundering towards her. The sunlight was behind him so that she couldn't see his face, but she knew that it was Wilfred Hilton on Titus, his beloved black gelding, who according to Eli he loved more than his own children.

'Good morning, Miss James,' he said, bringing the horse to a halt. He was a formidable man, tall and lean, with grey hair and a thick moustache covering his narrow mouth.

'Sir,' she snapped, glancing up at him briefly.

Wilfred Hilton had the same face shape as his son, but his manner was utterly different. Whilst Eli skipped everywhere he went and laughed at himself, his father walked with a heavy heart, looking over his shoulder at all times as if expecting to be pounced upon. Though he owned most of Lewes, he wore a permanent frown like someone who hadn't two pennies to his name, and he held his cane permanently in his right hand, ready to swipe anything that got into his path.

Bella focused on her breathing so that he wouldn't see her shaking.

'Sir, my mother hasn't been found guilty yet; this is our home. Please leave,' she said firmly.

'Not any more. I served your mother notice the day she killed Evelyn,' Wilfred said simply.

Bella immediately felt tears sting her eyes. Wilfred had wanted to get rid of her and her mother for years, but Evelyn and Eli had stopped him. Now that his wife was gone, her body barely cold, he had seized the opportunity to snatch the house back.

Nervousness began to creep through her as Wilfred hovered like a prophet of doom. Why had he served her mother notice when he knew Eli wouldn't allow it? The war was so nearly over, and if talk was to be believed, the fighting men would soon be home. But she hadn't heard from Eli for weeks – his last letter had been in the autumn – and suddenly she was frightened. She knew why Wilfred was here. She could feel his eyes on her, hear his heavy breathing as he began to speak the words that would end her world.

'Eli is dead. I had a telegram last week. The spell you and your mother have cast over him and our family for so long is broken. You are no longer welcome here.' He pursed his lips, saying no more.

Bella turned away, trying to stop herself breaking down in front of a man she hated. She had not let herself think about why she hadn't heard from Eli; she didn't have the strength. All that had been keeping her going was the thought of him coming home and being a father to Alfie, of them marrying and finally being a family so that she could leave her job in Portsmouth and come home.

Now Wilfred Hilton was telling her that the love of her life was dead.

'This war has taken Alfie's father. He is all you have left of Eli; why do you hate him so? He is your grandchild.' Bella fought back tears, refusing to break down in front of a man who would enjoy her suffering.

'He is a bastard. You were never married. How am I to be sure he is even my son's child? He looks everything like you, with his black hair and blue eyes, and nothing like my fair-haired boy.' Wilfred's voice wavered slightly as he spoke of Eli, then he set his glare on her again.

Bella glared back. 'I have nowhere else to go. My employer won't have me back with Alfie, and if my mother is found guilty, she cannot care for him. You have so much, and if you do this, we are destined for the workhouse, we will be separated. I beg of you, please give us a little more time.'

'You should have thought of that before taking my son into your bed without a ring on your finger. We are not a charity; you would have been out on the street a long time ago were it not for my wife's kindness. I have a reputation to protect. I see women coming and going in the dead of night. I know why they come here, wanting your mother to bring on their miscarriages, and some would say that is murder. I want nothing more to do with the James family witchcraft and I want you gone.'

Ever since her mother had become a midwife, women had begged her to help them bring on miscarriages for babies they didn't want or couldn't afford. Mostly she refused, but occasionally, if the circumstances were extreme, she would consider it. Bella remembered one woman who was carrying a baby that wasn't her husband's. She told Tessa she'd been raped by a soldier, and when her mother examined her, she could see she was torn inside. She told Tessa that if she didn't help her she would kill herself, if her husband didn't kill her first, leaving her five children motherless.

'Eli wanted Alfie to have The Vicarage, Mr Hilton. If you let us stay until the trial is over, I will go without a fight.' Bella's voice shook as she wiped her tears away, her heart breaking at having to beg, but knowing it was her and Alfie's only chance of survival. 'You will never see me again. Please, sir, it is what Eli would have wanted.'

There was a long pause, as Wilfred Hilton considered her proposal.

'I want your word, on your son's life, that you will have no visitors at all.'

'You have my word.'

'And I will never see you again?' He spat, glaring at her. Bella nodded, forcing herself to look up at him. 'Very well, you have until the day of the verdict. Then I never wish to see you in Kingston again, Miss James.'

His words took away the only strength she had left in

her, and she lowered herself back down onto the bench to stop herself from falling. In a heartbeat, Wilfred Hilton had erased them from his life completely; taken their home, their security, their freedom. Because Eli was dead.

She watched him ride away, wishing she could stop breathing and make it all go away. She held her breath for as long as she could, until she felt her lungs would tear, before letting out a piercing scream from the pit of her stomach. It started to snow, but still she sat there, unable to find the will to move. She could no longer feel her hands, her face or any part of her. Soon she stopped shaking, and all she could hear was the sound of her mother singing as she picked the herbs in the garden. She could see herself as a child, sitting in the long grass while her mother worked around her, growing tomatoes and runner beans and spinach.

'Mummy, you're cold.' She could hear Alfie's voice now. 'Get up, Mummy, come and sit by the fire.' His little hands reached out to hold hers. 'Don't cry, Mummy. You're getting too cold, your tears will freeze.'

But she couldn't get up. Her breath became shallow, her heartbeat slowing in her chest.

'Mummy, wake up! I need you!' Alfie shouted, and she jolted awake. Slowly she sat up and looked around for her son but no one was there. On shaky legs, she stood and went back inside, where Alfie lay sleeping, and threw some kindling on the fire.

As she watched her son's breathing, she began to thaw out, her despair melting into fury. She found some crackers and honey in the pantry and began to eat. Then she picked up the bucket of water warming over the fire and walked up the stairs into her mother's bedroom. There she found an old sheet and washed away as much of the blood as she could from in between her legs. She wrapped her bloodied clothes in the sheet, then dressed herself in her mother's skirt, jumper and black boots, putting one of her shawls around her shoulders.

Bella looked around the room, feeling the warm cocoon of her mother's love fill her with strength and resolve. She turned and walked down the creaky wooden steps, past the secret room that had kept Alfie safe, and bent down to a basket of garden tools lying by the front door and picked up a trowel, then turned and scooped up the bloody blankets and clicked open the latch of the front door.

The sun was warm, the dawn of a new day giving her strength. Bella walked slowly to the corner of the herb garden, where she knew the soil would be softer from her mother's constant tending, then she knelt down and began to dig, her eyes repeatedly drawn to the hedgerow and the nightshade hidden inside.

Chapter Ten
Vanessa

New Year's Eve 1969

Vanessa climbed the steps and stuck her head through the hatch, waving her torch beam around. The tree house was empty. Blankets, cushions and sweet wrappers littered the floor. As she backed down the steps, worry started to creep in.

'Alice, are you out here?' she shouted, listening to the sounds of the night as the pianist began to play in the distance. As Vanessa walked towards the house, the gates opened and a Rolls-Royce pulled into the driveway. It was starting; they were all arriving, and she wasn't even dressed. Alice must be in the house, there was no other explanation.

Walking at speed, she hurried back through the front door, ignoring the waiting staff milling around, kicked off her boots, then took the stairs two at a time and launched herself into Alice's bedroom. 'Alice? Darling, are you here?' Goosebumps roared up her arms, and as she stood staring at the chaos of her daughter's bedroom, she began to feel extremely uneasy. She turned and left, running to her own bedroom and pulling her dress from the velvet hanger.

In the time it took for her to zip up her dress, wrap her feather boa around her neck and put her earrings in, her irritation turned to deep concern. Richard appeared at the door, still fuming at the ordeal he had been through – fixing the lights, the driveway, the general carnage from the snowstorm – and began crashing around, every movement making her flinch.

'I need a shower,' he said, striding across the room to their en suite.

'I can't find Alice. She wasn't in the tree house, she's not in her room.' She felt her face flush in panic as the words made her concern real.

'She'll be in the house somewhere, try the kitchen – she'll be raiding the food.' Richard strode over to the window. 'There's another car pulling in now. I've never needed a drink more.'

'Leo's out there in the snow too,' Vanessa said, a feeling of worry refusing to settle.

'Please don't get into one of your panics. Alice is fine. I'll wring her neck for worrying you, but she's fine. Leo will be back in a minute, and he can keep an eye on her so you can relax.'

'I wish you hadn't sent Leo out like that. That bloody storm, and now Alice – it's all made me feel like there's a terrible omen hanging over this evening. Where is she? Why is she hiding from me? I wasn't that cross with her, I just told her to get dressed. She's impossible!'

'Vanessa!' Richard said, glaring at his wife. 'Don't start.'

Vanessa slipped on her heels and sprayed on her Chanel No. 5 before reaching for the door handle. She stepped out onto the landing, and looked down into the hallway where two waitresses with trays loaded with champagne glasses were waiting for the first arrivals. 'Alice! Alice, please come out. I don't care if you want to wear your dungarees, can you please just come out now.' She ran from room to room along the upstairs landing, opening doors into the darkness behind them.

As she walked down the stairs, the front door opened and the first guests appeared. Vanessa beamed at them as the couple stepped over the threshold. She felt suddenly nauseous.

'Bill, Olivia, how wonderful to see you,' she said, walking towards them. 'Thank you so much for coming. You look absolutely stunning, Olivia. Can you believe this storm, we nearly had to cancel. Please have some champagne.' She leaned in to kiss them both. A young man in black tie stepped forward to take their coats.

'Thank you, Vanessa. Look at your dress! My word, it's breathtaking. It was so lovely of you to invite us. We have been looking forward to it for weeks.' Olivia swept a glass from the tray that was offered to her.

Vanessa glanced along the hall, hoping to catch sight of Alice, then turned to one of the waitresses. 'Can you please search the house for my daughter; she's six and is wearing a red dress. And come and tell me when you've found her. If you can't find her inside, take a torch and look for her outside.'

'Do you not want me to serve the champagne?' The waitress looked slightly startled.

'No, I want you to find my daughter. Quickly, please. I'll be in the drawing room.'

'Um, of course,' said the waitress, flushing red.

'Is everything okay, Vanessa?' asked Olivia.

'Yes, silly really, I can't seem to find Alice. I'm sure she's in the house, but she's having a tantrum; she doesn't want to wear the red dress I got her for the party.'

The doorbell rang again, and a stream of people began to arrive. Vanessa's heart fluttered anxiously in her chest as she greeted couple after couple on her own. All the time, her body was desperately pulling at her to get away and look for Alice. Finally, as Richard came down the stairs, the waitress reappeared, shaking her head. 'I'm sorry, Mrs Hilton, I can't find her anywhere.'

It was then that the world appeared to slow down. The warm, welcoming noises of the party began to screech in her ears; the piano, the chatter, the heat. Vanessa turned to her husband. 'They can't find Alice, Richard.'

'For goodness' sake, Vanessa, she will be hiding somewhere in the house. She's doing it on purpose. George, Martha, how wonderful to see you,' he said, stepping forward to shake hands with the latest arrivals.

'I'm sorry, Richard, I have to look for her. Something doesn't feel right.' Vanessa smiled politely at her guests, leaving Richard on his own as she began to walk at speed down the hall, her heels clicking loudly on the tiles, calling out Alice's name as she went.

The kitchen was filled with steam and a smell of food that turned her stomach. She ran through to the back of the house, turning her ankle painfully in her heels as she reached the storeroom. 'Alice!' Fumbling with the back door, she opened it into the garden, where the outlines of Alice's toys were visible everywhere in the darkness.

'Alice!' Her heels sank into the mud as she ran round to the bike shed and opened it. She felt around in the dark, unable to see, until she found the light switch. *Click.* She recoiled as her eyes adjusted to the brightness, her stomach lurching at the near-empty bike stand. Only two bikes where there were usually four; a space where Alice and Leo's should be. Her heart began to thud so hard that she struggled to breathe as she ran back out into the garden and through the gate at the side of the house that led to the driveway at the front.

Her last conversation with her daughter echoed in her ears: *I can't find Snowy.*

As a trail of cars queued along the driveway, she rushed towards the front door in her red heels, hearing a hubbub of voices, laughter, snippets of words: *good evening . . . beautiful house . . . delighted to be asked . . .* Richard was standing in the doorway shaking hands, and she ran up to him. 'Something's wrong, Richard. We should drive round and look for them. I think maybe Alice has gone after Leo to The Vicarage, looking for her puppy. Her bike is gone.'

'What are you talking about? Our guests are arriving, we can't leave! For God's sake, is she definitely not in the garden? If she has gone after him, at least they'll be together.' He was trying to smile at the guests, some of whom were frowning with concern.

'Leo probably didn't even realise Alice was following him. Richard, please, I'm worried. Something doesn't feel right.' She plunged her nails into her husband's arm, which he pulled away as he smiled apologetically at the guests in front of him.

'You always worry too much,' he hissed at her. 'You've got no reason to be concerned. Don't do this to me now. Do you want to ruin the evening for me?!'

'Our daughter is missing, Richard!' Vanessa raised her voice so that several people turned to stare.

'Oh gosh, Vanessa, I'm so sorry.' An older woman in an emerald-green gown reached out for her arm. 'Goodness, Richard, how awful, can I do anything to help?'

Richard looked around, taking in the sea of faces staring at him expectantly, then turned to the waiter standing behind him. 'Can you and two of your staff please walk around the grounds with torches looking for my daughter, Alice. She's six years old and wearing a red dress, is that right, Vanessa? I'll check the house. Please try and stay calm, Vanessa. She'll be all right.'

'I'm going to go down to the lane, see if there's any sign of them,' said Vanessa, kicking off her shoes and pulling her wellington boots back on as she fought back her terror.

The drive was gridlocked now with cars, the slanting snow illuminated in the beams of their headlights. A couple of guests lowered their windows as she rushed past, waving and calling out cheerfully.

As she reached the end of the drive, she saw Leo and Bobby walking towards her past the queue of cars. 'Leo! Oh, thank God.' She rushed over to him, slipping as she launched herself at his handlebars. 'Leo! Where's Alice? Have you seen her? We think she might have followed you to The Vicarage on her bike.'

Leo looked at her, his face frozen, his nose and ears red from the cold. 'No, I haven't seen her. What's wrong, Mum?'

'Are you sure? Oh Leo, where is she?' She tried to control the panic from taking over as her eyes raked the front lawn, the beams of several torches sweeping through the snow as staff shouted her daughter's name. She felt her legs start to go as Leo let his bike drop and helped her over to a snow-covered bench just as Richard came hurtling towards them.

'Where's Alice, Leo? Bobby? Did she follow you? Richard barked.'

Leo's eyes widened at this scene of mayhem greeting him. 'I just went to get Bobby like you asked. I haven't seen Alice!' He was shaking from the cold, snow covering his hat and coat so they had turned white.

'Well, she's not in the house, and they can't find her in the grounds. She must have followed you!' Vanessa glared at her son. 'I think she's worried the puppy ran back to The Vicarage.'

'She can't have. I cycled too fast,' Leo said, his eyes wide.

'We definitely didn't see her, Mrs Hilton,' added Bobby.

Vanessa felt herself cave then, starting to suck in waves of hysteria as the blizzard engulfed them. 'You need to go after her, Leo! You need to find her and bring her back.'

'I'll go,' said Richard, taking the bicycle off his son and buttoning up his coat.

'If you go down the lane, I'll walk back through the woods the way we came,' said Bobby.

Vanessa felt her voice break. 'What do we do, Richard? I don't know what to do. Where is she?' She looked pleadingly at her husband as he turned the bike around. 'It's so cold.'

The waiters that Richard had sent outside appeared. 'We've looked everywhere, Mr Hilton, in the sheds, the grounds, the gardens. She's not out here and she's not in the house.'

Richard looked at his wife as he began to pedal away. 'Call the police, Vanessa. Now.'

Chapter Eleven

Vanessa

Thursday, 21 December 2017

'Sienna, where are you?' Vanessa shouted into the darkness, which was closing in frighteningly fast. She stepped back down onto the snow-covered grass and looked around her. The icy wind was rushing in her ears, but she could hear Helen shouting Sienna's name from the back of the house as the removal men stood watching hopelessly as the two of them dashed around in a panic. She told herself to breathe and stay calm. Sienna hadn't been gone for long; surely she would come running round the corner any second. She wasn't missing, she was just hiding. They could not lose another child; it could not happen again.

She heard the crunch of tyres as the gates opened and Leo's Volvo pulled into the driveway. The ground spat stones out around her feet like firecrackers as the car edged towards her. He pulled to a stop next to Vanessa and opened his window.

'What are you doing out here, Mum? It's nearly dark.' Leo frowned, the warmth of his car leaking out into the freezing air around her.

'Do you need some help looking?' shouted one of the removal men.

'Yes, please!' Vanessa called back, walking towards him

and ignoring Leo, unable to face him. 'She's wearing a red coat.' She felt her body shaking violently.

'What's going on, Mum, who are you looking for?' Leo's eyes were wide and darting. 'What's happened?'

Vanessa turned around and looked at her son, forcing herself to answer him. 'We can't find Sienna. She was out here playing in the snow.'

'What? What do you mean, you can't find her?' He was frowning, trying to take it in. 'How long have you been looking for her?'

'I don't know, not long. Helen came to find me in my bedroom and asked me where she was. I just went to get my gloves.' She started to cry.

'Mum, it's okay, she'll turn up. I'll meet you by the house, you need to get inside, you're freezing. I'll look for her. She's probably just hiding.' He glanced up at the house nervously.

'She was out here. Playing. She can't have gone far,' said Vanessa, but Leo had already driven off toward the house and parked up, jumping out of the car. She watched through her tears, unable to breathe properly, as Helen appeared again at the front of the house. It felt unreal to her, like a black and white film of that night fifty years ago, with the night setting in and the snow on the ground. Leo and Helen gesticulated frantically at one another; it was like watching herself and Richard that night. Like she had gone back in time.

This cannot happen, this cannot happen again, she said to herself, over and over.

As she reached the house, Leo had his arm around Helen's shoulders. 'I'll find her, Helen, I'll find her,' he was saying as he glanced over at Vanessa who was shaking from the cold.

'Can you take Mum inside, Helen?' he asked, before breaking into a run to look around the outside of the house, calling Sienna's name over and over.

Crying uncontrollably, Helen walked towards Vanessa and took her arm, leading her inside to the kitchen. Vanessa felt the warmth of the Aga hit her as Helen pulled a chair up in front of the fire and eased her into it. The removal men were standing around looking slightly stunned, not knowing what to do. Helen took Vanessa's coat off and put a blanket over her knees.

'I'm sorry,' said Vanessa quietly. 'I just went to get my gloves.'

'Stay here,' Helen snapped in an unfamiliar tone.

Vanessa sat staring at the floor, her brain unable to process what was happening, as the voices and noises surrounding her stabbed at her like needles.

'Sienna!' she heard Helen calling again, outside the window. 'Sienna, where are you? If you're hiding, it's not funny. Mummy and Daddy are very worried.'

Time began to blur as the night descended completely. Someone brought her a cup of tea and put some slippers on her feet as people continued calling out Sienna's name. She didn't know how long she sat there, but suddenly the kitchen lights came on, and the brightness of them made her wince.

'It's dark, Leo, we need to call the police,' she heard Helen say. 'It's freezing out there.'

'I'll go into the woods with the dogs and the removal guys. She could have fallen down and hurt herself.'

'She's seven and it's snowing. She could be dead in an

hour.' Helen started to cry again. 'I don't know what to do. Where is she?'

'I had a thought.' Leo panted. 'She could have gone to Dorothy's house.'

'I called her, she's not there.'

'But have you been down there to look? She could be hiding somewhere, in Peter's shed or something. Just go there, maybe, and have a search. She was upset about leaving her. Shit, if this gets out, we're finished.'

'What are you talking about?' Tears continuously poured down Helen's face, her eyes red raw.

'I've signed everything today; we are in it up to our necks if anything jeopardises this planning meeting tomorrow. What if the press get hold of this? They'll bring Alice up all over again.'

'I don't care about any of that. I'm going to Dorothy's,' said Helen. 'And if she's not there I'm calling the police.' She stormed out.

'Mum? Mum?' Leo knelt beside Vanessa. 'When was the last time you saw Sienna? You said you were going to build a snowman.'

'What?' she said.

'You told Helen you were going to build a snowman, but then she found you in your bedroom. Why did you go in?' Leo asked.

Vanessa started to cry. 'I don't know, I don't remember.'

'For God's sake.' Leo stood up and paced frantically. 'Did you see her from the window? Mum? Did you see Sienna from the window?'

Vanessa stared at her son. 'When?'

Leo's eyes filled with tears. 'Today, when you were in your bedroom. Before Sienna went missing.'

Vanessa tried desperately to rewind. She could see the image of Sienna in the hallway like a photograph. Leo's pacing was making her feel sick. She started to remember: she had needed something, she had gone back inside to get something . . . 'I needed my gloves. I remember now, I needed my gloves. I went to my bedroom. And I watched that man walking up the drive from my window.'

'What man?' Leo's gaze fixed on her.

'The man who was in your study.' The afternoon started coming back to her in random images, out of sequence. 'He had blue eyes.'

'Who did? Who was in my study? Was he one of the removal men?'

'I don't know.' Vanessa felt blood rushing in her ears as she struggled to bring it back. Her memory was like a locked door she had a hundred keys for. 'He didn't have the uniform on. I told him you wouldn't want anyone in your study, and he left. He walked up the drive.'

'In the direction Sienna went? Towards the tree house?' Leo was watching her intently.

'He walked towards the gates. I think he left. He was alone, he seemed . . .'

'What, Mum? What did he seem?' Leo snapped.

'Out of place,' said Vanessa.

'Can you remember what he looked like?'

'Not really, apart from he had very bright blue eyes.'

'Stay here in the warm, Mum. I'll be back soon.' Leo rushed from the room.

The door slammed. She could hear people calling for

Sienna, but their voices were fainter; they were getting further away. The room grew colder, but still she sat there, tears rolling down her cheeks. And then, another voice, one she didn't recognise.

'Mrs Hilton? Can you hear me?' She looked up to see a man with dark hair and a moustache pulling up a chair next to her. 'I'm Detective Inspector Hatton. Is it all right if I sit here with you?'

Vanessa looked at the doorway, where Leo was standing, his eyes dull and narrow, then back at the policeman. 'Have you found her?' she said. 'Have you found Alice?'

Chapter Twelve
Willow

Thursday, 21 December 2017

Willow sat back in the armchair in her living room and pressed stop on her mobile phone recording app. After walking back into her boss's office and handing Leo Hilton his mug of tea, she had feigned surprise that she had left her phone on the desk while making the drinks and returned it to her pocket.

Before she left the office, she had gone through her planning application again on the office system and had been horrified to find a blank folder she had not noticed before and, hidden inside it, a report she had never laid eyes on, entitled 'Earth Excavation Report'. It was an entirely separate document from the desktop survey, which Mike had shown to her at the very start of the project. Mike must have commissioned the Earth Excavation Report behind her back, Willow concluded. It was written by a man called Dr Edward Crane at Pre-Construct Archaeology in Portsmouth and was roughly ten pages long, with the final paragraph summarising that in five separate areas the layer of soil directly beneath the topsoil to the rear of The Vicarage had been removed – but that no human remains had been found. Dr Crane had concluded that there was no reason to believe the graveyard mentioned in the desktop survey was of any significant size, and that if there were any human remains, which were to be expected on a project of this magnitude on previously undeveloped land, they should be easily excavated.

Willow's heart had lurched at this piece of information. *The graveyard mentioned in the desktop survey.* She remembered very clearly Mike doing the desktop survey before she came on board and saying that it hadn't shown anything up. Her hands shaking, she printed out the report for herself.

She hadn't had much experience of archaeological desktop assessments, but she knew that they didn't consist of any digging, and were simply a case of collating library evidence of the area. If there had been a Roman settlement on the land, for instance, or if artefacts had ever been found on the site, they would show up.

She racked her brains to recall the conversation she'd had with Mike about the desktop survey. 'Developers always wait until the contractors have dug the foundations, and then they inspect those excavations to see if there are any archaeological artefacts,' he'd told her, very casually, when she'd asked. 'So they wouldn't know anything was below the surface until they actually starting doing the digging for the foundations.'

As she sat reading the report again now, she felt sick. She had asked Mike if she could read it at the time, and he had printed it out for her, but the document in her planning application file and the one he had given her were not the same. There were at least two pages missing from the one she'd read, one of which stated that a local map, dated

1895, showed a small grey area labelled 'graveyard' in the grounds backing onto The Vicarage.

She had sat at her desk in the office feeling utterly floored; it was proof that Mike had been playing games, but at the same time, it wasn't enough to confront him. He could still deny it, make up a story about doing the report to help her or to save time. She needed more.

She felt sick at her stupidity for trusting him, but she'd had no reason to doubt him – until now. After making her excuses to Mike about needing to work from home for the afternoon, she had sat and listened to the ten-minute recording of her boss and her client discussing the project she had been working on with them for a year.

Leo had begun by singing her praises, saying what a great job she had done, how she'd got the community on board better than he'd dared hope. Mike had agreed that she had been the perfect choice, as it was her first major project and she was keen to prove herself. He referred to her as 'malleable', and said that her charm offensive with the villagers had proved a good distraction.

It was then that the conversation had turned to the graveyard and she felt her world shift.

'So Blakers definitely aren't insisting on their own excavation before they sign?' Leo had asked, referring to the developers to whom he was about to sell planning permission for the Yew Tree development for five million pounds.

'No, proper archaeological digs cost hundreds of thousands of pounds,' Mike's voice had been quiet, 'and they wouldn't invest that kind of money unless they had reason to. I've known Ed at Pre-Construct since we were at uni together; he understands how these things work and was happy to excavate in the areas I asked him to. Luckily the area the old map showed wasn't where you said the graveyard was – it was in the field next to it – so we were able to work around it.'

'And Blakers can't sue us?'

'Nope, we had an Earth Excavation Report done. They could have chosen to have a much more extensive one but they didn't want to fork out a hundred grand. Every time you build on undeveloped farmland, it's a risk you take. They know that. Also the application is in Willow's name, and if anything did happen, I could argue it was her first project of this type. And that she didn't follow the right protocol and get me to oversee Pre-Construct's dig. But it won't come to that.'

'She would go along with that, would she?' said Leo. 'She'd lie for you?'

'Definitely. I've got to know her pretty well and she won't be a problem. She's pretty keen to get on in this industry. And even if she did, it would be my word against hers. Her signature is on the file when she submitted it, so its contents are her responsibility. She'll look incompetent if she puts up any resistance and she won't want that.'

Willow had rewound and replayed the conversation several times, making notes, until she couldn't bear to listen to it any longer. For a year she had busted her balls to get this project over the line, using every contact she had, bending every rule she could think of, meeting councillors and villagers and even her boyfriend's parents, charming everyone she needed to get the planning application through. All this time she'd thought she had Mike's respect, that they were in it together, that she was finally being taken seriously.

And it was all a lie. Not only that, but they were using her name to falsify an application, which was a breach of planning control that could get her struck off.

She put her phone down and rummaged through her bag, pulling out a copy of the Archaeological Desktop Assessment, which, trusting Mike's word, she hadn't given her full attention to before now.

She sat and read the twelve-page document, making sure she didn't miss a word. Then, as she turned to the final page, her heart skipped a beat. There was a photograph of a metal tin, about the size of a large jewellery box, with the name 'Bella' in black sloping handwriting, presumably burnt into the lid. Next to it, a small brown leather-bound notebook. The text below it read: *Metal tin, bound notebook, circa 1945. Found April 1987 by metal detectorist beneath the large Willow Tree in the East Field, Yew Tree estate, near The Vicarage. Tin stored at Brighton Museum, notebook stored at The Keep, Lewes Road, Brighton.*

Willow sat back in her chair. 'Bella,' she said out loud. She was sure that was her great-grandmother's name: Bella James. She knew the family had lived at The Vicarage for generations, but like everything, her father had shot her down for asking any questions about his past. She remembered searching Google for 'Bella James' once but nothing had come up. So, with little to go on and knowing her father would disapprove, she had given up. Seeing the tin was a stark reminder of why she had agreed to take on the project in the first place; the Yew Tree estate was a treasure trove of her family's history, and here, right in front of her eyes, was potentially a big slice of the puzzle.

Willow sat back in her chair and tried to think

rationally. Maybe she was being naïve about her outrage; maybe you did have to screw the system a bit to get a deal as big as this through. She didn't like the fact that Mike had lied to her, but when he'd told Leo he knew her pretty well, he actually had little clue who she really was and what her motive was for taking on the Yew Tree Project. If she was being honest with herself, Willow reflected, Mike wasn't the only one who had been deceptive. The fact was, though, that he had picked on the wrong girl. If push came to shove, she wasn't scared to confront him and Leo, and she wasn't afraid to fight her corner. She had worked too hard to just take it lying down; she needed to keep her head, stop acting like a victim and stay focused.

A plan began to form. The Keep in Brighton, where the notebook was stored, was also where they kept all the old maps of the area. She could find out for herself if there was any sign of the graveyard behind The Vicarage. Then, armed with that information, she would go and pay Dorothy a visit at Yew Tree Cottage and find out what she knew. Perhaps the graveyard was small, just a couple of headstones from centuries back, with any human remains eroded away. She couldn't confront Mike and Leo until she had her facts straight, but what she did know was that she needed as much information as she could get her hands on before the planning meeting in less than twenty-four hours.

She stood up to get herself a glass of water, breathing through the urge to vomit until it subsided again. She hadn't eaten properly all morning, and she was completely exhausted. As soon as all this was over, she was going to take a few days off, get away, sleep and rest.

Her phone beeped and she looked down to see a message

from Charlie. *Hi babe, just checking in, we missed you at lunch. Hope you're okay? You looked tired this morning. Well done again. Love you.*

She let out a weary sigh, kicked off her heels and walked across the sanded wooden floorboards to her bedroom. She needed to take off the suit she had worn for the meeting and get into some comfy clothes. As she sat down at her dressing table and removed her make-up, she looked at her reflection in the mirror. She looked more and more like her mother every day: her heart-shaped face, her narrow lips, and the dark hair cut in a blunt fringe to hide her worry lines, which in recent months had begun to look more like the ones her mother had carried her whole life. Her light blue eyes were her father's, though; piercing as Charlie called them.

She looked around the bedroom. She had only owned her flat for a year, but it was already her favourite place in the world; her haven. Charlie had helped her with so much of it. They had painted the bedroom together as they got pissed on cheap cider; shopped for her wrought-iron bed from an antique shop in North Laine (after trying and failing to haggle the price down); chosen and framed the black and white photographs of their travels around the world that ran along the hallway. She had stretched her budget to the max buying the Victorian conversion on the borders of Hove, which meant that she'd had to do all the renovation work herself, at weekends and after work. So far she had only managed to do the bedroom, and the wooden floor that ran from the kitchen through to the lounge. It had taken her and Charlie the best part of two months to sand back, restore and oil it, but it looked beautiful. Off the kitchen was a small balcony overlooking a shared garden, where they sat on summer evenings. She knew Charlie had wanted them to get a place together, but she needed her own space, somewhere she could hide away and not have to smile and pretend she was okay.

She took off her work clothes and walked through to the avocado bathroom, which had yet to make it onto the renovation list. She turned on the shower, waiting for it to steam up before she stepped in. She felt the urge to confide in someone, but Charlie was a worrier and there was a danger he'd make her feel worse. And she couldn't talk to her dad, because she still hadn't told him she was working on the Yew Tree development for the Hiltons – the ultimate betrayal.

She closed her eyes and pictured her father's face when she told him what she'd done. The more she thought about it, the more she realised she had to face what had happened to her head on; she had danced with the devil taking this project, why was she surprised that she'd got burnt?

She climbed out of the shower and dried herself off, rubbing cocoa butter into her tired skin and pulling on jeans and a soft hoodie. She sat on her bed to dry her hair, and after texting Charlie back, she opened up her laptop. As the cursor hovered over the search engine, her conversation with Charlie's mother came back to her. *No one talks about Alice any more. Poor Vanessa, it must be a living hell never knowing what happened to her.*

Nervously she typed in *Hilton, Kingston, Lewes*. The first result was a *Lewes Gazette* cutting dated 7 January 1970:

The great unsolved mystery of missing Alice Hilton. Below the headline was a black and white picture of a little girl with ringlets and dark ribbons in her hair, smiling at something off in the distance. It was the same portrait that still hung in the hallway at Yew Tree Manor, a picture that had become synonymous with Alice's disappearance. Willow read on:

> On a frozen morning in January 1970, a week after she had gone missing, hundreds of volunteers given the day off work to look for a missing six-year-old girl walked across the snow-covered Sussex Downs until the sun went down. It was a sight to behold as each participant stood twenty-five yards apart in a mile-long line, combing ten square miles as part of a search party coordinated by Detective Inspector Mills of Sussex Police; a painstaking event during which every volunteer took great care not to miss any tiny clue that may give police some idea as to the little girl's whereabouts.
>
> 'Volunteers need basic training before they can undertake such a search,' said DI Mills, the lead detective on the case. 'It has to be done incredibly carefully and slowly. Even a torn piece of clothing or a glove can be evidence that makes or breaks an entire case.'
>
> A week ago, little Alice Hilton disappeared from a New Year's Eve party at her parents' home in Kingston near Lewes. The search party this week was one of the largest ever seen in England, and Alice's mother, Vanessa Hilton, still holds out hope that she's alive.
>
> 'We can't stop looking. She may be injured somewhere, or lost, or being held captive. Please, if you were in the area on New Year's Eve, take a moment to think. It just takes one

> person to remember something that could give us the key to her disappearance. If you saw anything, however insignificant you think it may be, call the police incident line.'

Willow scrolled down to a picture of Vanessa and Richard Hilton huddled together at a press conference. Ashen-faced, wide-eyed and bewildered, they sat at a long table in front of a large sign saying *Sussex Police*, a row of microphones in front of them. She could imagine the press conference vividly: the stark white room, the deafening noise of the camera shutters and the cacophony of shouting journalists. The article continued, as they always did, making mention of the prime suspect in the case.

> An unnamed witness who was the last person to see Alice alive is currently helping the police with their enquiries. Police have confirmed that a handkerchief was found by police officers with Alice's blood type on it near to where she disappeared and are therefore treating the child's disappearance as suspicious.
>
> Dorothy Novell, a local woman involved in the search, told our reporter, 'We are all terribly concerned for Alice, she is the sweetest child, and we are all praying she turns up safe and well.'
>
> DI Mills thanked everyone involved in the search and has urged the public to remain vigilant.

Willow felt her heart quicken as she read the quote from Dorothy again. Perhaps Dorothy had known Bobby as a child and would be willing to chat to her about her father when she asked her about the graveyard.

She sat back against her pillows and returned to the articles in the search engine. Another piece came up, dated 14 July 1980, which was accompanied by a black and white photograph of her father as a boy, and the headline: *Vanished: Alice Hilton – Ten Years On.*

Ten years on from that fateful night on New Year's Eve 1969, and despite an extensive police investigation and thousands of man hours searching for little Alice, Vanessa Hilton is still no closer to finding out what happened to her daughter.

'It is hard to say which is worse,' says Vanessa Hilton, 'knowing your child has been kidnapped and killed, or knowing they've disappeared and could be anywhere, undergoing any sort of terror, and never getting answers about what happened. While having that bit of hope that your child is alive somewhere could give you a reason to keep on going, the lack of closure and the constant wondering could very well drive one mad.'

Willow went back to the search engine and noticed an article from the *Lewes Chronicle* dated 8 February 1968, the year before Alice went missing.

A dairy farmer in East Sussex is 'completely devastated' after his herd of dairy cows had to be slaughtered following the detection of bovine TB.

Richard Hilton, from Kingston near Lewes, says they will have to start again after routine tests detected the disease. Nearly half the cows that were killed were pregnant with calves, which made the situation even more difficult.

Mr Hilton said, 'I just can't put into words how it feels to see a cow that you have reared from a calf destroyed. My wife was in tears. I've been there since the day they were born.'

She looked up at a picture of her father on the mantelpiece opposite her. She knew very little about the day that Alice had gone missing, but what she did know was that Bobby and his father had spent the day destroying their herd because of an outbreak of TB. Reading the article, it stood to reason that her grandfather's cows, and Nell, had probably been infected by the Hiltons' herd.

Willow let out a heavy sigh as she began gathering her stuff to take to The Keep. Mike's deception was getting to her so much more because the project was so personal to her. She had spent a year not telling her father about the project, knowing that he would be angry, and yet she'd been burnt anyway. Perhaps this was karma punishing her for deceiving him. She had done nothing wrong in taking the project, but she should have been honest with him. It was time to tell him about the project and get his blessing, so they could both move on.

Willow made up her mind as she walked towards the front door that she would go to The Keep, then head over to her dad's flat. She dialled his number and listened as it went to answerphone. 'Dad, it's me, I need to talk to you about something. I'll be over around six; maybe we can get a takeaway or something.'

As she ended the call, she felt another rush of nausea and got to the bathroom just in time as the small amount of food she had managed to eat that day came back up. Afterwards, she wiped her mouth and walked to the kitchen to get herself some more water. Great, she had a bug, she was utterly spent, but she had to push on, the past couldn't wait any longer. She picked up her keys, slipped on her trainers and opened her front door. She felt overwhelmed with nerves at the prospect of seeing her father but, she told herself, there was a vague chance he wouldn't be angry. That he would be proud of her, and willing to talk about his life at The Vicarage, about Nell, the graveyard and Bella James. If that was the case, a huge weight would be lifted from her shoulders, but the intense butterflies in her tummy told her that her father letting her off the hook was very unlikely.

Chapter Thirteen
Nell

December 1969

'Has she kept any fluids down?' the doctor asked, taking the thermometer out of Nell's mouth. Nell watched as he peered at the reading over his half-moon glasses. He looked very old to her; his beard was nearly white and his hand shook slightly.

'Nothing since yesterday, I don't think,' her father said quietly as Nell looked out of the window at the clouds, searching for her mother's face again.

She couldn't remember a time in her life when she had felt so poorly. Bobby had sat by her bed and held her hand as her father called the doctor. She had started to drift off and then woken and looked out of the window, seeing shapes in the clouds – animals at first, then slowly, very clearly, a face with a nose, a mouth, long flowing hair. As she stared harder and harder, a hand had appeared, a fist and five fingers, one of them beckoning to her.

'Bobby, I can see Mama in the clouds,' she'd said.

She'd drifted off again after that, and woken to see a man standing at the end of her bed with a stethoscope around his neck. He was whispering to her father, who was looking very pale and worried.

Now she looked down at the bed and imagined her mother sitting by her, stroking her hair, holding her hand. She wanted her there so badly. How was it possible to miss someone she had never known so much?

Her father had hidden all the photographs of her mother, but she had found two in his bottom drawer amongst the crumpled clothes. In one of them, her head was tipped slightly to the side, her eyes crinkled, like she had been laughing so hard it made her tummy hurt. Her eyes were sparkling, all-knowing and wise; Nell imagined she said everything with them, without speaking. Her hair was soft waves, long and blonde, and her skin was fair, with freckles on her nose. Just like Nell herself. She had sat on the rug in her father's room and stared at the picture until her legs went numb, then turned her attention to the second photograph, of her mother and father at their wedding, dancing together, their cheeks touching. She had run her fingers over her mother's long wedding dress, imagining how the lace felt and how it moved, how her mother smelt. She didn't like to ask her father about her mother, but she asked Bobby whenever she got the chance. He was seven when she died, so he remembered her quite well, though not as clearly as he used to; like watching scenes in a film that he was scared were starting to fade.

'Dad smiled a lot when she was alive,' he told her. 'I remember him laughing more. The house felt different, warmer, cosier. There were flowers on the table at dinner time, and I remember us sitting by the fire in the rocking chair. She would sing songs as I went to sleep. I remember her saying she hoped you were a girl. I remember her tummy moving, with you inside her.'

'You don't blame me, do you, Bobby?' Nell had asked.

'For what?'

'That Mum died having me.'

'It's not your fault, Nell. Having babies is a dangerous business. Everyone knows that,' he said, trying to sound more grown up than his thirteen years.

Nell didn't know that, and she doubted that Bobby knew it either. It sounded like something their father had said when he was trying to change the subject and didn't want to answer any more questions. She'd once heard Bobby asking what happened to their mother when she died, to which Dad had replied, 'She's gone, son, I know it's hard, we just need to accept it.'

Dr Browne began to speak again, dragging her back to the present. 'She needs to go into hospital, Alfred, she needs to be on a drip. She's very unwell.'

'I'm cold, Dad,' Nell said, her teeth chattering in her head, making a rattling sound like they might all fall out.

'Her blankets are wet, Dad, because she's sweating so much.' Bobby leaned over her, his face creased with worry.

'I don't want to go to hospital,' Nell said. She was trying to be brave, but it was all so frightening, so strange.

'It's okay, Nell, everything will be all right. We'll change your nightie again and get you comfortable,' said her father.

'What's wrong with her?' Bobby asked.

'If she's coughing up blood, it could be TB; we'll need to run some tests,' the doctor replied, putting his hand on Bobby's shoulder. 'If that's the case, the hospital may send her to the Mayfield sanatorium in Portsmouth for treatment.'

'Has she caught it from the herd?' said Bobby, glancing at his father desperately.

Nell watched the small cluster of bodies discussing her, looking at her, as her body shook under her damp covers.

'What's he talking about, Alfred?' Dr Browne asked.

Her father shook his head. 'The cows have been unwell; the vet says it's TB. We've caught it from Hilton's herd.'

'Are you sure about that? Is he going to compensate you?'

Alfie let out a snort. 'No, quite the reverse. He's trying to kick us out. He's sold this place to a developer and is digging up the land around our feet before we are even out, but we aren't leaving. Wilfred Hilton wanted me to have this house.'

'Wilfred Hilton, as in Richard's father?'

'Yes, Richard has always tried to ignore the fact that this is my land as much as his, it's part of me, it's in my blood and one day the Hiltons will have to accept it.'

'What if it doesn't work, what if Mr Hilton makes you leave and I never come back here after the hospital?' said Nell, tears starting to splash onto the pillow.

'We're not going anywhere,' said her father. 'Over my dead body.'

Dr Browne cleared his throat. 'I'll send an ambulance later this evening, or in the morning, once I've spoken to the hospital and worked out what's best. They'll need to X-ray her lungs. Keep a close eye on her until then, and call me immediately if she gets any worse.'

Alfie led the doctor out, then turned to Bobby. 'I need to feed the cows, and that fence in the top field has blown down again. Can you stay with Nell?'

'Of course, but can you manage on your own?'

'It's okay, Bobby. I'll be all right on my own for a little

while. You go,' Nell said, reaching under her pillow to check the key was still there.

'Are you sure?' asked her father.

'Yes, I'm tired, I think I need to have a little sleep.'

'Okay, we'll be back soon.'

As soon as the bedroom door clicked closed, Nell sat up, so quickly it made her dizzy. She paused for a moment to cough, excitement giving her the energy to pull herself out of bed. On wobbly legs she walked over to the window and looked out. Her dad and Bobby were heading towards the cowshed; they would be gone for a little while.

If she was going to the hospital in the morning, she had to see the room. She might not get another chance. She would just look, she wouldn't go in.

Nell felt a surge of strength, the thought of the secret room spurring her on. She had so wanted to discover the secret room with Alice, but there was no time now. She would have to write to her from the hospital.

She walked slowly on wobbly legs along the landing until she reached the top step, where she had seen her father climb out a few nights before. She checked out of the window again, to make sure the light was on in the cowshed, then sat down and ran her finger under the lip of the step, and pulled up. It didn't move. She was sure it couldn't be locked as she still had the key.

Perhaps she was too weak, she tried again, then ran her fingers underneath the step until she found a tiny catch hidden to the left of the keyhole. She pulled it and *click!* The step popped up.

Carefully, her head spinning, she opened the landing step to another world.

She couldn't risk going right into the room in case she fainted, but there were two steps down, and she lowered herself onto the first one. The smell hit her first, musty and thick with damp, like old furniture. She wrinkled her nose, then shone the light in, slowly moving the torch around.

It was a tiny space, barely room for the mattress and small trunk it contained. There was a blanket at the foot of the mattress. The darkness made it difficult to see, but there looked to be a window in the far wall. She immediately pictured the glass bricks at the end of the house, which she had always wondered about, and smiled to herself. There was a book by the bed, one she recognised as her father's, and a half-empty whisky bottle. He obviously came in here when he was upset and needed somewhere to hide.

As she shone the torch around, she spotted some names written on the wall: Clara, Sara, Megan. Who were these girls and what had they been doing in here?

She began to cough again. She needed to get back to bed – what if she fainted, and her father came back in and found her lying in the entrance to his secret hiding place? But the trunk was too much, it was drawing her in. What was in it?

Listening out for the sound of voices, she took a deep breath, then eased herself down to the bottom step. Although the space was small, it wasn't claustrophobic; it felt like a den, like Alice's tree house. She crawled across the mattress until she reached the trunk, then slowly clicked it open, her heart beating fast. As quickly as she could, she lifted the lid and peered in.

It was mostly full of old magazines and newspapers, but as she shone her torch in, something caught her eye in the corner: a leather-bound book. She reached in and pulled it out, opening it to the first page. 'Tessa James, Patient Notes,' she read slowly, running her fingers over the words. The writing was slanted and hard for her to make out, but amongst the text, which looked to her like spiders running across the page, she managed to make out a few words: *birth, baby, stuck*. And one whole line: *There was nothing I could do*.

Nell had little idea what to think. She knew it was all to do with babies – every other word was 'baby' – but she didn't know why there was a whole notebook about them. She flicked on, every page a new entry – March, April, May, it went on in years to 1942, 1943, 1944 – and more words she didn't understand: *crowning*, *baby blues*, *breech*, *baby turned*.

Suddenly she heard the door bang and voices downstairs. They were inside, taking off their boots. She returned the notebook to the trunk and darted back across the room. As she climbed out, Snowy was waiting for her at the mouth of the room. She eased the lid down and pressed down until it clicked shut, then picked up the puppy and tiptoed back across the landing. She could hear her father on the phone downstairs. Her head was spinning again now and she felt quite faint.

'Okay, Doctor, I understand. We'll pack a bag for her now.'

As she climbed into bed, she suddenly started to cough again, the exertion of her adventure finally catching up with her. She clutched the puppy to her as Snowy licked her face and she began to panic at the idea that she wouldn't be here to look after him.

Bobby and her father appeared at the door. 'That was the

doctor, little one,' her father said, picking her up in his arms. 'They've found you a bed in Brighton Hospital for tonight.'

Bobby tucked a blanket round her, and her father carried her downstairs, the steps creaking as they went. As they reached the front door, he stopped dead, and Nell looked up at his face, which had a worried expression.

'Hello, Alice,' he said.

Nell turned her aching head to see her friend standing in the doorway and her eyes filled with tears. Alice looked as beautiful as always, in her smart red coat, with red ribbons in her hair.

'I just came to see how Nell was,' she said quietly.

'She's having to go to hospital, I'm afraid, Alice,' Alfie said.

'Oh, I see. I'm sorry to hear that.' Nell could hear that Alice's voice had gone wobbly.

They all stood in the doorway, not moving, until Snowy began to yap at their feet. Slowly Alice bent down and picked her up. 'Would you like me to look after Snowy, just while you're away? I know my mum won't mind because we were going to get one of Snowy's brothers or sisters, remember?' the little girl said hopefully.

'Would that be okay, Daddy?' said Nell. 'I've been worried about it.' She was feeling very tired again now, and tucked her head into her father's chest.

'If that's what you want, Nell,' said her father. 'You be sure to let us know if it's a problem with your parents, Alice.'

Alice nodded as Nell smiled up at her friend, 'Can I say goodbye to her first?'

Her father nodded and eased Nell down on the chair by the fire, as Alice lifted the puppy onto her lap, searching for its collar. If her father did have a key, and locked the secret room, Alice would need hers to get in there.

Alice stood next to her, and noticing what Nell was doing, blocked the view of Bobby and her father, who were waiting by the door.

'Please take really good care of her, won't you?' Nell said, and Alice watched, eyes wide, as Nell pushed the key onto Snowy's collar and fastened it back on.

'Of course I will. I won't let her out of my sight, I promise.'

'I'll write to you as soon as I can and let you know how I am.' Nell winked at her friend.

'Come on, young Nell,' said her father, as Nell handed the puppy to Alice.

Being carried towards the ambulance parked in the lane by their house felt strange. The blue lights were on, but the sirens weren't, and they turned the ground and all the hedges blue too. It was weird to be outside. Nell's skin felt like paper, and she started shaking so violently it was making her feel sick again. As they laid her down in the ambulance, her father climbed in and held her hand. 'You okay, Nell?'

'Where's Bobby? I want Bobby to come,' Nell said, starting to cry.

'Bobby needs to stay here to look after the cows. He can come and see you in hospital soon,' said her father as they started to close the doors.

'Bobby, I want Bobby with me!' Nell felt panic rising at the thought of being apart from her brother. 'Bobby!'

Bobby stepped up into the ambulance and kissed her forehead. 'Be brave, Nell, you'll be home soon,' he whispered as the engine started up.

'See that Alice gets home safely, Bobby,' Alfie said, 'and make sure Mrs Hilton is all right to have the puppy for a few days.'

As they closed the ambulance doors, Nell could see Alice standing next to Bobby, tears rolling down her face as she clutched Snowy, the ornate key swinging from the little dog's collar.

Chapter Fourteen

Bella

January 1946

Bella pulled at the skin around her fingernails and looked down at the emerald engagement ring on her left hand. She never usually wore it, especially not when she was hoeing the field behind The Vicarage, which she had done a great deal in order to survive for the past year. She had been unable to work as leaving Alfie at The Vicarage was an impossibility, so they had worked together growing vegetables: potatoes, runner beans, cabbages, onions and strawberries, just as her mother had done when she was a child, and set up a small stall at the end of the lane, giving them just enough income to buy firewood, milk and bread.

The trial had not been easy to watch, she had sat in the courtroom every day with Alfie, listening to the lies they had told about her mother. Despite writing to her every week, begging her to reconsider, her mother refused to take the stand and defend herself. Added to which, her mother's barrister had declined to meet with her, refusing to let her be a character witness in her mother's trial. Bella had not been around at the time of Evelyn Hilton's death, Mr Lyons had said in a letter to her, or for nearly a year prior to that, and he felt that she would be too emotional, possibly say things that would harm her mother's defence and which would end up going against her.

But the trial was not going her mother's way, all the expert witnesses were siding with Dr Jenkins' version of events and no one had spoken in her mother's defence. She had decided to try her mother's barrister one last time, sitting and waiting for the past week in the police station.

Which was where she sat now, her hands shaking as Alfie sat on the chair next to her, swinging his legs frantically. She reached out and laid her hand on his knee to stop him, and smiled gently.

'Are you all right?' she said

He nodded, and looked up at the police sergeant sitting behind the counter at Lewes police station, who had been ignoring them for the best part of two hours.

'I wish we didn't have to come here,' he whispered. 'What if they take me away?'

Bella squeezed his hand. The last policeman Alfie had seen had taken his grandmother away and had then sat in The Vicarage for most of the night like a beagle waiting for a fox to come out of its den.

'They won't take you away, Alfie. I'm your mother, nobody can take you away from me.'

She crossed and uncrossed her legs, trying to stop her foot from tapping on the parquet floor, and glanced at the clock on the wall for the fifth time in as many minutes. It was coming up to midday, and she knew the summing-up was due to start soon. The policeman looked up and glared at her irritably over his wire-rimmed spectacles, as he had done a dozen times since she arrived.

'Is Chief Constable Payne going to be much longer? I've been trying to see him for a week now. It's the final day of my mother's trial, and I desperately need to speak to her barrister.'

'I'm afraid the chief constable is over at the courthouse, and he could be there for some time. I have telephoned and notified him that you are here. You could possibly try him there, or I can make an appointment for you to come back another day,' the sergeant added hopefully.

I can't come back another day, it will be too late then! she wanted to scream, but knowing it would get her nowhere, she smiled weakly and said, 'I've tried the courthouse, but they said he was here. That's fine, if you're expecting him back, we'll wait.'

She looked around the waiting room, which had two uncomfortable wooden benches and large Georgian windows overlooking the cobbled stones of the high street, then back at the smartly dressed policeman, who was doing his best to ignore her. She glanced at the clock again, the second hand moving too fast; the window of opportunity to help her mother closing fast.

'Miss James?' A tall, grey-haired man in a navy suit had appeared suddenly, holding out his hand to shake hers. 'I'm dreadfully sorry to have kept you waiting. My name is Jeremy Lyons, I'm representing your mother. Would you like to come with me?' He turned and walked away as fast as he had appeared, his boot heels cracking like a whip as he strode across the wooden floor.

Bella stood as quickly as she could manage and took Alfie's hand, following the lawyer down the corridor.

'Miss James, please take a seat. It's a pleasure to meet you, and who is this young man?'

'This is my son, Alfred,' Bella said, as Mr Lyons pulled up another chair for him.

'Well, it's very nice to meet you both, albeit under such sad circumstances.' He smiled warmly, oozing charm. 'Can I get you a drink? Tea, perhaps? I can't believe it's lunch-time already; where has the day gone? It'll be getting dark soon.' He sprang up again, charging over to the small window and closing the blind before turning on the light and returning to his seat.

'No, thank you,' Bella said quietly.

'Obviously my presence will be needed in court before long, as the summing-up is due to start in less than an hour. But when your mother heard that you were here, she wanted me to grant you an audience.' He spoke as fast as he moved, gesticulating constantly, which was meant to give the impression that he was a very busy man who could not be detained for long.

'I want to speak in her defence before they sentence her,' said Bella.

Mr Lyons stared at her for a moment, then shook his head, smiling. 'I'm afraid that won't be possible. We have heard from all the witnesses now; it is done.'

'But surely *I* should have been called as a witness?' Bella spoke slowly.

'A witness for what exactly? You weren't there, Miss James.' He cleared his throat and sat back in his chair.

'No, but this is a crime against my mother. Many people in our community have taken very strongly against her; this is a storm that has been building up for some time.

There is a great deal more to it than what is being reported in the papers, and in court.'

'Miss James, I have to tell you there is little doubt that it was your mother's action in cutting Mrs Hilton that ultimately led to her death.'

'Why?' said Bella. 'Why is there little doubt she cut Mrs Hilton? She doesn't own any medical instruments; she believes in waiting for nature to do its job. She would never have cut her so that she bled to death.'

Mr Lyons snorted. 'Why would two people entirely independently say that she did?'

'With all due respect, sir, of course they are going to say that. Sally, the Hilton's house servant, will lose her job if she doesn't, and she has a little girl to think of. And Dr Jenkins would be struck off. I must be allowed to speak on behalf of my mother, to tell the jury of the doctor's behaviour towards her.'

'What behaviour do you speak of, Miss James?'

The room was hot and stuffy, Bella felt as though she might faint, and gripped Alfie's hand for strength.

'Dr Jenkins has a vendetta against my mother. He wants her out of the way because women prefer her to deliver their babies. Because they are frightened of him, because he cuts them and uses his instruments on them.'

The lawyer's face fell. 'I'm sorry, but it's far too late. And to be brutally honest with you, Miss James, I'm not sure I believe you myself. Dr Jenkins is a man of impeccable character with an untarnished reputation, and trying to do damage to him on the stand could work against your mother rather than help her.'

'Untarnished reputation? He moved to the area just two

years ago, with little or no actual experience of birthing babies. In his care, many women have died birthing babies who should have survived.'

'Which women? This is the first I've heard of it.'

'Because you have not listened, sir. If you had spoken with me, I would have told you their husbands' names, so that you could have spoken with them and asked them to testify.

'My mother has been delivering babies in Kingston for nearly thirty years. Why are you not speaking to the countless women whose lives she has saved? Why would she cut Mrs Hilton so that she bled to death? When she had never cut a woman in her life before? It makes no sense.'

'Because on the afternoon in question, Wilfred Hilton served her notice on The Vicarage. They fought, bitterly, and she told him she was putting a curse on his wife's birth.'

Bella sat back as his words sank in. Tears stung her eyes, which she angrily wiped away as Alfie clung to her hand even more tightly.

'That isn't true. She would never say that. Wilfred Hilton often speaks of my mother in such a way. His great-grandfather drowned a dozen witches in his lake, many of whom were said to be midwives, and he has convinced himself that my mother is descended from one of them and is seeking revenge. Despite the fact that she saved the lives of his two older children, one of whom is Alfie's father. It is Wilfred Hilton's paranoia; it has no merit or truth whatsoever.'

'Miss James, I must get back to court,' the barrister said, standing up as if to end their conversation.

'Please, sir, I don't want to fall out with you or speak out of turn. But I have to do something.' Bella felt her voice shake and tried to stay composed. 'It's not over yet. I cannot just sit here and wait for the verdict without doing something.'

'We still have a chance for clemency. You can write to the Home Office.' He straightened his jacket.

'So you think she will be found guilty?' Bella started to cry then, and Alfie stood up and wrapped his arms around her.

'Miss James, it's too late to do anything about it.'

'But I have tried time and time again to reach you, you know I have! You wrote to me yourself, months ago, to decline my request to be a witness. It isn't over yet. There has been no verdict. I don't understand why you aren't trying to save her life. Does it not count, all the lives *she* has saved in the past? All the mothers and babies she has helped? Why have none of them spoken in her defence?'

'Because she did not want me to pursue that avenue,' he said.

Bella sat back in her chair and stared at him in disbelief. 'Why?' she said quietly.

'She wouldn't tell me, Miss James. She also has to take the stand herself to plead her case, or to provide any witnesses for us to cross examine. That, along with the evidence stacked against her, has made my job of defending her almost impossible.'

'But why would she not try and save herself?'

'I have no idea. Perhaps you can ask her yourself, when she finally grants you an audience.'

'Well, have you asked her? Tried to persuade her to rethink? Or are you being paid by someone for whom my mother's incarceration is rather convenient? Like Wilfred Hilton.'

'I beg your pardon?'

'My mother can't afford a barrister, or a solicitor for that matter.'

'I am giving my time voluntarily.'

'I don't believe you.'

'Miss James, I think you need to be careful.' He glared at her now, his eyes flashing with anger.

'Why? The worst that could have happened has happened. I'm afraid of nothing now.' She spat out the words.

'Not even of losing your son?' he said slowly.

Bella glared at him. 'Are you threatening me?'

'No, I'm just pointing out that you are hysterical, and I have absolutely no intention of putting you on the stand. You could end up in contempt of court, and then what would happen to Alfie?' He looked at the boy. 'You are all he has in the world.'

'I want you to speak to the judge; to request that I act as a character witness for her before the verdict is given.' Bella didn't move from her seat.

Mr Lyons looked at his watch. 'I'm sorry, Miss James, I have to get back to court. I have a meeting with the judge in ten minutes that I need to prepare for.'

'What if I were to go to the newspapers? If you aren't interested in my story, perhaps they might be,' she said quietly. The interview room was so airless, she could feel the pain and misery of all the people who had sat in there before her, and she had to take deep breaths to stop it from spinning as Mr Lyons glared back at her from the doorway.

'I wouldn't advise you to do that, Miss James,' he said coldly.

'I'm sure you wouldn't. But I have my mother's notebook here, detailing all the things Wilfred Hilton has said to her and threatened her with. Not to mention Dr Jenkins himself, and Father Blacker, our parish priest, who thinks it's God's will that women suffer in childbirth.'

'They wouldn't print it. Mr Hilton is a man of influence.'

'Perhaps, but a lot of it would be easy to prove. There are a great many women who would testify in my mother's defence. Not that you have bothered to speak with any of them. I think it may make for interesting reading that you gave up so easily.'

Lyons stepped away from the door. 'I don't appreciate your threats, Miss James, and I think you will find that a woman of your class has little influence. Your mother asked me to give you this.' He threw a small envelope on the table in front of her. The sight of her mother's familiar slanting handwriting made Bella's legs go weak.

'Now if you'll excuse me, I must get back to court for the summing-up. I presume you will be attending, though it may be better not to bring the boy. I'm hoping the jury will be a long time in their deliberations; a swift verdict is never a good sign. Good day, Miss James. I will be in touch about a time for you to visit your mother when it is convenient for all parties.'

As she and Alfie slowly made their way into the cold January sunshine, outside the courthouse, crowds were already gathering. Her legs shaking, she sank onto a nearby bench outside a small tea room.

A young man in black robes came out of the court and crossed the road and walked towards the cafe.

'I'm so sorry to trouble you, but could I ask you a question?' she said as he approached.

'Of course,' he replied, frowning slightly.

'How do I find which barristers offer themselves for volunteer work?'

'There are schemes run by volunteer solicitors and barristers to advise the poor for free. You can speak to the administration office at the court where the trial is due to take place, and they can issue you with a list of names.'

'Thank you,' said Bella. As the young man went on his way, she turned and looked up at the courthouse before plunging her hand into her pocket and retrieving her mother's letter.

'I'm hungry, Mama,' said Alfie.

She reached into her bag and took out a chunk of bread and an apple and handed them to her son. Then she slipped the letter into the bag. It could wait until later. It would be unfair to read it in front of Alfie when she knew it would break her heart.

As she looked up at the vast Georgian building in front of her, the world a blur through her tears, she heard someone shout her mother's name. Men, women and children were starting to arrive, jostling to push their way inside, desperate to grab front-row seats for the final act of the drama.

It was time for the summing-up. Bella stood on shaky legs and took Alfie's hand; then, holding on to him for dear life, she started to make her way towards the courthouse.

Chapter Fifteen

Alfie

New Year's Eve 1969

Alfie James held his gun to the temple of Lola, his favourite cow. She sniffed it nervously, then pulled her head violently away from the rope tying her to the gate as the calf growing inside her kicked hard in her stomach. Alfie turned away, holding his breath, the biting cold stinging his eyes, his ears and the finger that curled around the metal trigger, which he slowly started to pull. Lola turned her head to look at him, her breath escaping in terrified puffs.

He had been there the day she was born. She had a beautiful nature, and had already produced several calves, which she always tried to hide from him in the long grass in a vain attempt to stop him taking them away. He pictured her walking up to him in the mornings as the sun came up, her udders heavy, needing to be milked. He would open the gate and round the animals up, several of the others pushing and fussing about him, but not Lola, never Lola. And now here she stood, tied to a gate, surrounded by the carcasses of the herd they had been forced to slaughter all day. Eyes wide with fear, she had watched the other cows being killed around her; she knew what had happened and what was coming. Her nostrils flared at the smell of cordite from his shotgun and the blood of her friends.

Alfie looked over at his thirteen-year-old son, a trail of tears pouring down Bobby's dirt-covered cheeks, which he wiped away with his sleeve as his father forced his paralysed finger to pull the trigger. He closed his eyes momentarily as the deafening boom echoed across the snowy fields surrounding them and Lola crashed to the icy ground, blood exploding from her temple like a firework. It was done; they were all dead, the herd he had spent twenty years nurturing.

The calf inside its dead mother began to kick frantically, fighting for life, and unable to watch, Alfie turned away towards the heaps of carcasses that Bobby had moved to the end of the field, ready to be burned, their dead limbs gathering snow as they stuck out like frozen branches. He could suddenly taste metal, and realised that his tears had mopped up the spatters of blood on his face, which were now trickling into his mouth. He ran to the well, frantically wiping away the blood with the icy water.

As Bobby continued to move the carcasses, Alfie sat down on a pile of firewood and tried to gather himself. He looked up at The Vicarage, the moonlight reflecting off the small window that always seemed to him like an eye on the world. Nobody had ever noticed the square glass brick, which his grandmother had slotted into the wall when she'd first discovered and renovated the little room beneath the stairs.

He had always kept the room a secret; not even Nell and Bobby knew about it. It was something he didn't want to share with anyone; a place he went to when he felt low and needed to remember his grandmother. His cocoon from the world. It had kept him safe for seven days and nights when she was arrested when he was six years old, and he felt great affection for it, as if it were a person who had protected him.

He still had memories of the women who had come to the house – sometimes in the dead of night so that they wouldn't be seen – staying in the secret room to hide and recuperate. Over the years, women who couldn't afford to pay to have their babies delivered had come back time and time again to Tessa James, who would never turn away a woman in need. Mostly they were poor and their husbands violent. They would arrive in the early stages of labour, often with a young child or two in tow. Tessa would always take them in, sit them by the fire and give them soup for strength to push their babies out. Then, after their babies were born by the fire, she would hide the woman and her newborn away, in the secret room, for a day or two so they could rest. She would feed the other children and play with them, darn their clothes and wash their faces. Alfie remembered their husbands coming to claim the wives, hammering on the door of The Vicarage, demanding Tessa hand them over. But they never found them and Tessa's hiding place stayed a secret; the women kept her secret, and she kept theirs.

The local priest, Father Blacker, would come knocking too, demanding that Tessa return the men's wives and chastising her for dragging the area down. The midwives' methods, their knowledge of herbs and their ability to find ways to alleviate pain during pregnancy and childbirth were reviled by Father Blacker, who would try and shame the women Tessa tried to help before his grandmother gave him the rough edge of her tongue and sent him on his way.

Before the women left, she would encourage them to leave their husbands when they beat them or took them by force when they weren't yet recovered from childbirth. But they never did; they had no money and there was nowhere for them to go. Sometimes, though, a night or two in Tessa's secret room was enough to give them the strength to carry on.

'No one does more harm to the Church than midwives,' Father Blacker would say to her as he accosted her walking into town past the church that backed onto her home. She would always smile and wish him a good day, never wanting to give him ammunition. But she knew that too many people hated her, that her life was made up of sand racing through an hourglass.

That one day they would find a way to take her away in handcuffs, lock her up and throw away the key.

That day was one that Alfie still remembered, when his grandmother had left him alone in the secret room. Over the following six days and nights, he had felt as terrified then as he did now of being taken away from The Vicarage; from everything he knew and loved, from his mother and grandmother.

He hung his head at the memory of the letter that had arrived that morning from his solicitor, the final nail in the coffin. He had fought as hard as he knew how, but Wilfred Hilton had left it too late. In the words of the solicitor: *I suspect that despite writing to you to notify you about his will, Mr Hilton was too frail to read the will properly at the time of signing and failed to spot that it did not accord with his wishes.*

Still, he was not ready to give up. This house and its land

was rightfully his. His father and grandfather had wanted him to have it, and he could not let his mother down. To allow The Vicarage to be demolished was tantamount to erasing her memory and admitting he was a bastard, rather than the beloved child of Eli Hilton.

'*I am Eli Hilton's son,* say it.' Those had been his mother's last words to him as they tore him away from her at the workhouse in Portsmouth where they had ended up when his mother couldn't get work. 'You must go back to The Vicarage and claim what is yours. Promise me.'

It was the only place he could sense his mother's presence, and the only place that had ever felt like home. The day he had left the children's home when he turned fourteen in the summer of 1953, he had hitched a ride to Lewes, then made the rest of the journey to Kingston by foot and asked the way to The Vicarage. It had been just as he remembered it. Just as it was now. He could picture the pretty white house on a sunny winter's day, his mother trimming the jasmine around the freshly painted black oak door, sweeping the dust from the tiled kitchen floor, humming to herself as she dug the flower bed and planted the pansies and daffodils that hugged the outside of the cottage. He had never told the Hiltons who he was – they hadn't laid eyes on him since he was six years old. He had just asked for work, and then, later, if he could rent The Vicarage from them. It was only over time that Wilfred Hilton had worked out who he was.

'Bobby! Bobby!'

Alfie looked over his shoulder to see Leo Hilton, Richard's son, running towards them, pushing his bike across the snow. He was tall and blonde like his father, with the same air of entitlement, which meant he carried himself with his head tipped back, looking down on everyone he met.

Bobby jumped down from the tractor and hurried towards him. 'What is it?' he asked.

Leo stopped in his tracks, looking at the dead cow at his feet, the snow dyed dark red around her temple. 'Dad needs you,' he said quietly, glancing away from the bloody mess. 'He's having some trouble with the lights for the party and wants you to take over.'

Bobby looked at his father.

'I can't spare him at the moment,' Alfie said.

'Dad won't be happy about that,' Leo snapped.

'It's okay, Dad, I won't be long. I could do with a break anyway.'

'I need you here.' Alfie felt his body start to shake with anger.

'Bobby works for us now, so I don't think it's up to you.' Leo grinned.

Bobby looked at him and shook his head. 'Thanks, Leo. I haven't said yes yet, Dad. Richard offered me a job at Yew Tree Farm. I thought it would help us out.'

Alfie turned his back on him, kneeling down in the snow to tie Lola's legs together with rope. 'Get the tractor. I can't manage this on my own.'

Bobby's eyes flashed. 'Maybe I've earned this; maybe Richard respects me.'

Leo looked down and kicked some dirty snow over Lola's face. The grey sludge slid down her bloodied cheek.

Slowly Alfie turned. 'Is that why he let you take the blame for the fire Leo started in their barn?'

Leo stepped back and frowned, then turned and walked away. 'I have to get back.'

'What did you say, Dad?' Bobby walked up to him.

'I said Leo started that fire. And I'm pretty sure he drowned those puppies too. But Richard Hilton, who you have grown so fond of, has seen to it that his son gets off the hook and that the police think you are responsible. And yet you still believe he respects you. He doesn't, Bobby, he's a Hilton, he'll throw you to the wolves if it helped him or his family.'

Bobby shook his head. 'You've got him wrong, Dad. He wants to help us. He's suggested that Nell stay at Yew Tree Manor when she gets out of hospital, while we get settled in our new home.'

'Over my dead body.' Alfie glared at his son. 'Can we just get this done?'

'Why? So you can yell at me and criticise me? You never thank me, you never tell me I've done a good job. You treat me like a slave.'

'Don't take that tone with me. Get on that tractor and help me, you ungrateful bastard.'

Bobby stared at him and shook his head, then turned and walked after Leo.

'Bobby, the Hiltons aren't your friends!' Alfie shouted after him.

'You're wrong, Dad,' Bobby said proudly.

'If you go now, don't bother coming back,' he called out, immediately regretting his words.

Alfie continued to tie Lola's legs, listening to Bobby's footsteps crackle in the snow as he walked away. He stopped and waited for them to return. But as the minutes passed, the silence grew deafening. He looked up into the distance; his son was gone.

He buried his head in shame at the tears he couldn't stop, and walked with heavy legs towards the tractor. It wasn't going to be easy to shift Lola on his own. The pile of carcasses was almost completely covered in snow now, and in the short time since Bobby had turned off the engine, the tractor's tyres were thick with ice.

He stepped onto the metal platform and looked across into the distance. Bobby and Leo had nearly disappeared into the white-out. He turned the ignition and the engine coughed slowly into life. The shuddering motion of the tractor shook him violently, and he started to cry great racking sobs. Richard Hilton had taken his herd, his livelihood, his home and now his son. He pushed the lever into gear and then pressed down on the accelerator, the cabin rocking violently as he moved towards Lola's still body.

As he reached her, he lowered the jaws of the digger and attempted to get them underneath her. He tried repeatedly, but each time her frozen hooves clattered against the steel mouth and the digger skidded and struggled in the ice. He pressed down harder on the accelerator, knowing he should leave it, but if he didn't move her onto the pile with the others before morning, she would be frozen solid and they would probably have to resort to drilling her out of the ice.

He put the brake on and jumped down, leaving the engine running to try and warm the ground beneath her. Tears still running into his mouth, he wiped his streaming nose with the back of his gloved hand and tried to focus on moving Lola closer to the digger. He bent down, pretending she was still alive and just sleeping, and leaned into her for a moment, feeling the warmth leaving her.

He should never have come back here; he should have found work in Portsmouth, ignored his promise to his mother and moved on with his life. Nothing good had come of it; everything he had gone through in the workhouse, his mother's death, was in vain. Richard would never give him what was rightfully his, and he didn't have the strength to fight for it. He should have let his ghosts lie and tried to find happiness elsewhere. All he had done by coming back here was make his daughter sick and lose Bobby to the Hiltons.

Counting to three, he let out a cry and pushed with everything he had, trying to move Lola with his shoulder, but she was a dead weight and there was nothing he could do to get her nearer to the tractor. He stood up and walked over to the barn to fetch a shovel. If he could dig a hole next to her, maybe he could get the digger's mouth underneath her.

He raised the shovel and brought it down on the ice, but he was exhausted and the ground was like cement. His body shook violently; from the cold and the shock of shooting all his cattle. His arms ached, and every time he brought the shovel down, a shooting pain ran up into his shoulder.

He climbed back up onto the tractor, pushing so hard on the accelerator that the wheels spun and burned with the friction. Slowly the digger lifted Lola until she was in place. But then her head and leg slipped, and before long she was sliding off again. In a panic, Alfie rushed to put the brake on and jumped down, bending beneath her head and shoulders to try and ease her back on.

Buckling under the strain of her dead weight, as if he were fighting to keep his whole world from crumbling, he cried out. He could picture the party in full swing at Yew Tree: the music, the drinking, the shouting, the laughter. Bobby being patted on the back by Richard, persuaded to have his first beer, to stay for a while. 'Your dad will be okay. He'll come round. You've both had a difficult day.' He heaved at the carcass so hard his head began to throb and silently he begged for someone, anyone, to help him.

He didn't know how long he'd stood there trying to take Lola's weight before he realised that the tractor had started rolling towards him. It was a strange noise at first, a sliding, rushing sound that he thought was snow falling from the branches next to him. He was moving too, being pushed slowly at first, then faster. He tried to get out of the way, but seven tons of tractor was gaining momentum, pressing down on him, tipping over sideways towards the ditch lining the field. He tried to jump out of the way, but he was trapped between Lola and the teeth of the digger, with the ground too slippery for him to grip onto anything in his path. His foot tangled beneath him, twisting and catching so that his knee screamed with pain and he felt his thigh bone snap. He cried out in agony, begging for someone to help him, the excruciating pain soaring up his broken leg and through his whole body, but the rushing noise grew louder and louder and the wheels screeched as they gathered momentum.

Panic flooded through him as the pressure became unbearable and he felt his ribcage buckle. He was completely powerless to stop it as the digger began to tip over on top of him, Lola's weight stopping him from being able to force himself out from underneath it. Slowly he realised that he was completely trapped now between the metal teeth and the ground, with no way of getting out. He turned his head, desperately looking around for help, and saw Leo Hilton walking towards The Vicarage.

'Leo!' he shouted. 'Leo, get Bobby, help me!' The screaming pain all over his body was draining his strength – he could barely breathe – but if Leo ran to the road he might be able to flag down a car. Alfie's mind raced, trying to stay focused and not lose consciousness; two men could probably pull him out. If Leo acted quickly, the boy could still save him.

But as he got nearer, Leo stopped and stood motionless, a strange look on his face. The same look he'd had when Bobby had found the drowned puppies in the sack.

'Help me, Leo!' Alfie's lungs were screaming for air. The tractor was pushing him deeper into the ice-filled ditch, metal crunching, the engine revving harder and harder. He was upside down now, his mouth filled with black muddy ice, a ton of metal pressing down on him.

Suddenly he turned his head, and through a gap in the digger's teeth he could see a little girl in a red dress, running towards him. The icy ground crunched under her feet as she bent down and reached her arm in, trying to help him.

'Alice, let go! Come out of there!' Leo shouted as she strained her tiny body to help.

The tractor engine burned with the effort, belching out a plume of black smoke. As he lay in the snow-filled ditch, sucking in tiny gasps of air, he felt the little girl tugging at his arm.

'Help me, Leo, help me. He's trapped.' He could hear

her groaning with exertion, and when he looked up, he saw that her face was red with panic, tears streaming down her cheeks, fear in her eyes. He tried to move, but he couldn't. He was pinned down, his chest cavity crushed, his heart swelling under the pressure.

He was being buried alive.

'Help him!' the little girl screamed.

'Alice!' shouted Leo. 'Take my hand!'

The voices became muffled as the tractor groaned its final breath and his vision began to blur. He fixed his eyes on her red patent, sludge-covered shoes, which were level with his eye line. He pictured her trying to lift the tractor on her own, like a superhero in a cartoon.

Just as the tractor came crashing down on top of them, the burning, twisting metal letting out a deep, screeching wail, like an animal in agony, Leo heaved the little girl away and the world went black.

Chapter Sixteen
Vanessa

Thursday, 21 December 2017

'I'm very sorry, Mrs Hilton,' said Detective Inspector Hatton, 'but we haven't found Alice. We are looking for your granddaughter Sienna, who was out playing in the snow this afternoon.'

Vanessa looked at him and then at the clock; she watched the second hand whizzing round, time going so fast she couldn't stop it or turn it back. She felt like she was on a train, and it was pulling away, too fast for her to get off, leaving Alice and Sienna side by side on the platform, watching her go.

'Can you tell us again exactly what happened after you last spoke to Sienna?'

Vanessa looked up at Leo, who was sitting at the kitchen table. Suddenly his phone sprang into life, making them both jump. It vibrated on the wooden table, making a horrible drilling sound, and he grabbed it and answered it, walking out of the room. Detective Inspector Hatton watched him go, frowning at his back as he walked away.

The policeman's eyes were a dull grey, and his shirt looked to Vanessa as if it hadn't been ironed very well. She glanced down at his shoes; they were tatty-looking, not polished, and his coat, which he'd kept on, was too big for him. He looked young, single; she could imagine him in a flat on his own, eating meals for one late at night, working long hours to get ahead. Why had they sent someone so young and inexperienced? The thought added to her feeling of panic.

'I just went to get my gloves, I wasn't gone long,' she said quietly.

'So you were in your bedroom the entire time Sienna was outside?'

She nodded as the detective made a note in his pad.

Vanessa turned to see a female police officer in uniform standing at the kitchen door, looking at her quizzically. As Vanessa stared back, the woman looked away, her cheeks flushing slightly. Vanessa hated all these people in the house, it was just like the night Alice vanished. Maybe she was having a nightmare, maybe it wasn't happening and any moment she would wake up and hear Sienna's voice downstairs.

Leo walked back into the kitchen, running his hands through his floppy fringe as he always did when he was irritable. He threw his mobile on the table. 'Bloody thing, never stops.'

The detective gave Leo a lingering look which spoke volumes. Vanessa could tell he didn't like her son; he was looking at Leo the same way Detective Inspector Mills had looked at Richard the night Alice went missing. 'We would like to do a press conference, Mr Hilton, with you and your wife. The first twenty-four hours are crucial when a child goes missing.'

Leo sprang to his feet as the intercom for the main gate buzzed as it had done repeatedly over the past hour since the press had arrived. He walked across the kitchen and pressed the button as the video camera came to life. 'Yes, hello?' he said desperately.

'Mr Hilton, my name is Hannah Carter, I'm from the *Daily Mail*. We would like to offer our sympathies at this difficult time, and were wondering if there had been any updates on your daughter. Or any comments to make?'

'No comment. And please don't press the intercom; we need to keep it free for the police. Christ, how do they get here so fast?'

'We need the press, they are a necessary evil, I'm afraid. It's the lead story on the evening news.' Detective Hatton watched Leo as he paced the kitchen. 'And we've put out a public appeal, voicing our increasing concern for her safety.'

Leo walked over to the television and switched it on. A picture of a smiling Sienna appeared on the screen. It was a photograph of her on a picnic in the garden – taken by Helen the summer before – that captured a moment in time. No one could have imagined its significance, that it would one day be the image plastered over newspapers and television screens across the country.

'A missing child would be unimaginable for any family,' said the reporter from the gates at the end of their driveway, 'but for Leo Hilton and his family, it is one they are re-living. On New Year's Eve 1969, six-year-old Alice Hilton went missing from here, Yew Tree Manor, the family home, where Sienna was last seen yesterday, just before she vanished. Alice has never been found and her disappearance remains a mystery to this day. Anyone who sees Sienna should notify the police immediately. She is described as having blonde hair and green eyes and is just over four feet tall. She was wearing a red puffa jacket and a black hat and gloves.'

'Mrs Hilton,' said the detective, turning his attention back to Vanessa, his pen poised. 'If we can just go back to the last time you saw Sienna. It was from your bedroom window, at the front of the house, is that correct?'

Vanessa looked at the man, she could smell onions on his breath. Her whole body felt like an exposed nerve, like her skin was slowly being peeled off her body.

'Mrs Hilton, do you think it would be possible to go up to your bedroom window, so you can point out to me the exact place in the garden where you saw Sienna?'

Vanessa looked away from the detective inspector at her reflection in the kitchen window as the snow came down outside. An old woman was staring back at her. In her dreams, she was always the age she was the night of the party. She could still run and dance and swim. She looked down at her hands; they were an old lady's hands, but inside she still felt thirty years old.

'Mrs Hilton? Can you hear me?'

'Please, can you leave my mother be?' Leo said. 'She has trouble with her memory and she doesn't remember anything. Can we focus on the search? A lot of friends and villagers are asking if they can help, but there doesn't seem to be anything being coordinated at the moment.'

'It's impossible to search in the dark, Mr Hilton. We will of course start again at first light, and we will be putting up a tent for volunteers to sign in. We have also scheduled a press conference for eight tomorrow morning, so you and your wife will need to prepare a statement.'

'Well, I'm not sitting and writing a statement while Sienna

is out in this. I'm going out again now to look for her.' Leo looked up at the kitchen clock. 'It's only six. I can't just sit here doing nothing until morning.'

'The family liaison officer is here now, so she can look after your mother,' the DI said.

Vanessa looked up to see Helen walking in. She was white and shaking violently. The female officer pulled a chair up to the Aga and eased her down onto it. 'I'll make you a cup of tea,' she said, before looking over at Leo. 'Do you have any blankets?'

'I think they've all been packed, but I'll have a look upstairs.' Helen curled into herself, as if wanting to disappear; she didn't acknowledge anyone, or even look up.

'I noticed all the packing boxes, when are you moving house?' said the detective to Leo as he walked away. Leo stopped in his tracks, then turned back slowly.

'We were meant to be going to France tomorrow, but obviously that won't be happening now.'

'Has the sale gone through? I mean are there buyers waiting to move in?'

'No, the house is being demolished. We're in the process of selling the land for development.'

'I see, what sort of development?'

'Ten houses and a community centre.' Leo shook his head. 'How is this relevant?'

DI Hatton nodded, scratching away at his pad. 'It might not be, but perhaps Sienna was upset about all the change and moving away. Was there anyone she was sad about leaving in particular, do you know?'

Leo closed his eyes. 'She mentioned Dorothy and Peter, but we checked there already.'

'Who are Dorothy and Peter?' asked Detective Hatton.

Leo flashed a look at Vanessa and let out a sigh. 'They are my wife's parents – she's adopted. They live at Yew Tree Cottage, at the end of our drive, but we don't see much of them. As I say, we've checked there.'

Detective Inspector Hatton looked at the family liaison officer. 'Ask one of the lads to go down to Yew Tree Cottage and double check Sienna isn't there. So you have planning permission? It's all gone through?' Detective Hatton asked, turning back to Leo.

'No, the planning meeting is tomorrow. Shall I get the blanket for Helen or not?' Leo snapped, to which the detective eventually nodded. As Leo walked out, his phone started to ring again.

Vanessa's attention returned to the television in a desperate bid to stop her brain whirring. 'Some people will no doubt be asking,' the reporter continued, 'whether there are any connections between the two girls' disappearance, despite almost fifty years passing. We contacted Sussex Police this evening to ask whether witnesses who were questioned on the night Alice Hilton disappeared on New Year's Eve 1969, from the exact spot where Sienna vanished, will be re-interviewed.'

Vanessa stood and walked over to the screen as a picture of Bobby James appeared. 'Witnesses such as local farmer Bobby James who, aged thirteen, was the last person to see Alice alive. Bobby James was never charged with any crime relating to Alice's disappearance, but, as the last person to see Alice before she vanished, remains a name synonymous with hers.'

'I'll see you later, Mum,' said Leo, returning with a blanket and wrapping it round his wife's shoulders. 'I'm going back out. The policewoman will look after you.'

'He was here, in the house,' Vanessa said quietly, pointing to the television as Leo walked past on his way out.

'What was that, Mrs Hilton?' said the detective inspector.

'That man on the television, he was in the house earlier today.' Vanessa looked up at her son.

Leo frowned at the television. 'What? When?'

'When you were out, I told you, there was a man in your study, going through your things. He wasn't one of the removal men, he didn't have the uniform on.' Vanessa felt her heart rate quicken at the memory which had made her so uneasy.

'Who was on the television just now?' Leo barked at the policewoman.

'They were talking about your sister Alice going missing. Witnesses who were there that night.'

Leo's eyes were wide. 'Bobby?' he whispered. 'Were they talking about Bobby James?' Leo picked up his phone and started tapping frantically at the keys, then he walked over to Vanessa and showed her a picture. 'Was this the man who was in the house, Mum?' he asked.

Vanessa reached out to touch the screen. 'Yes, that's the man I saw. When I went upstairs, he was in your study.'

'When Sienna was outside?' said DI Hatton, looking at Leo and then at his colleague.

'Yes, I think so. Just before she went missing.' Vanessa's voice was shaking.

'Helen?' said Leo. 'Helen? Did you hear what Mum just

said?' Helen didn't react; just pulled the blanket tighter around her, like she was cocooning herself from the explosion that was about to take place. 'Helen?' Leo shouted.

'All right, sir, calm down, please.'

'I won't calm down. You need to find this man now! He was the last person to see my sister before she disappeared, and now I'm being told he was here. Today, just before Sienna went missing. For God's sake, he might have her.' He grabbed Helen's arm and shook it. 'Did you hear what Mum just said? Do you know anything about this?'

Helen looked up at him with tears in her eyes. 'No, Leo, I don't. Thanks to you, I don't speak to him.'

Leo clutched her shoulders. 'Why was he here, Helen? Why?'

'Mr Hilton, I won't tell you again, calm down,' said DI Hatton.

'Why aren't you doing something? You need to find him! He could have seen Sienna, he could have taken her.' Leo turned back to his wife. 'Tell me why he was here, Helen, now!'

Helen stood up, glaring at her husband, her reddened, exhausted eyes full of tears, then ran out of the room, as Detective Inspector Hatton grabbed Leo's arm, to stop him running after her.

Chapter Seventeen

Willow

Thursday, 21 December 2017

Willow pulled up outside her father's block in Moulsecoomb and retrieved the bag of takeaway coffees at her feet. She still felt nauseous and her coffee tasted funny, but she wasn't poorly enough to put off facing the music; no more excuses, it had to be done.

After registering at The Keep and getting a membership card in order to be able to take photographs with her mobile, she had stayed until closing. It was an impressive modern building, an archive centre containing legal documents, newspaper cuttings, historical records and maps up to nine centuries old.

After being shown through to the library, she had asked to see any Ordnance Survey maps they had of the village of Kingston near Lewes. The softly spoken woman had looked up the reference numbers for her on the system and Willow had filled in the form, waiting patiently with her heart pounding. She looked at her watch; with only about seventeen hours until the planning meeting, she was certainly leaving it late to research such a crucial piece of information. Kicking herself for trusting Mike, it occurred to her that it was exactly a year since Mike had given her the project, and she realised, as a film of sweat formed over her body, that The Keep should really have been her first port of call rather than her last.

Soon afterwards, the helpful woman, with glasses on a chain and a shirt as crisp as unbroken ice, had appeared with three maps and asked her to handle them as carefully as possible. She had spread them out on the large white tables in front of Willow and opened them up for her, then smiled kindly before walking away. Willow scanned the village for the familiar landmarks she knew so well from a year of drawing up plans with Mike, Leo and the developers: the village hall, the church, Yew Tree Manor and The Vicarage. The cemetery backing onto the church was clear to see in all three maps, which dated back to 1853, but there was no sign of a graveyard next to The Vicarage. Although this meant she was none the wiser, it was a relief to know that she hadn't missed something blindingly obvious.

Scanning the most recent maps more carefully, she discovered three small grey areas in the fields surrounding the church labelled *Extra-Mural Cemetery* and goosebumps ran up her arm.

Pulling her mobile phone from her bag, she took a picture of them, and a quick Google search told her that they were the solution for overflowing cemeteries at the time.

> The population of Lewes expanded rapidly in the early nineteenth century and the churchyard of St Nicholas's became severely overcrowded. In 1893, the Privy Council prohibited burials in or around the churches and chapels

in Lewes under the Burials Beyond the Metropolis Act 1853 and purchased twenty acres in the adjacent fields.

It would stand to reason, Willow thought, as her eyes ran over the three surrounding fields, that if the church graveyard was full and the land that backed onto The Vicarage was being used as a kind of overspill cemetery, some of the graves could also have spread onto The Vicarage grounds.

Her conversation with Kellie in the car that morning came back to her: about how the graveyard Dorothy had mentioned could have been where paupers who couldn't afford a proper burial were laid to rest. Pauper graves would probably have gone under the radar, and it would make sense that only locals would know about them. They wouldn't have come up in any Ordnance Survey maps, or indeed the desktop survey in her file.

She returned the map and thanked the woman before turning her attention to finding the notebook. For that she had to go to the archive section. She walked through a huge futuristic sliding glass door and handed over the reference to the girl behind the desk, waiting for a short time until a blue paper file with a string around it was put down in front of her.

Notebook of Tessa James, midwife, circa 1930–1945.

Willow walked to the nearest available table and slowly opened the file; goosebumps prickled up her arms as she pulled out a small leather-bound book. Time and damp conditions in the soil had done away with much of the beautiful slanted handwriting, but she could tell that the entries ran from 2 April 1930 to 4 January 1945. Small notes, clearly written by her great-great-grandmother, about whichever birth she had attended that day. The first few entries were too damaged by water and dirt for her to read, but several pages in, she made out a paragraph:

She was too young for childbirth, and the boy who held her hand throughout promised he'd never again put her through such pain; a promise rarely kept.

It is lovely to hand over a baby to such a loving couple. I have helped too many mothers with six children under her feet she cannot afford to feed and a drunk for a husband. But not these two; it was their first, and tears ran down his cheeks. 'She's a beauty,' he whispered after he cut the cord.

A few more pages in, another passage was legible:

A woman birthed twins last night. It was a long night and she struggled terribly. A boy and a girl. The girl was born dead. 'I'm glad,' said the mother. 'I've got five others. I can't take care of them all. My husband says best the boy lives, because a girl ain't worth nothing.'

A mother out in Lewes is now pregnant again with five mouths to feed and a husband who beats her. She asked me to perform an abortion, but knowing how weak she is, I refused. It might kill her. Later the woman drank bleach to try and bring on a miscarriage and bled to death leaving all her children without a mother. I wish I'd helped her, as she'd asked. Those children haunt my dreams.

She continued to read as it grew dark outside. Some pages were a blur of smudged ink, and she was only able to make out the occasional word. But sometimes whole paragraphs were legible.

Dr Jenkins has told the husbands of Kingston they ought to have a man attend their birthing; that I am no better than a witch with my old-fashioned remedies and healing ways. It is God's will that a woman suffers in childbirth, he says, and it is not my place to interfere with God's will – though he will happily interfere with his forceps and scalpels so he is home in time for dinner.

Too soon, the woman behind the counter announced that they were closing, and Willow began gathering up her things. She had photographed all the pages that were legible and was walking back to return the notebook when she noticed the corner of a piece of paper sticking out from the back. Slowly she pulled it out and opened it up. It was a note, in a child's handwriting.

TO MY BEST FRIEND ALICE,

I'M SORRY I DIDN'T MEAN TO RUIN EVERYTHING. I MISS YOU SO MUCH.

NELL X

Willow stared at it in shock and realised she was holding her breath. She couldn't believe her eyes, the note she was holding in her hand was to Alice. The source of her obsession for the past year, and beyond, the very sight of her name, her fingers touching something that Alice had possibly touched, made her feel like she had seen a ghost. Her eyes scrolled down to the person writing the note: Nell. This had to be Bobby's sister – her aunt Nell – writing as a little girl; it was too much of a coincidence not to be. It made sense that she and Alice were best friends; they'd lived right next door to each other and were the same age.

She read the note again, more slowly this time, trying to drink in the past, picturing the little girl writing it. It was such a sad letter to her friend, and it made Willow well up as she studied the childish handwriting. It was the closest she had ever got to Alice and to Bobby's sister Nell and it felt like a small window into their world.

She went to put it back in the notebook, but found it impossible to part with. It was like a ticket to the past, to Alice and Nell and everything she had ever been desperate to know about for as long as she could remember. If only she could reach in and speak to Nell, she would do anything to meet her, to talk to her. She didn't understand how she could miss someone she'd never known so much. Willow's eyes darted to the desk as she made a snap decision, and checking that the woman wasn't watching, she slipped the note into her pocket.

'You asked for any articles on Tessa James,' the woman said cheerfully when Willow walked over, feeling intensely guilty about what she had just done. 'There were quite a few, so I printed a couple off for you. But you may want to come back another time to read the rest.'

Willow had thanked her and glanced down at the article

lying on top of the pile. It was from the *Sussex Times*, dated February 1950: *Was Convicted Midwife Innocent? Exclusive by Milly Green.*

A driver pressed on his horn as Willow stepped out onto the road outside her father's block of flats. She jumped back as the car roared past, her heart thudding in her ears. She had been so lost in thought, overwhelmed by her day, and as she looked both ways, she stepped out into the road again, tried to calm down and ignore the butterflies creeping into her stomach. Her mobile started ringing in her bag, and knowing it was probably Charlie checking up on her, she left it. She didn't want to lie to him, or have to explain things over the phone. Once she had spoken to her dad, she would hopefully feel better and would call him back. But telling her dad about her work on The Vicarage was a conversation she was dreading, and one she had no idea how to broach.

Willow started walking up the steps to his flat, the aroma of urine on the stairwell making her nausea return. It had taken a long time for the council to find him somewhere to live, and for a while it had looked like he was going to have to stay with her after he left prison in order to avoid ending up on the streets. But eventually they'd found him a rundown one bedroom flat, and although it wasn't exactly cosy, Willow had picked up a few bits of furniture and crockery from a local charity shop and they'd painted the living room and bedroom together. She felt better knowing he was settled, and that as long as he managed to stay out of trouble, his parole officer would leave him in peace.

As she reached his corridor, she began to feel panicked and started to rehearse the conversation in her head. Her mind flitted back to a meeting she'd had with the family liaison officer who had interviewed her when Bobby was due to be released on parole and had nowhere else to go.

'We know that you and your father have had a strained relationship, Willow, but we need an address for him, otherwise we can't release him. You're his last hope; if you can't have him, he'll have to be recalled.'

She had said that of course she would take him in, but admitted that she sometimes found him tricky to deal with. 'We all do, Willow,' the woman had responded. 'We work hard to build relationships, but some people don't like the system, they don't like any members of staff, they keep their heads down and don't engage. Your father is one of those.'

'Can I ask you something? Why wasn't he given probation earlier? I mean, people usually serve only half their sentences, don't they?' Willow had felt disloyal, prying behind his back.

'Your father's behaviour in prison would be the reason he stayed longer than he needed to. He's confrontational, struggles with authority and fails to follow rules.'

'But why? I mean, why does he want to make life harder for himself than it needs to be?'

The woman had paused and looked at her colleague, then back at Willow. 'As he was serving a longer sentence, he had a psychological assessment, and his trauma came up.'

'From his time in the youth detention centre?' Willow had asked, knowing it was a rhetorical question.

The woman had nodded. 'Unfortunately when someone has been institutionalised as long as your father has, they have a skewed view of the world. Nothing is ever their fault; there is always an excuse – that if this hadn't happened, or that person hadn't let me down, everything would be fine. Don't let him make you feel guilty.'

Willow had nodded. It had sounded all too familiar.

'And very often it's the family members who pay the price for this; in a sense, you are the victims as well, worn down by his repetitive offending and broken promises.'

'I know he's trying his best. I want to help him, I really do. We only have each other now.'

'That's good to hear, Willow, but you must try to protect yourself as well. He may find it hard to see things from your point of view for a while. Prison makes people focus on themselves, and they find it difficult to realise that others may experience things differently.'

Willow had nodded nervously. 'We're here to support you if you need to talk to us. Reintegrating yourself into society isn't easy, and he will need a lot of help. He's been inside institutions for most of his life. A lot of repeat offenders can be quite childlike; they expect things to fall into place and have little resilience.'

'I understand,' she had said, starting to feel quite uncomfortable.

They had explained what his behaviour might be like, and had told her that he would have a curfew and be unable to associate with certain people or to go to the town centre. She had an obligation to report him if he wasn't sticking to the terms of his probation; if he was breaking his curfew or drinking too much. And as his release date approached, she had started losing sleep, worrying about losing the sanctuary that was her home; that she would do something wrong, say something to upset him, and he would end up falling off the wagon and going back to prison. So when they'd phoned two days before he was due to move in with her, to say he was being given a council flat, she had cried with relief.

As she stood in front of his front door now, she lifted her closed fist and took a deep breath, then knocked three times. She could hear the television on inside his flat, but he hadn't replied to her text message to say she was coming, so perhaps he would be surprised – and not pleased – to see her. The butterflies began to take over in her stomach. She'd raised her fist to knock again when suddenly the door opened, and in front of her, in a sweatshirt and shorts, stood her father.

He was a tall man, with prominent cheekbones, a narrow mouth and a mop of black hair. His cool blue eyes were so bright they often made her uncomfortable. Her looks were entirely his; her long black hair and sky-blue eyes were often commented on, which had annoyed her mother intensely as a constant reminder of the father who was rarely around.

He always looked tired, and didn't smile often, but when he did, it was all in his sparkling eyes and rarely reached his mouth. If you got a smile from Bobby James, it counted. But now, standing in the doorway, he was scowling, clearly thrown by her presence, and his darting glance made it look as if he had something to hide. He hadn't shaved, and he had black circles under his eyes and creased skin on his left cheek like he'd just woken up.

Willow felt shocked at the sight of him in such a bedraggled state and tried to force herself to smile. 'Hi, Dad!'

'Hey, kiddo, how's it going?' He looked shifty and distant, as if he'd just bumped into someone he hardly knew in the street.

'I'm not sure if you got my message, but I need to talk to you.' She bit her lip.

'Oh, right. No, sorry, I didn't get it,' he said, clearly searching for a viable reason not to let her in. She could smell alcohol on his breath even from where she stood, and the smoke from the cigarette he was holding wafted up in front of her, making her feel nauseous again.

'It won't take long. We can go for a walk if that suits you better? I can wait here while you get dressed.' She was keen to walk in the fresh air rather than sit in a smoke-filled flat.

'No, it's fine, come in,' he said.

She tentatively followed him along the swirly brown carpet into the front room. The television was blaring eighties soft-rock music videos, and a bottle of cheap-looking wine sat on the table, with half the contents poured into a tumbler next to it and a pile of cigarette butts stacked in a side plate on the floor. The coffee table was filthy and covered in old newspapers, and the curtains were drawn. Takeaway containers littered the floor, along with a pile of discarded clothes and empty beer cans. The room smelt of damp, and despite the smoky air, all the windows were closed. Her father stood at the centre of it looking haunted.

Willow immediately felt a stab of guilt that she hadn't been to see him in over a month. She had been so busy at work, and avoiding him because of the conversation she had to have with him now.

'You okay for a minute while I get dressed?' he said, looking back at her as she found a space on the sofa and sat down.

'Sure,' she said, looking round at the carnage, trying not to go into a spin of guilt at the state of her father and his home. She was a bad daughter; it had been her job to look after him, and she'd failed. She took deep breaths and tried to talk herself back from the precipice; don't let him make you feel guilty. He was not a child; he was a grown man and not her responsibility. Maybe he'd just had a bad week. As long as he hadn't violated his parole in any way, it would be okay. She had been working hard, but the project was nearly over, and now she could take some time off to be with him.

Trying to distract herself, she looked down at the piles of paperwork and letters strewn about and her eyes fell on a box of photographs at the foot of the couch. She glanced at the photo on the top: a black and white picture of a woman in a wedding dress dancing with her groom.

Bobby reappeared, half dressed, and took a cigarette from a packet on the table. 'Make yourself a coffee,' he said.

'I brought you one.' She held up the takeaway bag.

As he disappeared again, she glanced back at the photos, then leaned down and picked one up. It looked like her father as a boy, around thirteen years old, leaning on a gate that a little girl with dark hair was sitting on. The girl had a beaming smile and was looking at him adoringly. In the background, a herd of cows was coming up the lane towards them.

Willow looked more closely. She was sure the girl must be Nell. She had never met her aunt, and her father refused to talk about her. All she knew was that Nell had hurt him deeply, which meant that, as was his way, he had shut down and cut her out of his life. Willow thought of the note she had discovered, burning a hole in her pocket. She could see that Nell looked like Bobby; they had the same heart-shaped face and the same smile, the same eyes. She would have loved to have known her.

Bobby walked back into the room. 'This is a lovely picture, Dad. Is this Nell?' He paused, then nodded, and she put the picture down, reading the usual signs that the subject was out of bounds.

'How have you been, kid?' There was something about his demeanour that was making her uneasy.

'All right. I feel a bit sick; I think I might have a bug.' She sipped her funny-tasting coffee again.

'Not preggers, are you?' he said, winking at her.

Willow laughed. 'No, God no. No chance.' She frowned to herself as she took the idea in.

'How's yer fella? Charlie, isn't it?'

Willow, still stuck on his last question, paused before answering. 'Good, he's been helping me with the flat. We finished sanding the floor and painting the bedroom. It's really starting to feel like home now.' She put the picture back on the pile.

'That's great. He's a good guy, I like him. You know I can help any time,' he said, pulling a cigarette from the packet and running his fingers through his greasy hair. 'I don't know why you never ask.'

'Dad,' she said quietly, 'there's something I need to talk to you about. I'm not sure if you're going to be very happy with me, but I want to be honest with you.'

'Sounds ominous,' he said, searching for a lighter.

'I just . . .' She stopped, her heart thrashing in her chest, her voice starting to shake. 'I just want you to know that what I'm about to tell you was a really big deal for me, and it wasn't a decision I took lightly.'

'Okay.' He sat back in his faded armchair and crossed his legs, which made him feel far away. He had the look that made her nervous, when he seemed to completely cut off his emotions by sheer will. Her mouth went dry as she tried to go on.

'So, I've been working on a project for nearly a year now based in Kingston near Lewes.'

She smiled, trying to break the tension, but he was still now, and staring, frowning at her intently.

'Dad, the Hiltons – as in your old neighbours – are pulling down The Vicarage and building ten houses and a new community centre on the site. And my firm, my architecture practice . . . well, I've been working with Leo Hilton and running the project.'

Bobby's eyes dropped to the floor as he lit his cigarette and inhaled deeply. Finally, when she couldn't bear the silence any longer, he spoke. 'I know.'

Of all the things she had expected him to say, that one had not even crossed her mind. In the space of only a few seconds, she went from shock to anger. So he had known – for how long? Secrets, as always, between the two of them. Things left unsaid, difficult conversations put off. It was the story of her life.

He looked down at his cigarette, which had burned down to the butt. 'I'm not an idiot, Willow.' His lips twitched as he looked away. 'People talk, and it's been in the local paper. I would have preferred to hear it from you first, though, I have to say.'

Willow felt the nausea lurch in her stomach again. 'I

wanted to tell you sooner, but I didn't know how you'd react.'

Her anger intensified. As always, the onus was on her. It was always someone else's fault with him; he took no responsibility for talking to her. For trying to understand the pressure she'd been under. Her heart raced and her hands shook. It had been so long since she'd seen his temper flare, she had almost convinced herself he didn't have one any more. But it was always there, lurking under the surface; nothing had changed.

He sat in silence, cigarette ash dropping on the floor at his feet, and she continued, her voice quiet now. 'My boss asked me to run the project, and I wanted to do it. I was worried how you'd react, but I've been waiting for a project like this for years. I've worked so hard to get to this point; if I'd turned it down I might not have got another chance.'

'So you've been working with Leo Hilton. Does he know who you are?' Bobby's face was white.

'No, he doesn't.' Willow felt like she was going to be sick again. She'd known he might be hurt, but she hadn't expected this. 'Look, Dad, I can see you're upset, that's why I've been avoiding telling you.' She felt tears spilling over. 'I needed this job. I don't have the luxury of turning down work; I don't have anyone I can turn to for financial help.'

'Oh, right, so you're saying you had to take the job with the Hiltons because I'm a shit father? Did you ever think that maybe the Hiltons, and what they did to me, are the reason for that?'

'I didn't mean it like that. I was just saying I have to put myself first sometimes, because I've got used to being the only person I can rely on.' She felt her tongue tying itself in knots, the words coming out all wrong. 'Perhaps I can explain a bit better where I'm coming from, I mean why I agreed to run the project.' She brushed the tears away, trying to control herself.

'If I'd known back at the start, I could have warned you to stay away. They'll use you, then cast you aside; that's what they do.' He took another drag on his cigarette as his anger turned to sadness. 'It happened to me. I turned my back on my father, my own blood, for the Hiltons on the day he died.

'I left him on his own that night, to help Richard Hilton with some bloody lights, and he died. He had slaughtered all his herd and I left him. I'll never forgive myself, and for what? To help a man who threw me to the wolves. Dad warned me about the Hiltons, but I didn't listen. Be careful, Willow, you have no idea what they are capable of.' He took a drag of the cigarette, his eyes dead. 'And you're demolishing The Vicarage?'

She nodded. 'It's a ruin, Dad, nobody's lived there since you left.'

'What about the graves? What's happening about them?'

Willow felt her stomach plummet again. 'I didn't know about the graveyard until today,' she said quietly. 'There's no record of it on any of the local maps – which Leo is banking on, I think.'

'There wouldn't be. They used to bury the poor there, and unmarried mothers who died in childbirth. And a witch, if folklore is to be believed. None of them had a proper headstone, just bits of rock or wooden crosses. The witch's grave was piled high with stones. Apparently the locals did it to stop her coming back to life. Nell was fascinated by that grave,' he added, lost in thought.

'I only found out about the graves today by accident, from a villager. It sounds from what you're saying that there are a lot of human remains on the site, which means I'm completely in the shit, unless I lie about it to protect Leo.'

'Don't ever lie to protect Leo. I did that and it landed me behind bars.' His voice was grim.

'What do you mean? What did you lie about?' Willow said, her eyes wide.

'Never mind, I don't want to talk about it.'

'There's a surprise,' she mumbled under her breath.

Her father shot her a look. 'Just don't trust him, and never, ever take a bullet for him. Promise me, Willow.' He had a way of staring at her that made her uncomfortable, as though he could read her thoughts.

'Okay, I promise.' Willow sighed, close to tears.

'Does Nell know about The Vicarage coming down?'

Willow frowned. 'Nell? I don't know, Dad. I've never even met her.'

He let out a snort of laughter and shook his head, his anger returning. 'It would help if you stopped lying to me now, Willow. But okay, whatever you say.'

'I'm not lying.' Willow watched her father as he stood and began to pace. 'I don't understand. How am I supposed to have met her? You've never introduced us, I have no idea where she lives, or even what she looks like.' She couldn't help the tears escaping now. She desperately wanted a father who would reach out to her, hold her, tell her he was proud of her. They could spend as much time as they liked decorating her flat, walking together, building bridges, but when things got messy, the shutters always came down.

'Dad, why don't you see Nell any more? You obviously loved her so much.' She looked down at the picture of Nell sitting on the top of the pile. 'What did she do to you?'

'Why don't you ask her yourself?' he spat.

'How can I ask her? Where is she?' The tears were flowing now. 'Why are you being so cruel?'

'Because I know when someone is lying to me,' he snapped.

'I'm not lying! It took a lot of guts to come here, Dad. I thought we could actually have an honest conversation, so I wouldn't have to hide things from you, or lie to you. You know, Dad, one of the main reasons I took this project on was to get closer to you. To try and find out about where you came from, and what really happened to you to make you the way you are. So don't talk to me about being lied to. You've never been honest with me about anything since the day I was born.'

Bobby stopped pacing. 'I don't know why you want to hurt me like this, but I think you should go.' He spoke calmly, with no emotion.

'Dad, please don't shut me out again.'

'I am proud of you, Willow. That house brought nothing but misery to my mother and grandmother. I'm glad it's being ripped down. Maybe now I can put the past behind me once and for all.'

At that moment, the doorbell rang, piercing the tense atmosphere between them. Bobby looked at Willow and frowned, then slowly walked down the hallway and opened the front door.

There was a sudden explosion of crashing and shouting and Willow rushed out into the hallway to see what the commotion was. The door was thrown open and two police officers launched themselves at Bobby, pushing him against the wall and putting him in handcuffs. Two other policemen started racing round the flat, opening cupboards and wardrobe doors, crashing through the bedroom shouting out Sienna's name.

'What's going on?' Willow stood in front of one of the officers.

'A seven-year-old girl has gone missing from her home in Kingston. Your father was seen in the grounds of the child's house today, around the time she went missing.'

'Wait, what? Where are you taking him?' she demanded.

'Lewes police station for questioning,' the officer said, as Bobby was escorted out of the flat.

Another policeman walked past her, speaking into his radio. 'She's not here. Repeat: Sienna Hilton is not at the suspect's property.'

'Okay, I'll inform the parents,' came the reply.

None of the officers even acknowledged Willow as they half walked, half dragged her father out of the front door, the thunder of footsteps, shouting, banging doors and then silence.

Willow stood in her father's flat, swallowing tears of shock before forcing herself to walk over to the remote control and turn on the television. She flicked through the channels until she found the news, then turned up the volume.

'Seven-year-old Sienna Hilton is still missing after vanishing earlier today from the garden of her parents' house in the village of Kingston, East Sussex. A man who was seen in the grounds has been arrested on suspicion of abduction and taken for questioning. Sienna Hilton is the daughter of businessman Leo Hilton, whose sister Alice famously disappeared from the same house nearly fifty years ago, in a missing persons case that has never been solved.'

Willow turned the television off and ran to the bathroom, throwing up the coffee she'd drunk earlier. She sat on the side of the bath to catch her breath, turning on the cold tap to splash water on her face. She reached into her pocket for a tissue, her fingers closing round the note she'd taken from The Keep.

There was only one person who could help her now: Bobby's sister, Nell James. Someone who she had never met and who she knew nothing about – despite her father insisting she did. A woman who – judging from the note Willow clutched in her hand now – may have known what happened to Alice that night and could clear her father's name once and for all. Nell James – a woman she didn't have the first clue how to find.

Chapter Eighteen
Nell

December 1969

Dear Bobby,

I never thought I could miss someone as much as I miss you and Dad and the farm. They are kind to me here, but everything sounds and feels and smells different to what I am used to. And it is so cold! They are very keen on keeping us as cold as possible, and in bed, and so that is what I do all day - complain of the cold and lie in bed, not so different to how I am at home!

Nell bit down on her lip as she said the word 'home', and looked over at her friend Heather, who was sitting up in the bed next to her, writing the letter for her. At twelve years of age, Heather was a big girl and Nell adored her. She had blonde curls, and porcelain skin, like a doll in a toy shop, and she had looked after Nell since the day she arrived. Heather could do no wrong in Nell's eyes: she read to her, played cards with her, and held her hand when she felt bad, which was a lot of the time. And she was much better at writing than Nell; her handwriting was tall and beautiful, just like her.

Nell looked round the long room with its wooden floorboards and rows of beds and open windows where she had spent the past few weeks, and ached for her father to walk in and carry her away.

She knew from Dad's arguments with Mr Hilton that it would not be The Vicarage she would be going home to, but she tried to be brave about that and not mind too much. Home was wherever Bobby and Dad were, and she needed to stay strong until they came for her. Heather knew how she felt, she really missed home too, because she had been at the sanatorium for over a year. Nell didn't know how poorly Heather was but she knew she wasn't going home any time soon. She'd had an X-ray of her lungs done the other day and was told the TB was back. Nell had heard the doctors talking to Heather, saying they were going to try a new treatment on her. But when Heather went for her X-ray, the doctor said there was a lot of damage to her lungs. Heather had been very upset and had cried for several days, and Nell had given her her teddy bear to try and cheer her up.

Finally Heather's parents had come and it had made her feel better. Nell liked Heather's parents; they were very kind, and often brought some sweets, which Heather had shared with her. Her mother was called Emma and her father was called George. Heather had a smile which went from cheek to cheek. Her mother's smile was just the same, but her father was upset and didn't smile at all, just looked down at his hands. When Heather had gone to the bathroom, Nell heard her mother say to her father that he'd better not come next time if he couldn't at least try to be cheerful for Heather's sake.

It had been lovely to see some parents, even though she was terribly jealous that they weren't hers. No one told her why her father or Bobby didn't come. She cried herself to sleep most nights worrying that they were cross with her, or that she had done something wrong. Heather's mother had told her that the train fare was very expensive and perhaps her family couldn't afford it, but that she was sure her father would be there soon to see her. She looked over at Heather, who was waiting for Nell to continue, her pen poised.

The other children here are nice. I have a friend called Heather who is very kind and shares her sweets with me. I am coughing quite a lot still and my chest hurts. The doctor took an X-ray of my lungs. It doesn't hurt but the metal screen is quite cold when you stand next to it as you have to take all your clothes off apart from your underwear.

Please write to me, Bobby, I want so much to hear from you how Alice is, and how Snowy is doing. The doctor says I am getting better, and that the medicine they are giving me is working, so hopefully I can come home soon. I bet it is quiet there without me! Lots and lots of love, Nell.

'That's a lovely letter, Nell,' said Heather. 'Do you want to sign your name?'

Heather handed over the letter and Nell used her most grown-up writing to sign her name.

'My parents are coming this weekend,' said Heather, taking the letter back from Nell and sliding it into an envelope. 'So they can post it for you.'

'Maybe Dad will come this weekend too,' said Nell hopefully. 'We have to move out of our house, so he may know where we are going to.'

'Well, there you are,' said Heather cheerfully, 'that's why he's been busy, it's a lot of work moving. I'm sure he'll be here soon. Did you want to write any more letters today, Nell?'

Nell paused, knowing she had yet to write to Alice, but not wanting to share the secret room with anyone else. 'I do, but I think I might try and write that one on my own.'

'Good for you, Nell, shall I lend you my writing paper and pen? Here, you can lean on my book too,' said Heather, laying everything down on Nell's bedside table.

'Thank you, Heather,' said Nell, smiling at her friend adoringly.

As Heather lay down to have a nap, Nell picked up the paper and pen and slowly started to write as goosebumps darted along her arms at the thought of Alice reading it.

Dear Alice,

I hope you are okay and keeping Snowy warm and playing with her. I miss you so much that I can't really think about it too much or I will cry. I can't wait to see you again and show you the secret room I have found under the stairs in The Vicarage – that is what the key is for on Snowy's collar.

You would never know the room is there except for a tiny keyhole under the top step. It opens up like a lid to a secret world with a bed in and a chest and a candle with matches. But I don't know where we will live next or if we will ever be together in the secret room now. If you see Bobby or Dad, please tell them I miss them and tell them to write to me. I can't wait until we can be together again. You are my best friend in the world.

Love Nell xxx

Nell slid the letter in to an envelope and wrote *Alice Hilton, Yew Tree Manor, Kingston – PRIVATE NOT FOR ANYONE ELSE* – in big letters on the front, then she licked the flap and sealed it tight.

Chapter Nineteen

Bella

January 1946

'Bring up Tessa James!' the clerk bellowed as the din in the courtroom lowered to an audible hum.

Bella held her breath as she watched her mother being brought up into the dock. She was so close, she could almost reach out and touch her frail slumped shoulders. She looked down at the bruises creeping around her mother's wrists like snakes, from being in handcuffs for hours on end.

The atmosphere in the court was electric, like a throng baying for blood. Bella could almost feel their glee at the prospect of a life sentence. It was not their wish to find out that Tessa James was innocent; where was the entertainment in that?

Had they not had their fill of horror and pain on the battlefield? Bella thought. As her eyes scanned the benches of spectators, she could see several of the men with scars on their faces, or with or their arms in slings. Hadn't they had enough death and misery?

After walking with Alfie from the police station to the courthouse, Bella had battled her way to the entrance as the gathered crowd booed and shouted her mother's name.

'Excuse me, I'm Bella James,' she had said to the policeman standing there. He didn't hear her, and she stepped closer. 'Excuse me, sir, where should I go? I'm Tessa James's daughter.' As the policeman finally heard her, so did several others. She could feel the mood of the crowd shift, sense their eyes on her and Alfie.

She had turned her panicked gaze to the copper, who tried to get her through the doors as the shouting and pushing increased. A man behind her shoved her hard in the back, and she stumbled on the top step. Pain shot through her leg as it bashed against the cold stone, and as she struggled to right herself, a smart-looking young woman with wavy red hair wearing a white blouse and a long black skirt forced herself through the crowd and helped her and Alfie through the door.

'Thank you,' Bella said quietly as the doors closed behind them. 'Are you okay, Alfie?' she said, and the little boy nodded up at her.

'Glad to be of service. You need Court Number One,' the woman said, smiling kindly.

Bella had brushed herself down and rubbed her painful knee before walking with a heavy heart along the red-carpeted corridor.

'Excuse me?' she said to a woman cleaning the windows at the end of the hallway. 'Could you please tell me where the administration office is?'

The woman turned and looked at her; she seemed irritated to have been interrupted. 'Up the stairs, first on the left,' she said before returning to her task.

Bella looked around to check no one had noticed her presence and set off slowly up the wooden staircase, as Alfie clutched her hand. Finally she reached the top and knocked on the door ahead of her. A well-spoken voice called to her to come in, and she turned the handle and opened the door to reveal a large woman with her hair in a bun and spectacles on a long string resting on her bosom.

'Hello, I was wondering if you could help me.' She smiled nervously. 'A relative of mine has to appear in court in the next few weeks, and I was wondering if you had a list of the volunteer barristers available in the area?'

The woman looked at her for some time, then opened a drawer and pulled out a file. She flicked through it, extracting a piece of paper.

'You'll be lucky. There aren't many and they get very booked up,' she said, handing it over, 'so if it's only a few weeks away, you may not be in luck.'

Bella scanned the page. 'Thank you. Is this definitely all of them?'

The woman nodded. 'I'm afraid so. Justice is expensive. Some barristers volunteer their time, but most of them never work for free.'

Bella thanked the woman, folded the piece of paper and put it in her canvas bag before slowly walking back down the stairs towards the door of Court Number One.

As she reached out for the brass handle, a female voice from behind her made her jump. 'Miss James? I'm sorry to trouble you, but could I speak with you for a moment?'

Bella turned to see the young woman who had helped her up the step. She seemed young – in her twenties, she thought – and danced from foot to foot as she spoke, as if she had so much energy she didn't know what to do with it.

'My name is Milly Green, I'm a reporter at the *Sussex Times*. If you ever wanted to speak about your mother's trial, give your side of the story, my door is always open.' A red curl fell in front of her green eyes as she handed Bella a card with her name and telephone number on it. 'I know she has always protested her innocence, and I'd like to get to the truth.'

Bella's eyes fixed fiercely on the young woman. 'I doubt fact sells as many papers as fiction,' she said.

The girl smiled wryly. 'It depends on the story. Nobody wants the life sentence of an innocent woman on their conscience and, if she's been wronged, I want our readers to know about it. Your mother deserves to have her voice heard. My office is opposite the courthouse, if you ever want to speak to me.'

'How convenient for you. Please can you let us through.'

Milly Green moved aside, and Bella and Alfie entered the court. It was already crammed with people: journalists, lawyers and spectators. Many of them turned to stare as the two of them sat down on one of the hard wooden benches. Bella clutched Alfie's hand tight, giving her strength, and felt her heart break as she watched her beautiful mother being ushered into the dock.

She scanned the crowd for Wilfred Hilton. He was sitting on the other side of the courtroom, opposite the jury. She stared at him, but he immediately looked away as the court clerk began to speak.

'Members of the jury, it is my task to sum up the statements of the prosecution and the defence and to remind you of the evidence you have heard. In order for you to convict the defendant of voluntary manslaughter, you must be convinced that the victim died as a consequence of her actions, and that she had the intention to cause serious harm.'

Bella stared intently at her mother, willing her to turn around, the need to reach out and put her arms around her shoulders so overwhelming that she had to sit on her hands to stop herself.

She sensed the whole court holding their breath, rubbing their hands in glee, desperate for the result they all wanted: life imprisonment, something her mother would never be able to survive; a cell without access to any of the things she lived for.

Bella's eyes lifted slightly to the men in black gowns and cream wigs. The judge, in red, scowling down at her mother from his throne. She could feel a presence in the room. Something was moving amongst them. Bella reached down and felt the deadly nightshade berries in a cloth in her pocket. Death was sitting next to her. Was she really going to give them to her mother? It was as good as killing her herself.

As she watched her mother tremble with fear in the dock, Bella felt her whole body slump. A policeman caught her and stopped her falling to the floor in front of the packed courtroom. She clung to the bench and closed her eyes as Alfie squeezed her hand tightly.

Bella held her breath and looked around the room. The rows and rows of spectators were glued to the action as if they were watching a film in the cinema. Their enjoyment was palpable. Alfie looked up at her with tears in his eyes and she pulled him close.

'It is the task of the prosecution to prove that the accused is guilty of voluntary manslaughter. I put it to you that our three witnesses have proved the case. We have heard from Sally White, the house servant at Yew Tree Manor, who was there that night. She saw what happened, and corroborated what our second witness, Dr Jenkins, told us. Why would two people entirely independently say the same thing? That Tessa James took the scalpel from the doctor's bag and cut Mrs Hilton. Miss White saw it for herself, standing at the door looking in; her view was clear.'

Bella looked over at Sally, a tiny slip of a girl, with no income for her or her daughter if the Hiltons were to sack her. The family had been good to her, letting her stay on with a child in tow; no other household would have done that, and she knew it.

'How can you trust a woman whose entire defence has been to criticise Dr Jenkins? A man of impeccable character, a well-known doctor with an untarnished reputation, a pillar of the community who would have no reason to make an unwarranted accusation against the accused.

'This is a woman who, as we have heard from Father Blacker, has a reputation not for saving life, but for bringing on miscarriages in loose women and in wives who are tired of bearing children. A midwife who hides pregnant women away in The Vicarage, where their husbands cannot find them, and sets upon them with instruments she claims not to own in order to make them bleed. Deciding which children will live and which will die. Just as she did on the day of Mrs Hilton's death, after Mr Hilton told her he would no longer turn a blind eye to the illegal activities taking place on his land and that she was to leave immediately. Members of the jury, whether you think this would give a woman intent to harm his wife is a matter for you. A woman who is known to take the law, and the lives of unborn babies, into her own hands.'

Bella watched the judge raise his eyebrows, in response to which a couple of the jury members smiled. She looked over at the woman typing the transcript of everything being said; in black and white it sounded innocent enough, but it was clear where the judge's opinion lay.

She felt the fury rising inside her, and glanced at Jeremy Lyons, her mother's barrister, who throughout the trial had done little to try and prove her mother's innocence. Bella hung her head in despair, her mind screaming at the injustice unfolding in front of her eyes and the lies that were going unchallenged by her mother's barrister; the grandeur and majesty of the court process making justice for her mother impossible.

'Members of the jury, when Dr Jenkins left Tessa James with Mrs Hilton, she was very much alive. The house servant saw the midwife use a scalpel to make the cut – she supports him on that – but again, this is a matter for you. The Midwife's Act of 1902 was created to regulate the profession of midwifery, but unless you, the jury, convict women like Tessa James they will continue to disregard it. Taking babies from us is God's will alone. I fear Heinrich Kramer & Jacob Sprenger may have been right when they said that no one does more harm to the Catholic Faith than midwives.'

Stunned silence fell over the crowded courtroom as they waited for Mr Lyons to begin. Bella watched as her mother's barrister stood up, struggling to swallow her fury, knowing before he uttered a word that he would not do her mother justice.

'Members of the jury, you may think there is little doubt that the actions of the accused in making the cut that caused the bleed ultimately led to the death of poor Mrs Hilton. But if that is your conclusion, that is not sufficient.' The barrister thumped his fist on the table. 'In order to convict the accused, you have to also find she had the necessary intent. And, members of the jury, I put to you, she did not intend to kill. Tessa James didn't even have the intention to cause serious harm. Mrs James's only crime is that she didn't follow protocol. She didn't follow the Midwife's Act of 1902, which was created for this very purpose, to regulate the profession of midwifery, requiring that midwives attend normal births only. And it stipulates that they transfer care of a woman in labour to a physician in complicated cases such as this, and restricts them from using instruments such as forceps and scalpels. Tessa James did not want to kill Evelyn Hilton. But she is a proud woman, a midwife who has practised for over thirty years, and asking for help went against everything she stood for. It was pride, not malice, that stopped her transferring Mrs Hilton's care to Dr Jenkins until it was too late. Times are changing, pregnant women want a qualified doctor at their bedside, and midwives such as Tessa James are against the number of medical men now practising midwifery. She bitterly resented this invasion of her territory, but does this make her a killer?'

He banged his fist again making Bella jump. 'I ask you, ladies and gentlemen of the jury, does this make her evil? She has served the community of Kingston her whole professional life, many women sitting here today are testament to that, her life has been about preserving life, not shortening it. I put it to you that Tessa James simply made a mistake, she thought that, with her thirty years experience of saving the lives of mothers and babies in childbirth, she could cope, but she couldn't. And Evelyn Hilton paid for that mistake dearly.

'So, it falls to you, ladies and gentlemen of the jury, to decide if she needs to go to prison for life for that mistake? There is little doubt that it was the actions of the accused in making the cut that caused the bleed that ultimately led to the death of poor Mrs Hilton. But if that is your conclusion, it is not sufficient, because in order to convict the accused you have to also find she had the necessary intent. And members of the jury, she did not have intent to kill, or even to cause serious harm. Tessa James is owed a great debt by the community of Kingston and today we must focus on the hundreds of lives she has saved and not the one she, ultimately, couldn't. There is no doubt that midwives such as Mrs James need stringent regulations but they do not need imprisonment. So I put it to you today that you find it in yourselves to return a verdict of not guilty.'

Bella burned with the desire to stand up and defend her mother. If she didn't say something and her mother was given a life sentence, she would never forgive herself.

'Sir, excuse me, please!' Bella stood, and the entire court turned to look at her. 'If I may be allowed to say a few words in my mother's defence?'

There was an audible gasp.

'You may not!' the judge bellowed.

Bella ignored him and looked pleadingly at the jury, her eyes full of tears. 'My mother has delivered a thousand babies and has never once used a scalpel. She would never do such a thing. Dr Jenkins regarded her as a threat, because local women loved her and she was taking business away from him. I myself heard him say that he was determined to bring her down. My mother would never have hurt Evelyn Hilton. They were friends; she delivered her other two babies and cared a great deal for her.'

'Sit down, young lady, now! Or I will find you in contempt of court!' He slammed his gavel down so hard that it sent a jolt through her and she reluctantly took her seat again. Her mother turned to look at her, and their blue eyes locked for a moment before Tessa began to cry and turned away so Bella could not see.

As the judge began his summing up, Bella could not stand to listen to any more lies, so she took Alfie's hand and stood on shaking legs and walked towards the door. Her mother's barrister glared at her, his face puce with rage.

She had been told it could be hours, days even, before a verdict was reached, and she sat on a bench outside the courtroom door, focusing on Alfie's little hand as she squeezed it tight. Alfie lay down on her lap and she stroked his hair, the tracks of his tears still visible on his beautiful face. He looked like Eli, she thought, so much like Eli but with her blue eyes. Soon the crowds in the courtroom began to file out, chatting animatedly about getting cake and tea as if it were the interval of a play.

She didn't know how much time had passed, but too soon there was the rustle of activity, the murmur of something happening. It couldn't be time already, could it? Jeremy Lyons' words came back to her, sending a surge of panic through her body. *I'm hoping the jury will be a long time in their deliberations; a swift verdict is never a good sign.*

A man's voice bellowed along the corridor where she sat, 'Verdict, Court One.' Alfie and Bella looked at one another, and Alfie threw his arms around her. They stood on shaking legs and joined the stream of spectators filing back in, and took their seats on the cold wooden bench. As the jury shuffled back in and took their seats, none of them would look at her. Bella closed her eyes and clung to Alfie's hand.

'Foreman of the jury, would you stand. I understand you have come to a verdict.'

'Yes, your honour.'

'And is this the verdict of you all?'

'Yes, your honour.'

'Do you find the defendant guilty or not guilty of the voluntary manslaughter of Evelyn Hilton?'

'Guilty.'

Bella closed her eyes and tried to focus on not being sick as the bile in her stomach rose into her throat. She looked over to her mother, whose legs had gone from under her. The guard caught her and lowered her onto a chair. For several minutes there was chaos in the courtroom as the masses erupted, shouting and jeering, banging their hands on their seats. Alfie jerked awake with the uproar and looked up to his mother, who wrapped her arms around him so he couldn't hear.

'Stand up, Mrs James!' ordered the judge. The policeman pulled Tessa up so she was standing in the dock. 'You have been found guilty of voluntary manslaughter. I am asked by your counsel to show mercy on the basis of your previous good character, but I cannot ignore the fact that several witnesses have reported that you induce miscarriages, an act which is strictly prohibited in the eyes of the law. Your daughter also gave scurrilous evidence as to the character of Dr Jenkins, which I found unbelievable and which has not helped your position now in terms of my thinking you have not taken account for your mistakes. Added to the criminality and malice of your action in causing the death of Mrs Hilton, you have worked hard to destroy the reputation of Dr Jenkins, a pillar of our community and a man to which we owe much gratitude.'

Bella felt violently sick and tried to steady her breathing. Murmurings from members of the public became louder, the scratch of pencils on journalists' pads like fingernails down a blackboard. Milly Green's intense stare was focused on her and making her uneasy. She looked over to Wilfred Hilton, who kept his eyes firmly on the judge. Tessa's gaze remained fixed on the ground. Suddenly, without warning, a ray of sunshine fell through the stained-glass windows, lighting up the grey room and the dark mahogany benches. Time stopped, the reporters squinting up and staring hungrily at her mother.

Bella reached out to steady herself as the judge spoke, his voice deep and slow, calm and considered.

'This was a selfish crime, putting your ambitions as a midwife before the well-being of a woman and her baby, for which there is but one punishment. Despite your continued protestations of innocence, the evidence against you is overwhelming. Mr Lyons has, on countless occasions, referred to the women whose lives he claims his client has saved. Sadly for you, Mrs James, your barrister has been unable to persuade a single one of them to take the stand in your defense. And you refuse to take the stand yourself.

You caused terrible suffering to Mrs Hilton and her baby, and we must make sure no other mother suffers the same fate.

'Tessa James, you have been found guilty of voluntary manslaughter. The sentence of this court is that you will be taken from here to the prison cell whence you came, where you will begin to serve a life sentence. Let us hope this acts as a deterrent to other midwives taking the law into their own hands.'

As jeers of elation erupted, Bella stood and walked over to the dock. Every eye in the courtroom turned and watched her.

'Mama, Mama, it's me, Bella.' She couldn't stop herself from breaking down at the sight of her strong mother having to be supported by a prison guard. The strain too much, tears rolled down her cheeks. 'Mama, I'm here,' she said more loudly.

Tessa slowly turned to her daughter in a state of shocked stupor, her blue eyes flashing. The judge began to shout over the noisy crowd.

'Order, order! Get away, young lady, or I will find you in contempt of court.'

'Mama, I love you,' said Bella, holding out her hand, which her mother took. In it was a small linen bag, too small for anyone else to notice, containing twenty berries. Her fingers curled around a palm as familiar as her own as her mother stared at her intently, her eyes holding all the memories of their life together. Bella looked at the guard and eased Tessa away from him and into her embrace, her mother's hair, her body, her spirit enveloping her. As she breathed her in for the last time, they were back by the fire at The Vicarage, sheltering from a storm. 'I'm always with you, Mama,' she whispered.

As Tessa collapsed into her, Bella felt her mother's panicked heartbeat slowing, and for a second they were one, at peace, until the prison guards tore Tessa away and the judge slammed down his gavel.

'Get that woman out of here; lock her up for the night!' he boomed.

A police officer pulled Bella away, separating them for the final time, and she watched helplessly as her mother was carried down the steps of the dock.

As the officer took her arm and steered her through the courtroom, jeering men booed and cursed her name, bloodthirsty men whose wives her mother had helped, often for no money. Bella looked back and saw Wilfred Hilton walk over to Alfie, and she began to scream, blind panic flooding her body. With Eli dead and her in police custody, Bella knew that Wilfred would say he was the boy's legal guardian. As they dragged her away, she begged the judge to let her go, that she was sorry, that she would do anything. But as she screamed her son's name, Wilfred smiled down at the boy, encouraging him not to look at her, then calmly took Alfie's hand and led the boy away.

Chapter Twenty

Vanessa

New Year's Eve 1969

'Has your daughter ever run away before?' Vanessa looked at the dark-haired police officer across the table, then over at her son staring into the fire, a thick woollen blanket wrapped around his narrow trembling shoulders.

'No,' she said. 'Well, sort of, but it was just a silly game, a misunderstanding.' She stood up and began to pace again, the detectives at the table twisting round to face her.

'Could you explain what happened on that occasion, Mrs Hilton?'

She didn't know what to do with herself; her body was so fired up with adrenaline and panic that she wanted to run. She would have run all night if it meant getting to Alice. But there was nowhere to run to, nothing but dead ends and a burning ball of panic in the pit of her stomach. It was one o'clock in the morning, and her daughter was still missing. The blizzard had stopped, replaced by a flat, silent white sheet over the entire village, a blank canvas covering all tracks. She had been out in the snow for nearly two hours, running up and down the lane through the village looking for her child, until she was so frozen she could no longer feel any of her body.

A few well-meaning guests were still milling around the house helping to coordinate a search party, coming back in to warm up, to gather strength, drinking hot drinks, talking. She knew they needed to regroup, but she wished they would go back out. The noise of their chatter, maybe enjoying the drama, the clink of coffee cups infuriated her: 'Isn't it awful?' 'I don't understand it.' 'Such a beautiful child, no one would do anything to hurt her, surely?' The only sound she wanted to hear was Alice, shrieking, laughing, giggling, and the absence of her in the house was sending her to the brink of madness.

'Can I get anyone another cup of tea or coffee?' The waitress who had found her earlier that night to ask about the champagne was still hovering, her face ashen. She had been one of the last people to see Alice alive; when Vanessa had told her beautiful daughter off for not getting ready. All she had cared about all year, all Richard had obsessed over, was this bloody party, the event, the show, for business colleagues, acquaintances and the villagers. While the two people who mattered most, whom she loved more than anything in the world, were increasingly ignored. As she looked down the hallway, she felt such a rage at the house that had stolen so much of her life that she wanted to scream, pull over the Christmas tree, tear down the decorations, smash the vases full of blood-red roses. What if the past few weeks, of her being so absent, so distracted, so cross and stressed with the decorators and party planning had been her last with Alice?

'Mrs Hilton, would you mind telling me what happened when your daughter ran away last time?'

'She didn't run away!' Vanessa snapped. 'She went to the

tree house. It was just a silly quarrel; she was upset because I wouldn't let her friend Nell stay the night. So she packed a picnic basket and put her cat in it and a blanket, and while I was cooking dinner, she ran to the tree house. I found her almost straight away. She's six; we argue sometimes, it didn't mean anything. This is different. She would never want to be away from home – from us – in the snow, alone.'

'So would you describe your daughter as naughty?' The detective looked up, his pen poised expectantly; the assumption that Alice was up to something mischievous seemed the focus of all their time and efforts. While the seconds ticked by, they weren't taking it seriously. She wanted to shake them, throw their notebooks in the fire: listen to me, something bad has happened to Alice, for God's sake do something.

She tried to keep breathing, focused on the rise and fall of Leo's shoulders as he sat in the chair beside the fireplace. Vanessa knew he should be in bed, but that would mean acknowledging the day was done, then soon afterwards it would be dawn, and a sense of dread would start to prevail. Only when it was the following day and Alice hadn't returned and it was too late would they start to realise she wasn't just being naughty, that she was in a ditch somewhere. She could hear it on the radio now: 'A six-year-old girl has gone missing in the small village of Kingston near Lewes. She vanished from the family home at seven o'clock yesterday evening and hasn't been seen since.' While they sat here asking her question after question, that vital time when Alice could be found alive was passing them by, like sand through a timer, and she was slipping further and further away. From the last time Vanessa ever saw her baby.

Everything was slowing down, the detective's voice, the fire crackling, the clock on the wall. It scared her that her hysteria was starting to pass; she felt herself becoming quieter and more withdrawn, her brain unable to handle the overwhelming emotions and beginning to shut down.

'She was just . . . she's just wilful.' It was a slip of the tongue, referring to her daughter in the past tense, but suddenly she began to feel vomit rise in her throat and she started to retch, running to the sink as her stomach spasmed over and over. She turned the tap on and splashed cold water on her face, taking gulps of air, trying to right herself, to keep it together, for Alice's sake.

'I don't understand why you're not looking for her.' She turned back to the detective. 'Why are we in here? There's been a snowstorm, she's six, she went out on her bike looking for her puppy. She followed her brother and got lost, or fell off; she's lying in a ditch somewhere, in this bitter cold, probably dying. Right now. For God's sake, please do something. I can't stand this sitting around doing nothing!'

They all looked up to see Richard walk in, his face burning red from the cold, his hat, coat, gloves, scarf all caked in snow.

'Nothing,' he said. 'There's police everywhere now, the whole fucking village is looking for her. She's vanished. It's minus two out there. Unless she's found somewhere to take shelter, there's no hope. Goddammit. Where the hell is she?' He smashed his fist on the counter, sending a champagne glass tumbling to the floor, where it shattered into splinters.

The detective stepped forward. 'Mr Hilton, I know this

is a very difficult time, but if we could possibly ask you a few questions . . .'

'I can't talk to you now, I need to get back out there!' Richard snapped.

'I know it's hard, but it won't take long and it could help us to find her. Please try not to think the worst. Most missing children are back home in twenty-four to forty-eight hours.' The man spoke matter-of-factly.

'I don't like sitting here doing nothing, we should all be out there – looking for her!' Richard barked.

'If you could just sit down so we can talk, we may be able to work out together where she might have gone.' The detective gestured to a chair at the kitchen table.

'I don't want to sit down. I only came back to see if she'd turned up.' Richard walked over to the fire, put his hands on the mantelpiece and leaned over the flames to try and warm himself. 'Well, go on then, what do you want to know?'

'Okay, Mr Hilton, please don't take offence at our line of questioning. We just need to try and get an idea of Alice's mindset before she went missing; we just want her home, as you all do.'

'Yes, yes, get on with it, will you,' Richard snapped, looking up at the clock.

'Has Alice argued with either you or your wife today?' the detective said carefully.

'She's six years old, for pity's sake; every day there is a disagreement of some sort.' Richard took his hat off and shook the snow from his hair.

'Okay, let me put it another way. Have there been any tensions at home lately that would make her frightened to come home?'

'If you're asking if I hit her, or if she'd be scared of me, then no. I've never raised a hand to her. She had a silly squabble with her mother and went off in a sulk.'

'So there was a squabble? Can I ask what it was about?'

Vanessa sighed. 'It was nothing. She didn't want to wear the dress I'd bought her for the party, but it was all fine in the end.'

The detective nodded. 'Okay, so could you tell me how the dispute played out?'

'Well, I was dealing with a problem with the champagne and didn't have time to sort it out myself, so our nanny helped Alice get dressed.'

'So Alice agreed to wear the dress in the end and you made up?' The only sound was the scratching of his pen on the notebook.

'Yes, the last time I saw her, she was running across the front of the house wearing the red dress. Alice is a strong character, but we are very close, we never fall out for long. Do you have children? You must know what it's like.'

The detective kept writing in his notebook without replying to her question. 'So am I understanding it right that your nanny was the last person to speak to her? That we know of?'

'I suppose so, yes,' Richard answered.

'And is she still here? Can we talk to her?' said the detective.

'No, she was here all day looking after the children while I got ready, but she left just before the party began. She's local, though, she lives in the village,' Vanessa said quietly.

'So she left around the time Alice went missing? And

did you speak to her about your daughter when she left? She was helping her into her dress, you said?'

'Yes, she got Alice changed. I wanted her to stay and look after the children during the party, but she was in rather a hurry to go; she had dinner guests coming. And I was stressed about the champagne. It sounds so unimportant now, but it had been such a hectic day. Everything had gone wrong.'

He nodded, looking down at his notes. 'What is her name?'

'Dorothy Novell. She lives in one of the terraced cottages at the end of our driveway, Yew Tree Cottage.'

The detective turned to his colleague. 'Can you go to Dorothy Novell's home and bring her here now. Wake her if you need to.' He ripped out the piece of paper he had been scribbling on and handed it over.

Leo watched him go, then stood up and started making towards the door.

'Where are you going, Leo?' Richard asked.

'Just to change my jumper, it's wet.' Leo was deathly pale and his teeth were chattering.

'Come straight back,' Richard barked.

'He will, Richard,' said Vanessa. While her husband had never laid a hand on Alice, he hadn't been so restrained with Leo. She didn't want the fact that he sometimes hit their son coming out, putting a spotlight on their family, wasting time pointing the finger at them rather than looking for Alice.

'I really don't know how this is helping,' Richard said, scowling at the detective. 'Dorothy doesn't have anything to do with this.'

'I'm sure you're right. I'm just trying to map out Alice's

movements as much as possible. Could you tell me, when you saw her run across the front of the house, which direction did your daughter go?'

'My wife saw her. She was heading for the tree house in the front garden. It was the first place Vanessa looked, and when she wasn't there, that was when she started to worry.'

'And where was your son at this point?'

Vanessa took a sip of water. 'Richard had sent him out on his bike to fetch Bobby James from The Vicarage to help with the lights. We think Alice may have followed him; if she was in the tree house, she would have heard us say that Leo was going over there. She couldn't find Snowy, her puppy, and maybe Alice thought she had run back to The Vicarage where she was born. But Richard retraced Leo's steps a dozen times and there's no sign of her.

'Okay, it would be helpful to talk to your son about his journey there, if that's okay. And to speak to Bobby James as well, to see if he saw Alice at all.'

'Of course,' said Richard, walking to the kitchen door. 'Leo! What are you doing? Can you come down here?' he yelled.

'Richard, go easy on him,' said Vanessa quietly. 'He's pretty cut up about all this. He told me he blames himself.'

'Why would he blame himself?' said the detective, frowning.

Richard shot Vanessa a look and shrugged. 'Because she was probably right behind him and he didn't even notice. He lives in another world.'

'Why would he be looking behind him for Alice? We don't even know that she was following him. You're always so hard on him!' Vanessa started to cry again.

As silence fell on the room, Vanessa looked up to see the detective's eyes fixed on her.

'Okay, can we go back to the tree house?' he said. 'That's at the front of the house, is it?'

Vanessa nodded. 'Yes, on the front lawn, quite near the driveway. If she was in there, there's every chance she would have seen Leo leaving; he would have been lit up by the car headlights that were coming in for the party. I remember it was exactly seven when I saw her run towards it. I looked at my watch because I heard Alfie's gunshots go off again and I was worried they wouldn't stop before the party started.'

'Alfie's gunshots?' The detective's ears pricked up.

Richard shot his wife a look. 'Alfie James, one of my tenant farmers, had to shoot his herd today. There's been gunfire going off all day.'

'Were there gunshots when Alice disappeared?'

'If you're implying that Alfie shot my daughter by mistake, he wasn't hunting, he wasn't firing at rabbits in the woods, he was shooting cattle at point-blank range.' He picked up his keys. 'I'm going back outside.'

When Richard had left the room, the detective turned back to Vanessa.

'Would it be possible to look in Alice's bedroom?'

'I suppose so,' said Vanessa. She led the way out into the hall and past the enormous Christmas tree and grand piano at the bottom of the stairs. As she looked up the vast staircase, she felt the floor below her start to move. She reached out to grab the banister, feeling unsteady.

'Are you all right, Vanessa? Here, let me help you.'

She turned to see Dorothy standing at the front door.

It was only six hours since Vanessa had last seen her, but her entire world had changed in that time. Dorothy looked sleepy-eyed, and her hair, usually scraped back in a neat ponytail, was unbrushed. Normally very well put together when she came to look after the children, she had obviously dressed in a hurry when the police arrived and was wearing jeans, a creased jumper and trainers with no socks. She had no make up on and she looked very different, thought Vanessa; like a stranger. Vanessa felt a surge of irrational anger towards her. It was no use her being here now; if she had just stayed when she had been asked to, none of this would have happened. Alice would be asleep in her bed and the party would be in full swing. Instead Vanessa was living a nightmare. She wished the police hadn't brought Dorothy here.

She turned away, ignoring her, and started to climb the stairs, pausing several times to catch her breath. As she looked up at the landing, the memory of the last time she had spoken to her little girl, standing at the top of the stairs looking down at her in her grass-stained dungarees, made her body icy cold. She could hear her own voice saying the last words she had ever spoken to her: 'I'll be back in five minutes, and I expect you to be dressed and ready for the party.'

Suddenly the front door banged and someone called out for Detective Inspector Mills.

'Here!' he replied as Vanessa rushed to follow him back down the stairs.

'What is it? Have you found her?' Vanessa asked frantically.

'I'm afraid there's been an incident.'

'What are you talking about, lad?' DI Mills snapped.

'A man's been crushed by a tractor in the field behind The Vicarage – Alfred James, I understand his name is. His son Bobby found him and managed to pull him out, but I'm afraid he's dead. My officers found Bobby in the snow by the body.'

'Oh God, no,' Vanessa said, collapsing onto the stairs.

The young policeman glanced at Vanessa before taking a breath and continuing. 'Bobby James is saying he saw Alice just before he found his father and that her head was bleeding. But when she saw the accident, she ran off. He said he doesn't know where she went.'

Vanessa looked at the policeman, then let out a primal scream as her little girl's beautiful face burned through her mind's eye. The windows rattled with the returning snowstorm that her daughter was probably lost in, in her red party dress and shoes. Vanessa stared at Dorothy with an overwhelming sick-inducing feeling that she would never see her daughter alive again.

Chapter Twenty-One

Vanessa

Friday, 22 December 2017

'Have you written your statement, Mr Hilton?' Detective Inspector Hatton looked at Leo across the breakfast table, their coffee cups and plates of toast barely touched.

'What statement, Leo?' Vanessa asked.

Leo let out such a heavy sigh that she knew she must have asked him that question already. 'For the press conference this morning, Mum. To appeal for information about Sienna.'

She looked at her son, his eyes bloodshot, his hair unkempt, his shirt crumpled. 'What about Sienna? What's wrong, Leo? You look terrible.'

Leo put his head in his hands. 'She's missing. I've been out looking for her since first light, Mum, walking through the woods, driving around the lanes, stopping the car, calling for her, driving on, shouting her name over and over.'

His mobile phone started to ring and he jumped up and walked out of the room to answer it. 'Hi, Philip. Yes, I'm aware of the deadline, but things are quite difficult here . . .'

'What does he mean, he's looking for Sienna? What's happened?'

'Your granddaughter is missing, Mrs Hilton, but we're doing everything we can to find her. Please try not to worry.'

Vanessa felt tears sting her eyes, and she looked away and out of the kitchen window onto the bright winter's morning rising over the lake. Her brain felt like a thick fog; she had lain awake most of the night, drifting in and out of sleep, listening to Helen crying.

She remembered now. Sienna was missing. But every time someone reminded her, it felt like finding out all over again. She was exhausted, but sleep had been impossible. The police had stayed in the house all night, their walkie-talkies receiving updates, people coming and going into the early hours, talking and slamming doors. At one point she had dozed off into a nightmare about the lake turning to ice. Alice had been trapped underneath it in her red coat, and Vanessa had been too weak to crack the ice to get to her. The front door had slammed so loudly it had woken her up with a start. Every time she fell asleep, her brain reset to the night they lost Alice.

'Do you think we should call a doctor, get her something to help her sleep?' She had heard her son's voice on the landing outside her room.

'I don't want to sleep, I can't sleep until I have my little girl back. Where is she, Leo?' she had shouted. Leo had promised he would keep looking, taken her back to her bedroom, but she could not be calmed or soothed. At first light, they had all given up trying to sleep and gone out again to look for Sienna.

Leo walked back into the kitchen, and threw his phone down on the counter. He let out a groan of frustration and poured himself a coffee. 'I can't believe this is happening,' he mumbled.

The detective cleared his throat. 'Mr Hilton, if we could discuss your statement for the press conference. The main point to stress is that we want to encourage you and your wife to be yourselves, so Sienna recognises your tone. This press conference is for her, after all; that's who we're appealing to. We want to reassure her that she's not in any trouble. Something along the lines of please come home, we miss you terribly, you've done nothing wrong.'

Leo frowned. 'What if she's been taken? Aren't we addressing the person who has taken her?'

DI Hatton looked at him. 'If you're referring to Bobby James, we are questioning him at the moment, but we don't believe he knows where she is.'

'Obviously you're not getting anywhere with him or we'd have Sienna back by now. I'm referring to the fact that I've heard the public appeal you made this morning and the statement suggests that Sienna has run away. She's seven years old; where would she run away to?' Leo snapped.

Vanessa listened to the conversation with rising dread. It appeared to her that police procedure had not changed much in fifty years. They still seemed to assume that someone in the family was guilty, and the press conference would be an opportunity for the police to watch Leo and Helen – analyse their behaviour and body language to see if they were hiding anything – as it was to reach out to the public. The way the detective was looking at Leo was identical to the way Detective Inspector Mills had looked at Richard on the night Alice went missing. She felt a stab of guilt that she hadn't warned her son about it, but there was little point. He didn't listen to her anyway, and the idea that he'd had anything to do with Sienna's disappearance was ridiculous. Leo was far from perfect, but his love for his daughter was beyond reproach.

'At the moment, we are addressing Sienna.' DI Hatton continued. 'We're appealing for her to come home. We are also appealing for anyone in the area at the time she went missing to come forward with information, however insignificant they feel it might be. The purpose is to promote public awareness that Sienna is missing, issue a description and try and get people calling in.'

Leo hung his head. He didn't say anything, but reached into the drawer and pulled out two paracetamol, which he gulped down with a glass of water.

DI Hatton looked at him, then continued. 'The DCI leading the investigation will be sitting in the press conference with you. He will make an appeal to Sienna or anyone who might know where she is to get in touch. After he speaks, he will give a number the public can call. We have a team of people manning the phones.'

'Are you expecting many calls?' Vanessa asked.

Leo's phone rang again. He looked at the number and put it on silent.

'You get a lot of time-wasters. It's a case of sorting the wheat from the chaff, but if something solid comes through, there would be a very quick response, and if someone phones to say they've seen her, we'd be there in minutes.'

Leo nodded and started to pace. 'I'm getting a lot of calls from friends and villagers wanting to help. We've had no confirmation of any clear search plans. Many of them have decided not to go to work today to help us, but they're just standing around waiting.'

'Once we've done the press conference, we will start the search. It's just being planned now, and we will update everyone as soon as we're able. We are aware people are waiting to help, but they need to be briefed. We need to cover the area methodically and they need to know what to look for and how to deal with anything they do find.'

'So Bobby James isn't saying anything? Why was he here at the house?'

'I'm not able to discuss that, but he's saying he knows nothing about Sienna's disappearance.'

Leo closed his eyes and rubbed his temple.

'Mr Hilton, when we get back, it would be helpful if we could go through your bank statements,' said DI Hatton.

Leo looked at him aghast, the colour draining from his cheeks. 'Why do you need to do that?'

'The family liaison officer can go through them with you – yours and Helen's and your mother's, if possible. We need to see if there has been any unusual activity on your accounts, if Sienna took one of your cards or someone else has stolen them without you realising. If anyone has withdrawn money, we can find out where that was, and there is usually CCTV at bank machines.'

'I only have one bank card and I know it's in my wallet. I used it last night to get petrol.'

'All the same, we need to go through everything. There could be a forgotten card in a drawer.'

'There are no cards I've forgotten.'

An awkward silence fell between them. The detective broke it.

'Well, we can discuss this with you and your wife later. It's just a precautionary measure. Is Helen on her way down, do you know?'

'Poor Helen must be utterly exhausted,' said Vanessa. 'She seemed to be up all night.'

'Yes, she's coming now,' said Leo.

They all stood and went into the hallway. Vanessa looked up to see Helen walking down the stairs with a police officer by her side. She was so pale the veins in her forehead were visible, and it was clear she had been crying. She was shaking violently despite the heavy woollen cardigan wrapped around her, and was clutching a sodden handkerchief.

As she reached Leo, he attempted to put his arms around her, but she flinched and walked towards the front door without saying anything.

'I don't know how long we'll be, Mum. The police liaison officer is going to stay and make sure you're okay.'

'Do you not want me to come?' asked Vanessa.

'No, you stay here and hold the fort, in case Sienna turns up.' Leo followed Helen out to the police car that was waiting for them on the driveway.

Vanessa watched the cars go, the house suddenly turning from a buzz of activity to an empty, silent shell. Then she turned and walked back into the empty hallway, the only thing left propped against the wall was the portrait of Alice that Helen had asked the removal men to leave.

She stopped and stared at it, then lowered herself down onto the floor, ran her finger across the little girl's cheek and began to cry.

Chapter Twenty-Two

Willow

Friday, 22 December 2017

Willow drove past the throng of journalists at the end of Yew Tree Manor's driveway and watched the two policemen in fluorescent waistcoats trying to keep them back. Normally she had no trouble parking, but the sea of reporters desperately trying to get an update, or a glimpse of Helen and Leo Hilton, was clogging up the the whole of Yew Tree Lane.

She finally found a space at the top of the path down to The Vicarage and turned off her engine. She put her head in her hands and took several deep breaths. After a sleepless night worrying about her father and Sienna, she had woken early. She had absolutely no idea how she was supposed to find Nell; she didn't even know if she was still alive. But her father's comments, accusing her of having met Nell, made her suspect that she was.

But where was she? Obviously Bobby hadn't been able to find her, so what hope did Willow have? She had phoned the local council when they opened in an effort to find out how to trace someone when you have virtually nothing to go on, except their childhood name and address. She had spoken to a woman named Claire who had said she was fairly new and had no idea but that she would ask a colleague her advice and call her back.

Not wanting to go into work early, she had instead driven over to The Vicarage. She didn't know why she wanted to go there, but somehow she felt that being near Bobby and Nell's childhood home would make her feel closer to them and help her think more clearly.

As she climbed out of the car, she was hit by the freezing temperature of the early-morning air. Her mobile started to ring and she looked down at it. Charlie's name flashed on the screen, but she returned it to her pocket and let it go to voicemail. Her head was spinning, and after her father's arrest, she knew Charlie would be full of questions she didn't have the strength to answer. Her thoughts kept darting to Sienna, now missing for an entire night, in freezing temperatures she couldn't have survived. She pulled on the walking boots she always kept in the back seat, buttoned up her coat and wrapped her scarf twice around her neck. Then she started down the ice-covered track, the hedgerow to her right hiding Yew Tree Manor. The sounds and smells of the countryside surrounded her, and she made herself breathe in the crisp morning air to try and calm herself down.

When she reached the end of the hedgerow, she looked to the right and saw it: the majestic Georgian manor house two fields away, surrounded by police cars and removal lorries. The Hiltons' land stretched as far as the eye could see, The Vicarage the only break in the estate. She took a deep breath, feeling as if she were about to see a long-lost friend, and as she cleared the hedgerow, The Vicarage came into view.

She was surprised to see two diggers already poised by the little house, as if waiting with bated breath for the green light. Bright yellow demolition signs were attached to each wall in anticipation; Leo Hilton wasn't wasting any time.

She had been here only once before, on a site visit with Mike, and had made herself stay detached as they walked around it, working out the logistics of the demolition. She had not let herself think of it as her father's childhood home. Nobody had lived in it since then, and it had gone to rack and ruin. Ivy was crawling up every wall, and there was no glass left in the windows.

Now, after her talk with her dad, she turned and faced it full on, as if forcing herself to look at her father's childhood home for the first time. It was smaller up close than it seemed looking at it from the edge of the Hiltons' land, and despite its desperate state, it was still brimming with charm: a peaked porch roof, small windows with thick sills she could imagine adorned with flower boxes, and a veranda wrapping around the entire front of the house. It had been painted white at some point in time, but was now so covered in dirt it had turned almost black.

Slowly Willow walked up to the heavy wooden door, which was hanging off its iron hinges. After several pushes, she managed to lift it open. She waited for her eyes to adjust to the dark, and turned on the torch on her mobile phone to look around, shining it into the corners as she stepped inside.

There was no sign of the cosy home her father had occasionally spoken of; no hint of the life that had been lived here by Alfie and Bobby and Nell. Nothing but a damp, empty space, a stone floor that had crumbled over time and a hole in the wall where the fireplace had been. A large chunk of the roof was missing, and pigeons were nesting in what was left of it.

She pictured her father here as a boy, possibly sitting at a table by the window, or by the fire with his sister. Willow recalled the photo of the dark-haired, blue-eyed girl she had found in her father's flat and tried to picture her in the space where she stood now. She was still completely thrown by him accusing her of having met Nell; how was that going to happen without his help? Had Nell told him she'd been in touch with her? Had she missed an email or letter at her flat because she'd been so busy lately? He had been so adamant about it; it had seemed impossible to him that their paths hadn't crossed. But how?

The damp of the cottage started making her feel sick again, but as she walked to the door to get out, she realised it had jammed shut. She pushed her shoulder against it, struggling to get it open, and felt her tears returning. Wherever she went, whoever she was with, however much she pretended she was all right, she always felt as she did now: cold, alone, pushing against life and never feeling any sense of peace. Eventually, after one final shove, the door gave way and she fell out into the winter morning. As the cold air rushed into her system, she began to hurry away, trying to get the sadness of the house out of her system.

Soon she began to realise that she was walking, in reverse, the path Alice Hilton would have walked that night. As she headed in the direction of Yew Tree Manor, she pictured the girl in the red dress a little way in front of her, stomping through the snow looking for her puppy. Reaching the hedgerow at the end of the field, Willow found a break in the foliage and pushed her way through, the thick branches catching at her coat and scratching her hand. As she emerged onto the field at the end of Yew Tree Manor, she immediately saw the vast willow tree, her namesake, where she knew – from Nell's note to Alice – that Nell had buried the tin box with the notebook in. But why did she have the notebook in the first place? thought Willow. And why did she bury it where nobody would find it?

The willow tree dominated the landscape, a lone figure marking the end of The Vicarage land and the start of the Yew Tree estate. Its long arms seemed to stretch out and draw her in.

As she listened to the sound of her own heavy breathing, something caught her eye at the bottom of the tree. A plastic tag, pushed down into the roots. She walked over to it and bent down, plucking it out of the ground. She recognised what it was immediately: a marker from the Earth Excavation Report with the company name 'Pre-Contstruct Archaeology' on it. She put it in her pocket; more proof if he tried to deny it.

She pressed on through the woods towards the house, unsure what was drawing her in. The thought of little Sienna missing and the anguish Helen and Leo must be going through suddenly hit her hard as she reached the mouth of the woods and saw three police cars parked outside the house. She suddenly felt angry with herself for going to Yew Tree when the family were going through so much; she didn't belong there, and it wasn't her place. She turned back, retracing her steps until she reached her parked car, the events of the past twenty-four hours catching up with her as she scrambled to find her keys in her bag. It had been wrong to come here; she felt panicked and overwhelmed after her conversation with her dad. Finally she clambered into the safety of her car and, as she struggled to catch her breath, a police car roared past her with Helen Hilton in the back seat. Whenever they had met in the past, Helen had been eager to please, offering them tea, smiling, but always distant with Willow, disappearing as swiftly as she had appeared. Now, as she raced past, she looked entirely different: drawn and haunted.

Willow's phone suddenly rang, making her jump. It was a local number.

'Hello? Willow James speaking.'

'Hello, it's Claire from Lewes Council; we spoke earlier.'

'Yes, thank you for calling me back so quickly.'

'Well, I'm afraid I don't have much news for you. I spoke to my colleague, and apparently they're not allowed to give out people's married surnames – it's due to the privacy laws.'

'Well, can you find out if she was adopted or went into care after her father died? It's my aunt, we're family. I've got her maiden name.'

'I'm sorry, I can't. But if you have proof you're family, you could apply to the court for access to her records.'

'I don't have time for that. I need to find her quickly. All I know is that she was sent away to a sanatorium in the late sixties. But I don't know what happened to her after that.'

'Well, I'm no expert, but could you try the sanatorium records? Sometimes they were converted into hospitals and still keep their old records on site. If you're family, they may agree to let you see them, but you'd probably have to go there in person, with ID. Do you know where it is?'

'Mayfield Sanatorium in Portsmouth, I think,' said

Willow, already trying to work out if it would be possible for her to take the day off. Mike had emailed to say that Leo had requested the planning meeting go ahead without him, and that she wouldn't be needed, freeing up her whole morning.

As Willow ended the call, a loud bang behind her made her jump and spin round. Dorothy, the woman she had met at the village hall meeting yesterday, was putting her rubbish out in front of her cottage at the end of the Yew Tree driveway. Willow got out of her car and waved.

Dorothy frowned and looked at her.

'It's Willow, from the planning meeting yesterday.'

'Oh yes, Willow, hello.'

Willow crossed the road towards her. 'I'm sorry to bother you. I was wondering if I could have a quick word?' Dorothy looked very different today, she thought, tired and pale.

'It's not really a good time, I'm afraid. Peter's not well.'

'I'm sorry to hear that. I hope it's nothing serious?' Willow asked.

'No, just a migraine, but I'd best get back to him.' Dorothy turned and walked away.

'Isn't it awful about Sienna?' Willow called after her.

'Yes, it is. Poor little thing, I hope she's all right. Peter and I are worried sick.' The woman shook her head and continued walking back towards the house.

'Dorothy, can I ask you something, just quickly?' Willow walked towards the house as Dorothy turned back, letting out a curt huff. 'You mentioned at the meeting yesterday a graveyard next to The Vicarage. I started looking into it but I can't find any evidence of it, but my father remembers it too.'

'Your father?' said Dorothy. 'Is he a local man?'

Willow felt her cheeks flush. She had never told anyone in Kingston who her father was, but it felt now like something she needed to share if she was to have any hope of finding Nell.

'Yes, he used to live at The Vicarage; his name is Bobby James.'

'Bobby James is your father?' Dorothy stared at Willow wide-eyed and visibly shocked. 'But you've been working for Leo, does he know?'

Willow frowned, slightly taken aback. 'No, he doesn't.'

'Well, I don't think he'd be very happy if he did. You need to be careful, Willow.'

'Careful? What do you mean?' Willow felt uncomfortable suddenly.

'Because of Bobby's history with the family, there's a lot of bad blood there. Vanessa still thinks he knows what happened to Alice.' Dorothy stared at her intently.

'But my father had nothing to do with Alice's disappearance. Or Sienna's, for that matter. If I can just find his sister, Nell, I think she may know something about the night Alice went missing.'

'Nell? Nell doesn't know anything,' Dorothy snapped.

'You sound very sure. Do you know Nell?' said Willow, slightly taken aback. 'Or do you have any idea how I can get hold of her?'

Dorothy frowned at Willow. 'What do you mean, how you can get hold of her?'

'I need to track her down somehow, but I've got no idea where to start,' said Willow, baffled by Dorothy's question; the last twenty-four hours were playing havoc with her brain, she was exhausted. 'I've found a letter Nell wrote when Alice disappeared, which makes me think she may have some information that could help my dad.'

'I wouldn't start digging up the past, Willow. You don't want to get on the wrong side of that family. I should know.'

Willow stared at the woman, shocked. 'On the wrong side of the Hiltons, you mean? Dorothy, please talk to me. They've arrested Dad again.' Willow felt her voice break and looked up to see Peter frowning down at her from the upstairs window.

Dorothy shook her head. 'I know, I'm sorry, love, he was a lovely lad. He had nothing to do with Alice's disappearance. Vanessa blames everyone but herself for her little girl going missing. She let everyone in the village know that she asked me to stay that night and look after Alice and I refused. And they believed her, nobody ever questions a woman who has lost a child; she is untouchable.'

Willow leaned in, intrigued, the freezing wind biting at her cheeks. 'I'm sorry, Dorothy,' she said quietly, 'that must have been awful.' Willow looked up again at the window, where Peter was still glaring down at them, and he started to walk down the stairs towards them.

Dorothy nodded, seemingly relaxing for a moment. 'Of course, what she didn't tell anyone was that I had been there all day looking after the children, from seven in the morning until seven in the evening. I was exhausted, and I had to get home; I had my sister coming to dinner. It hadn't occurred to her to invite me, of course. I worked for Vanessa for ten years – I knew Alice from the day she was born – and Peter had worked tirelessly for them as their gardener; nothing was too much trouble when it came to Richard. For a year I had to listen to nothing but preparations for the party: the house decorations, what they were eating, wearing, the invitations. Everyone was invited, the villagers, all their friends, all of Richard's suppliers, everyone but Peter and I. We put up with so much from that family, and we thought they cared about us, but we weren't good enough to be one of them, even for a single night.'

She looked up, her eyes wide with anger at the memory of it. 'Until the moment she realised how much she needed me. Just as the party was starting, the penny dropped. And I admit it, I was pleased as her panic set in. I was glad that me not being there was finally going to make an impact. But so help me God, I never thought anything would happen to Alice. I loved that little girl.'

Suddenly the front door opened and Peter shouted out to his wife. 'Darling? What are you doing out here?'

Willow glanced up. He didn't look very well, she thought. 'Nothing, Willow was just leaving, Peter. Go home,' said Dorothy, pulling her cardigan tight around herself and turning to walk back inside. 'I know Bobby didn't hurt Alice, or start the fire – they do anything to protect their own family – but you need to stay out of it; you can't change the past. And you're wrong about Nell. She doesn't know what happened. You need to leave her in peace.'

'Wait, you know about the fire? Please tell me where Nell is. Don't go!' said Willow desperately.

Dorothy reached the door, and Peter glared at Willow as his wife walked inside. 'Don't come back here please, Willow,' he said, before closing the door to Yew Tree Cottage.

Chapter Twenty-Three
Nell

February 1970

Nell stared at the door seeing a stream of visitors coming into the ward, as they did on the last Sunday of every month. It was the third time she had sat there hoping with every beat of her breaking heart that this would be the day Bobby or Dad would appear, smiling at her, with arms full of presents. She daydreamed about them sitting by her bed, holding her hand and telling her why it had taken them so long to get to her; why they had not written.

She lay down, turned her back to the door and pulled the blankets over her head. She couldn't bear to watch the other girls' parents arriving any more, or the prying eyes staring at her as she looked down at her hands, trying not to cry. She had overheard one of the nurses talking about her when they thought she was asleep: 'Poor little thing. It's a long bus ride for some people and they just don't have the money or can't take the time off work. It's all right for the adults, but for the children it's terrible. A few of them just get dumped here by families who have twelve other children and can't afford to keep them. No one ever visits them, or comes to collect them, even when they're better. From here they go off to the children's home.'

Nell had started to hate the sanatorium. At first she'd seen it as a nice place to rest for a while until she got better, but it had started to feel like a prison from which she would never escape. She hated the sounds of the place: the trolley being wheeled round on the hard parquet floor with the medicine or the bed baths; the constant coughing of the other girls. The nights terrified her the most, because it was at night that the poorliest girls died. One day they would be there, and the next morning their bed would be empty and they would be gone. The nurses would lie to her to try and make her feel less frightened, and say the girl had gone home, but after a while she realised the truth.

'Hello, Nell,' said her friend Heather's mother as she stood over her bed. She was always kind to Nell on visiting day, and brought her little presents too, but it made Nell feel almost worse that they pitied her. She could imagine them talking about her on their way home, about how cruel her parents were not to visit. She hated the idea of them thinking badly of Dad and Bobby.

'Hello, Mrs Parks,' said Nell.

'Please call me Emma; we're friends now, aren't we?' She put some sweets on the bed next to Nell before sitting down and stroking her hair. 'Are you all right, Nell? Heather said you'd not been eating. You must eat, or you won't get better.'

'I'm okay,' Nell said quietly, not wanting to look at the woman in case it made her cry. Emma was the loveliest lady in the world: kind, softly spoken and beautiful, just as she dreamed her own mother would have been.

She hated herself for it, but she had prayed earlier in the

week that Heather wouldn't get better and leave. Sister Morgan had come to Heather's bedside and said that if her X-ray was okay, she could go home with her parents that Sunday. Heather had gone to the X-ray department with a smile on her face, but an hour later she had come back crying so much she couldn't be comforted by anyone. Eventually her gut-wrenching sobs stopped when she fell asleep.

'Is Heather all right?' she asked now, turning to face Emma. 'She was very upset before.'

'I know, they thought she might be coming home today, but unfortunately she's had a relapse,' said Heather's mother.

'What's a relapse?' Nell looked over at Heather, who was sitting up talking to her father.

'The TB has come back, I'm afraid. But I hear you're doing really well and might be able to go home soon.'

Nell looked up at her. 'It's my fault about Heather,' she said, starting to cry. 'I was so scared about her leaving that I prayed to God she wouldn't go. It's my fault she's poorly again. I deserve it that nobody comes to see me. I'm a horrible, horrible person.'

She buried her head in her pillow as Emma stroked her hair. 'I'm not surprised you want her to stay,' Emma said. 'She's your friend. You are not a horrible person, Nell. You've been very brave.'

Nell turned and looked up at her just as a woman appeared at the door behind them, the very last of the visitors. She had red hair, and was dressed in a cardigan, a long skirt and black shoes. Nell had a feeling she knew her, but couldn't think where from. She had definitely never seen her at the sanatorium before, and her heart began to race as the woman looked around the ward. Finally, her eyes fell on Nell, and she began to walk towards her, her shoes tapping on the wooden floor as Nell's heart began to race.

'I'm sure you'll get some news soon,' Emma continued. 'I know they're trying to contact your family. We asked about you as we were worried, and they said they had been notified someone was coming to collect you.'

'Hello, Nell,' said the woman, who was now standing at the end of Nell's bed. She was pale and was wearing red lipstick, and she was clutching a purse nervously in her hands. Nell stared at her, her eyes still blurred with tears, trying to work out who she was. 'Do you remember me?' the woman said, smiling.

The visitor looked at Heather's mother and half smiled. 'Hello,' she said rather curtly.

Emma nodded at her, then patted Nell's hand and went back to her daughter's bedside.

Nell sat up, stunned to see she had a visitor. The woman sat down next to her awkwardly and laid a teddy bear on the bed. 'This is for you, Nell. How are you feeling?'

Nell looked at the woman, drinking her in. Someone was sitting on her bed at last, but it wasn't who she'd thought it would be. She didn't know where Dad and Bobby were; why had this woman she hardly knew come to see her?

'I'm all right. I'm feeling better, I suppose,' she said, scared to ask any questions in case the woman ran away.

'Well, that's wonderful news,' said the woman, playing with her hands nervously, before finally answering the question buzzing around in Nell's head. 'So, I was wondering if you'd like to come and stay with me and my husband for a while. I called a week ago to see how you were and they think you're ready to go home. Would you like that, Nell?'

Nell's head was racing; she didn't know what to make of this visitor. 'Why can't Dad come and get me?'

The woman looked down at her hands and waited for a while before she replied. 'Your father had an accident, Nell.'

Nell felt tears sting her eyes. So this was why he hadn't come. 'What sort of accident?' she asked.

'It was an accident on the farm. It was nobody's fault.' The woman looked away.

'But he'll be all right?' Nell pleaded, knowing already that he wasn't all right.

'No, Nell, I'm sorry. He's in heaven with your mummy now.'

Nell felt the cold room fill with heat. She pulled her knees up and buried her head in them and started to sob. She tried to muffle the sound as the woman put her arms around her, but she knew everyone could hear her. The sanatorium was normally deathly quiet, apart from the coughing and the murmuring of the doctors on their rounds, but on visiting days, the stairs and corridors were full of people and a cacophony of chatter filled the room. Now, everyone fell silent.

She didn't know how long she cried for, but eventually she ran out of steam. She held her breath for a long time, wishing she could go back, just five minutes, to when she thought Dad hadn't come because he was too busy or couldn't afford the train ticket. She closed her eyes and an image of her brother flashed in front of her eyes.

'Where's Bobby?' she managed.

'He's gone away for a little while.'

'Can't I go and stay with him?'

'Unfortunately not, they only allow boys where he is. But I'm sure he'll be home soon.'

'Can I see Alice?' said Nell.

'We'll talk about that later. Let's get you dressed. I'll ask the nurse to get your things together.'

As the woman walked away, Emma looked over at Nell and smiled kindly. 'Are you going now, Nell?' she asked.

'I think so,' said Nell, wiping her tears away with her nightie and climbing out of bed on wobbly legs. She picked up the teddy bear the woman had given her and slowly walked over to Heather, who was lying down looking very pale.

'Thank you for looking after me, Heather. I really hope you feel better soon.' She put the teddy down next to Heather's face.

Heather smiled. 'Thanks, Nell. Will you write to me? You're so good at writing now.'

'Okay.'

'Right, here you go, Nell. Do you want to pull your curtain round while you get dressed?' The woman had returned and was smiling at her.

As Nell pulled on the clothes her father had packed for her, she noticed they smelt of The Vicarage still, soapy from when Bobby had washed them in the bath and a little bit smoky from being dried by the fire; a tiny piece of home.

'We will really miss Nell,' Emma said to the woman on the other side of the curtain, as Nell pulled her woolly jumper over her head. 'She's a lovely girl. Can we get your address so Heather can write to her?'

There was a long pause. 'Of course, that would be lovely. It's Yew Tree Cottage, Kingston.'

'And your name?'

'Yes, of course. My name is Dorothy, Dorothy Novell.'

Chapter Twenty-Four
Bella

January 1946

'Where is my son?' Bella glared at the officer behind the counter of Lewes police station. She had just been released from her unbearably long, uncomfortable night in the cells for contempt of court.

'He's with his guardian,' the man said, finally looking up from his paperwork.

'Guardian? He's my son, why did you let someone else take him?' She tried to keep the hysteria from her voice.

'He said he was the boy's grandfather,' said the policeman.

'I'm his mother,' Bella cried. 'You had no right to hand him over without my consent.'

'We had every right, young lady. It would have been advisable to have thought of your son before insulting the judge presiding over your mother's case. I would be grateful if I were you; the boy would have been taken into care were it not for his grandfather.'

'I didn't insult him,' Bella said quietly, looking at him. She knew she was utterly powerless. If she made a scene, she could be arrested again, and then she would have no chance of getting Alfie back before Wilfred Hilton sent him away somewhere she would never find him.

She walked outside, blinking in the winter sunlight, and looked down the road towards the courthouse, remembering her last moments with her mother. She had no idea if Tessa would take the deadly nightshade berries she had given her, but it had been a last act of love; to let her know that she understood the depths of her pain. It was the hardest thing she had ever had to do, but having spent just one night in a cold, damp, foul-smelling cell, she knew more than ever that it had been the right decision.

She knew what she had to do next, but she had no clue as to how she would get to Yew Tree Manor, or how she would steal Alfie back. The house was full of servants, and Wilfred would have made sure he was hidden away somewhere she couldn't find him.

Bella sat down on the steps of the police station and pulled her knees up to her chest, trying to cocoon herself away from a world she couldn't cope with. She didn't know how long she sat there for, but when she eventually looked up, she couldn't feel her hands or face for the cold. She glanced at the clock on the spire above her. She had to get back to Portsmouth soon, or her employer would not take her back and then she would be out on the streets. She had no money for the train. She needed her mother; she was utterly lost without her.

'Miss James,' said a female voice from above her on the steps. 'I'm sorry to trouble you. I've been in a café over the road, waiting for them to release you. Would you care for some breakfast? You must be hungry.'

Bella looked up. She recognised the girl standing there, but could not remember where from.

'Who are you?' she asked, starting to shake from the cold.

'We met yesterday, at court. My name is Milly Green, I'm a reporter at the *Sussex Times*.' The girl was blowing warm breath into her cold hands whilst hopping from foot to foot. 'I was in court yesterday when you spoke about your mother and Dr Jenkins. I'm hoping you might want to speak to me about the case and give your side of the story. Now that the trial is over, we can print it. I know she has always protested her innocence.'

Bella shook her head. 'If the trial is over, what is the point? She has been found guilty in case you weren't there for the verdict.'

'I was there, Miss James, every day of the trial. I listened to what you said, and I believe you, and our readers will too. Your mother deserves to have her voice heard. And there is still the chance of an appeal. Particularly if we can start a campaign. Shall we go and warm up inside?'

Bella nodded, weak from the cold and lack of food. She stood up slowly, wrapping her mother's shawl around her.

They crossed the road and entered a small, cosy café. 'Would you like a cup of tea and some toast?' Milly asked.

'Just tea, thank you.' Bella pulled out a chair and lowered herself down onto it.

The bell over the door tinkled, and she looked up as a young family came in from the cold: a pretty woman and her husband, with a small child. The husband had lost his leg from the knee down and was struggling with his crutches. He cursed to himself as the door swung into him, and his little girl looked up at him and then cowered behind her mother. Bella moved a chair out of his way, and he looked up and thanked her with his eyes, which were dull and lifeless.

'There you go,' Milly said, putting a pot of tea down on the table and pouring her a cup.

Bella picked it up and took a sip. It was too hot, but it felt good to hold something warm. She was shaking, frozen through. 'Thank you,' she said quietly. 'I didn't know there were women reporters.'

'Well, there aren't many of us,' said Milly, taking her coat off and putting it on the back of her chair before sitting down. 'I only get to go to court and cover the crime stories because so many of the male reporters didn't return from the front. Before the war I was on women's features or covering the local fete or Women's Institute stories.'

Bella nodded. 'I think since the war ended it's been very hard for a lot of women to go back to how things were before.'

Milly paused. 'I'm very sorry about your mother's sentence.'

Bella nursed the cup as the warmth spread through her frozen fingers. Eventually she looked up. 'My mother didn't hurt Evelyn Hilton. She believed in natural births, letting nature take its course. She would never have cut Evelyn like that; she believed in waiting until a baby was ready to come into the world. She would sit all night, for days sometimes.' She felt tears coming again. 'She won't survive in prison; they are as good as murdering her.'

The young reporter pulled her notebook from her coat pocket and rummaged for a pencil in the other one. 'Do you have anything that could help us prove she's innocent?'

'If you knew Tessa, you'd know she was. A hundred women would vouch for her, but her barrister said she didn't want any of them to have to take the stand. I don't know why, but it was typical of her to put others first.' Bella tried to quash the memory of her mother in the dock as she watched Milly start to write. 'This isn't just about Evelyn Hilton. This is about doctors trying to put midwives out of business because they cost them hundreds of pounds a year in lost earnings. It is about discrediting the profession of midwifery by regulating them and limiting what they're allowed to do, requiring them to transfer care of a labouring woman to a physician when a birth becomes complicated – which is exactly when women like my mother come into their own.'

'Go on,' said Milly, pinning her long red hair into a bun on top of her head so she could write more easily.

Bella shook her head and looked out of the window at the bitterly cold morning. 'It's the physicians who often cause the complications in the first place. They force women to have babies lying on their backs with their legs in stirrups. They use painful equipment in medicalised environments where the women aren't listened to and feel scared. They have no patience: they break a woman's waters when the baby isn't ready to come, they yank babies out with forceps rather than turning it in the womb, they don't want to sit by a woman's bedside all day and night, talking to her, soothing her; they want to charge in at the last possible moment, deliver the baby and take all the glory.'

Milly was scribbling away eagerly. 'And what has all this got to do with Evelyn Hilton's death?'

'Evelyn wanted my mother at the birth, but her husband, Wilfred Hilton, wanted a doctor. When the baby was breech and it went badly wrong, Dr Jenkins, in a panic, called for her.'

'Dr Jenkins called for your mother?' Milly Green stared at her wide-eyed.

Bella nodded, and reached down into her bag, pulling out the letter her mother's barrister had given her. 'He framed her. Read it for yourself.'

Milly looked down at the letter. 'This is from your mother?'

'Yes, it's her account of what happened.' With shaking hands, Bella picked up the letter and read, 'I would never cut a woman like Dr Jenkins did. That night is for ever burnt in my mind, however hard I try and forget. He butchered Evelyn's tiny body, and starved her baby of oxygen, then got Sally to call for me at The Vicarage when he realised what he had done. He left me there to watch them both die and take the blame.'

Milly finished frantically making notes then looked up at Bella.

'Dr Jenkins didn't mean to kill her, but when he realised she was going to die, he needed a scapegoat. And Wilfred Hilton has wanted to get rid of my mother for years.'

Milly read the first few lines of the letter, then looked back up at her. 'Why?'

'Because we rent a house on his land – the house where I was born. My mother delivered his wife's first two babies and saved her life, so Evelyn always insisted he let us stay.'

Milly was making notes fast now, as Bella picked up a sugar cube to put in her tea.

'Wilfred Hilton doesn't like the desperate women my mother helps on his land. They come to us broken, hungry, beaten and pregnant; often they've been raped or abandoned. She has always let it be known that her door is open, even to women who couldn't afford to pay.'

'Why didn't your mother's barrister call any of these women as witnesses in court?'

'Because his fee was paid for by Wilfred Hilton.'

'Are you sure of that?' Milly looked up, pencil poised.

Bella nodded. 'He denied it, and said he was a volunteer barrister, but he's not on the list.' She pulled out the sheet of paper she had collected from the administration office the previous day. 'His name is Jeremy Lyons and he's not there. My mother didn't want to put any of the women she had helped on the stand, and Mr Lyons didn't try and find another way. He wanted her to be convicted so they are all rid of her and her witchy ways.'

Milly read the rest of the letter before handing it back to Bella. 'Your mother sounds like an extraordinary woman.'

'She is,' Bella agreed. 'I have to leave now, Miss Green. I have some urgent business to attend to with regard to my son. I hope you will write about this.'

'Is there anyone at all who you think might talk to me so that we can find some proof?' Milly asked as Bella rose to go.

'Sally, the Hiltons' house servant, who was the prosecution's key witness, knows the truth. Mr Lyons could have cross-examined her, got the truth from her, but he chose not to.'

'Do you think she might talk to me?' said Milly eagerly.

Bella shrugged. 'She relies on the Hiltons for her livelihood and she has a small daughter. She can't afford to lose her job. But maybe in years to come she might talk to you. It will be too late for my mother then, but it would be comforting to think her name might be cleared one day.'

'What do you mean, it will be too late?' said Milly, frowning up at her.

'Because her life, as she knew it, is over. I must go and attend to some urgent family business. Good day, Miss Green, good luck with your career. I hope you get to be a voice for women like my mother.' Bella turned away so that Milly Green wouldn't see the tears in her eyes, then walked out of the warm café and began the long walk back to Kingston.

Chapter Twenty-Five
Vanessa

New Year's Eve 1969

'Where is Bobby James now?' All eyes fell on Vanessa as she began walking to the door. 'I need to talk to him, I need to know exactly what happened and what he said to Alice before he let her go.'

The police constable who had broken the news of Alfie James's death looked at his superior.

'Well, lad, where is he?' snapped Detective Inspector Mills.

'They're taking him to the station for questioning, sir, but his dad has just been killed so he's in shock – he ain't saying much so far.' The young constable was wide-eyed, and despite his thick coat and gloves, he was shivering from the cold.

'I need to see him.' Vanessa angrily wiped away the tears that were falling.

'Mrs Hilton, I assure you that if he has any information, we will get it from him.'

'No! I know this boy, I need to speak to him. I'll know if he's hiding anything. I'm coming with you to the station.'

'Mrs Hilton, please, it would be much better if you were

to stay here. We will update you as soon as we have any news.' DI Mills stepped in front of her.

'I want to know exactly where they found Alfie James. Are your officers looking there? She's fallen down and hurt herself looking for that puppy, I know it. Oh God, she's out there. He left her out there in the snow.' Vanessa started crying again.

'There are officers covering every inch of the area around where Alfie James's body was found,' the detective insisted.

'I want you to take me there. I want to help look for her. I can't sit here any more, I'm losing my mind.' Vanessa pulled on her boots and grabbed her fur coat from the stand in the hallway.

DI Mills looked over at his colleague. 'Porter, call the station and tell them we've gone to the field by The Vicarage. Then track down Richard Hilton and tell him to meet us there.' He opened the front door, and a gust of bitterly cold air blasted in.

'Where is Leo?' Vanessa looked at Dorothy, who was at the foot of the stairs.

'He's probably gone out with Richard to join the search,' said Dorothy. 'Don't worry, I'll let him know where you are if I see him.'

'Oh God, Alice, please, please be there,' said Vanessa out loud as she followed DI Mills outside towards the police car that was parked next to the lights for the party, which had taken all of her and Richard's attention when she saw her daughter for possibly the last time in her life, running across the front of the house in her red dress. She would give anything, anything on God's earth, to go back to that moment; to run to her daughter, grab hold of her and never let go. DI Mills opened the passenger door for her, then climbed into the driver's seat and started the engine. It coughed into life, and as they headed down the driveway, Vanessa looked up and saw that, in the distance, the crimson dawn was beginning to break.

The short journey through the winding lanes that she had done a thousand times since she had lived at Yew Tree Manor seemed to go on for ever. She sat clutching her seat as the car skidded twice on the black ice before righting itself again. As they took the blind bend that led to The Vicarage, the road narrowed and they met the headlights of another car that came hurtling towards them. Mills slammed on the brakes, screeching to a halt just before they hit the other vehicle head on. He wound down the window, waving his hands frantically and shouting 'Move!'

As Vanessa glanced over at the detective, she felt her heart shatter. She had tried to ignore it, but it was obvious as the hours passed that DI Mills's concern was growing. The questions that had revolved around Alice being naughty and running away had stopped, replaced by the quest for another explanation. A much more disturbing one. She had wanted him to take Alice's disappearance more seriously, but now that he had, his concern was terrifying her: asking for Alice's nightie so the sniffer dogs could try and track her down; officers going door to door, waking the villagers from their sleep to check their sheds, bashing at the snow-covered hedgerow with their canes. It was suddenly agonisingly obvious to her that they had stopped looking for a missing little girl and were now looking for a body.

Mills swore under his breath as the oncoming vehicle

backed up into a gateway opening on Vanessa's side, plunged into the dawn shadows as it waited. It was almost impossible to identify the driver, but as they passed, Vanessa realised it was a vehicle she knew. The flickering headlight and the canvas roof that leaked whenever it rained identified it as Richard's Land Rover that had been hurtling at speed away from The Vicarage.

Mills stopped, and Vanessa wound down her window. 'Any news?'

'Nothing,' Richard called back.

As Mills ploughed on, Vanessa glanced into the cab of the Land Rover. It was only a second, but the sight of two figures sitting there staring straight ahead made her stomach turn over. Leo was in the passenger seat, and next to him her husband. Leo didn't look up, his head was hung; it was obvious to her that he'd been crying.

In a split second, they were gone.

Vanessa bit her lip hard, her fingers white from gripping the seat. She couldn't bring herself to think about how cold she was, a grown woman inside a car, wrapped in a fox-fur coat. Alice had been out in the bitter cold all night, in a red dress and shiny red shoes. If she had fallen into a ditch, there was no way she could have survived in these temperatures, but if she was trapped somewhere inside, there could be hope – if they found her soon. Maybe she had made it as far as The Vicarage and had gone into the barns to look for the puppy and fallen. 'Please be there, Alice, please be there, please be there,' Vanessa chanted under her breath in an effort to try and stop herself from losing her mind.

As they turned the corner into a narrow lane caked in snow, DI Mills slammed on the brakes again. 'There are fresh tyre tracks,' he said breathlessly. 'Someone's just driven up here. They could have taken Bobby James in already.' He climbed out and trudged over the uneven ground towards the gate ahead. As he wrestled with the bolt, bursts of his frozen breath punched out with the strain of trying to open it.

Vanessa couldn't help but picture her little girl struggling with the gate in the snow, her small hands shaking with the cold, desperate to find the puppy; abandoning the bolt, perhaps, climbing over and running the rest of the way. She shook the image away from her mind's eye as the detective finally got the gate open and rushed back to the car. He put the vehicle into gear, and its snow-covered wheels skidded into life again.

'I can see blue lights by the house. That might be them bringing Bobby James in now,' he said, pointing to where the red dawn met blue police lights ahead of them.

Vanessa's eyes fizzed from exhaustion as the car rocked like a boat over the uneven ground. She looked around frantically for any sign of her little girl's footprints in the snow. Mills pressed the accelerator, and the hedgerow cleared as The Vicarage came into view around the bend ahead.

She hadn't visited it for years, and as she looked at it now, she saw that it was much deteriorated. It was a beautiful house, warm, with exposed oak beams, carved wall panelling, pretty tiled fireplaces and flagstone floors. But in the past six years, it had lost its sparkle and stumbled into neglect as Alfie struggled to run the farm and look after the children. Now the honeysuckle around the door was straggly and untended, the paintwork was chipped and peeling, and the path was covered in months' worth of mud and leaves.

Her eyes followed the tracks in the snow to the far side of the cottage, and the field beyond, where lights were pulsing out into the morning. She held her breath as the figure of a young lad appeared through the mist-filled dawn, dressed in a long black coat and woollen hat. His head and shoulders were hunched, his arms locked behind him, and he was flanked by two large police officers who half walked, half dragged him across the snow to the waiting police car. The sight of him knocked the air from her lungs, and as he walked past the car's headlights, she could see he was shaking violently. At that moment, he looked up and saw her, his face as white as a corpse, his eyes unblinking.

Bright blue eyes, Vanessa thought to herself as her belly burned with rage. Eyes that had been the last to see her little girl.

Chapter Twenty-Six

Vanessa

Friday, 22 December 2017

Vanessa lay on her bed watching the snow come down outside her bedroom window. She could hear the sniffer dogs barking and the police whistles piercing the woods where they had been searching for Sienna since dawn.

She looked over at her alarm clock, which told her it was two in the afternoon. It would be getting dark soon; another day was slipping away and they hadn't found Sienna. The house had been packed with people for two days – first the removal men and then the police – but now it was still and deathly quiet. She knew that Helen and Leo had gone out, but she couldn't remember where, or when they were coming back.

Watching the snow falling was making her sleepy, but when she closed her eyes, all she could see was Alice and Sienna holding hands, side by side, calling her name. She had hardly slept; she needed to doze just for an hour, and then she would go out and join the search before it got dark.

Her eyes were heavy. She had gone upstairs on the pretext of lying down, but her main motive had been to get away from the family liaison officer who had been assigned to her. She was a blonde woman with very straight white teeth and a scraped-back shiny ponytail. She kept going over and over the minutes before Sienna went missing, none of which Vanessa could remember clearly. When she had finally given up, she had started asking questions about the family. Was Sienna a happy child? Did Leo and Helen ever argue? Would Sienna be scared to come home for any reason? She had made endless tea and smiled warmly, but it was a smile that reminded Vanessa of the crocodile in *Peter Pan*.

The days and nights when Alice had gone missing were a blur, but the behaviour of the police had stayed with her to this day. As she'd paced the house, inconsolable about her missing daughter, the female police officer assigned to them had comforted her, held her hand, built up her trust and convinced her that she was her friend. The police had spent a great deal of time telling her and Richard that they were working with them, that they would update them immediately on any developments and on how the search was going. They were charming and comforting and warm, and they slowly cajoled her into talking, sharing, confiding.

But it had dawned on her as the hours and days dragged on without success that she was the one doing all the talking, the over-sharing, the confiding, and the police were telling them nothing; less than the press, in fact, who would often know about any developments before they did. They would read in the newspaper, or see on the news, that an item of clothing had been found, or there had been a potential sighting of Alice somewhere, and Vanessa would break down and shriek and cry about the fact that they were the last to be told anything.

Now, laying down in her bedroom, she heard the family

liaison officer talking quietly on the telephone at the bottom of the stairs. 'She's asleep, she's exhausted . . . No, nothing really, she's very closed off, won't talk about either of the parents. Any developments with Bobby James? . . . Have forensics gone over his flat and his car yet? . . . Shit. Maybe he's hiding her somewhere else.'

Bobby James's face as a thirteen-year-old boy jumped to the forefront of her mind, he was unrecognisable to her – apart from his bright blue eyes, which were as piercing now as they were then. She remembered that he had been here, in Leo's study, just before Sienna went missing. What had he wanted? She hadn't seen him for nearly fifty years, not since she had been taken down to the police station to watch through a one-way mirror as he was questioned. She had begged repeatedly to see Bobby, accused them of keeping information from her, but they had refused to let her speak to him. Eventually, when she had completely broken down and threatened to stop cooperating with them altogether if they didn't give her the opportunity to talk to him, they had agreed to let her listen in on his interview for five minutes, after warning her that it could be very distressing.

She had sat in the hot, stuffy observation room with six police officers, all crowded round peering in at the detective inspector chosen to interrogate him. The table and chair in the middle of the interview room were empty, and Bobby, still in the clothes he'd been wearing when she saw him last, was pressed up in a corner by the detective. He looked awful, his eyes bloodshot and bruised, his lip swollen and covered in blood, and he appeared to have a cut on his head too.

'You need to tell us what happened to Alice, Bobby. This

is a very serious situation and you're not being honest with us.' The man had stood so close that Bobby had to turn his head away.

'I've told you, I don't know! Please can I sit down, sir? I've been standing for hours,' he pleaded, his face so dirty that Vanessa could see the tracks of his tears.

'You can sit down when you tell us where Alice is.' The man pushed his face right up to Bobby's. The detective had slicked-back black hair and a tattoo on the side of his neck, partially hidden by his shirt collar. He was holding up a picture of Alice that Vanessa had given the police. 'Look at her, look at this little girl. What have you done to her?'

'Nothing, sir, I wouldn't hurt Alice. Please let me sit down, my legs are going to give way.'

'No.' The detective slapped Bobby around the head, hard, and Bobby yelped in pain and started to cry. 'We know you were the last person to see her, so you'd better tell us the truth. Where did you take her?'

'I didn't take her anywhere, she ran off to get help,' cried Bobby.

'Which way, boy? Which way did she run?' He shouted in Bobby's face, bits of spit escaping from his mouth.

'I don't know! I'm sorry, I was trying to help my dad.' Bobby sobbed, before the man slapped him again.

'We need you to focus, Bobby. You were seen with Alice; what were you doing with her? Do you like playing with little girls, Bobby?' The man leaned in even further.

Tears streaked down Bobby's chin and dripped onto the ground. 'She was upset, her head was bleeding. I gave her my handkerchief.' His voice began to shake and he started to cry again. 'That was when I saw my dad trapped under the digger. I told her to run and get help.'

'Why are you crying, Bobby? Are you ashamed of what you've done? Was Alice crying when she died? Was that what you wanted? To see her suffer?' The detective glared at him.

'No! I went to help my dad. I didn't hurt Alice. She ran away, I didn't see her again. Why do you think I did something to her?'

'Because there was a handkerchief in the snow with your initials on it, covered in her blood. And your hands were covered in her blood when we found you. You're known to us, Bobby James. This isn't the first time you've been in trouble. You have clearly got a problem with the Hilton family; you set fire to their barn.'

'No, that wasn't me, it was Leo. Mr Hilton told me to say it was me, but it wasn't.'

'So you lied to the police? That's a very serious crime, Bobby. Are you lying to us now too, Bobby? What did you do to Alice? Why was there so much blood?'

'Her head was bleeding before I got to her, she was upset. I put my handkerchief on her head to soak up the blood. Then I saw my dad. Oh God, Dad. I'm sorry.'

'What are you sorry about? Did you hurt her head? Did you hit her, Bobby? How did she hurt her head? Did you kill her and put her somewhere?'

'No! No, I told you I would never do anything to hurt Alice. Please let me sit down.'

The officer slapped Bobby hard again, then held up the photograph. 'Look at her face, Bobby, look at it. We know there was a legal dispute going on between your dad and Alice's father; we know everything.'

'I didn't hurt her. Please let me go. I'm sorry I didn't take her home, but I had to help my dad. He was trapped. I didn't hurt her, I promise you. Please.'

Vanessa woke with a start as the front door slammed so hard the house shook. She heard Helen's voice on the landing; she sounded different, hysterical.

'It's starting to get dark, I can't do this for another night. She's dead, I know she's dead. I'm never going to see her again.'

'Helen, that's not true, we will find her.' Vanessa heard Leo's voice, coming up the stairs.

'How? How will we find her? She could be anywhere! I can't bear this. Where is she?!'

'Is there anything I can do?' Vanessa heard the liaison officer say.

'Just give us a moment,' said Leo, trying to keep the anger out of his voice.

'Leo, help me. I don't know what to do. I can't stand it, I'm losing my mind.' It sounded as though Helen was pacing up and down outside Vanessa's room.

'Helen, don't do this, please. If you fall apart, it won't help Sienna. She needs us,' Leo begged.

Vanessa pushed herself up and swung her legs over the side of the bed. She stood up slowly, shaking away the sleep, then walked to the closed door and stood by it, listening to Leo and Helen's conversation.

'It's just like Alice all over again. We'll never find her and we'll be stuck here and never able to leave. We'll rot in this godforsaken house waiting for her to come home, going mad, just like your mother. I'm being punished. We're both being punished. For what we did.'

'Helen! Keep your voice down, someone will hear us,' Leo hissed.

'So what? Why does it matter? Nothing matters now. Sienna's gone,' Helen cried. 'She's dead, I know it.'

'She's not dead! We will find her, I promise.'

'No, we won't. Don't touch me! Leave me alone!' she screamed. 'I hate this house. I hate this house!'

Vanessa heard a crash outside on the landing and opened the door. A silver-framed photograph of Alice had smashed into splinters where Helen had thrown it against the wall.

'I don't care about anything any more,' said Helen, glaring at Vanessa then back at Leo. 'The worst has happened, I've lost my baby. I don't care what you do or say to me; you can't bully me any more.' She collapsed on the floor, shards of glass from the portrait cutting her hands, and as Leo tried to pull her away, she screamed like a vixen caught in a trap and clawed at his face, the blood from her cuts leaving trails on his skin.

Slowly Vanessa walked past them and down the stairs, where several policemen were standing around. She looked at the family liaison officer and beckoned her into the sitting room.

'I need to talk to Bobby James,' she said quietly. 'I think it might help me remember.'

The woman shook her head. 'I'm afraid that won't be possible. He's still being interviewed.'

'I thought you were meant to be on our side. Time is running out.' Vanessa felt a burning rage rising in her stomach, fifty years of built up fury and helplessness reaching the surface. 'Do you want me to walk out and tell all those journalists at the end of the drive that you won't help me find my granddaughter? Because, so help me God, I will, and you won't come out of it well, my dear.'

The family liaison officer stared at Vanessa, then slowly nodded, picking up her walkie-talkie before turning towards the front door. 'I'll see what I can do.'

Chapter Twenty-Seven
Willow

Friday, 22 December 2017

It was raining heavily as Willow pulled up outside the old Edwardian sanatorium building in Portsmouth and paid the driver. It had been converted into a slightly shabby three-star hotel, and when she had called ahead about seeing old patient records, a cheerful receptionist with a sing-song Welsh accent had told her it wasn't a problem. Hopefully the caretaker would be available, she'd said, to show her round the wing of the hospital that used to house all the TB patients – and which hadn't been touched since it closed its doors in 1971.

As she ran towards the entrance with her coat over her head to protect her from the rain, Willow glanced up at the Gothic turrets, pointed spires and long, narrow wrought-iron windows staring down at her. She opened the front door to a cacophony of chatter, clinking glasses and music, and as she pushed her damp hair out of her eyes, two little bridesmaids rushed past. A girl in a low-cut white shirt beamed at her from behind the reception desk.

'Can I help you?' she said.

Willow looked around as two guests in wedding outfits

and fascinators rushed past her. 'My name is Willow James. I called earlier. I was wondering if you'd had any luck finding the patient records for the old sanatorium.'

'I'm sorry, no, I haven't. I spoke to my boss and he said that most of the patient notes were destroyed in a flood. I think the council have some, but you'd have to write to them, I suppose.'

'Oh, right,' said Willow, her heart sinking at her wasted journey. 'I've spoken to the council and they said to come here.'

'Did they? I'm not sure why they'd say that. I'd better give them a call and tell them we don't have any records here, save anyone else being disappointed. Do you still want a tour of the sanatorium? I thought that was what you were coming for; we get a lot of people asking.'

'Yes, I suppose, as I'm here, that would be great. If you don't mind. Sorry, I didn't realise there was a wedding today. Probably not the best time for you!' she added.

'Oh, that's no problem, there's always a wedding on here.' The receptionist giggled happily. 'Let me call Sam, our caretaker, to come and get you. Do you want to sign here and then take a seat,' she added, handing over a visitors' book and a pen.

Willow took a seat in the hallway and glanced through into a large reception room, where scores of guests were chatting and smiling at one another as a string quartet played in a corner. They weren't the most stylish of wedding guests, she thought – a lot of bosoms spilling out of shiny lilac and pink dresses, and ill-fitting tuxedos with carnation corsages – but they were definitely the happiest. Peals of laughter repeatedly burst out, and an army of kids ran amok amongst their happily tipsy parents. The longer Willow watched, the harder she found it to look away. There must have been sixty or seventy people in the room, but they all seemed to know each other intimately: old friends, aunts and uncles and grandparents and grandchildren huddled together in groups, chatting warmly: comfortable, happy, content. And though their laughter was infectious, Willow felt her heart ache, knowing that being part of an extended family, the feeling of protection, unconditional love, belonging, was something utterly alien to her.

'Willow James?' said a male voice, and she looked up to see a small, shy-looking chap in his twenties standing in front of her. He had long, wavy brown hair and wore a grey sweatshirt covered in paint, and baggy jeans that sat low on his hips.

She sprang up and held out her hand, smiling warmly. 'Nice to meet you.'

'I'm Sam. I hear you're wanting to head up to the old hospital?' He was already beginning to move past her towards a double door.

'Yes, that would be great, thank you! If you're sure you aren't too busy.' She grabbed her bag and followed him.

'No, it's fine. I like taking people up there.' He spoke quietly as he flicked his fringe away from his face.

'Do you? I thought you'd get rather bored of showing people round.'

'Nah, it's really interesting. It's barely been touched since it closed, and it's still got all the old beds and X-ray equipment. I don't like going up at night, mind, it's a bit creepy.' The sights and sounds of the wedding began to fade into the distance as they walked along the corridor.

'Do you get many requests to see it?' Willow asked, picking up her pace as they went through several sets of double doors and the freshly painted walls and newly laid carpets gave way to cracked skirting boards and peeling wallpaper.

'Quite a few, yes. Mostly older ladies who used to be patients here as kids. They always get a bit overwhelmed coming back. I like hearing their stories, although they can be quite sad. Their parents had to leave the kids here and were only allowed to visit them once a month.' He looked back at her and flicked his fringe again. 'I like old people, they're always really cool. There's no bullshit with them.'

Willow smiled appreciatively as she followed him down a corridor lined with black and white photographs of Portsmouth Dock.

'Some of the guys in catering go up to the old male ward to do the Ouija board after the bar closes,' he continued, 'but I've tried that shit once and I ain't ever doing it again.' He stopped abruptly, opening a door that led up to the next floor. 'We need to go up here – mind your head.'

'Thanks,' said Willow, stepping onto the dark, narrow staircase.

'The lights don't work, so mind how you go. Here, I'll put the torch on my phone on.'

Willow made her way carefully up the wooden steps, which creaked as she walked. At the top, she was greeted with a long, narrow corridor with various rooms leading off it. She peered into the first one, which was packed to the ceiling with what appeared to be junk: black bin bags, cardboard boxes, and plastic containers full to the brim with Christmas decorations and other paraphernalia. Next to it was a tiny room with a sink, and smashed tiles falling off the walls.

'The women's ward is down there,' Sam said, pointing to the end of the hallway.

Willow nodded and moved on, walking past several other smaller rooms crammed with chairs and filing cabinets and general junk, until she reached a vast room with high ceilings and floor-to-ceiling windows leading onto small balconies.

'This is it,' Sam said. 'I think they all sat in the beds, lined up along the walls, kinda facing each other, judging by the curtain tracks on the ceiling. The male ward is the next floor up but the floor has been eaten away by dry rot so we can't go up there.'

Willow looked up to see that in certain sections of the room the rails from which the curtains around the beds must have hung were still fixed to the plaster.

'I had an old dear in last month who said that she was here for two years, from the age of ten. Her bed was over there in the corner. She made a good friend while she was here who died. Really sad it was; you got used to people dying in their sleep, she said.'

'Ten? That's so sad,' said Willow quietly. 'I get the impression that no one really told kids anything in those days.'

'Nope. A lot of the people I've met said they thought they'd done something wrong, or been abandoned by their parents. No one told this woman why her parents couldn't stay with her, or when they were coming back. She wanted to see her friend's grave and pay her respects, because she'd never been back.'

'There are patients buried here?' Willow asked.

'Yeah, just over by the woods. I can take you there in a minute,' Sam said enthusiastically, as if they were planning a jolly treat.

She walked to one of the windows and looked out at the bare trees. The ice-cold wind blew dead leaves across the grey balcony floor. 'Did they really put patients out there?' she asked quietly.

'Yup, the cold was the only treatment back in them days. Quite a few of the old ladies remember it. They never let them close the windows, ever. Even if it snowed. The cold stopped the TB from spreading, see.'

Willow looked round the room where Nell must have stayed, the heart of so much sadness and loneliness, yet just a room, with no real sense of the past contained in its high ceiling. There were two or three metal beds pushed up against the walls. Peeling paint and a parquet floor that had faded to grey. It was bitterly cold, and despite her thick woollen coat, hat and gloves, she began to shiver.

'The people I've shown round said they weren't ever allowed to get up and out of their beds. The nurses were very strict, even with young kids.'

'I can't believe children were sent here without their parents. It's unimaginable now.'

'I know, and some of them for two or three years at a time. And like I said, visits were limited to once a month to reduce the risk of visitors spreading germs. Some people never had visitors at all, even the kids.'

Willow bit down on her lip at the image of those abandoned children watching while visitors flocked in to see other patients. She spotted a door at the end of the room. 'What's through there?' she asked.

'That's the old X-ray room.' Sam pushed open the heavy door and walked over to a set of wooden shutters, pulling them back to reveal a room with three long beds on wheels.

Smiling cheerfully, he strode over to the other side of the room. 'Check this out,' he said, opening a high cupboard and wheeling out a large X-ray machine on tracks. 'You stood behind this screen here, and the machine took an X-ray of your lungs. Cool, eh? And the morgue is just through here, in the next room.'

Willow suddenly felt very sick again as Sam opened the door to the next room. It contained four large trolleys and a wall with twelve openings just wide enough to slide a body into. 'There's a lift at the end of the room,' he said. 'It doesn't work any more, but it went straight down to the back of the building where the graveyard is.'

'I think I might need to get some air now, if that's all right,' said Willow. Despite the freezing temperatures, her scarf suddenly felt too tight, and her forehead was sweating under her hat. She was sure she was about to throw up again.

'Sure, we can go down to the emergency exit and check out the graveyard, if you like. It's pretty shabby, mind, just to warn you. Don't think a lot of people come back here to tend to the graves.'

The staircase leading to the emergency exit was tight and poorly lit. Sam held his mobile-phone torch in front of them again, and Willow made her way down slowly, holding tight to the hand rail, tripping at one point but catching herself before she fell. By the time they reached the exit, she felt quite breathless and sick, and as Sam shoved at the door to get it open, she began to feel panicked.

'Sorry, it's not normally this stiff,' he said, letting out a nervous laugh and giving it another push.

Finally it opened and they spilled out into the grey day. The rain had finally stopped, leaving a trail of puddles across the staff car park at the back of the hotel that led to the woodland beyond.

'This way to the graveyard; it's just at the entrance to the woods. I might have to leave you to it, as I've got a team meeting in five minutes,' said Sam as they left the shadow of the old hospital and headed towards the dense woodland.

'Of course, no problem,' said Willow.

They trekked across the car park towards two concrete pillars flanking a crumbling stone wall and a narrow concrete path leading into the woods. She could see the tops of the gravestones over the wall as they approached.

'So I'll say goodbye if that's okay?' said Sam, beginning to back away.

'Thank you so much for your help,' she said, then she took a breath and turned back to the entrance of the graveyard.

The silence of the woods engulfed her as Sam's footsteps faded into the distance, and she started to shiver. She took several deep breaths, then walked purposefully past the concrete pillars. It was strange to see a graveyard out in the middle of nowhere. There was no logic to it; just cracked stone plinths and crosses scattered about the place.

The path was well kept, as were the first few yards of grass at the entrance, but as she ventured deeper, the roots and undergrowth began to take over. She looked around, overwhelmed and unsure of where to start. She couldn't possibly read every gravestone; there were too many of them. She looked up at the hospital, and at the windows where she had just been standing, and pictured the patients watching the burials from the balconies. She began to scan the inscriptions: *Katherine Harper 1937–1950. Beloved daughter, sister, granddaughter, niece.* Some gravestones were smarter than others, but most were crosses with small inscriptions, which Willow imagined the sanatorium organising for poorer families.

As she made her way through the undergrowth, she began to notice that there were clusters of headstones that had been put up at similar times, the mid-thirties and forties further back, and then, as she made her way to the left of the wood, another area from 1955 to late 1959.

As she gazed at the dates, a thought suddenly occurred to her. She knew that Nell had been at the sanatorium when Alice had gone missing in 1969. Perhaps if there were any graves of children who had died around the time she was there, their parents could be alive and might remember Nell. It was only fifty years ago, so even if the parents had been in their late twenties then, they would only be in their mid-seventies now. It was a long shot, but not impossible. She began searching in earnest for gravestones in the late sixties, and early seventies.

Connie Walbrook, November 1968, In Loving Memory, she read as she stepped from grave to grave, crouching down to run her fingers over the lettering on some of the stones that had almost faded to white. Even though it was starting to rain again, she felt her heart race at this new flicker of hope. The trees above her started to rattle as raindrops pattered onto them, and she moved deeper. *In Fond Memory, Helen Kerry, 1935–1953. Taken too soon. Rest in peace.* Only eighteen years old.

She carried on, working her way deeper into the abandoned graveyard until the cold became unbearable. Just as she thought she might have to turn back, she spotted a small semicircular piece of stone jutting out from the ground, half hidden under a pile of brambles. As she walked over to it, her heart began to thud. She used her foot to ease back the thorns, but one of them managed to get through, and she let out a gasp as blood oozed out onto her sock. Ignoring the stinging pain, she looked down at the faded words on the grey limestone plaque: *Heather Parks, 1958–1971. Beloved daughter to Emma and George. Taken too soon, for ever missed.*

She stood for a moment staring at the stone, unable to believe she had actually found someone who was there at the same time as Nell and might actually have known her. As Willow stared at the grave, she noticed a decaying bunch of flowers next to it, with a faded yellow ribbon tied around them, telling her that Heather's parents, or someone close to her, had been here not too long ago. Willow pulled out her phone and took a picture of Heather Parks's gravestone.

'There you are. Everything all right?' A familiar voice came from the wood behind her, making her jump.

'Oh, hi. Yes, fine, thanks,' she said, despite trembling now from the bitter cold. 'Can I ask you something? Do you think there is any way I could get hold of the death records of someone who died here?'

'Not sure,' Sam said. 'Maybe the council? I know a lot of patients went home to die. Particularly children. Their parents came to get them. And I think there might be a reunion group for this place on Facebook. Worth a shot, maybe?'

Willow nodded. 'Okay, thank you.' She looked at her phone again and saw that she had a message. The rain was getting heavier now, pouring through the trees.

'I'm heading into town if you need a lift anywhere,' said Sam. 'Save you getting a taxi.'

'Great,' said Willow. 'That's really kind, I was worried about missing my train.' She took one more look at the flowers next to Heather Parks's grave before turning away and hurrying to catch up with Sam.

Chapter Twenty-Eight

Nell

November 1970

'Why can't I see Bobby? I don't understand.' Nell looked across the table at Dorothy, who was putting out the breakfast things.

'It's complicated, Nell,' Dorothy said, letting out a heavy sigh.

'Why? Why can't you tell me where he is? I want to see him. I miss him. Did you send him my letter?'

'Yes, Nell, I did.'

'Then why doesn't he reply to me? I put my new address on it, here at your house.'

'*Our* house. It's your house too, Nell, we are your family now. You need to try and move on and make new friends at your school. It's been a while now since you came to live with us.'

'I don't want to make new friends. Everyone I love dies.' Nell started to cry. 'It's my fault Alice died.'

Dorothy sat down on the chair next to her and put her arm around her. 'Of course it's not your fault. You weren't even here, Nell. And anyway, we don't know that Alice died. She's still missing. She could just be with another family somewhere.'

'She's not, I know she's not. She's dead.' Nell buried her head in her arms.

'Nell, please don't say that. Come on, you need to eat something.'

'I'm not hungry,' said Nell, getting down from the table and running up to her room, where she threw herself down on her bed and sobbed. She had written to Bobby so many times, letters that Dorothy promised her she had posted, but she had never had one reply. She had begged Dorothy to tell her where Bobby was so many times, but she had given up now because she always gave vague answers. She and Peter whispered all the time about Nell when they thought she wasn't listening. They were so different to Bobby and Dad, never telling her anything, keeping her locked away and putting her to bed when it was still light. She had no animals to play with and nothing but a doll's house to entertain her. She desperately missed life on the farm. She wanted to run around in the mud, helping Bobby and Dad, feeding the cows and chatting to the milk tanker driver while she sat on the fence eating apples.

Dorothy and Peter's house was so strange to her. Everything was cream – the carpet, the cushions, the rugs – and she wasn't allowed to touch any of it. It was like a picture they had to live in but not mess up. They were obsessed with everything being clean. Nell had grown up on a farm, covered in mud from head to toe, but all Dorothy ever said to her when they went out was don't get your dress dirty, don't jump in that puddle, be careful, Nell, don't go near that fence, don't fall. Then as soon as they were back, it was bath time, wash your hands, wash your face, tidy your room, bedtime, lights out. Dorothy was forever hoovering and wiping and cleaning. Everything smelt of fake flowers, stinking lavender and bleach. Nell missed the dirt and the mess, the happiness and chaos and warmth of her old life. Muddy boots, and crackling fires, cowsheds and milking time and falling asleep by the fire, stories and washing once a week and belly laughter. She missed her old life so much her tummy ached constantly.

Nell stood up and walked over to the window of her lilac bedroom without a book or toy out of place and stared into the distance, where the end of Dorothy's garden met the Hiltons' land. She looked at the driveway of Yew Tree Manor and pictured her and Alice skipping up there holding hands as Bobby walked in front of them telling them to hurry. As she stared, willing the past to come to life, she saw Leo, Alice's big brother, walking towards the woods. He was throwing a stick for Snowy, her puppy, who was now fully grown, with a white fluffy coat, and enormous paws that made him look like a polar bear.

Nell crept down the stairs and pulled on her wellingtons by the back door. Dorothy was at the kitchen sink, talking to Peter.

'I just don't know what to do with her any more. Sometimes I feel it was a mistake bringing her back here, but I had to help her, I couldn't just leave her alone in that awful place, with no one ever coming to visit her. Vanessa's made it quite clear she wishes I hadn't done it. She thinks someone else would have adopted her, but then Bobby wouldn't have been able to find her.'

'Don't worry about what Vanessa thinks. Heaven knows

she has enough to deal with; losing a child is enough to make any woman lose their mind. Just give her time, she'll settle. She's been through a lot.'

Nell grabbed her coat from the hook and ran out of the back door, closing it quietly behind her before Dorothy started making a fuss about not getting muddy and asking where she was going and when she would be back. She ran down the path and through the back gate, and crossed the driveway of Yew Tree Manor, heading towards the woods in the same direction that Leo had been heading.

As she walked, the empty branches curled over her head like witches' fingers. She could hear Leo calling out for Snowy, and hung back so that he wouldn't see her.

Soon everything went quiet, and all she could hear was the wind whistling through the bare trees and her own heavy breathing as she got to the edge of the woods and looked down at The Vicarage. She glanced around, but there was no sign of Leo and Snowy. Nell gazed longingly at her old house. It had changed so much already; Richard had ploughed all the fields surrounding it, all the gravestones were gone and he had started to convert the cowshed into a hay storage unit. She pictured Bobby on the doorstep, kicking the mud off his boots, and their father slapping the cows' bottoms at the gate to make them move.

She swung round as she heard a twig snap, and looked over to see Leo standing a few feet away from her. Neither of them spoke, but they stared at each other for a long time.

'Hello, Nell,' he said finally.

'Hi, Leo,' Nell said, crouching down to stroke Snowy and noticing that the key was missing from his collar where she had left it. 'She's grown,' she said.

'Yeah, she's nearly one now,' said Leo.

Nell nodded, then kicked the ground at her feet awkwardly. 'I better get back. Dorothy will be wondering where I am.'

'Do you know what the key was for that was on his collar?' Leo asked as she turned away.

Nell stopped in her tracks and felt her whole body start to tremble. She slowly turned back to face him. It had only been a few months since she had last seen him, but he had changed. He'd always been tall and slim like his dad, Richard, but now he looked less like a boy and more like a young man. He was twelve, she worked out, his voice had got deeper, and he had some fuzzy hair around his mouth and chin. His eyes looked sad, though, and his shoulders were hunched. He had lost the swagger she remembered, and it had been replaced with something more unsettling.

'Do you still have it?' she asked.

He stared at her without blinking and watched her mouth as though he was waiting for her to say something else, then he reached into his pocket and pulled out the key. It was exactly as she remembered it, ornate, beautiful, like something out of a fairy tale. 'What's it for, Nell?'

'Have you told your parents about it?' she asked.

'Mum found it tied to Snowy's collar. But nobody knows what it's for. Do you?'

Nell nodded. 'I found it under the willow tree in a tin that had been turned up in the mud by the digger.'

Leo stared at her, waiting for her to go on.

'What does it unlock, Nell?'

Nell stared over his shoulder at The Vicarage. 'I'm scared to tell you,' she said quietly.

'Why?' said Leo slowly. He was watching her intently, rooted to the spot.

Nell started to walk towards The Vicarage. Her stomach felt like a bag of snakes, but she pushed herself on. She could hear the crunch of Leo's shoes on the ground as he followed behind her, and Snowy panting heavily as he scampered along beside him. When she reached the front door she knew so well, she froze, her hand refusing to turn the handle. She hadn't been back here since she had returned, she couldn't bear to. Nell's body began to tremble, as Leo reached round her and opened the door for her. *Click*.

She looked at Leo, who was standing too close, his hot breath on her neck.

'What are you waiting for?' He snapped, as she bit down hard on her lip and stepped inside.

It smelt different, damp from water leaking in through the windows, which nobody was here to mend, meaning the wooden frames had started to rot. The furniture was gone, showing all the gaps in the floor where the mice had got in and eaten the curtains without Snowy to chase them away. Nell felt her heart stop at the shell before her, which used to be her home, and pictured her and Bobby at the breakfast table, her father coming in and putting his boots by the fire, her old self chatting and eating her porridge with honey. Giggling and laughing without a care in the world.

'Are you going to show me or not?' said Leo.

'I'm frightened to, Leo.' Her voice was shaking. She gazed at the stairs; they felt like a mountain she had to climb. She forced herself to look up at the landing. Then at the top step. The way the lip curled round, it was impossible to see the keyhole unless you knew it was there.

'Nell, whatever it is, you need to show me,' said Leo firmly.

She nodded, and started up the steps, which creaked as she moved, one foot in front of the other. It was a journey she had dreaded making since she had first heard that Alice had disappeared. The thought dawning one terrible night about where Alice might be, and then implanting itself in her mind over several days and weeks until she could think of nothing else.

As they reached the top step, Leo looked at her. 'What is it?' he barked. 'For God's sake, Nell, show me.'

She held out her hand, her palm open. He looked down at it, then slowly reached into his pocket and handed over the key.

Slowly she sat down on the top step and reached under the lip, as she had done when she had first discovered the room. The room that she had written to tell Alice about. The secret room they had never got to be in together. Every night since Dorothy had adopted her, she had lain in bed dreading this moment, hoping and praying that she was wrong about Alice being in there. That it was all a terrible dream, a nightmare.

Slowly she slid the key in and turned it, until it let out a loud clicking sound and the step popped up. 'I can't look,' she said, turning to Leo. He stepped forward and lifted the lid.

Panting with fear, Nell forced herself to look as her eyes slowly adjusted to the dark. The first thing she made out was a small shape, like the hand of a ghost, lying on the floor by the latch. A bracelet with the initial 'A' lay on the floor next to it. She stared at it, paralysed; her heart stopped beating, she couldn't breathe. Alice was here, she had been here all along. Everyone had been looking for her, and all this time she had been locked in this room, where she had died alone and terrified.

The second thing she saw was a piece of paper lying next to Alice's bracelet, a letter written by her that had led her best friend here, into this room, where she had locked herself in and not been able to get out again. They would never have known she was in here, she had died alone in the dark. It was all her fault, by sending the letter, she had killed her best friend.

She went to scream, and Leo put his hand over her mouth. He shook his head, his eyes fixed on her as they stared at each other desperately. Finally Nell managed to pull her eyes away, and they both looked at Alice's hand again in utter disbelief. She had suspected, and worried that Alice was in the secret room, but she had never really believed it was true. It was impossible to take in; she felt utterly overwhelmed with shock and sadness. They both stood paralysed, staring at each other, until Leo reached in and grabbed the letter, then slammed the lid shut and locked it.

As Leo stood rooted to the spot, poring over the letter Nell had written to her best friend, Nell ran outside and stood on the top step as her breakfast came pouring out of her. Leo followed soon after, putting his hands on his knees and taking deep gulps of air. 'If the key was around Snowy's neck and Alice was locked in there, how did Snowy get out?'

Nell looked at him, then walked slowly round to the back of the house and pointed to the blue glass bricks, about five feet off the ground. One of them had smashed, leaving a hole. 'There's a window in the room. Look, it's broken,' Nell said, pointing up to it.

'Snowy must have jumped out and run back to the

house.' Leo stared up at the window, then looked back at Nell and shook his head. 'You must never tell anyone about this, Nell. They will blame you.' He looked down at the letter as Nell started to sob, then handed it to her before turning and walking away. 'Get rid of that; burn it. Don't ever let anyone see it.'

Left alone, Nell sobbed until she had no more tears then sat down on the step and looked at the letter in her hand.

Dear Alice,

I hope you are okay and keeping Snowy warm and playing with her. I miss you so much that I can't really think about it too much or I will cry. I can't wait to see you again and show you the secret room I have found under the stairs in The Vicarage – that is what the key is for on Snowy's collar.

You would never know the room is there except for a tiny keyhole under the top step. It opens up like a lid to a secret world with a bed in and a chest and a candle with matches. But I don't know where we will live next or if we will ever be together in the secret room now. I feel like I don't know anything any more. If you see Bobby or Dad, please tell them I miss them and tell them to write to me. I can't wait until we can be together again. You are my best friend in the world.

Love Nell xxx

Chapter Twenty-Nine
Bella

January 1946

Bella stood next to the willow tree at the edge of the farm and held the tin with her name burned onto it. She placed the key inside it, then kissed it before closing it tight. Picking up the trowel, she dug a hole as deep as she could manage in the frozen earth, then put the tin inside and covered it up. When she had finished, she walked across the field towards Yew Tree Manor, the thick mist covering the frozen ground a blanket for her to hide behind.

As she crept closer, moving between the shadows of the huge oak trees lining the fields, she began to hear sounds from the house. Yew Tree Manor was aglow, every one of the ten bedrooms lit up, and she could hear the yells of the stable boys as they rushed around in panic. They were familiar sounds, ones she had heard many times before from her vantage point at The Vicarage: hounds barking in the yard and building into a frenzy, the roar of cars up the driveway of the grand manor house, honking their horns, their drivers shouting with excitement.

It was the day of the annual hunt. Though the country was in a deep depression, food supplies were desperately short and a great many people had lost their homes and farms and were physically and mentally scarred, Bella was not surprised to see the meet going ahead. No doubt the servants' rations would have been cut for weeks in order to provide the feast for Wilfred's wealthy friends, who were all over the age of enlistment and no doubt welcomed the distractions the day would bring from the post-war depression.

As she reached the flint wall marking the boundary between her mother's land and the Hiltons', she was unable to feel her frozen feet through her boots, which kept sliding on the icy ground. She followed the wall down to the entrance to the stables, where the panicked voices of the boys in the yard became more audible. She stopped and listened, her icy breath piercing the winter morning.

'Sid, where's the body brush, I need to groom Brandy still.'

'Major still isn't tacked up. They'll be coming down soon – get a move on.'

'Has anyone checked Titus's saddlebag?'

Bella carefully peered round the corner to see six horses tied up outside the stables, thick blankets on their backs, hot breath bursting from their nostrils, all eating hay from nets whilst the grooms rushed around them. At the far end was Wilfred Hilton's black gelding, Titus. His coat shone as he stood calmly while the world rushed around him. He was a solid horse, the Rolls-Royce of horses, as Eli's father had described him once to his son. From the speed at which the stable boys moved, and how they were snapping at one another, it was obvious that the pressure was on and they didn't have long before the horses needed to be ready.

Bella had to get to the house quickly and find Alfie before it was too late.

Bella continued to hug the wall that ran around the back of the rose garden and past a pergola under which she and Eli had sat on summer's days when Wilfred was away on business. Her eyes followed the path to the back door of the house, where she could see one of the servant girls hurrying inside with a basket full of logs.

The servants would have been up for hours, she thought, dashing about, their faces pink from the effort, lighting fires in every room, polishing the silver, slicing the bacon and collecting eggs from the yard for Cook to prepare a breakfast for the hunt guests.

She tucked herself behind the neatly trimmed hedge that ran the length of the garden and started walking towards the back door. She could hear laughing and shouting coming from the dining room; pictured the guests dressed in their smartest hunt attire: white shirts, buff-coloured jodhpurs, their blazers hanging on their bedroom doors next to their polished black boots and top hats.

She pressed herself up to the window. Breakfast was already in full flow, as Cook rushed around red-faced, flour on her apron and hands from making pastries. Bella could hear the clatter of plates as orders were shouted. The range was aglow with bubbling pots of porridge and milk, cake stands stacked high with scones and jam, the butler piling himself up with plates ready to head into the dining room whilst trying to avoid Cook's wrath.

Bella finished scanning the room through the steamed-up window. There was no sign of Alfie, and she began to feel panic rising in her stomach. He could be in any one of the dozens of rooms, upstairs or downstairs. Soon the horn would go to signal the start of the meet, the servants would be everywhere, and she would be seen and the police called.

She walked along the side of the house, staying out of sight and passing the dining room, where about twenty older gentlemen sat around a huge oak table eating their breakfast feast. The atmosphere was charged, port was being poured into tumblers by the butler and she could almost feel the anticipation of the day's riding ahead as the guests slapped each other on the back, threw their heads back laughing and built each other up into a state of frenzy. At the head of the table sat Wilfred Hilton, smiling and refilling the glass of the man next to him, his friend Dr Jenkins; a round-faced, greedy-looking little man with egg in his beard. As Bella watched them, she felt the rage rising inside her to the point that she felt tempted to pick up a rock from the ground next to her and hurl it at the glass.

But the thought of finding Alfie spurred her on, and she continued to make her way round the entire ground floor, peering in at every window, until she reached the servants' quarters at the back of the house, which were completely empty due to the frantic efforts to feed all the visiting guests. There was no sign of her little boy anywhere.

Her last chance was Wilfred's study, a huge room at the front left of the house, meaning that she had come full circle. It overlooked the vast expanse of grounds and the lake. She peeked in at the room, with its leather chairs, Chesterfield sofa and large mahogany desk, the walls lined from floor to ceiling with books. With the shouts from the kitchen and dining room a distant din now, she scanned each nook and cranny as best she could. It was empty, no sign of life at all. She began to feel the panic rising again. Perhaps they had sent him away already. Or he was locked in one of the bedrooms upstairs. Tears began to sting her eyes as she tried to gather herself and work out what to do next. She would have to go into the house; she had no other choice. If it meant being caught, so be it.

As she stood to make her way back to the servants' entrance, her eyes fell on a large sighthound in the corner of the room, a long-haired scruffy-looking grey dog stretched out on the rug. Knowing Alfie's love of dogs, her heart began to thud, and she shifted her position to get a better look. She rubbed at the steamed-up window with her fist, spotting the corner of a book poking out from behind the dog, then a small black boot, and finally Alfie's head resting on the dog's stomach as it slowly moved up and down in its sleep.

For a moment she stood frozen to the spot. It had only been a day since she had last seen him, but she'd been so terrified she wasn't going to see him again that she was struggling to stay composed. Fighting back the tears as she looked around, checking no one had seen her, she tried to gather her thoughts.

Making Alfie jump up and rush out to her would be a disaster; she needed to stay calm and catch his eye, but not in such a way that he would shout her name or attract attention. Slowly, her heart racing, she began gently tapping on the window. For a little while he stayed in his own world, slowly turning the pages of the atlas that seemed to be gripping him. She clutched her frozen fingers into a fist and tapped a little harder. Immediately his head spun round and his brow furrowed; it was clear that he was unsure what he was looking at. She raised her finger to her lips, and just as he stood and began to walk over to her, a man came thundering into the room, making both Alfie and the dog jump.

'What are you doing in here? I told you not to come into my study.' Wilfred Hilton strode towards Alfie in his full hunting gear and slapped him so hard around the head that he immediately started to cry.

Bella watched in horror as he then pulled Alfie up by the ear and dragged him out of the room. She ran along the side of the house, hearing Alfie crying out in pain, powerless to help him. When they reached the kitchen, Wilfred threw him in. 'I said to keep the bastard out of my way until they collect him.'

The housekeeper, at whose feet Alfie had landed, was clearly stressed from her morning's labours, and upset at having her master shout at her.

'Go and make yourself useful and get a dozen eggs from the chicken coop,' she barked at Alfie, throwing him outside by his ear as Wilfred stormed from the kitchen.

Alfie exploded from the back door, crying great sobs, and Bella, having tucked herself around the corner, grabbed him by his little wrist and pulled him to her. At first he was terrified, not realising who she was for a moment, still clutching at his ear in pain, but as Bella pulled him close to her, she whispered in his ear.

'It's okay, Alfie, I'm here, Mama's here, I'm going to take you away from this place.'

The child collapsed into her, sobbing uncontrollably, and Bella held him tight. She could hear the noises from the house beginning to rise like the mist, the atmosphere and tension building as the riders prepared to leave for the hunt. As Alfie's sobs started to subside, she kissed the top of his head and squatted down to his level.

'Alfie, you need to do everything I say, okay? We have to move quickly.'

He nodded, his little tear-stained face gazing up at her, and she grabbed his hand and pulled him towards the stables. Riders in all their regalia were starting to appear from the house now, shouting and laughing as the stable boys began bringing the horses out one by one, the hounds dashing around their feet, excited by all the activity. Bella hung back as the last of the boys took the final horse to the riders, leaving only one tied up in the yard: Titus, Wilfred Hilton's gelding.

Bella had no time to hesitate; she ran over to the mounting block where Titus stood, unhooked him and pulled his blanket off. She could hear the stable boys coming back, shouting that the master was waiting, as she swung Alfie onto the saddle and threw the blanket over him.

The horse didn't flinch as she clambered on, accustomed as he was to different stable boys riding him to keep him fit. She gave him a squeeze with her legs, then, with her right arm around Alfie's middle, she took the reins in her left hand and broke straight into a canter as they climbed the bank around the back of the stables.

Her heart was hammering, knowing they only had seconds before the stable boys realised that Titus was missing. As they reached the grass alongside the driveway, she urged the horse into a gallop. Alfie clung to her arm wrapped around his body, not saying a word. He felt warm and calm; they had ridden together a hundred times, and his little body gave her strength.

She could hear the other riders beginning to shout in the distance now, commotion breaking out as they realised Titus was gone. Then came the first yells as they caught sight of her galloping down the drive, and she glanced back to see two riders setting off in pursuit.

Bella's heart thudded loudly in her ears as she kicked Titus harder and clung tighter to Alfie. She knew the property well enough to be aware that at the end of the driveway there was a cattle grid, which most riders would not dare to jump. If they didn't make it, it would break the horse's legs, and possibly kill her and Alfie as well. But as she galloped towards it now, she knew she had no choice.

She looked back again, over her shoulder; they were gaining on her. If she could get over the cattle grid, they would never catch her; she knew the woods and the estate too well, and there were a dozen places they could hide. Bella's core felt weak, she hadn't ridden for two years, but Titus was strong enough for both of them. She pressed her heels down and kicked him hard in his ribs, and as she clung to Alfie, she closed her eyes, and Titus jumped.

By the time they reached the woods, she could hardly hear her pursuers' voices at all. Wilfred Hilton's horse was too fast, and she'd had too much of a head start. She galloped to the edge of the Hiltons' land, just by the road into town, then jumped off, reaching up to help Alfie down.

'We made it, Mama,' he said, his little cheeks flushed red from the icy wind.

'Not yet,' she said, smiling gently down at him and

pulling the emerald engagement ring off her left hand. Bella pulled the envelope with her mother's letter from her bag, slid the ring in and sealed it, running her finger slowly over Tessa's slanted handwriting.

'What are you doing?' Alfie asked.

'Returning something that isn't mine any more,' she said, smiling down at the little boy.

She undid the buckle on Wilfred Hilton's saddlebag, slid the envelope inside and fastened it back up.

'Off you go!' she said, hitting the gelding hard on its buttock and watching as it galloped back towards Yew Tree Manor. It knew its way home, and the riders who had been pursuing her would stop as soon as they had Titus back.

'Come on, there's a car; let's see if we can hitch a lift.' She climbed over the wooden fence and waved down the vehicle, which slowed and came to a standstill next to them. Together they climbed into the front seat, Bella clinging to Alfie's hand as they bumped along the road. The winter sunshine piercing the windscreen felt like a sign from Eli that he was watching over them.

Bella tried not to think of what would happen when they reached Portsmouth. She could only pray that she could find a job where they would let Alfie stay too. He was seven now, and used to growing vegetables in the fields; if she was lucky there was a chance someone could find a use for him. If not, it would leave them with only one option: the workhouse, a place where they would be separated.

They watched the fields rush by, and as they passed The Vicarage, she whispered in Alfie's ear, 'That house is yours, Alfie, don't ever forget it.'

'I won't, Mama,' he said.

'Come back here one day and take it back, you hear me?' she said, kissing his rosy cheek. 'Promise me.'

'I promise, Mama,' he said. Clutching her little boy tight, Bella closed her eyes and prayed that this little joyful moment, which she feared would be their last together, would never end.

Chapter Thirty

Leo

New Year's Eve 1969

'Alice?' Leo looked around. Everything had gone quiet suddenly; after seeing Alice's puppy from the road, and hearing Alice calling out to it, Leo had walked towards The Vicarage trying to find them both.

'Alice, where are you? Answer me! Mum's really worried about you, we need to go back to the house, now!' Leo shouted, letting out a sigh of frustration. He'd heard her calling out to Snowy, so he knew she was okay, she was just being a pain – as usual. He just needed to find her and drag her back to his frantically worried mother. His parents were so obsessed with Alice, he thought, looking round the snow-covered ground for any sign of her footprints and let out an irritable sigh. If he went missing, he doubted they would even notice – or care.

Through the eerie silence of the night a strange noise distracted him from his search, a strange screeching, groaning sound, coming from the field behind The Vicarage. Leo followed the noise to the back of the house, to see Alfie struggling with the tractor, trying to get the huge mouth of the digger underneath a cow's carcass. The digger skidded and struggled in the ice and the tractor engine strained and growled angrily as Leo watched him transfixed.

Leo turned back to The Vicarage and shouted Alice's name again. It was pitch black now, and he didn't dare to go back without her.

'Alice! You are going to be in big trouble if you don't come out now!' shouted Leo, listening to the deafening silence. Suddenly he heard the puppy barking again, from inside The Vicarage.

'Alice, where are you?' he said, cupping his hands at the window to try and see in as Alfie let out a yell.

Leo rushed back round the house, to where Alfie had now climbed out of the tractor and was trapped between the cow carcass and the teeth of the digger. Alfie was struggling frantically, trying to push himself out of the hole he got himself into. Within seconds he spotted Leo standing, watching him, and Alfie began shouting out to him for help. But Leo was unable to move or take his eyes off the disaster unfolding in front of him. He felt powerless to act. He felt like his father's fury was holding him back, stopping him from helping Alfie, who had refused to leave The Vicarage for the past year, making Richard's life impossible.

As Leo listened to Alfie's anguished cries, he began to burn with a feeling of excitement. Was this his opportunity to make his father love him? Was this the thing, his chance, to change everything? To make his father look at him like he looked at Bobby?

'Help me, Leo!' Alfie shouted to him desperately, blind panic in his eyes as the digger buried him alive in the mud and slush.

But Leo couldn't move. What if his father didn't want

him to help Alfie, what if he found out that he could finally have been rid of him, and Leo helped him. He would never forgive him.

Suddenly, Alice appeared from nowhere and began running towards the tractor. She was in a red dress, and red party shoes that were covered in slush and mud, but she ran towards him as if she were wearing trainers. 'Alfie! Leo, help him! Why aren't you helping him?'

She moved like lightning, scrambling across the snow-covered field, with no thought for herself, tripping and falling once, before getting up again, and hurling herself towards the digger, which was screaming like a trapped animal as the metal twisted and turned.

Awakened from his trance, Leo began to run, trying to catch up with her, and grabbing at her hand. But she managed to break away, throwing her tiny body, with no thought for herself, under the gnashing teeth of the machine which was on the brink of falling.

Leo watched in horror as she began pulling at Alfie's clothes in an effort to free him. She was tiny but utterly determined, crying out with the strain of her efforts. Before Leo reached them, her dress caught underneath the digger, taking Alfie and Alice with it, as it slid down the bank, sinking deeper and deeper into the ditch bordering the field. Soon she became trapped herself, as she was pulled down with the digger and it sank deeper and deeper into the ditch bordering the field.

'Alice, let go! Take my hand!' he shouted. He could see her face filled with panic as she tried to pull herself out, but the teeth of the digger had her in their grip. He began kicking frantically at the ground underneath her, until slowly he moved enough frozen earth so she could free herself. The tractor engine burned with the effort, belching out a plume of black smoke.

'Help me, Leo, help me. He's trapped.'

'Alice, let go of him,' he said. As he pulled her by the waist with all his might, a tooth of the digger came crashing down on top of them, striking Alice on the head. She let out a cry of pain as a trickle of blood ran down into her eyes.

'Alice, for God's sake, take my hand. I have to pull you out or you'll be killed.' He shouted, barely able to be heard over the crashing metal.

Finally, she let go of Alfie's hand and with one last almighty heave from Leo, she was free. Seconds later, the tractor groaned its final breath and the digger came down with an almighty crash on top of Alfie.

Alice looked at Leo, her face awash with tears. 'Why didn't you help him? Why did you just stand and watch? I hate you, Leo, I hate you.' Blood was dripping into her hair and eyes, mingling with the tears.

Leo stared at his sister, panting with the shock and terror of what had just happened.

'I don't know, I'm sorry. I don't know why I didn't help.'

Alice looked at the wreckage next to her and began to sob, 'He's under there, Nell's daddy is under there.'

'Alice? Alice, are you out here?'

Leo and Alice looked over to see Bobby coming through the clearing. Without hesitating, Alice began running towards him. 'Bobby, help!'

For a moment Leo looked down at the wreckage, not able to face Bobby and what he was about to discover. He could hear Alice crying, telling Bobby what had happened, he had to get out of there. He had to leave. He turned and began to run in the direction of the road, up the lane as fast as his legs would carry him, back to Yew Tree Manor where his frantic mother was giving up hope of ever seeing her daughter alive again.

Chapter Thirty-One

Vanessa

Friday, 22 December 2017

Vanessa sat on a chair outside the interview room where they had taken Bobby James for questioning.

'We have applied to the magistrate for an extension, because of the seriousness of the crime,' said DI Mills, 'but he's not talking, and there's no incriminating DNA in his flat or his car. So we can't hold him for much longer.'

'Has he said what he was doing in our house when Sienna went missing?'

'No, he won't say. If you can get him to tell you that, we'd have a breakthrough.'

'Can I go in now?' Vanessa asked. 'Alone?'

'We'll be watching through the mirror,' Mills said.

Vanessa stood, feeling very shaky. Here she was, almost exactly fifty years after the night Alice had vanished, when she had begged them to let her talk to Bobby James and all her hopes of finding her were pinned on him – just as they were now. She opened the door and then closed it behind her.

Time had not been kind to Bobby James. He was a tall man, with a drawn face, a narrow mouth and black hair that was starting to thin. He was deathly pale, making his cool blue eyes look almost synthetic in their intensity.

He was leaning back in his chair, his legs stretched out in front of him and crossed at the ankles.

'Hello, Vanessa,' he said.

'Hello, Bobby.' She pulled out a chair and lowered herself into it.

The two of them sat for a while saying nothing.

'They tell me you aren't cooperating again,' said Vanessa. 'I really think it would help you to at least tell us why you were at Yew Tree yesterday. It's a bit of a coincidence, don't you think?' Her voice trembled.

He looked at her and smiled. 'It would help *me*, would it Vanessa? I see you haven't changed a bit.' He shook his head.

'Meaning what exactly?' Vanessa asked curtly.

'Meaning that, even after everything you've been through, all the pain you've suffered in the last fifty years, you'd still prefer to believe that I had something to do with Alice's disappearance and stay in the dark than be honest with yourself.'

She recoiled. 'You're a cruel liar, Bobby James, and you deserve to go to prison for the rest of your life for what you've done to our family.'

He shook his head and let out a sad laugh. 'You know, Vanessa, I have never, ever lied to you. I can picture myself as a young lad fifty years ago; I think this may even be the same interview room. I can see myself standing in the corner while that man slapped me around the head. Begging and pleading for them to let me sit down or to just be given a glass of water. They told me you'd been there watching. You did nothing, when you knew I would never hurt Alice, any more than I had burned down that barn Richard made me take the blame for, or drowned those puppies. I don't know how you can live with yourself. You're the one weaving a web of secrets and lies, letting them send me away to Borstal, to be brutalised, when I worked my fingers to the bone for you and put Richard before my own father, a man who took his home, and everything he loved, and was entitled to, away.'

'Just tell me where Sienna is. Please, Bobby. I'll do anything. Anything you ask. You can have The Vicarage. Is that what you're saying? Is that what you want?'

'Go to hell, Vanessa. None of this would have happened if you had been watching your own kid.'

'How can you sit there and torment me like that when my granddaughter is missing!'

'Me? Me torment you? I was a kid, I was a good kid, and you took my life.'

'Why were you at Yew Tree Manor yesterday?' repeated Vanessa. 'Tell me!'

Bobby looked away. Vanessa nodded and stood up and walked to the barred window.

'Don't you think I blame myself?' she said. 'Don't you think I lie awake every night, torturing myself about everything I did wrong that night? That I didn't cancel the party, that I didn't watch Alice, that I was too worried about the lights and the storm and the champagne when out of two hundred guests the only one I should have cared about was Alice.'

Bobby locked eyes with her. 'I'm not talking about Alice.'

Vanessa glared at Bobby. 'Leo? You're talking about Leo?'

'Have you ever sat down and asked him about what happened that night? Leo was there when my father died. Alice told me, right before she vanished. She tried to help my father and Leo pulled her away. Leo must have seen Alice hurt her head, and he watched my dad being crushed to death, and he did nothing to help.'

'Leo didn't have anything to do with Alice's disappearance,' Vanessa said sharply.

Bobby shrugged. 'Why are you here, Vanessa? You don't want to know your own family were responsible for Alice's death, not mine; if Richard had given my dad The Vicarage as he was supposed to, my father wouldn't have been so distressed and had the accident where Alice hit her head. If Leo had saved my father, Alice wouldn't have got involved; if you had watched Alice, she wouldn't have been at The Vicarage in the first place.'

'Tell me why you were at Yew Tree today!' She banged her fist on the table.

'Because I found out that you were pulling down The Vicarage. The last place I was happy. I went to say goodbye, and then Leo roared past me, out of the gates, and the temptation was too much. I hadn't walked up that driveway since the night Alice went missing. Or set foot through that door. It was easy; there were removal men going in and out. I just walked through the front door, and there was Nell. My beautiful Nell, who, because of you, I haven't seen for over ten years.'

'Stop calling her Nell; her name is Helen! She's not your innocent little sister any more; she's a grown woman and I don't trust her. I never have.'

'Well, you're right not to trust her, because it's all going to come out now, Vanessa. Nell knows all your secrets. She hasn't spoken to me for years because Leo won't let her, because he's so scared of what she knows. But it's all going to come out now. It's over, Vanessa.'

'You're a cruel man, Bobby James,' said Vanessa, backing towards the door.

He glared at her, his blue eyes burning. 'She's terrified of Leo, but her love for Sienna will overcome that; she'll do anything to get her back. And that includes telling everyone what you've been trying to hide for fifty years: that your son is a deeply damaged human being. She wouldn't do it for me, but she sure as hell will do it for her daughter. You can control most things, Vanessa, but you can't control the love a mother has for her child.'

Vanessa's whole body began to shake as she banged at the door with her fists. Bobby sat silently watching her tremble, as footsteps slowly came along the corridor towards them.

Finally the door opened and she rushed out, past the police liaison officer, hurrying along the corridor and through the entrance of Lewes police station, into the freezing night air which, as she clung to the railing, she gulped at desperately, like a dying fish on a riverbank.

Chapter Thirty-Two
Willow

Friday, 22 December 2017

Willow sat on the side of the bath, staring at the two blue lines on the pregnancy test she had grabbed at the supermarket on her way home from her tour of the old sanatorium.

Her period was nearly a month late, and she'd been feeling sick for days, but she'd put it down to stress with work, and the shock of having it confirmed was too much to take in.

Her phone began to ring in her bag, and she stood up and walked over to it.

'Hello?'

'Willow, it's Mike. Great news, we got the green light at the planning meeting today. It's all gone through. Huge congratulations, kiddo, it's all down to you.'

She felt her heart race as it throbbed in her ears. 'Thanks, Mike,' she said.

'They're going to start demolishing The Vicarage straight away. The developers are keen to get going.'

'Really? Even with everything that's going on? With Sienna Hilton missing, I mean.'

'Yup, they've cleared it with the police. She's definitely not in there, and it's far enough away from Yew Tree Manor not to be a problem. They just want to clear it now so they can start laying the foundations. We can't afford any more delays.'

'Okay,' said Willow. 'Though, as you know, they're about to face a lot more delays as soon as they start digging and find all the human remains buried there.'

Mike went very quiet. She could almost hear his mind whirring at the end of the line.

'I don't see why you felt the need to lie to me and screw me behind my back, Mike. I don't think it's a very nice way to behave.'

The silence until he spoke was excruciating. 'Don't take it personally, Willow. Sometimes you need to break a few rules to get to where you need to be. You should be proud of yourself: your name is associated with a groundbreaking development, knocking down two listed buildings on farmland, which they said couldn't be done.'

'My name is on a document that says there are no human remains in a plot of land where there are a lot of human remains. The development will be held up for months, if not years, at a cost of hundreds of thousands of pounds to the developer, and they are going to want someone to blame.'

'Why don't you come into the office and we can talk this over. Maybe get some dinner.'

'No thanks,' she said, her voice shaking. 'I need time to think. But I know I'm not the first person you've done this to.'

'I don't think I like your tone, Willow. I'm not someone you want to make an enemy of.'

'Well, maybe I'm not either.'

Her heart pounding out of her chest, she ended the call, then sank her head in her hands and started to cry. She had tried to sound strong, but she was heartbroken. Mike was an influential man in the world of architecture, and he would make sure she never worked again if she told the truth about what he'd done. And what difference would it make even if she did? It would just reflect badly on her that she hadn't checked all the documentation before it was submitted.

Whichever way she spun it, she came out worse.

But how could she let him treat her like that? It would be setting a precedent for the rest of her career. After a year of back-breaking work, she should have been over the moon that the project had got planning permission, but she felt utterly deflated.

The last twenty-four hours had thrown her entire life off a cliff. Sienna Hilton was missing, she still couldn't believe it. Her father had been taken in for questioning for child abduction, her career was on the line, and now she'd discovered she was pregnant.

She looked back down at the pregnancy test, racking her brains as to when it could have happened. She had been working so hard on the Yew Tree project, and had ignored a nasty tummy bug a few weeks ago that must have stopped the pill from working, but she and Charlie had barely seen each other, let alone had sex. Though once was all it took . . .

She let out a heavy sigh. She was always so careful, knowing that children were a long way into her future – if at all. She could barely look after herself, let alone a baby, and she had fought tooth and nail to have the career she loved. She didn't want to give that up or put her child into nursery from dawn until dusk. If she ever did decide to be a mother, it would be when she could do it properly and devote herself to it. Not now.

It was obvious that Charlie felt very differently. He couldn't wait to have a family, and would always smile and wave at babies he saw in shops and cafés. 'Babies just fit in around you,' he'd once said. 'They don't have to mean your life is over.' They had never sat down and discussed it at length, because, as with everything tricky, Willow tended to avoid the subject. But it was another reason she had turned down his marriage proposal in Barcelona.

She stood on tired legs and walked into the kitchen. Her visit to the sanatorium and the thoughts of what Nell had gone through had really shaken her up. On the train home, she had emailed the Mayfield Sanatorium's Facebook group in the hope of finding Heather Parks's parents, or anyone who was there at the same time as Nell and remembered her. She had left a message on her dad's voicemail on the way home, but when she had turned on the news, they were still no closer to finding Sienna, meaning he would still be in police custody.

She made herself a cup of tea, sat down in her favourite armchair and pulled out the press cuttings on Tessa James they had printed out at The Keep for her. As she opened the envelope, Nell's note fell out. Willow felt sick. She was so exhausted, she felt as if she could sleep standing up, but her dad needed her and that meant finding Nell – somehow. As she started to read the articles, the doorbell rang, and she let out a weary sigh and stood up to answer it.

'Hi, babe, I'm starting to think you're avoiding me.' Charlie stood in front of her, leaning against the wall.

Her heart sank at the sight of him. He looked tired, and he was biting his lip, which he always did when he was cross and trying not to say anything.

'Of course I'm not avoiding you. I've just had a hectic couple of days.'

'I know, I heard about your dad. It would have been nice to hear it from you rather than see it on the news. Can I come in?'

'Of course. I'm sorry, my head's been all over the place.'

She followed him down the hallway to the kitchen, and he took up his usual place in the corner, standing with his arms crossed. Except today it didn't feel comfortable, and for the first time ever, she didn't want him there and wished he would go.

'Are you okay?' he asked, frowning over at her.

'I'm really tired, this project has really taken it out of me.' She poured herself a glass of water.

Charlie shook his head. 'And I guess you're upset about your dad? Willow, please don't shut me out.' He bit his lip harder.

'I'm not shutting you out.' She walked out of the kitchen and into the bedroom, starting to undress and put her pyjamas on.

'Babe, your dad is all over the news and you haven't even called me. We're supposed to love each other, I'm supposed to be the person you turn to, but I haven't heard from you for two days.'

'Charlie, I don't need this right now.'

'Well, I'm sorry, but I do. I always bite my tongue when you shut down and try and give you space, hoping that one day you'll open up to me. But you never do. My parents keep asking if you're okay and where you are, and I don't know, I don't know what to tell them.'

Willow felt sick again, and like she was about to cry.

'Well, tell them you don't know because you haven't spoken to me.'

'I can't do this, Willow, I can't do this any more. You won't let me in. I love you so much, but there's this wall around you that I can't get past.'

'Fine,' she said.

He looked at her. 'Fine?'

'Yes, fine, I respect that. I'm sorry I can't give you what you want. It's probably best if you go.' She craved her bed. Craved sleep so she could stop thinking about her dad in a police cell, again, and her being unable to help him.

'Just like that?'

'What do you want from me?' She was so desperate for him to leave, her stomach was twisting in knots.

'I know you're not a cruel person, but the way you can just shut down your emotions scares me,' said Charlie quietly.

'I can't do this. Whatever it is you want, I can't have you come here and demand things of me now, tonight of all nights.' She stood at the bedroom door and went to close it in his face.

'All I'm demanding of you, as you put it, is that you let me be there for you. That's all I want.' He reached out his hand to the door so she couldn't close it.

'Why? Why do you want to be there for me?' she said, shaking her head.

'Because I love you.' His eyes filled with tears.

'No, you love the version of me that you want me to be. The version that you hope I will be one day. Well, I can't, okay? I can't be that person, she doesn't exist. You have to take me as I am.' She started to cry. 'You only love me because you don't know who I really am.'

'Maybe it doesn't matter to me who you really are, maybe

that's just for you. And maybe who I really am is just for me. All I care about is that you're happy, and feel good and succeed and that you become what you are meant to be. I love you, Willow, I don't really know why sometimes, to be honest, like right now I'd struggle to give a single reason, but love isn't a transaction, there's no logic to it, it's just . . . energy.'

Willow frowned. 'Energy?'

Charlie smiled. 'Yes, it's there or it's not, and it's definitely there between us, it always has been.'

Willow shook her head. 'Well, I think this energy of ours might vanish into thin air in about ten seconds.'

'Why?' Charlie bit down on his lip again.

She stared at him with her bright blue eyes. 'Because I'm pregnant, and I don't want it. I don't want to be a mother.'

Charlie leaned back against the wall and stared at her, then slowly put his head in his hands.

'And you can't change my mind. So don't try,' she added, her voice shaking.

Silence fell between them, then slowly Charlie reached out and took her hand.

'Thank you for telling me,' he said quietly.

Willow looked at him wide-eyed. 'I can't be a mother. I don't want to be a mother. I'm sorry, but I just don't have it in me and I don't know if I ever will.'

He nodded. 'Okay. Okay. I hear you. I just need a minute to take this in.' He closed his eyes and wiped away the tears with the back of his hand. 'Can I hug you?' he said.

'Yes, but I'm not going to change my mind.'

'Okay, I understand.' He turned to her and wrapped his arms around her. Willow was tense at first, her hands by her sides as he held her tight, then slowly she began to collapse into him. 'It's okay, babe. It'll be all right. I'm here for you, okay?'

'Okay,' she said quietly.

'Can you just tell me what's going on with your dad?' he asked after a while. 'I've been so worried about you.'

Willow wiped away the remnants of her tears. 'He was at Yew Tree Manor yesterday when Sienna went missing. They think he took Alice fifty years ago and now they think he took Sienna too. He didn't, I know he didn't, but he won't talk to me. He will never talk to me.'

'Like father, like daughter,' said Charlie, smiling feebly.

'I found a note to Alice that Nell wrote when she was a little girl, saying she was sorry she'd ruined everything. Look.' Willow stood up and walked over to her bag, pulling out the envelope of press cuttings.

Charlie took the note and read the faded child's handwriting.

TO MY BEST FRIEND ALICE,

I'M SORRY I DIDN'T MEAN TO RUIN EVERYTHING. I MISS YOU SO MUCH.

NELL X

He let out a heavy sigh, then glanced down at the articles that had spilled out of the envelope. He picked one up and looked at it.

'Who's Tessa James?' he asked.

'She's my great-great-grandmother; she was a midwife,

and she used to live at The Vicarage, where my dad grew up. I don't know much about her other than that she went to prison because one of her deliveries went very wrong, a mother and baby died in her care.'

Charlie frowned at the headline. *Midwife facing life imprisonment for manslaughter.* He picked up another cutting. *Midwife found guilty of manslaughter.*

Willow leaned over to look at the articles: *A midwife who caused an innocent mother to bleed to death has been found guilty of manslaughter today. Tessa James, who practised in Kingston for thirty years, took a scalpel to Evelyn Hilton when a breech birth went badly wrong.*

She flicked through the articles, then began to read one from the *Sussex Times*, dated February 1950: *Was Convicted Midwife Innocent? Exclusive by Milly Green.*

> Tessa James was a well-respected midwife in Kingston near Lewes until tragedy struck. During the birth of a much-longed-for little girl, the baby turned and became stuck. James was found guilty of causing the fatal injuries that killed both mother and child, and tragically took her own life in prison.
>
> James refused to take the stand at her trial, a move that ultimately cost her her freedom. She pleaded not guilty, but without cross-examination, the jury were unable to hear her side of the story and chose to convict her.
>
> But there was another person present that night, a servant, Sally White, a vital witness in Tessa James's conviction, and five years on, we have tracked her down.

As she read, Willow heard her mobile phone start to ring. It was a number she didn't recognise.

'Hello?'

'Hello, is that Willow James?' said a woman's voice.

Willow's heart missed a beat before she even knew for sure who it was. She had emailed the Mayfield Sanatorium Facebook group asking if anyone knew of an Emma Parks, and had received a generic reply from one of the members saying that Emma wasn't on Facebook but that they would email her Willow's contact number if she wanted to forward it. That had been this morning, and she had been concerned that she wouldn't hear back for several days, but the voice on the end of the line immediately gave her hope.

'My name is Emma Parks,' said the woman, her voice slightly shaky. 'I received an email earlier today from an acquaintance of mine who said you were looking for someone who was at the sanatorium at the same time as my daughter Heather.'

'Yes, that's right. I'm so sorry for your loss, Mrs Parks,' Willow said feebly.

'Thank you, dear. Time eases the pain but certainly doesn't take it away. And I wouldn't want it to. So, who is it you are looking for?'

'Um, it's my aunt, actually, my father's sister. Her name is Nell. Nell James. She was there at the same time as your daughter, and I realise it's a long shot, but—'

'I remember Nell very well, she was in the next bed to Heather. She became quite good friends with my daughter during the months she was there. She had the most dazzling blue eyes – I'll never forget them,' Emma added.

'Oh, that's wonderful to hear,' said Nell, relieved that her trip to Portsmouth hadn't been entirely wasted. 'I don't suppose you know what happened to her?' She waited, holding her breath.

'She was adopted, I believe. A woman came to collect her.'

'I see. It is a long time ago, I know, but can you remember anything about this woman? What she looked like maybe, or a name?'

Emma paused. 'Yes, of course. She was very smartly dressed and spoke well, and Nell seemed to know her. I used to worry about Nell terribly. No one ever came to see her. We actually enquired about adopting her ourselves; she was such a sweet child.'

As Willow waited for her to continue, she looked at Charlie, who was still absorbed by the newspaper cuttings.

'What was her name? She gave us her address, so Heather could write to Nell. Let me see, I think I still have it.'

Willow felt a huge rush of adrenaline flooding through her body as she waited for the name that could lead her to Nell.

'Her name was Dorothy Novell, and I believe she lived in Yew Tree Cottage, in Kingston near Lewes.'

Chapter Thirty-Three
Nell

November 1970

Nell's alarm clock went off under her pillow, and she startled awake with a jump, turning it off quickly for fear it would wake Dorothy and Peter. She rubbed her eyes and stared at the digital display: 3.50 a.m., just as Leo had told her. She had ten minutes to pull her warm clothes and wellington boots on and let herself out of the back door.

She swung her legs over the side of the bed and held her breath, trying not to make a sound for fear of being found out. She pulled her small rucksack out from under the bed. She had packed it carefully the night before: a torch, her ear muffs, gloves, the notebook, and the tin she had found buried under the willow tree just before she got sick. She looked at the notebook one last time, then picked up her pen and quickly wrote a note to slip inside the back cover, desperate to say something to her friend.

TO MY BEST FRIEND ALICE,

I'M SORRY I DIDN'T MEAN TO RUIN EVERYTHING. I MISS YOU SO MUCH.

NELL X

She stared for a long time at the key she had found inside the tin. If she had never found it, would Alice still be alive? Was it really all her fault, like Leo said? It had kept her awake night after night, and she decided that the only way to make sure no one discovered what she had done was to bury it again, with the notebook, in the tin. In the same place, just as she had found it.

But something was stopping her.

She didn't want to part with the key. It was like it was alive, a passage from the past. It had brought her closer to her dad, finding the room that was his secret place. She looked at the clock again. In that split second, she decided she would keep it. She would hide it with the letter she had written to Alice. She would keep it under the loose floor-board in her bedroom, and nobody would ever find it. Maybe one day she would need it.

She folded the letter around the key, secured it with the ribbon she had tied around Snowy's collar, then popped up the floorboard under her bed and slid it in.

She looked out of her window across to The Vicarage. She loved her little room in the eaves of the house. Peter had made it for her, with a hatch, and a ladder that dropped down. You would almost never know it was there from the landing. But it was torture being able to see the house where Alice lay every day.

A few days after their grim discovery, Leo had come knocking for her and asked if she wanted to go for a walk in the woods. Dorothy hadn't seemed very keen on her talking to him and had told her she'd prefer her not to go. 'Why does he want to go for a walk with you?'

'I don't know,' Nell had said, plucking her coat from the

hook and hurrying out before Dorothy could stop her. Dorothy had stood by the kitchen window watching them go, pulling the net curtains back until they disappeared out of sight.

'I'd prefer it if you weren't friends with him, Nell,' she'd said later. 'I want you to make friends your own age.'

'I will, Dorothy, I just like hanging out with Leo sometimes.'

But it wasn't true, she didn't really like hanging out with Leo. She had had a sick feeling in the pit of her stomach since her greatest fear had come true: that Alice had used the key she gave her to open the hatch into the secret room and hadn't been able to get out again.

'You know they'll blame you for not saying anything,' Leo had said as they walked through the Hiltons' fields. '*I* don't blame you, but if they ever found out you'd given Alice the key, my mother would never be able to forgive you.'

She had started to cry. 'But shouldn't we tell them where she is? Won't it be better than them worrying that something awful happened to her?'

'What's more awful than being locked in a tiny space on your own and not being able to get out? And dying that way, all alone? She must have starved to death.'

'Don't say that. Dorothy said her head was bleeding when Bobby found her, so maybe she knew nothing about it.'

'We'll never know, will we? Nobody went back to that house after the night she went missing; she could have been calling out for days.'

Nell hadn't been able to sleep since seeing what was left of Alice's hand, and when she did, she had nightmares about Alice hammering on the door, trying to get out, calling her name.

'Luckily you've got me,' Leo had said. 'I won't tell anyone, I promise.' He looked down at the ground. 'We need to stick together, Nell, do you understand? You can't trust anyone else.'

'I miss her so, so much. I bet your mother does too.'

'Yes, Alice was their favourite. They wouldn't want to see her like that, though. It's better they don't know any of this. They'd want to remember her how she was.'

'Oh Leo, it's so sad. I wish we could do something, have a little funeral for her. I can't bear it.'

'Well, we can. I mean, we can't move her, but we can go to the willow tree where you found the key in the first place. We need to bury it again, Nell, you know that, don't you? But it will have to be at night, while everyone is asleep, otherwise someone might see us, and we can't risk that. This is our secret, Nell, nobody must ever find out. It's very serious, you understand that, don't you? If Dorothy or anyone discovered what you'd done, they'd send you away. Like they did Bobby.'

'Okay,' she had said. 'Thank you, Leo. I think you're right about Dorothy, I don't think she would understand. She doesn't seem to like me very much.'

'She doesn't really understand children because she hasn't got any of her own. She loved Alice, like everyone did, but she didn't like me. You mustn't listen to anything she says about me, Nell. She makes things up. She's a busybody.'

Now Nell slid the loft ladder down and crept downstairs, just as the clock in the hall began to strike four. She was late, and Leo was going to be annoyed with her. Her heart thudded in her chest. He had told her to meet him under the willow tree, where they would bury the key and say goodbye to Alice together. She would have to lie and tell him the key was in the tin; she could do that, he wouldn't check, he trusted her.

Something about Leo made her do everything he said. He had a way of staring at her when he spoke, a long, lingering look. He had told her that she couldn't have known Alice was going to die in the secret room, but that they could never tell anyone because other people might not feel the same way, might not forgive her as he had done.

He didn't like her making new friends. She had to be careful, he said: what if she slipped up and said something about Alice? He knew everyone at school and warned her off people he said weren't good for her. She was lucky to have him, he told her. And she knew he was right.

'Hello, Leo,' she said, as she spotted him standing underneath the willow tree. He was kicking the ground; she could tell he was annoyed. 'I'm sorry I'm late.'

He had already dug a hole; it was all waiting for her. She placed the tin inside, then picked up some soil and threw it in.

'Now nobody ever needs to know about that room,' Leo said. 'It's impossible to find if you don't know it's there.'

'Okay,' agreed Nell.

'It's just you and me now. You and me against the world.' His eyes narrowed.

'And Bobby, when he gets home,' Nell added.

'No, Nell, you need to keep Bobby away. We can't risk him finding out about this; he could tell someone. It will always be just you and me now. We never need anybody else. Do you understand?'

'Yes, Leo,' she said meekly. She didn't want to make him angry.

He began to replace the soil he had dug up, piling it into the hole.

'Goodbye, Alice,' Nell said as the tin disappeared from sight.

Chapter Thirty-Four

Alice

New Year's Eve 1969

'Bobby, help!'

Alice's heart leapt at the sight of Bobby running towards her in the snow.

'Alice, there you are. Everyone is looking for you. Where have you been?' He smiled down at her. 'We need to get you back to your mum, she's really worried.'

'I was looking for Snowy, she ran home to The Vicarage.' He was so different to Leo, she thought immediately, always so kind to her. He would be so upset when he saw his dad's accident. She didn't know what to say, she didn't know how to tell him; she felt dizzy, and something wet was dripping down her face.

'Alice, my God, your head is bleeding. What happened? Here.' He pulled his white handkerchief from his pocket and held it to the side of her head.

Alice took it from him. It was already wet with blood, and her head was throbbing. She pulled it away to look at it and gasped. The sight of the bright red blood made her cry.

'We need to get you home,' Bobby said. 'You've really

hurt your head. You need a doctor.' He put his arm around her and started to guide her back towards the house.

'No, Bobby, your dad is trapped. You have to help him first,' she said.

His face fell. 'What do you mean, he's trapped?'

'Over there, under the digger. I tried to help him but Leo pulled me away.' Alice was starting to feel sick. She held the handkerchief to her temple, but it was so wet, blood was leaking through onto her hands.

Bobby ran towards The Vicarage. Alice stayed where she was, her blood dripping onto the white snow at her feet. She was beginning to feel very strange, the world around her starting to spin.

'Dad!' She could hear Bobby, but she couldn't bear to go round the corner and look. She had tried to help, but she wasn't strong enough. Why hadn't Leo helped, why had he just stood there watching as Nell's dad struggled and pushed and fought? If he had helped sooner, they could have got him out.

She had always stuck up for Leo, even though he was always so mean to her, calling her names and making her cry. She watched how Bobby was with Nell, carrying her on his shoulders, tickling her, letting her win races and playing marbles with her, and it made her green with envy. She had always made excuses for Leo. But Dad was right, he was a bad apple. How could he have just stood and watched Nell's dad be crushed? She could still hear Alfie's cries, hear the metal crunching. There was nothing she could do to save him.

She felt dizzy, dizzy and sick. She had hit her head so hard the world was starting to go blurry, and she needed to lie down.

Yap! Yap! She looked up to see Snowy standing in the doorway of The Vicarage. Maybe she could go into Nell's bedroom and just lie on her bed for a little while.

Her vision beginning to blur, she dropped the handkerchief in the snow where she stood and walked towards the house. She could hear Bobby shouting for help, but she knew there was nothing she could do. She needed to get to Snowy before the dog ran away again. Her face felt sticky with blood. She put her hands up to her head; it was all in her hair and, thick like treacle, dripping into her eyes.

She walked through the front door and followed Snowy up the stairs. The dog had started scratching at the top step. She was looking at Alice, the key dangling from her neck. Nell's secret room, of course. Alice had put Nell's letter in her coat pocket; she carried it with her everywhere, so that no one could find it. She didn't want Leo knowing about the room; he would tell Mum and Dad straight away – any opportunity to be cruel.

She reached out and took off Snowy's collar. She could hide in the secret room until she felt better. She needed to get away from the accident, from Bobby and Leo; she couldn't bear to see it any more.

She would come out when it had all gone away.

She found the keyhole just where Nell had said it was, and slid the key in and turned it. *Click*. She lifted the step and peered inside. It was warm and dark in there, and she was longing to just lie down and sleep.

She could still hear Bobby shouting outside and it was making her cry. When would somebody come and help him? She couldn't bear to listen to it any longer.

She climbed inside, and Snowy jumped in after her. She

closed the lid and locked it, then tied the key back around Snowy's collar so that it would be easy to find when she woke up. Then she lay down on the mattress, watching the moon through the blue window at the end of the small room. She pictured Nell in there with her, playing teddy picnics or snap. Hiding under the blankets and telling ghost stories. She missed her friend so much.

Her head was bleeding onto the blankets now. She didn't want to make a mess, so she looked for the handkerchief but couldn't find it. She must have dropped it in the snow. Her head was throbbing and aching, and the room was spinning. She just needed to sleep, then she would feel better.

Bobby's cries for help were fainter now, she felt safe.

She thought of her mother's beautiful face, her hair in curlers, her nails painted blood red for the party. She loved to try her mother's perfume, and she would choose her jewellery for her from her collection in the box that played a tune when you opened the lid. As she lay in the dark, her whole body started to shiver. She pulled the blanket around her and wished her mother was lying next to her, as she did every night when she tucked her into bed and read her a story.

'Everyone is looking for you. We need to get you back to your mum.' Bobby's voice sounded echoey and far away in her head.

'I'm coming, Mummy, I just need to rest for a little while,' said Alice out loud, as she closed her eyes and dreamed of laying under the willow tree, with Nell and Snowy, on a perfect summer's day.

Chapter Thirty-Five

Sienna

Friday, 22 December 2017

Sienna Hilton sat on her bed in the eaves of Dorothy's house and looked over at the big diggers and the crane, like a huge giraffe, standing next to The Vicarage. She knew nobody lived there any more, and her mummy had always forbidden her from going in there, but it always looked so pretty to her. Like it could be the prettiest house in the world if someone loved it.

She let out a heavy sigh. It was the second night she had stayed here since Dorothy had walked up to her on the driveway while she was making a snowman and asked her if she'd like to come to her house for a little while to get warm and play with her mummy's old toys. She had happily said yes, but now she was starting to get bored. She didn't know why she couldn't go out, why Dorothy kept bringing her food to her room, but she was really starting to miss her mummy. And her granny. It had been a long time since she had been to Dorothy's house. She knew Daddy didn't like her and Mummy going there any more, and it was hard not being able to come and play like she used to.

She had tried to open the hatch last night to tell Dorothy she couldn't sleep, but it was locked from the other side. She had been bursting for the toilet and had called out and knocked on the door, but nobody had come. In the end she had weed in a plant pot in the corner. In the morning Dorothy had said it didn't matter, but she was very embarrassed.

She reached out and opened the window onto the flat roof, but the window had a lock on it so it wouldn't open very far. It was nice to get a little bit of air, though, as the room was starting to get very stuffy.

Dorothy had given her her own television and an iPad and lots of sweets to eat, and at first she couldn't believe how lucky she was, but after a while her eyes had got sore and she didn't want to watch the screen any more. She had played with her doll's house and made her mummy a card, but she was starting to feel like she wanted to leave. She knew Mummy would be missing her. If she went to stay at people's houses ever for a sleepover, she always spoke to Mummy before bed. But Dorothy had said there was no need and that she would see her soon.

She looked around the room for something to entertain herself. Dorothy had given her a box of marbles, and she opened it and looked at all the different colours. She laid them out and started to play with them, but they began rolling all over the floor in different directions. One rolled under the bed and into a hole in the floor, and she stuck her finger into it trying to reach it. As she pulled her finger out, the floorboard lifted up.

Hidden under the floor was a wooden box, which she carefully lifted out. She felt like she had found some treasure as she pulled open the lid and peeked inside to see a piece of paper, a hand-written note and a beautiful key engraved with a picture of a Willow tree.

Dear Alice,

I hope you are okay and keeping Snowy warm and playing with her. I miss you so much that I can't really think about it too much or I will cry. I can't wait to see you again and show you the secret room I have found under the stairs in The Vicarage - that is what the key is for on Snowy's collar.

You would never know the room is there except for a tiny keyhole under the top step. It opens up like a lid to a secret world with a bed in and a chest and a candle with matches. But I don't know where we will live next or if we will ever be together in the secret room now. If you see Bobby or Dad, please tell them I miss them and tell them to write to me. I can't wait until we can be together again. You are my best friend in the world.

Love Nell XXX

She read the letter again. She couldn't believe it: a secret room in The Vicarage. She had heard her mummy and daddy talking once when they thought she was asleep about a hidden room. She was half asleep so she thought she must have dreamed it, but now she knew it must be true. She was determined to find it, then she could show them that she knew where it was! Now she really had to get out.

Dropping the letter by the bed and putting the key in her pocket, she walked back over to the window, suddenly desperate to get outside and start her adventure. She started to push the lock, and then fetched a knife that Dorothy had brought with her lunch and wedged it underneath. After a few wiggles, it gave way, and the window opened far enough that she was able to squeeze through and climb out.

It was lovely to be outside. She had watched from the window as Peter cleared out the drains the day before and had left his ladder up against the side of the house. Sienna walked along the roof towards it, then slowly and carefully began to climb down. Her legs felt wobbly on the steps, but she made herself keep going. She would find the room, then go home and tell Mummy about it.

Keen not to be seen by anyone, she climbed quickly down the ladder and ran for the hedge by The Vicarage. Two men were talking by one of the big tractors parked up outside, and she waited until they turned their back on her before running as fast as she could, under the yellow tape surrounding the house, and through the heavy wooden door.

It was dark inside, and very cold, and she suddenly felt quite scared. But she really wanted to make her mummy proud, so she made her way across the damp stone floor towards the small staircase in the corner. There was enough light coming in from outside for her to find the keyhole that Nell had talked about in her letter, and she took the key out of her pocket and slid it in.

Click, it turned. She lifted the step, and her heart skipped a beat. It was so exciting! She had found the secret room that nobody else knew about! She eased the door up, then climbed in. The springs were rusty and it was a huge effort to keep it open long enough to get her whole body through the gap, but finally she did it.

Then, before she could stop it, the heavy lid slammed down on top of her with such a bang that when she turned back to push it open again, it was completely jammed shut.

Chapter Thirty-Six

Willow

Friday, 22 December 2017

Willow sat in her car at the end of the stone pathway up to Dorothy Novell's pretty terraced cottage with its immaculately manicured garden waiting patiently for spring.

It had been less than half an hour since she had received the phone call that had brought her right back to where she'd started yesterday. Dorothy Novell had adopted Nell from the sanatorium. The woman she had spoken to at the presentation at the village hall; a woman who had lived in Kingston all her life. It was Dorothy who had told her about the graveyard and set off the chain of events that led to her finding the notebook.

She had immediately thought back to a conversation with Charlie's mum, Lydia, the morning of the presentation. *Helen is Dorothy's adopted daughter, but they're estranged, I believe. It's all rather complicated.*

Now she looked at Dorothy's front door as if it were the entrance to another world.

'Lydia, it's Willow, how are you?'

'Oh hello, dear, yes, we're fine, thanks. Are you all right? We were so sorry to hear about your father being arrested. We're thinking of you. If there's anything I can do . . .'

She was such a sweet woman, thought Willow; it would be good to get to know her better, without her husband around always dominating the conversation. 'Thank you, Lydia, there might be something actually. Can I ask you a question?'

'Of course, dear, fire away.'

'I don't know if you remember, but the morning of the presentation we spoke briefly about a woman called Dorothy Novell in the village.'

'Yes, I remember vaguely.'

'Well, you mentioned that she and her daughter are estranged. Do you know why, by any chance?' She glanced up at the front door, which was decorated with fairy lights and a huge holly wreath. She looked at her watch: 3.30 p.m.

'Well, I'm not one to gossip, Willow, but I think a lot of it was to do with Helen's husband, Leo. Apparently he and Dorothy didn't get along, Dorothy says he can be very controlling, but he's so charming I find that hard to believe.' Lydia hesitated before continuing. 'And Dorothy can be rather intense. She could never have children and I think that affected her a lot. I believe she was very upset about the four of them going to France without her after the deal went through. Particularly little Sienna.'

Willow could hear some crashing noises in the distance; they had started on the demolition already. Blakers Homes weren't wasting any time.

'Yes, I'm sure that would have been very hard for her. Thank you, Lydia, you've been very helpful. I look forward to seeing you soon.'

She opened her car door and climbed out. Dorothy's house was quiet, no sign of life, and Willow looked around.

Earlier, when Dorothy had spoken to her about Nell, Willow had been putting the rubbish out and a thought suddenly occurred to her. Making sure that nobody could see her, she ran over to the bin and pulled out the black bag on top. Then she squatted down on the ground out of sight.

She tore it open, fishing through Dorothy and Peter's rubbish – bits of paper, plastic wrappings and juice cartons – until she came to what she was looking for: a Peppa Pig yoghurt pot, sandwich crusts and an alphabet spaghetti tin.

And underneath, with bits of orange sauce spattered across it, a drawing of a woman and a little girl holding hands, and in the corner, in a child's spidery handwriting, *Mummy and me, by Sienna.*

Staring at it in disbelief, Willow looked up at the house, her heart thudding uncontrollably. She dropped everything in the road and started running towards Dorothy's front door.

Chapter Thirty-Seven

Vanessa

Friday, 22 December 2017

Vanessa walked through the woods, the air bitterly cold as the branches whispered above her.

'Leo? Leo?' She looked around. Night was closing in, the second without Sienna. There was no way that if she'd been outside all this time, if she had fallen and hurt herself, they would find her alive.

She wandered deeper into the woods, starting to feel disoriented, when she spotted Alice, in her red dress, in the clearing ahead. 'Alice?' Vanessa tried to speed up, but whenever she got too close to her, she would start to run, the gap between them never closing enough for her to touch her. Alice stopped again and beckoned her to follow.

She reached the edge of the woods and looked down at The Vicarage. She stopped, the sound of her own breathing in her ears. 'Mummy! Over here!' She turned in the direction of the willow tree, alone on the landscape, and under it saw a figure lying on the ground.

Alice was standing next to the tree in her party dress. She put her finger to her lips and pointed at the ground, where

Helen was lying, still and silent. Slowly, Vanessa walked over and stared down at her daughter-in-law.

'Where is Leo, Helen? I need to talk to him urgently about Alice,' Vanessa snapped.

'I don't know,' said Helen.

'Well, when is he coming back?'

Helen looked up and shook her head. 'I don't know and I don't care. I hope I never see him again.'

'I went to see your brother at the police station this afternoon. He seems to think Leo knows what happened to Alice.'

Helen was clutching Sienna's teddy to her. She closed her eyes as a tear streaked down her cheek.

'Is he right, Helen? Does Leo know where my little girl is?'

'Just leave me alone, Vanessa. You never cared about me; all you care about is your own flesh and blood.'

'Helen, please, this is important. Where is Leo?'

'He's probably run away, like he always does when things get hard. Like he did on the night Alice died. Do you know how much debt he's in? He owes hundreds of thousands of pounds, and the police know all about it now that they've been through his bank statements to see if Sienna took one of his cards. He owes more money than this whole deal is worth.'

'What's that got to do with Alice and Sienna?' Vanessa snapped. 'I'm going back to the house to call him.' As she turned to walk away, there was a massive crash.

'What was that?' she gasped.

'They've started the demolition. The developers want it to go ahead,' Helen said simply.

'Couldn't Leo stop them? We can't have that going on while we're looking for Sienna.'

'It's not up to us; it's not our land any more. The planning went through and we signed all the paperwork. It's done. Besides, Leo's glad.'

'Glad about what? Helen?' Vanessa had to shout to make herself heard over the noise.

'Glad that The Vicarage is being torn apart. He was desperate for them to tear up the graveyard.'

'Why? Why does he want to get rid of the graveyard? What are you talking about? For God's sake, Helen, tell me!' She grabbed Helen by the shoulders.

Helen sat up and stared at the house, tears escaping as the wrecking ball smashed into its side. Slowly she looked up at Vanessa with her piercing blue eyes.

'Because that's where he buried Alice.'

Chapter Thirty-Eight
Willow

Friday, 22 December 2017

Willow's hand was shaking as she reached out to ring the bell of Yew Tree Cottage.

She had travelled all the way to an old sanatorium in Portsmouth to find a woman who had been hidden in plain sight.

Dorothy Novell opened the door without a smile, and Willow held her breath.

'Hello, Dorothy. Sorry to just turn up like this, but I was wondering if I could have a word.'

'I'm afraid it's really not a good time. Could I call you later?'

'It's quite important, actually. It's about my aunt, Helen Hilton – your adopted daughter, I believe.'

Dorothy let out a sigh. Willow could hear the crashing of the wrecking ball in the distance. If the noise was loud from this far away, it must be deafening up close.

'I promise it won't take long.'

'Who is it, love?' said Peter, appearing behind Dorothy.

'It's Willow, from Sussex Architects. She wants to talk to me about Helen.'

'Helen?' said Peter, frowning.

They had been so warm at the coffee morning; Peter

had been so helpful setting out the chairs, and always doing what he could to help, but they both looked entirely different now. Peter was scowling at her through the small opening, and Dorothy had her foot firmly against the door.

'It's really not a good time, Willow, we're very upset about Sienna going missing. Could we possibly speak to you tomorrow?'

'I'm sorry to push,' said Willow, 'but my dad, Bobby James, is sitting in a police cell, accused of taking Sienna, and I really need you to help me.'

Dorothy opened the door wider. 'Very well. Let's go in the conservatory.'

Willow followed her along the hallway to the far end of the house. She knew why she was being led down there, away from any sign of Sienna. She knew the little girl was somewhere in the house; she just had to find her.

Dorothy turned on a lamp, crossed her arms and stared at her. The conservatory glass was fairly thick, but she could still hear the boom of the demolition going on at The Vicarage.

'As you know, I've been trying to find my aunt Nell, and I learned today that you adopted her when she was seven years old. After she went to the sanatorium.'

'Yes, that's right.'

'I found a note from Nell addressed to Alice, apologising to her for spoiling everything. Do you have any idea what she might have meant?'

Dorothy glared at her. 'I'm sorry, I wouldn't know anything about that. You'd have to talk to Helen.'

'Yes, I will, but obviously I can't at the moment. She and the family are rather preoccupied. I thought that over the years you might have heard conversations or suspected things. Does Vanessa ever talk to you about Helen?'

Dorothy let out a sarcastic snort. 'Vanessa wouldn't talk to the likes of me about anything personal. I haven't been in her house since the night Alice went missing. I told you she blames me. I'm sorry, Willow, I don't think I can help you. People like us are kept at arm's length, unless the Hiltons want anything, of course.'

'It must have been very hard for you when Alice disappeared. You looked after her all her life, and then suddenly she was gone.'

Dorothy nodded. 'Vanessa and Alice adored each other, but Vanessa was always busy, in a rush, on to the next thing. I used to play with Alice for hours. I loved her so much, and nobody even asked me if I was okay after she disappeared. I was just pushed aside. It was always Vanessa, Vanessa, Vanessa.' Dorothy looked up at Willow. 'And now it's happening again: everyone is talking about how hard it must be for her that Sienna is missing. How much they adore each other. But I'm Sienna's granny too. Nobody thinks of me, or thinks to ask how I am.'

'I'm sure Helen does,' said Willow, reaching out and putting her hand on Dorothy's arm. Willow racked her brains, desperate to find a way in, then she remembered the comment Lydia had made about Leo. 'Seeing the two of them together over the past year,' Willow continued, 'I think Leo can be quite controlling of Helen.'

Dorothy looked up with tears in her eyes. 'I tried so hard to like him, but he made it impossible. He would say the most hateful, cruel things as a child. I felt sorry for him, though. Richard used to hit him; he would take him out to the cowshed so that Vanessa couldn't hear Leo crying. It was the reason he tried to burn it down.' She wiped her tears away with the back of her hand.

'That's terribly sad,' said Willow. 'Poor Leo.'

'The problem was Alice was so adorable. She was beautiful and sweet and tough with it. Everyone loved her, Richard most of all. I always suspected Leo might have known what happened to her, but of course I couldn't do or say anything, and Vanessa was so buried in her grief that I couldn't talk to her.'

Willow nodded, willing her to go on. Dorothy seemed to be relaxing, relieved to be finally able to talk to someone.

'When Leo started to show an interest in Nell, I was genuinely frightened. He was obsessed with her; she didn't stand a chance. He wouldn't let her see or talk to anyone else, and slowly but surely I lost her. When she told me they were getting married, I thought I'd never see her again – until I bumped into her and Sienna one day and we just clicked.' Dorothy's eyes started to well up as she looked at Willow.

'Sienna was just like Alice, so easy and funny and full of life. Leo had knocked the wind out of Nell completely, so she agreed that we could meet in secret. I blamed myself, you see, for bringing Nell and Leo together. I'd just wanted to help, but if I hadn't taken Nell in, she wouldn't have been anywhere near him. I made it worse. I've made everything worse.' She was crying hard now.

'It's okay, Dorothy, it will be all right.' Willow put her arm around the woman's shoulders.

'But it won't. They're going to take Sienna away. The four of them are going to France, leaving me behind without a second thought, like they always do.' Dorothy's face flashed with anger.

Willow took a deep breath. 'Can I see Nell's room?'

Dorothy looked at her, both of them knowing where this was going. 'Please don't go up there, Willow.'

'It's okay, Dorothy.' Willow backed out of the room before Dorothy could stop her. 'Everything will be all right.'

She raced upstairs and rushed along the landing, trying all the doors and putting her head round each one, but there was no sign of Sienna. As she looked around frantically, she suddenly saw the loft hatch. Grabbing a chair, she placed it underneath, then stood on it and unlocked the hatch, pushing it open.

'Sienna, Sienna, are you in here?'

She reached up and pulled the ladder down, then climbed the steps into a loft room painted pink, with a bed in the corner and a doll's house. There were toys scattered everywhere, and a tray of half-eaten food. At the end of the room was an open window. She strode over to it and looked out onto a flat roof.

'Sienna?' She leaned out to see a ladder propped up against the roof. 'Sienna, are you out here?'

Dorothy's head appeared at the loft hatch. 'Where is she?'

'The window was open. She's gone.'

Willow looked down to see a letter laid out on the floor next to the bed, in handwriting she recognised from the letter in the notebook. Nell's handwriting.

Willow picked it up and read it, panic rising in her as she realised exactly where Sienna had gone. Willow's entire body flooded with adrenaline and she looked up at Dorothy, her eyes wide. 'Sienna's in The Vicarage. Call the police. Now!'

Chapter Thirty-Nine

Vanessa

Friday, 22 December 2017

'You aren't allowed to be here. It's dangerous, you need to stay back!'

Vanessa was trying to push through the barriers and tape surrounding the grounds of The Vicarage. A man in a hard hat was shouting at her as she begged for him to stop the demolition work. The noise was deafening, tons of machinery that had been waiting for weeks to pounce now finally unleashed. She watched as a digger scooped up mounds of earth, tears pouring down her cheeks at the thought of what was left of Alice being torn to shreds.

Over the sound of the wrecking ball smashing at the side of the house, she heard someone shouting, and turned to see a woman running towards her, waving her arms. She was yelling at the man in the cab of the wrecking ball, frantically pointing at the house. Finally the driver saw and turned the engine off as Vanessa heard what the woman was yelling to him.

'There's a little girl in there! Sienna Hilton is inside that house!'

'What?' the man shouted at her, pulling his ear defenders away so he could hear her.

'There's a little girl in there!' she said, running into what was left of the house as Vanessa followed. Vanessa stopped dead, a wall of brick dust made it impossible to see as one of the men came running in after her. 'You can't be in here!' he said, tugging at her arm. 'It could collapse any second, we need to get out of here, now!' He was coughing desperately as Vanessa tried to look around; the brick dust was clinging to her nose and mouth.

As the dust began to settle Vanessa saw the woman starting to lift away the mounds of brick by the fallen staircase. Instinctively Vanessa walked over and sank to her knees, starting to lift the piles of broken cement and smashed debris away.

'Be quiet! Everyone be quiet!' Willow shouted as Helen came flying through the door crying and looking around desperately.

'We have to get you out, you could all be killed.'

'Be quiet!' shouted Willow, shocking the man into stunned silence.

Above the creaking of the breaking building they suddenly heard the faint sound of a child crying.

Helen screamed, realising that her little girl had been buried alive. She turned to the men standing in the doorway. 'Please help us! My daughter is under there.'

The mood in the room suddenly changed, as everyone blocked out the creaking sounds of the building giving way and launched themselves at the piles of bricks and rubble under which Sienna was buried, and began frantically digging.

The ceiling above them groaned from the strain of being held up by only two walls, as the pile of debris grew smaller and smaller. Every pair of bleeding hands moving as fast as humanly possible.

'The building is going to collapse, we have to get out of here!' shouted one of the men.

'Quiet!' called Willow again, and once more the room fell silent.

'Sienna?' shouted Helen.

'Mummy!' cried the little voice, as the building groaned again, with its final dying breaths.

'She's over here!' Willow shouted. 'Everyone, help me get this wooden beam up. Now!' Willow beckoned them all over, and on the count of three, they heaved the beam up and it crashed on to the ground next to them.

Suddenly through the smoke of brick dust, Vanessa saw a tiny hand appear.

'She's here!' Willow shouted, and taking Sienna's hand, she squeezed it tight. 'Hold on, Sienna!'

With a sickening groan, the third side of the house began to collapse. Some of the demolition workers rushed out of the building, but two stayed behind, scrabbling frantically at the remnants of the brick and beams to try and uncover the little girl.

Sienna was screaming and crying as they pulled at her trapped leg, desperately trying to free her from the ton of demolished stairwell which had collapsed on top of her. Helen and Willow frantically pulled at a beam which had fallen on a piece of the priest-hole door and finally it rolled back. They lifted it off, freeing the little girl as the roof began to give way.

'Get out of here now!' shouted one of the men as the other one scooped Sienna up in his arms, and the five of them rushed from the ruins as the building let out an almighty roar as the final wall of The Vicarage collapsed on itself and turned into a cloud of smoke and dust.

Chapter Forty
Helen

Friday, 22 December 2017

Helen sat between her daughter and her brother in the hospital corridor. Sienna had been given a pink cast for her broken ankle, which she was busy showing off to Bobby.

'The nurse said I was the bravest little girl she had ever met.'

Bobby looked down at her and smiled. 'Did she now? Your mummy's very brave too. She went away to hospital when she was about your age, all on her own.'

Sienna nodded. 'Will you sign my plaster?' she asked Bobby, pulling a pen out from her pocket.

He smiled. 'Of course.'

'Any news of Leo?' he asked Helen as he began to draw on Sienna's cast.

'Yes, they got him just as he was boarding a flight. He's at the police station now, being interviewed. He's been borrowing against the house for years and owes a great deal of money, and he's been lying to a lot of people. He and the architect falsified documents for the application.'

'The architect? But that's Willow, isn't it?' Bobby frowned.

'No, someone called Mike, Willow's boss, who worked

closely with Leo on it. Apparently they forged all kinds of things to get the planning approved. They're charging them both with fraud.'

'Oh dear. Is Willow caught up in it?' Bobby asked, concerned.

'I asked the police about that, and apparently it was obvious to them that she knew nothing about it. Mike and Leo kept her in the dark on purpose. She's given a statement, but she's got so many fans in the village, I think they'd have a riot on their hands if they tried to charge her with anything.' She smiled. 'She's an amazing girl, Bobby, you must be very proud of her. She saved Sienna's life.'

'I am.'

'What is it?' asked Sienna as Bobby finished his drawing.

'It's a willow, my favourite tree.' Bobby smiled at her. 'According to my father, it represents the ability to let go of pain and suffering, to grow new, strong and bold.' He winked at Sienna, who smiled and wandered off towards the glow of the vending machine.

'And what about Alice?' he said, leaning into Helen.

She glanced over at her daughter, who was busy eyeing up the contents of the machine.

'He's admitted to moving her body, which is obstruction of justice apparently.' She looked down at her feet.

'And are they going to want to talk to you about that too?' Bobby asked gently.

'Yes, they have, but Dorothy has told them how abusive Leo was; they call it coercive control. Dorothy is in quite a lot of trouble for hiding Sienna. I'm really hoping they don't come down on her too hard, but the whole Sussex police force was involved in the search, so it's not looking good for her. I had no idea she had her. I still can't believe she'd put me through that.'

She looked down again. 'I'm sorry I never told the police about Alice. Leo made me feel like I didn't have a choice. He told me they'd put me in prison, and then later that they'd take Sienna away. He's worked on me since I was seven years old, and I believed him.' She started to cry.

'I just wish you'd told me,' Bobby said. 'We could have worked it out.'

'Dad only ever wanted us to have The Vicarage,' Nell said sadly. 'If the Hiltons had given it to him, none of this would have happened.'

Bobby took her hand. 'Well, my solicitor seems to think we've got a chance of getting our share of the estate. They can do DNA tests now, apparently. And prove Dad's paternity.'

'And Leo can't contest it?'

Bobby shook his head and took her hand. 'He can't hurt you any more, Nell. We'll be okay.'

'You can go in now,' said a nurse, appearing at the door.

Helen took Sienna's hand, and they all walked into Willow's room, where she was sitting up in bed smiling.

'You've got a cast too!' said Sienna, bounding over to the bed. Willow's shoulder was strapped up and her elbow was in plaster. 'How come you get purple? I want purple!'

Willow smiled. 'Hi, Sienna, how are you feeling? This is Charlie, my boyfriend.'

Charlie winked at her. 'Hi, Sienna, I've heard a lot about you. I hear you've been extremely brave.'

Sienna giggled. 'Are you two going to get married?'

'Nope! She doesn't want to marry me,' he said, pulling a sad face.

'But we are having a baby,' said Willow.

Helen's stomach did a flip, as she grabbed Willow's hand. 'You're pregnant? Did you know that when you went into the house to rescue Sienna?'

Willow nodded. 'It was when the world was crashing down around me that I realised how much it meant to me.' She looked at Charlie, who winked at her.

'Is the baby okay?' said Bobby, frowning.

'Yes, it's fine, it's got a good strong heartbeat.'

'Does that mean I'm going to be an auntie?' said Sienna.

'No, you're going to be a cousin.' Charlie smiled at her.

'I'm so sorry, Willow, I . . . .' Helen began, as her voice trembled.

'Stop, it's not your fault. None of it is your fault. I'm just glad we're all together finally.' Willow squeezed her hand tighter and looked at her father.

'How are you feeling?' Bobby asked, smiling warmly at his sister.

'Better than I have done in a long time,' said Helen. I'm so proud of you, Willow. I heard about your boss. I'm sorry. Is your job safe?'

She shrugged. 'I don't know, but I'll be on maternity leave before I know it, and then after that I can have a think. I wouldn't mind trying to work for myself although Dad tells me he's coming into a bit of inheritance so I think I might take a year or two off.'

'Easy!' said Bobby, laughing as Willow smiled warmly at her dad. 'Is Vanessa okay, have you seen her?' Willow looked over at Helen.

'Sienna and I are going to see her now,' said Helen. 'She's in a private room. According to the doctor, she's terribly confused; she doesn't remember anything that happened when you saved Sienna.'

'It must have been hell for you living with her all these years, trying to keep your secret.' Willow looked at her sympathetically. 'I understand that they've found Alice's remains, so we can give her a proper burial. She was in the graveyard that Leo and Mike were trying to hide from the developers. According to Tessa's notebook, there were a lot of women buried there – women she tried to help and who took refuge in the priest-hole.'

'Can we go and see Granny now?' Sienna was tugging at Helen's hand.

Helen looked down at her and smiled.

'We'll be back in a minute,' she told the others, and allowed herself to be pulled out into the hall.

Sienna skipped along beside her as Helen followed the signs to Vanessa's ward.

'Granny may call you Alice again, sweetheart; she's very confused now. Is that okay with you?'

'I don't mind,' said Sienna cheerfully. 'If it makes her happy.'

Helen smiled down at her daughter. She still couldn't believe she had her back. Every second together now felt like a gift. Like being reborn. A life like Vanessa's, torn apart with grief and pain, had so nearly been hers. It was terrifying to think about.

Finally they reached Vanessa's room and knocked on the door.

'Come in!' Vanessa's voice was faint.

Helen eased open the door and peered in. Vanessa was sitting up in bed, looking much worse than Helen had been expecting. She had oxygen in her nose, and her face was deathly pale. Helen was worried that Sienna would be upset, but she just bounded onto the bed like nothing was amiss.

'Granny,' she said, wrapping her arms round her grandmother's neck. Vanessa slowly lifted her arm and put it around her granddaughter.

'Careful with your cast, darling.'

Vanessa lay back and looked at the little girl. 'I missed you. We couldn't find you.'

'I know. I got locked in the priest-hole at The Vicarage, but they rescued me.' Sienna ran her hands through her grandmother's hair.

'I was so worried about you, Alice, my darling. We didn't know where you were.' A tear rolled down Vanessa's cheek. Sienna smiled up at Helen and winked. She understood completely.

'I'm okay now, Mummy. I'll be fine. You don't need to worry about me any more. I'm safe.'

Helen turned away so that Sienna couldn't see her crying. The empathy and wisdom of her little girl was almost too much for her to bear.

Vanessa started to doze off, clinging to Sienna's hand.

'You sleep now, Mummy. I love you.'

'I love you too, Alice. I love you so much.'

Fighting back her tears, Helen watched as Vanessa drifted off to sleep, then held out her hand for Sienna to take. The little girl kissed her beloved grandmother, then jumped down off the bed.

Helen took her daughter's hand and pulled her into her, clinging so tight she felt she would never be able to let her go. Then they took one more look at Vanessa sleeping and quietly left the room.

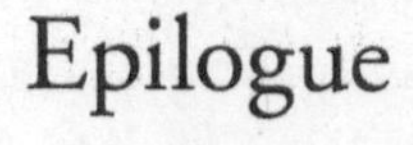

Epilogue

January 1946

My *darling Bella,*

By the time you read this, I will no doubt have been found guilty of manslaughter, and will be facing a life sentence.

But I knew as soon as I was charged with this crime I had no hand in that I could not take the stand. Being cross-examined would mean taking an oath where I would have to tell the truth, the whole truth and nothing but the truth.

I would no doubt have been forced to answer questions about the women I am proud to have helped during my life as a midwife. Women who came to me to tell me of their husbands forcing themselves on them days after childbirth. Of not being physically strong enough to bear another child. Girls too young to give birth who had been raped by their brothers or fathers, begging me not to tell of their shame. Girls I have helped by giving their babies away to women who wanted a child but were unable.

I promised these girls and women that I would keep their secrets, that I would guard them with my life.

Some of them will have been in court with me, sitting by their husbands, who would have beaten or even murdered them had I spoken their truths.

I am deeply sorry for what this means for you and Alfie. That I cannot take my place on the witness stand and tell the world that I loved Evelyn Hilton, that I would never cut a woman like Dr Jenkins did. That night is forever burnt in my mind, however hard I try and forget. He butchered Evelyn's tiny body, and starved her baby of oxygen, then got Sally to call for me at The Vicarage when he realised what he had done. He left me there to watch them both die and take the blame.

That day was the worst day of my life. It was the same day Wilfred told me that Eli had been killed, the day you lost the love of your life and Alfie lost his father.

And it was my last day as a midwife.

But I am not afraid. I am grateful. I love what I have spent my life doing. Being your mother and Alfie's grandmother is my greatest honour.

Do not be sad, my love. You are a James. We are not victims, we are free. I am at peace knowing that I helped to create a world that we can be proud of, and that I kept my word.

I told those women that I would take their secrets to my grave.

And I have kept my promise.

I love you, my darling, be strong until we meet again.

Mama xxxx

Acknowledgements

Thrashing out ideas with interesting, clever people – whilst trying not to disappear down rabbit holes – is the best part of writing books. Often those I talk to have no idea how much they've helped me, so with that in mind a huge thank you to Vicky Newman for her endless patience and sharing of medical knowledge, and also to Sarah Harris and Alexis Stickland for the midwifery chats. Thank you to the wonderful Marion Wilyman for our conversations about the changing face of midwifery over the decades, and to prison officer Danny for sharing his extensive experience about the HMS prison system. Also, to Anna Blowfield for her help with my prison chaplain queries and for steering me towards extraordinary prison chaplain Phil Chadder, who helped me hugely.

Huge thanks also to Marita Bianco who carefully pieced together my survey related issues and Asia Jedrzejec who gave endless time and a much-needed female perspective on my architecture strand. Thanks go to Jeremy Pendlebury (7BR chambers) and Valeria Swift who were both extremely patient in trying to help me understand criminal trials. As was Sue Stapely; always a font of knowledge and contacts. Thank you also to horse goddess Emma Lucas for her expertise.

Finally, thank you to my wonderful editor, Sherise Hobbs, who always brings out/extracts the best in me, and to my agent, Kate Barker. A debt of gratitude to my beloved, Steven Gunnis, for always digging me out of cold, hopeless plot holes. Thank you to my girls, Grace and Eleanor, for their patience in putting up with me living in other worlds rather a lot of the time, and to the dear friends – Rebecca Cootes, Clodagh Hartley, Harry De Bene, Suzanne Lindfors, Jessica Balkwill, Helen Tullis, Jessica Kelly, Kate Osbaldeston, Sue Kerry, Claudia Vincenzi and Sophie Cornish – who got me through lockdown; working with kids at home has not been easy on anyone.

I raise a glass to you all!

Author's Note

I, like many others, have always been fascinated by midwives. For as long as women have assisted other women in childbirth, many cultures have believed that midwives possess some supernatural secret wisdom. In the past, midwives have even been tried and killed as witches, so powerful was their knowledge of natural remedies and womanly ways. Indeed, no job title incites more fascination or interest than that of a midwife.

Midwives are there during the most powerful, emotional, traumatic and life-changing hours of a mother's life, and so it was for centuries; for her mother, and her mother's mother. They are there to share the elation when a baby comes out of its mother's body, or to comfort a woman who is told that her baby won't survive to draw breath – and everything in between.

Whilst midwives have existed for hundreds of years, midwifery didn't become legally recognised in Britain until 1902. Even then many midwives felt that childbirth was the domain of women and they were reluctant to receive training from male instructors. Also, many women were not literate, which made formal education near impossible. Beginning in the early 1800s, middle-class families started using doctors for childbirth. And by the early 1900s, delivery began shifting to hospitals. By the mid 1900s, midwives were only used for those who could not afford a doctor. It was seen as 'lower class' to use a midwife, but herein lay the problem; many doctors weren't trained sufficiently in midwifery; a fraction of their medical training was in childbirth and even less attending actual births.

Birth was viewed as a pathology that needed treatment. Babies were delivered with women lying on their backs with their legs in stirrups, in sterile and frightening medicalised environments, where the women weren't listened to. The number of medical men practicing midwifery increased rapidly and the midwives, namely Tessa in our story, bitterly resented this invasion of their territory. Most who started in general practice had only the dimmest idea of the conduct of normal, let alone complicated, births, and learned by hard, often bitter experience, killing mothers and babies who would otherwise have survived.

This idea fascinated me, because this pathological approach to birth echoes still in the modern day. The feeling of being out of control that so many new mothers who have their babies in hospital speak of. Of being not listened to, of intervention they didn't want or need. Sadly, birth trauma is not uncommon today; the idea that you are completely at the mercy of the medics at the birth of your own child. And often with no pain relief, something which is seen as a badge of honour. Or sometimes even refused it, with women being told 'it's not called labour for nothing – it's meant to be hard work'. Never in any other medical procedure would you be forced to suffer in unimaginable pain.

Our heroine, Tessa James, has been a midwife for thirty years. She has saved countless lives and often works for women who can't afford to pay. But she is born during a time of change, and our story begins just before the creation of the NHS, when women having babies were paying customers that the doctors wanted for themselves. There was a great deal of pressure on women such as Tessa James to step aside, women who often knew a great deal more about birthing babies than any doctor with his fancy degree.

As a midwife I spoke to put it: doctors have their place, and sometimes medical intervention is absolutely necessary. But sometimes it is better to wait it out. Midwifery is the most anxious and trying of all medical work, and to be successfully practised calls for more skills, care and presence of mind on the part of the medical practitioner than any other branch of medicine. I started to see this picture of a woman's plight, her midwifery knowledge as an immovable object meeting the unstoppable force of modern-day medicine. It was irresistible to me: a powerful story which I hope resonates with women to this day.

Reading Group Questions

1. How have attitudes to midwifery changed since 1945? What do you think prompted the move to a more medicalised birth experience around that time? And, with the foundation of the NHS three years later, in 1948, and therefore free access to medical treatment, do you think that slowed down or sped up the change of attitude to midwifery that is represented in the book by Wilfred Hilton and Dr Jenkins?
2. Letters lost and found are integral to this story – how might things have been different in today's world of instant (and endless) communication? And will future generations have as much insight into us as we have into past generations when so much of the evidence of our existence is ephemeral – literally, 'in the cloud' – rather than physical?
3. If Eli hadn't died and Bella hadn't miscarried the baby conceived through sexual abuse at the hands of her employer in Portsmouth, do you think Eli would have accepted a baby that wasn't his when he returned from the war? Or would Tessa have helped her daughter abort the pregnancy?
4. Do the events of our childhood set the pattern for our adult lives? Can people turn their lives around, despite a poor start? Was Bobby James doomed to a life spent

in and out of institutions and prison the moment he lied for Richard about the fire in the barn?

5. Helen, Vanessa and Evelyn Hilton all suffer at the hands of their respective husbands, despite the outwards appearance of prosperity and success. Tessa James, meanwhile, has no male protector, which makes her vulnerable to attack. Have the Hilton women bargained away their freedom and happiness for financial security and social acceptance?
6. Unless Willow decides to marry Charlie after all, her baby will be born 'illegitimate'. Compare and contrast how different things will be for Willow's baby than they were for Bella's son, Alfie (Willow's grandfather). Is there still a stigma to being born out of wedlock?
7. How do you think the newspaper coverage of Alice's disappearance in 1969 and Sienna's in 2017 would have compared?
8. It used to be that children were supposed to be 'seen and not heard', but this book shows that they often weren't told anything either. How do you think it was for the children, like Nell, on the TB ward who didn't understand what was happening to them and why no one came to visit?
9. In many families, history repeats itself over the generations. Discuss how this happens with both the Hiltons and the Jameses. Has history repeated in your own family?